# Fallen Tiers

The Blue Dragon's Geas

Cheryl Matthynssens with Co-Authors Theresa Snyder and Alex Hunt

Cheryl Matthynssens
895 Riverside Drive
Wenatchee, WA 98801
www.dragonologists.com
ISBN: 9781521309797

Book Layout © 2016 BookDesignTemplates.com

Fallen Tiers/Cheryl Matthynssens. – 2nd ed.

# DEDICATION

This book is dedicated to the Outcasts of the world.

## ACKNOWLEDGMENTS

A special thanks to Alex Hunt and Theresa Snyder. I was struggling with finishing the book during yet another round of chemo. They stepped up and helped me get this out. Also, Thanks to the fans who have stuck by me.

Jon nodded to the acolyte that took the reins of his lexital, smiling inwardly at the sudden stillness which descended over the crowd. It was not his robes, gray with travel dust, nor his unkempt hair which drew the attention of the entire stable yard. No, all eyes were on the tiny black dragon, whip tail wrapped like a choker around the mage's throat

He looked around in amazement. He had heard of this temple, all death mages had, but this was more than he ever imagined. It was fashioned similarly to the tiers of the capital, though the levels here were not as distinct, and black spires rose here and there, a sharp contrast to Silverport's glistening white stone. The courtyard where he had landed stood outside the main walls of the temple, and he wondered briefly what wonders lay on the other side.

The death mage was distracted from these thoughts when he spotted cave openings lining the far-off cliff walls. How many dragons had the High Priestess managed to gather? If they were all full, it was a concern he would have to relay to Alador. He cast a cleaning spell absently over his robes as he continued to take in the spectacular view.

His eyes caught the distant movement of three dragons flying together. They looped in and out of one another before making some diving run, displaying amazing in-flight choreography before dropping down out of sight. Nightmare sat up on his shoulder, crooning softly as though he too was watching the aerobatics, and Jon absentmindedly stroked the hatchling's small muzzle, bringing the usual response of a soft sigh.

As they left the stable yard, they joined the line of those making a pilgrimage to the temple. The journey here was not an easy one; most of those in line were travel worn, and proceeded with heads bowed. Nightmare looked about with the same curiosity as Jon, the little dragon hissing at any that dared draw too close. The crowd parted as the black robed mage made his way toward the main gate of the temple that rose above them.

The line stopped at the gate where the weary travelers could see a large inner courtyard which held a few privileged travelers milling about waiting for their turn to be admitted to show respect to the High Priestess.

The guards stopped him at the gate. "What business have you in the temple?" demanded the man who appeared to be in charge, his hand on the hilt of the sword.

Jon cocked an eyebrow at the man, who stood a head taller than him and twice as wide. "Either you are blind or inept. I bring this small hatchling for the High Priestess' flight."

The man actually looked at the small dragon, seeming unimpressed. "Is the High Priestess expecting you?"

Jon tipped his head, his eyes narrowing as he looked at the guardsman. "Obviously not, or you would not be standing there asking inane questions. I do not know how much more tolerance this wee one has before it starts spitting acid at people." Those that were close behind him took several steps back. "I suggest you send me through so that we can get him settled."

The man nodded at Jon as though the mage's words had finally brought him to his senses. He motioned one of his fellow guards over. "Take this mage to a private parlor and then let the High Priestess know that a dragon has come in."

The guard who had approached saluted, then turned to Jon. "If you will follow me, milord." He turned and led the way through the narrow gate.

Jon was content to be led wherever it was that he needed to go. Everywhere he looked he saw black robed acolytes tending the pathway gardens, weeding the side paths and sweeping the wide walkway - really a road - to the main building. He knew they were no more than simple attendants of the temple, for their robes were of common cloth with no embellishments.

There was a peace inside the wall that amazed him. He noted the sound of his own footfalls, the swish of the acolyte's brooms and the rustle of the breeze through the early spring leaves above his head. Those that were speaking here and there seemed hushed and equally aware of the strange calm. He was so absorbed in taking in the magnificence surrounding him that he almost ran into an acolyte sweeping.

Jon shook his head and followed the guard up the stairs and into the main receiving hall, where there was a bit more noise. People had ill family members with them on stretchers and handcarts. This was not a temple of healing, but a place of passage; for a substantial donation, one could buy a space in the crypt. However, the people that he saw seemed far too common for the most part to be here for that. It made him curious, but he shelved the question until he could ask the High Priestess or a talkative acolyte, if such existed.

He was placed in a simple room, holding a small table with a decanter of wine and two glasses, framed by three chairs. There was a large black fireplace that crackled merrily, taking the chill off the early spring morning. He moved to the fire to warm both himself and the small fledgling.

Nightmare had burrowed under his cloak for the flight, for the air had a bitter bite even when flying just over the treetops. Jon turned his back to the fire, where the warmth drew the small dragon out to hang by his tail, basking in the flames. Fortunately, he did not weigh much yet, so the tight constriction of the tail to Jon's throat was only slightly uncomfortable.

He had expected to wait for some time since Lady Morana was not expecting him, so he was surprised when the door opened only a short while later. Nightmare sprung up at the sound of the door, to curl back around the safety of Jon's shoulders.

Jon was caught completely off guard, despite Alador's warning that the woman who entered was not his goddess but her priestess. Her long hair was coiled in ringlets, most piled from the top of her head and cascading down. Her lips had to be painted, for their red was like blood first exposed to the air. Her gown was built in layers of voluminous black material, the bottom a series of cascades of silken material trimmed in gold thread. A corset was set over the top of the gown, laced with gold and decorated with gentle loops of black braids. The corset pushed her breasts up to perfect mounds that swelled just above the tight fabric. The sleeves were sheer and only closed at her elbow and her wrist, giving almost a winged appearance. It took him a moment to realize he was staring before he descended to one knee.

"Milady," he acknowledged.

"Rise, mage." The dry rasp of her voice was a startling contrast to her outward beauty, and only her confident tones kept him from rushing to offer her a sip of wine for her throat.

She looked him over with a critical eye. "What is your name?" She demanded, but her eyes had already shifted to Nightmare before he could answer. She took a step forward, "And pray tell, where did you acquire the hatchling?"

"I come from the bloodmine. It was assaulted. The dragons you sent to protect it fell under the onslaught of other flights." Jon gave a flat factual report. "This is the only one of the fledglings I could save." He paused and gave a slight bow. "I am known merely as Jon."

She put her hand up to the fledgling without even hesitating. Even more to Jon's surprise, Nightmare did not hiss. The little hatchling purred as she rubbed between its eyes, only protesting when she attempted to remove it from Jon's shoulder.

Jon winced as Nightmare's talons dug into his flesh. The little dragon drew back and let out a growl of warning that was really more of a whimper, due to its small size. "I fear, milady, that he has bonded with me during the trip to bring him to you."

"Do you need to return to the bloodmine?" Lady Morana asked, withdrawing her hand to calm the small beast.

"It fell completely. There is nothing to return to." Jon stated. "My loyalty is to Dethara, rather than to Silverport or its minister. I would prefer to stay with the hatchling." Jon knew that not all death mages were also priests. He knew that not all those seeking priesthood were mages. To be both would automatically place him in higher rank than the acolytes he passed on his way into the temple.

She was about to speak when Jon thought to add, "May I point out that I am also trained in blade use within the Blackguard?" It was possible he could get closer to over time if she believed he could protect her.

She nodded her permission. "I will have a cave assigned for your use. Each dragon's cave has a small quarter for its keeper. I think you will find it a pleasant enough space." Lady Morana was talking to him, but all her attention was trained on Nightmare. Her eyes only flitted to Jon's face on occasion, the greed within her gaze reserved for the hatchling.

"I am sure that it will more than suffice." Jon answered politely. "He has not eaten," he added in a questioning tone, caressing the small head that pressed into his hands.

"I will have a keeper sent to you to show you where the supplies are kept for those that live in the caverns above the temple." She finally turned her gaze away from Nightmare, her eyes moving from head to toe, assessing the young mage. "You will wait here until someone is sent to escort you. You said your name is Jon?" She asked to clarify.

"Yes, milady, that is correct." He gave a slight bow once more. "We will do as you have bid."

"Welcome home, Jon." Morana's voice held a strange silken edge rather than the rasp it had exhibited earlier. Jon felt a shiver go up his spine.

Though her words of welcome were proper, he felt as if a cage door had just swung shut behind him. Nightmare's weight was suddenly apparent, as was the tail about his throat. For a brief moment, he realized he felt much like a fly must feel in the spider's web. His eyes followed her as she turned and swept from the room. He took a settling breath as the door closed. He was in the temple as he planned. For a brief moment, he wondered if he should flee while he still could.

## Chapter One

Alador waited for Nemara on the veranda outside his office, where breakfast had been laid for them both. He stood at the rail overlooking the city; the sun was shining, but the air was strangely still and heavy. Still, it was spring, and the winter was finally behind him. He was so deep in thought that he startled at Nemara's touch, not having heard her soft tread as she joined him at the rail.

"What has you so deep in thought that I can sneak up on you?" she teased as she thumped him on the arm, but her smile did not make it to her eyes. Nemara had seemed different after her return with the egg. It had been two weeks since their return, and still she was not quite the woman that Alador had conspired with to bring down the bloodmines, a dragon bleeding facility. At times, he felt like she was doing her best to act 'normal' around him.

"Nemara, we can't keep the egg here," he replied, once again broaching the subject. They had already argued about this twice. Since she appeared with the dragon egg, she had become quite territorial; one would think it was her egg, the way she protected and hovered about it.

She bristled instantly. "Why not?" He looked over at her, marveling at how she could look so beautiful even when she first woke up. Her red hair was loose, falling around her shoulders; it glistened in the sunlight with glints of burnished copper in the dark cherry strands. She had settled for a simple gray skirt and a soft blue tunic. It brought out her copper eyes and hair.

He turned to face her, ready to do battle once more. "Nemara, someone is going to find out. I can't keep the servants at bay saying you're sick and likely contagious much longer." He gazed down at her, tenderly pushing a few strands of hair out of her glaring eyes.

"Where else are you going to find a pool to keep it warm that you can also protect?" She put her hands on his chest, a pleading look in her eyes. "We have to keep it safe. I promised Rena before she died." She almost choked out the words. This was another example of how she had changed since her return. She was so emotional.

"I am going to take it to Pruatra." he said firmly. "She is Rena's mother and will know how to care for it." Somehow Alador felt he needed to get the dragon dame involved. How had this ever happened? He couldn't fathom the magic that must have taken place, out of his control and as it would seem Rena's as well.

"I can care for it!" Nemara snapped, her hands dropping to her sides in defiance. "I can hear it move. Rena gifted me with the knowledge to take care of it."

"You have kept your promise, Nemara. You brought the egg safely to me." Alador reached out and gently touched her shoulder, "but I can't keep it safe, nor can I keep others from finding out." Nemara shook off his hand. "We have no idea how long until it hatches because of my influence in its creation," he persisted. "We have gone over this." He took her hands from her sides where they were clenched into fists and held them tightly. "Pruatra is the best choice we have."

Nemara searched his face worriedly, her eyes still threatening tears. "What if she refuses because... because it is partly a mortal's hatchling?"

"Then I will have to make her see reason." Alador leaned in and kissed her cheek. "I will make her see the connection to Rena."

"She might kill it if it's not a dragon, as she expects a dragon to be." Nemara visibly wilted.

Alador put his arms about her. "It might be as well if she did, Nemara. If it is some misshapen monster, it would be kinder."

She shuddered against him, struggling with his logic. He felt it when she finally relented, her body fairly sagging in his arms. "All right." Her answer was muffled against his chest. She looked up at him. "Are you going to send me away too?"

Her eyes held her concern as she waited for his answer. She seemed so attached to the egg and him since her return. It worried him.

"No. The High Master has released you from service at my request and you are free to stay with me as long as you like." He put a hand under her chin and looked into her eyes. "I can arrange for you to return to the caverns if you would prefer."

She shook her head vigorously to his suggestion. "I want to stay with you."

This was not the spirited woman he had met in the caverns. Something significant had changed her. "Nemara, did something happen while you were trying to get to the egg and back? You haven't seemed yourself at all, even after rest and proper food." He kept his hands at her waist so that she could not escape his question.

"It was just a hard journey, that is all." She wiped the hair back from her face. "Am I really so different?" Her eyes seemed to come alive.

"Yes." His simple answer lay between them, silence building the tension.

She reached up and brushed her fingers over his cheek before her hand dropped and she attempted to turn away.

He held her firmly. "Nemara, what happened?"

"I don't know," she murmured defensively. "I haven't felt the same since Rena gave me a picture of the path to the egg." She scowled and absently rubbed her brow.

Alador's eyes narrowed. Had Rena attempted to take over Nemara and only given the information for the egg when she could not do it? Henrick had indicated it was quite the process; surely Rena would not have attempted it.

"Dragons can do that to a person," he offered. He would have to watch her more closely and see if there was any evidence of Rena's presence. He had loved

Rena, but there was no way he would have sanctioned the stealing of another's place in life. He guided Nemara to the table.

"You still need more rest." His words held an edge of authority rather than a simple comment. "You are too thin. Perhaps we can start practicing with each other in our sword play. I could use the workout and it might help you build your strength back up." He scooted the chair in as she slid into it.

"I guess," her answer held the edge of doubt.

She watched as he added food to her plate. He purposely chose things he knew she favored. Only when her plate was filled, did he take his own chair. He was fairly hungry after the workout with Luthian the night before. They had been practicing deflecting spells again; Alador was getting faster and now could often parry his uncle's swift use of spells.

"When will you go?" Nemara asked. She pushed her food around her plate, not really eating any of it.

"I am not going to tell you if you do not eat," he insisted, waving his fork at her, absentmindedly shrugging his shoulders. The air felt almost oppressive this morning, as if it were bearing down on him.

She scowled at him and dutifully shoved a bite in her mouth. Alador nodded his approval. "Luthian is going to Whitecliff in a few days, and he has said I need not go as he will be meeting privately with the High Minister there." Luthian, his uncle and the High Minister over all of Lerdenia, had been a hard task master since the fall of the bloodmines. Alador knew Luthian suspected his nephew of being involved, but had been unable to prove it. It seemed his alternative to an accusation was to keep Alador too busy to cause trouble.

While Nemara did not appear happy at the news it would be so soon, for the first time she had not become volatile. Their discussions previously had ended with them both angry, and with no resolution. They both fell silent, each lost in their thoughts as they continued their breakfast. The only sound was the cry of the gulls overhead, riding the breeze that had come up.

Alador eyes drifted out to the harbor. The tall masts were rocking in the bay as if they were sailing on a full sea. The bare masts and docks swayed with swells that had made their way into the harbor. He would have thought a massive storm had hit the port, but the air was still pleasant. White clouds dotted the blue skies here and there. It had been this way for a couple days, but today the ships danced. He noted the docks were much emptier than he had ever seen them.

"Nemara, I have to work on the council tier. Something doesn't feel right about today; promise me you will stay at the manor." He rose and stared out at the sea, focusing in with the dragon's gift of far-sight. Off in the distance he was sure he saw a band of gray clouds; perhaps a storm was coming in. He had been here for large storms in the past, but he couldn't shake the feeling that today felt different somehow.

"Of course. I really haven't taken much pleasure beyond these walls," she answered with a nod, following his line of vision. She rose and moved to his side. "What is it?" She followed his gaze to the ships in the harbor as they rocked back and forth like apples in a water barrel game.

"I am not sure. Look at the ships in the harbor." He pointed to where the differing size ships rose and fell as they bobbed left then right. "I have never seen so much movement of the water in the actual harbor. I think a storm is coming."

Nemara patted his arm with reassurance. "Silverport has weathered many a storm. Do not fret." She grinned at his concern and reached up to smooth his brow with her fingertips. "You worry too much."

"But... something today feels different." He ran a hand over his face. "Maybe I am just dreading having to spend yet another day with my uncle," he admitted.

The young woman nodded her head in agreement. "I would dread that every time I had to do so. Why you don't just tell him you don't want to be involved in the city's politics?" She blew out a sigh of frustration.

"If I mean to see him removed from power, I will need to remain close to him. I haven't figured out a way to do this without a direct challenge," Alador huffed. "I have practiced with him enough to know that I won't win that way," he mumbled under his breath.

"Can't you just have Sordith kill him?" she suggested.

"Yes. Sordith and I have even talked about this," he admitted. "There is no guarantee that someone worse won't take his place, however. Most of the council are self-serving egotists." Alador watched the skyline as he spoke. He noted the flags on the spires as they began to rise and fall in the growing sea breeze. "It is why I am working to gain access to the actual council. Then I can help someone with true care and concern assume the mantle of High Minister."

"You could be High Minster," she replied, eyeing him seriously.

Alador let out a long sigh and shook his head. "I have no desire to lead. I know it is what Henrick is working toward, but I just want this geas done and to move on with my life."

"Will removing Luthian end the geas?" Nemara asked curiously.

"Gods, I hope so." Alador truly did not know when it would end. He knew that a leader that cared about dragons needed to be in place. Surely there was someone who regretted the division between dragons and Lerdenia! Someone who would not advocate to reopen the bloodmine. The problem was, he just hadn't found anyone in the city that wanted to end the practice except Lady Aldemar. It was a dilemma he had not been able to solve and would not today. He pulled his thoughts back to the present.

"I had best go, Luthian hardly likes to be kept waiting." Alador sighed and pulled her over to him. When she did not resist, he laid a gentle kiss on her brow. "Promise me you will stay in today," he whispered.

"I promise." Nemara's answer was soft and barely audible.

"Good. I will see you tonight then." He cast one more glance at the skyline and then turned and strode away. He still felt an ominous pressure; whether it was having to go to Luthian or the strange feeling in the air, he could not determine.

## Chapter Two

Sordith stood on the docks outside the trench, suffering in the warm, overly humid day. The sun refracting off the water nearly doubled the heat, creating rivulets of sweat within his leather armor. The docks were unsteady under his feet, rocking with the swells in the bay as he waited for the harbor master to join him.

The tide was predicted to be high, and Sordith had been warned that a summer storm was coming in. He had ordered the boats out of the harbor, but there had not been enough sober crewman to get the remaining six out. He knew the time needed for the boats to make it to the storm hole was swiftly closing.

The storm hole was a deep, narrow inlet. It had good anchor and mooring positions in a small bay surrounded by rock cliffs and trees. The harbor master, Ferand Wischard, assured him that the trading fleet would be secure in this location.

The two old sea hands the harbor master employed to warn of severe weather events were calling for a storm of higher magnitude than the port city usually weathered. However, it hadn't taken an expert to know something large was headed their way. By mid-day there was not a single sea bird flitting about the harbor and the wind was gusting stronger with each passing hour.

Ferand approached from the far end of the dock as

Sordith was looking over an older boat to his left. His tall boots struck the wooden dock like hammers on an anvil. "Lord Sordith, I hope you are not disappointed. I think we've got the best of them out to sea." The harbor master stuck his thumbs in the wide belt that encircled his sizable girth. He was pleased he had done as well as he did getting the ships he could to a safe harbor.

Sordith's eyes roved over the six remaining ships. Ships were costly and time consuming to build, especially the mammoths that High Minister Luthian ordered. "What of these that are left?" He pointed at the boats at his side.

"Gotta crew workin' on additional tie lines and wrapping the ropes where they rub boat and dock to try to keep them from breaking. Plus, dropping down some spacers to keep the two from bumpin'." Ferand shrugged. "Best we can do at the moment, 'm 'fraid."

"Well, let us hope that we are overly prepared." Sordith gave a nod of approval as he spoke. "Anything else I can do to help?"

"No milord. I believe I have it handled," Ferand said with a grim look. "As much as one can take on the weather." He stood looking out to sea, the shirttail of his tunic flattened against his rotund belly by the wind as it picked up speed. "What about that storm mage everyone talks about? Can ya get him to chip in?"

Sordith stood for a couple seconds staring at the man. He had not even considered seeking out his half-brother, Alador, to see if there was something the man could do to lessen the impact of the storm. "It can't hurt to ask him. I will look into that immediately."

The two men nodded their farewells. Ferand went back to checking on his crew and the remaining boats.

Sordith started up the stairs to the trench. Fortunately, it was a good ten feet above the dock line, so even with the tide as high as it was thought to become, his people would be safe. The only time he had known it to get high enough to impact the trench was a storm that created a backflow of the sewage for a few hours when he was a youngster. He remembered sitting on the steps to the first tier to stay above the filth.

Owen was waiting for him at the top of the stairs. "Got that old mine opened up for those that wanna get out of the rain just like you asked," he said as Sordith took the last couple of steps up to the trench.

"Good, get a couple of men to spread the word and then meet me at the stairs. We are going to the council tier." Sordith didn't even pause, expecting Owen to turn and keep up with him.

Owen grumbled. "I hate them upstart mages in all their fancy dresses."

"They are robes, Owen, not dresses." Sordith pointed out with a wry grin as he sidestepped a woman and her child hurrying down the stairs.

"It looks like a dress, it be a dress as I figure it." The big man backed up against the wall of a building avoiding the woman and her snotty nosed child. He hurried to come up alongside Sordith.

"Yes, well looks can be deceiving. A few of those

mages in their fancy dresses could kick your ass without a sweat." Sordith made his way to the steps to the trench hall then turned to look at Owen. The wind whipped his hair into his eyes. He raised a hand and pushed it back.

"Not if I be gettin' my hands on them," Owen pointed out.

"Hence, the reasons mages don't let men like us close to them." Sordith chuckled at Owen's response. "Start getting the word out. I need to clean up and then I will be right there."

Sordith turned at Owen's salute and took the steps two at a time. He was so used to climbing them that they did not even wind him anymore. The day he couldn't take them swiftly would be a day to worry about his end as Trench Lord. He was rather grateful for them today. The trench hall was higher up and less likely to be impacted by the trench then the denizens on a level with it.

He made his way to his suite. Keelee was nowhere to be seen; it was just as well, as he had given her a task and he was in a hurry. He had asked her to see about helping the trench orphans get to the cave he set aside for them. It was one on the leeward side of the city and would afford them safety and protection from the elements. Keelee was also going to see about getting it stocked with food and supplies for a couple of days. She had adjusted so well to her role as his lady and living in the trench.

Sordith had a soft spot for the city orphans who were too young to test or had failed their test. He too had been relegated to survival in the trench when he was a young boy. Starving, scavenging for food, sometimes thrown into servitude and beaten; this was the typical life of an orphan in the trench. It was a hard life even when the Trench Lord was generous, and Aorun had not been generous. Death in the trench was a daily event, but it stung when it was the young who were dying.

Sordith changed into clean clothes that would not smell of trench and fish. Since the day Luthian found Sordith and assorted females in Alador's bed, the High Minister had treated him coldly; it wouldn't do to make things even more strained by showing up filthy. The High Minister had established a very businesslike attitude toward the Trench Lord, treating him as though he was not worth his time, which suited Sordith just fine as he didn't want the powerful mage meddling in the trench. Unfortunately, Luthian would need a report on the security of the harbor. More importantly Sordith knew Alador would be there, as he always was lately.

Once properly attired for the upper tiers, Sordith set out. Owen caught up with him at the steps to the first tier, and Sordith had to give him credit, for it looked as if Owen had at least attempted to clean up a bit. They made their way through the city and up the winding paths to the upper tiers. It was not a simplistic system for getting from the top to the bottom, but it was an effective defense mechanism.

The city was bustling with its normal routines. Merchants hawked their wares. Ladies strolled about showing off their latest dress or jewelry. Most seemed oblivious to the weather.

Relatively speaking, Silverport was a rich city. A mine of medure beneath its towering height ensured that those with any marketable skill did fairly well within the cities confines. For the most part, even lower tiered denizens who had little to no mage skill but had found placement as a servant were doing quite well.

Upon arrival, Sordith was admitted into the High Minister's manor house with only minimal delay. He would have to step carefully if Alador and Luthian were together. Sordith didn't want to give away how closely he and his half-brother were aligned. Fortunately, having saved the young mage's life from Aorun, and then being present at his testing, had given him a little more room to maneuver.

He was ushered into Lord Luthian's receiving room by a guard, having left Owen in the hall due to the oaf's lack of social skills and somewhat "trench" flavor. The large room was as intimidating as he remembered it, lush and radiating the importance of its occupant. Luthian sat behind a massive desk in a calculated display of power that Sordith understood, having the same sort of setup in his own receiving chamber. Unlike his room, however, the walls here were lined with books and maps rather than weapons.

He approached to the proper distance and bowed low. "High Minister, thank you for seeing me." He glanced about and caught sight of Alador over to his far left at his own small work desk. He nodded briefly and turned his attention back to Luthian.

Luthian beckoned for the guard that had escorted him in to leave them. "You do not call without invitation. I figured the matter must be urgent." He laid down the letter he had been reading when Sordith entered.

Sordith got right to the point. "According to the weather watchers down at the harbor, there is a large storm descending on the city. I have the trading fleet out, but I was hoping I could borrow your storm mage to redirect the storm entirely, or at least soften its blow." He glanced over at Alador and back to the High Minister.

Luthian waved a dismissive hand. "I hardly see the concern. We weather such storms every descent to the winter turn." Luthian sat back in his chair.

Alador rose to join them. "If I may, Uncle, I too noted something is amiss with the storm that is approaching. I did not speak of it because I planned to check on it while you were in audience." The three were now triangulated as Luthian sat considering.

"You feel it is larger than most?" Sordith watched as Luthian's sharp eyes picked up the note of concern in Alador's voice as well as his words.

"I do. I also felt that there was something… unnatural about it." Alador replied uneasily.

"Unnatural?" Sordith asked, looking perplexed.

"Yes, I can't explain it. It just feels... wrong, somehow." Alador shrugged helplessly.

Luthian rose and went to the window. The storm had advanced, and while the weather was still quite warm, a wind had begun to pick up. The standards along the council tier were snapping firmly in the wind. A line of billowing black clouds was easily seen on the horizon. "Do you think we are being attacked by another storm mage?" Luthian turned to scrutinize his nephew.

"I don't know. It was too far off this morning to discern much more than that it was… off and very large." Alador admitted unhappily.

"Then it is time you took up the mantle you have trained for." Luthian nodded to Sordith. "Alador is free to assist you with this storm. Do what must be done to secure the harbor's safety." Luthian rose and picked up a couple of papers. "I would join you out of curiosity, but I fear I am needed to see to the complaints of the merchant class at the moment."

Alador bowed to his uncle's decree while Sordith gave a brief nod. "Thank you, High Minister. I will be grateful for his services." They both followed Luthian out of his office and parted in the hall to head down to the harbor.

"I will need to get my cloak." Alador grimly stated as he strode down the hall to the door.

"Afraid you might melt, milord?" Sordith winked at Owen. He couldn't call Alador brother, but his wit was rarely held back and he felt no concern at teasing his sibling.

"You're right," Alador conceded. "This storm is so big that a cloak is likely to be little help. Water rarely concerns me anyway."

"You are spending too much time on this tier." Sordith grumbled. "You are totally losing your sense of humor."

"I have been told I never really had one to begin with," the mage quipped back.

Sordith laughed. "True… matter of fact, I think that I am one who has cast such accusations upon you." The two men made their way off the council tier, with Owen following close behind in their wake.

Alador sobered, bringing the conversation back to serious matters. "I am a bit concerned about the tide combined with this storm. It appears that both will hit almost at the same time."

The two men moved swiftly through the city, bustling activity parting for them as the Trench Lord and the fifth tier mage who had broken the testing sphere passed.

Once down to the busy third tier, the main merchant tier of the city, Alador turned toward the Blackguard caverns rather than the second tier.

"Where are you going?" Sordith paused as they started to go different directions.

"The overlook outside the caverns. It has the best view of both the harbor and the ocean," Alador pointed out. He stopped and waited for Sordith and Owen to join him, and then the trio continued on.

Sordith lowered his voice so Owen could not overhear. "What could be unnatural about this storm?" He knew how to combat natural elements for the most part, but unnatural brought an unpredictable element. Sordith did not like the unpredictable.

Alador lowered his voice to a whisper. "Well, as Luthian suggested, it could be an attack from another mage.".

"And if not that?" Sordith asked worriedly.

"I don't know."

Sordith's brow wrinkled with concern and his voice dropped to an urgent whisper. "You are a storm mage, shouldn't you know what else it might be? What about those dragon memories of yours?"

The look that Alador flashed him held something of frustration and irritation. Sordith realized that for the first time, he had little room left to push his half-brother. There was an air about Alador that was different. A strange confidence in his tone and his walk, and even his small mannerisms had changed. How much of the impulsive lad he had first met was left? They had not been able to talk much since Luthian put him on such a short leash.

"Let me see what I can fathom when we get to the overlook," Alador snapped.

They all three walked in silence the rest of the way. The overlook was unoccupied when the men stepped out onto it. Sordith stood a half step back now to stand beside Owen. The storm had rolled in enough that he could clearly see the cloud line off on the horizon. There were flashes of lightning visible from even this distance. One thing he knew, whether natural or magical, they were in for a storm the likes of which he had never seen.

## Chapter Three

Alador stood on the edge of the parapet, his hands on the rock wall as he leaned forward to stare out at the horizon. The storm was visible to everyone now, but he needed to look at it from a different perspective. The storm was violent, and even from here he could tell it was stronger than anything he had personally weathered. He longed to see it from above; if he could only take wing like Renamaum and see how it was building, he might be able to combat the threat of its landing better. The idea of seeing it through a 'dragon's eyes' gave him the thought that he might be able to project his essence into the water as he had once in the past. He took a deep breath and pulled on his inner power.

Alador felt his inner self leave his body. He saw the wall of clouds black and boiling as his soul approached the edge of the storm, and he knew Renamaum had seen such cloud movements before. The memory surfaced like a breaching whale - the speed with which the storm rolled and coiled, accelerating as he watched, was there in their shared mind.. It almost appeared alive and very... very... angry.

He focused in and turned his attention to the air stones, which danced and collided with no discernible pattern. It was like watching a hornet's nest that had been poked with a stick. He redirected his view from the air stones and took in the ocean itself, plunging into the sea beneath the fast advancing bank of clouds.

Instantly, his vision was clouded by churning sand ripped from the ocean floor by the massive undercurrent of the sea. He could feel the surge; like a beast, it wrapped itself around him and propelled him forward. If he had been in his corporeal form, he would have been tossed about like a log in a river flooded by torrential rains. A deep memory of Renamaum's overwhelmed him, a memory of a storm, eons ago - a storm that was so violent it even drove dragons to cover.

He saw a massive wall of water inundate the shore. It was so tall he wondered if Renamaum's memory could even be trusted. If the wave was based on Renamaum's height, from his point of view, then Alador had no doubt the surge would breach the rocks that protected the small harbor from the normal movement of the ocean currents.

Sordith noticed his brother's silence and his stare, riveted out on the sea. He moved forward to the wall edge and touched Alador's arm. "Brother, what is it?"

Alador's soul was jerked back into his body with the touch of Sordith's hand. He leaned forward, his hands still clutching the rock wall. His knees felt weak, and he gulped in air as though he had been drowning.

"It's coming," he gasped.

Their eyes met. "What's coming?" The look of fear on Alador's face scared Sordith more than the storm.

"There is going to be a wall of water pushed by this storm." Alador pulled his gaze from the cloud bank speeding toward them and looked directly at Sordith. "It will be tall enough to flood the harbor without slowing down."

"Will it hit the trench?" Sordith became grave as he glanced at what appeared to him to be just a stronger storm on the horizon.

His brother almost whispered, "It may even hit the first tier."

"The first tier? That has never happened." Sordith glanced down. From here, they both could see the stairs to the trench level and even the edge of the first tier.

"Get your people out of the trench, Sordith." Alador urged, with an undercurrent of what almost sounded like panic. "Send them to the lee of the city. Send them to the upper tiers, but get them out," he hissed.

"How long do you think we have?" Sordith asked with concern. "Between the miners and the others, that is a lot of people to move."

"Maybe three...four hours, maximum." Alador replied. He was watching the storm's advance again. The threatening clouds crawled across the horizon, turning daytime into night. He could see the occasional lightning flash.

"Owen!" the Trench Lord called.

Owen's head snapped up from where he was concentrating on cleaning his nails with the tip of his dagger. He had lived in the trench for years. He had seen storms come and go. To his way of thinking, the Trench Lord seemed far too concerned about the arrival of this one.

"Yes?" he responded as he shoved his dagger home in its sheath.

"I need you to gather all the members of my guard, immediately. Meet me in the courtyard of Trench Hall as soon as possible."

Owen turned to comply. It was good to have something to do other than follow Sordith around with his Mage friend.

"Owen!" Sordith raised his voice over the wind that had picked up.

The man pulled up short and turned back with a slightly irritated look. Come… Go… which did the Trench Lord want?

"Hurry, man, we will need to move everyone from the trench."

Owen's jaw dropped. "Everyone from the trench - to where?" he asked in a perplexed tone.

"Higher ground… Much higher ground." Sordith glanced out to sea. The storm was now an ominous beast nipping at their heels. Soon it would take a chunk out of them, if his brother was right.

Owen did as he was ordered and hurried off.

"Can you stop it? Redirect it?" Sordith clutched the edge of the wall as if it might fortify his brother answer.

Alador shook his head. "Not by myself." He felt defeated before he even started. Renamaum's memory of the previous storm of this size filled his brain with anguish, even… fear. "It is too large and chaotic." He

looked at his brother. "I don't know, maybe with help."
Could he? Could he at least modify its impact?

"Can you shield the city?" Sordith knew that many
of the trench occupants would be hard to move. Only the
stubborn usually survived in the trench, making
management of them all that much more difficult.

"I don't know Sordith. Not alone..." He couldn't
do this alone. He wasn't strong enough. Renamaum's
memories told him to run, not fight. "My dragon memory
has a vision of such a storm and it is overwhelming. This
storm... It is... unusual and I can only guess that it's an
attack on the isle." Was it Dethara? Had she created the
storm? Was it some sort of revenge for the attack on the
bloodmines? Alador's tension increased. "I couldn't
make this type of storm, so if it is an attack, the mage is
stronger than I am."

"So, what do we do?" Sordith glanced down at the
opening to the trench. His eyes drifted out over the
harbor. The six remaining ships were swaying in the wind
even though their sails had been lowered and bundled.

"Block the opening is my first thought." Alador
offered, "but then, if it does reach the first tier..." His
voice trailed off.

Sordith stood looking at him. What horror was his
brother seeing in his mind?

"Either way, the floor level is going to flood.
Between the rain and sea, I don't see any way to prevent
it." Alador turned away from the storm and looked at
Sordith. "Will the storehouses resist water?"

"Yes, to an extent. Each is built up before burrowing down. If the water gets higher than the slant, the doors will let it through beneath." Sordith's voice held an edge of panic. "I have to get men moving things off the storehouse floors."

"Go... Go!" Alador urged. "I will see my uncle about sending someone to build a wall between the trench and the harbor."

Sordith nodded and turned. He did not walk - the man ran as if chased by minions of Dethara. Alador had worked with Luthian long enough to know that the city's wealth and stores were in those storehouses, and he had no idea how much of it could withstand a soaking in salt water.

Alador simply did not bother walking back to the council tier. If someone had been watching, they would have seen the mage walking away from the rock wall and then magically disappearing. He materialized in his uncle's office with the help of his amulet and a quickly conjured traveling spell, certain his uncle would still be attending to those seeking advice or decisions. He made his way down the hall to where Luthian held such audiences. He walked in the side door usually reserved for only Luthian.

Luthian looked up in surprise when the door opened. Alador met his gaze with serious intent. "Lord Guldalian, I fear there is a more urgent matter that needs your attention."

Alador knew that his uncle would understand that he would not interrupt him unless the need was dire.

Luthian rose and dismissed the merchant before him with a wave of his hand. When the man attempted to protest, the High Minister gave him such a powerful look that the words which might have been forming in the man's mouth dried on his tongue and he hurried away following the servant as order. He would come another day when the High Minister was in a more congenial mood and willing to receive.

Luthian turned to the servant scribe at his elbow and told him to send the rest away for the day, as an urgent matter had arisen.

Alador's uncle led the way back to the office, neither man speaking until the door to the library closed. The High Minister made for his desk as Alador began to speak behind him.

"The storm is intense, Uncle. It is bigger than anything I could manifest," Alador admitted, "but that is not the worst of it."

Luthian's eyes widened slightly. "Not the worst?"

Alador moved into a rest position typical of the Blackguard, hands clasped behind him. "There will be a wave such as we have never seen, which will likely swamp the harbor and the trench, possibly even the first tier."

Luthian swore under his breath. "I have never heard of such a thing. Are you certain?"

Alador nodded. "I can sense it." He was not about to tell his uncle he had actually seen and felt its power. "While I can't discern the actual height, I was able to make a rough estimate of the minimum." He paused, knowing his news was dire. "It *will* cross the harbor."

"How far up and down the coast? Will it hit other cities?" Luthian became all business. "And most importantly, can you soften its blow, or turn it?"

"I don't think I can alone. I might be able to with help." Alador stated.

"With help? If you cannot turn it, how could a lesser storm mage?" Luthian eyed Alador with a bit of confusion.

"I will meld our powers," the younger mage replied.

"Meld... your powers?" Luthian eyes widened and he slowly sank into the chair behind his desk. "That is unheard of!" His eyes met Alador's and his look became more than curious, it was accusatory. "Where did you learn such a thing?" he demanded.

Alador tried not to look shocked at the question, but he was surprised at Luthian's reaction and cursed inwardly. The melding of his powers with Rena's had happened so easily that he had wrongly assumed all mages could do such things. He had just erred in a major way and scrambled internally for an explanation.

"Unheard of?" Now he *did* put on an air of being shocked. "But my father taught me this skill!" Alador tried to sound alarmed. "It is not something you both know?" He hoped he could deflect the suspicion of his uncle from himself to Henrick. If Luthian thought his father was holding back such a power he would be more concerned about that than the fact that his nephew, who he felt he had control over, had learned such a valuable bit of magic.

"Noooo," Luthian drawled, eyeing Alador intently. "He somehow managed to keep that to himself." There was anger simmering just below this uncle's words.

"I am sorry I didn't mention it." Alador dropped his eyes. He had managed to sidestep the High Minister, or so he hoped. "Henrick offered to teach me, and I thought we might have use of it someday to further the cause of uniting the isle."

Luthian was quiet for a long moment. "This is something you know you can do? You have done it before."

Alador nodded. "Once or twice," he truthfully admitted. He shifted uncomfortably under his uncle's gaze and neither spoke for a long minute.

"Then, let us get busy," Luthian finally interjected. "I will find every other storm mage in the city and send them to you. Where do you need them?"

"The overlook outside the Blackguard caverns." Alador stated. "If you could also send mages down to help in the trench, I am sure that the flooding will overwhelm the storehouses. Plus, we have to get the people out of there. Sordith is going to need help."

Luthian nodded, considering intently. Alador felt unsettled by the look on his face. There was something in his gaze that was calculating. What was the High Minister planning now?

"Come to the map and show me the minimum edges of this storm." He rose and started toward the small room that held his detailed maps. "I will need to send orders to any cities in peril."

Alador followed him into the other room, relieved they had moved beyond the subject of melding magic.

The young mage was quick to point out cities on the coast that were likely to have their sea walls breached. In between were many small fishing villages, and he looked up at his uncle with concern. "Can we get word to them to move inland?"

"I can try." Luthian frowned at the map and the numerous locations that would be affected. "The cities all have scrying bowls, as you know. We will have the scryers send orders. I can also send my messengers out by lexital until the winds prevent flight."

Alador had a momentary shock when a memory from Renamaum unexpectedly surfaced of him careening through the last storm of this size – fighting the winds as if were another living being.

Luthian did not notice his nephew swallow hard and force down the fear that engulfed him. He was eyeing the map. "At least we have a bit of warning; I will do what I can." He looked up and squeezed Alador's arm. "Where is the main intensity of the storm going to land?"

Alador struggled to shake off Renamaum's memory. He leaned over and studied the map. He placed a marker down the coast. "Here." He placed another up the coast. "And here." Silverport was all but dead center of the two markers. He looked up at his uncle gravely.

"You are certain?" Luthian eyed the map.

"Yes. If I am going to divert it, the best I can do is maybe get the brunt of it up or down the coast. I am not going to be able to stop it from landing." Alador knew that the air stones were beyond his reach still and by the time they were close enough he was not going to be able to turn it back out to sea, if he could turn it at all.

"How long do I have before this surge?" Luthian was studying the map.

"Maybe two hours now." Time was flying by. The delay at the wall discussing it with Sordith, plus the minutes Luthian and he had talked about it here, had stretched into over an hour. He wanted to instill a sense of urgency in his uncle's actions.

The rain had begun a good half hour ago, and the pelting sound of the water hitting the windows tapped out a somber tune warning of what was to come.

Luthian yanked the bell and a servant appeared almost instantly. Alador noticed the reaction of the man when he saw the scowl on his uncle's face. The young mage had seen the looks of fear the servants had for their lord, and was glad that he did not have the same effect on his own serving staff.

"Get me the chief scryer." Luthian commanded.

The servant bowed quickly and scurried off to obey his master's order.

The High Minister moved to his desk and sat down. He pulled forward parchment and dipped his quill. "I will send orders for each city to move their residents to high ground and send bronze mages down into the trenches to seal the storehouses." His pen flew across the paper in between frantic dips of his quill in the ink bottle. "I doubt any other city has a storm mage to lead such an effort to forestall the impact of the wave." He scratched another line. "I will wish them luck."

Alador nodded. "Do you need me any further? If not, I will return to the overlook and do what I can."

Luthian shook his head no. "Your warning has given us time to mitigate the losses."

Alador considered. "You might want to send word to General Levielle, much of your army is in tents, and a tent will afford no protection against this beast. You might also use their manpower to fortify the wall between the harbor and the trench."

Luthian raised a brow. "Your choice of words is ominous." He put the quill down and sanded the parchment. "I will send word immediately to have the general attend me with haste. It is good to see you have been paying attention to my lessons in the city's management."

Alador smiled and could not help feeling a bit of pleasure at the usually harsh mage's praise. It was rare that Luthian had a kind word unless he was being manipulative. He nodded to his uncle and stepped back a few paces before turning to head for the door.

He stopped and gathered his cloak this time; he really didn't want to be soaked when he attempted this. He did not bother with his Blackguard armor, as Luthian would be sending mages to attend him and they would likely struggle to follow a half-breed as it was.

He sighed as he headed out of the manor. He had

gravely erred when he let Luthian know he could meld powers. He was sure that the discussion of that ability was not over, but there were just more pressing matters at hand. He would have to remember to speak with Sordith and Henrick about his slip up.

The moment he started down the steps, the wind on the high tier assaulted him. It was not strong enough to be dangerous, but it was moving well enough to drive the rain into his face. Fortunately, most of the way down he would not be facing the wind directly. He focused on the task at hand.

Each level he dropped through, he warned the guards he saw, Blackguard or Home Guard, of what was to come. He noted as he descended to the third tier, merchants were taking down the cloth awnings before their shops. Puddles were forming in each nook and dip in the walk. Citizens were hurrying here and there with cloaks pulled close. The rain was coming down hard enough to soak through clothing. He saw a stray hat fly by – caught by the wind and lifted from its owner's brow.

House after house was securing shutters. At least the people knew a storm when they felt it and were doing their best to prepare. They just had no idea how powerful this one was going to be. Most of the city was made of stone – it wouldn't wash away. Alador's concern was the wave he felt, and one he saw in Renamaum's memory. It could strip the tiers of anything not nailed down – maybe even things that were.

The young mage could part water into waves, but could he stop a behemoth even dragons feared?

## Chapter Four

Luthian sent a runner ordering General Levielle to attend him immediately. While he waited, he met with the head scryer and gave detailed instruction to send messages to the other cities in danger. The rain, driven by the wind, drew his attention to the window. It struck the panes so hard it sounded like pebbles rather than water. Luthian walked closer to see if the rain had turned to hail even though the temperature was not low enough to warrant that option.

The guard opened the High Minister's door and announced, "The General has arrived, milord."

Luthian turned, nodded and beckoned the man forward. "General, thank you for coming so quickly. We have matters of some urgency to discuss."

The man's face was red from the wind and rain, and despite the probable use of a cloak he was still quite sodden. Luthian moved away from the window, leading the General to the small map room. He did not look back, expecting the man to follow him.

As they entered, Luthian beckoned him forward to the table. The map laying on it was one Levielle had seen before. He moved up beside Luthian, hands clasped behind his back and eyes darting about with interest.

"What matters are concerning you, High Minister?" His tone was soft and inquisitive.

"I have been informed that we are about to be hit by a storm of never-before-seen size and strength. My nephew, the storm mage, has told me there will be an enormous wall of water when it comes ashore." He indicated the two markers that Alador put down for the minimum impact on the coastal communities. "It will affect the coast from here… to here. The strongest part of it will be directly centered on Silverport." Luthian looked at him with genuine concern. "I have called you here because your men are bivouacked in tents, and tents will not withstand this gale."

The General leaned over the map, his eyes taking in the breadth of the storm's impact. "Really that large? If it is of that magnitude, a good portion of the island will be hit." Levielle looked up at Luthian with a bit of fear in his eyes. "We have to evacuate the lower tiers. There will be flooding, and I will need to get my men to safety." He returned to studying the board intently, looking for a means of escape.

"My nephew suggested the lee of the city, where the wind will be less." Luthian looked over at Levielle.

The General nodded in agreement, still not looking up from the map.

Luthian cleared his throat in order to draw the man's attention back to him. When the General looked up he said, "I have no intentions of evacuating the lower tiers. In fact, I would like a contingent of guards on each tier ensuring order and preventing a mass push upwards."

A flash of confusion and concern appeared on Levielle's face. "Well, you could send bronze mages down to the trenches to raise a wall up between the city and the port. That way, the water and wind will break against it, minimizing the possibility of damage and injury to the trench and lower tiers." Levielle stroked his beard idly, then looked for a city map nearby. "That way you won't need to evacuate."

There was a city map on the wall to his left. The General moved toward it. Luthian followed the man's gaze. "I have mages down there assisting the Trench Lord and sealing the storehouses as we speak. However, I cannot put a wall up between the port and the trench. Where would the water go that drains down from the upper tiers?" Luthian's voice was even. "To let them all move up will cause panic. Each must stay upon their assigned tier. Your men will see to it."

Levielle turned to look at Luthian. "My men will be unable to block that many people from trying to move up the tiers." He pinned the High Minister with a steady military gaze that must have put fear in his troops. "Have you ever seen a mob before, High Minister?" he asked coolly.

The gaze did absolutely nothing to deter Luthian from the plan he was about to unfold. "I have… Is that not why your men have swords, to enforce the law and order of this country?" Luthian stared him down. "They will block and hold each tier," Luthian commanded a bit more formally. "With force, if they must."

"You expect me to command my men to kill friends and loved ones to protect the upper tiers?" Levielle repeated in a low, shocked tone. "If the storm is as mighty as you have been told it will be, they too will be swept away."

"Sometimes harsh choices must be made to secure order." Luthian stated with just as low a voice. "And they won't be swept away unless they are down in the trench itself. It has been some time since such a thorough cleansing has been done."

"Am I to understand this is not a matter of cleaning the city, but of the people?" Levielle looked at the map on the wall and pointed to the trench. "You are speaking about half the population of the city, plus all of my encampment and men outside the city." He stared at Luthian levelly, "These are lives we are talking about: Men, women, and children!"

"You exaggerate, Sir. The trench is hardly half the city. It houses those not in service to the upper tiers; maybe a quarter of the city's population, at most." He looked to where Levielle was pointing. "Mostly vagabonds, whores and thieves, and well you know it. The mages will close the mines, so we will not lose good men who know how to dig the city's fortunes." He tapped his lip thoughtfully with one finger "You have maybe an hour to get your men inland or into the lee of the city. If you wish, you can attempt to shelter a good portion in the testing ring.".

The General stood quietly, studying the map and thinking. The High Minister gave him a moment to mull over his orders. The room grew silent except for the sound of rain striking the window.

Eventually, Levielle spoke. "We could move all of

them to the first tier. I will have my men guarding the shops and the gate to the second tier. It'll get close, but at least we will save those that can help and assist." His eyes met Luthian's. "If the storm is as bad as you and Alador think it will be, you'll need all the laborers you can get, High Minister."

Luthian looked at him for a long moment. He studied the map where the rocky hook of land guarded the harbor. Alador had stated that most likely the first tier would be hit, as well; however, the boy had not told anyone else as far as Luthian knew.

The High Minister finally nodded. "You are wise. See it done." He stated firmly. He turned and walked back into his office and the General followed in his wake. "Get supplies into your permanent buildings or the ring. I will have the test master raise a dome to protect it. I would raise it for the whole city, but to be honest, I do not think the mages could hold it for long at such a size."

"Thank you, High Minister. I will see that all preparations are made post-haste." Levielle's relief was almost palatable. "The trench may be destroyed, but we can rebuild it quickly. Perhaps with the assistance of those bronze mages being used to protect the goods." His tone was one of request and inner thought.

Luthian's answer rang of dismissal. "Yes, that would be the plan. I have sent similar orders to have the storehouses sealed in other coastal cities." Luthian looked over at Levielle. "I have done what I can to warn the small outlying fishing villages, but I fear the lexitals may already be pushed to the limit by the wind as it is." He moved back to the desk. "See yourself out General, time is of the essence." Luthian did not look up.

"Of course, High Minister." The General saluted. "It seems I'll need to get my hands dirty in the trench again." He smirked and stepped to the door, his hand on the knob.

"General…" Luthian called a halt to Levielle's hasty exit. "I want you to remain with your men in the garrison or the testing ring; it would not do for my main commander to be hit in the head by flying debris. Send one of your other commanders to see to the tiers and trench." This time, there was no room for discussion in his voice.

After a brief but tense silence, Levielle nodded. "Of course, High Minister, I will see it done."

Luthian sat back with a frustrated exhale of breath as the door closed. He knew Levielle was the most efficient man he had in the service, but the man's damn honor was so high that it was sometimes frustrating to work around him. It was good that he was expecting another to see the storage areas sealed. If you could not hit a problem directly, you always had the option to see it done subversively.

He moved to the bell pull, a cold smile playing across his lips as he considered what he was about to do. It would make a few enemies, but if it played out as he had formulated, his hands would be clean. While others would suspect, none would be able to tie him directly to the matter. A servant appeared within seconds of the peal of the bell.

"Yes, High Minister? What service may I provide?" The man bowed low and waited his master's order.

"Lady Caterine is expected. Check the receiving room, and if she has arrived, escort her to me immediately." Luthian turned and walked back to his desk.

By the time he sat down, the servant was gone; he had not heard the man's affirming whisper, but he had no doubt there had been one. He pulled over Sordith's last report. The number of people in the trench could never be more than estimated; people came into and left the city on a daily basis. Those that had no status were limited to the trench access unless they had coin and business on an upper tier.

He looked up as the door opened. The lady was on time, and he could not have been more pleased to see her.

She was not an unattractive woman, but there was also nothing striking about her. Her matronly curves were slight, but like most high tier mages, her hair was white. Today she had it piled up on her head, with small curls escaping around her face. The shade of brown she wore to signify her sphere seemed to wash her face of further color.

Luthian rose and moved around his desk to her as she came forward. The servant bowed and exited, shutting the door securely behind him. Luthian took Caterine's hand and laid his lips gently upon it. He was pleased to see a flush of color brighten her cheeks.

Luthian indicated a chair by the fire. "I am pleased

you could attend me so quickly. My nephew has informed me that we are in for quite the storm; as the leader of the stone mages, I need you to send people down to seal our storehouses." He waited until she sat down to continue.

She frowned, her placid face worsened with the grimace. "Of course, I am fully aware that our staples are stored beneath the city, but we have had storms before. The water has never breached the storehouses, High Minister."

"Please, we are alone… call me Luthian." He smiled, but it was more because the calculated familiarity had its desired effect. The lady smiled demurely and dropped her gaze, her cheeks taking on the rosy coloring again. "Alador has warned me that there will be a wave of an unusual height. I also know that it will land when the tide is at its highest." He sighed with a bit of forced distress. "I would rather be safe for our people than regret a lack of action. We have little time."

Caterine rose immediately. "Then I had best be off to see the task done." She turned to head for the door.

Luthian caught her arm. "One moment, I think we might have an opportunity that would profit us both." He paused until she turned back to look at him, her face full of her confusion. "Do you still have ill will toward our Trench Lord?"

Caterine's face hardened at the mention of Sordith's title. With Luthian's order to assist in the covering of the trench, she had been insulted to find herself working under the Trench Lord's direction.

"He is not in my favor," she admitted, her voice hoarse with distaste.

"And those in the trench? Your thoughts on them?" Luthian pressed.

"It is filthy and contains a forsaken lot who are barely more than animals." Her fingers brushed across her robe as though the mere thought of the trench and its inhabitants made her feel dirty.

Luthian nodded gravely as she played into his hands. "I feel much the same. May I suggest a little foul play?" He dipped his head in acknowledgment as a conniving look flashed in her eyes. He had chosen his mage correctly.

"What did you have in mind?" she practically cooed.

"Send your troublesome mages, those you have concerns over, into the trench to seal the storehouses against the weather; that truly does need doing. Once they are fully occupied, you seal the trench from the first tier."

"I fail to see what good this will do either of us?" She eyed him a bit warily.

"I have been told the wave will fully engulf the trench. The falling rain…" he indicated the window, "needs an outlet as it drains down the tiers, so sealing it against this wave is not an option."

"You plan to drown them?" She considered the idea.

"It is such a fine opportunity, don't you agree? I can assure you that no mages will interfere. General

Levielle is even now giving the order that there is to be no movement between the tiers." Luthian's voice was soft and suggestive.

Luthian could tell that her calculating mind was already lining up as she realized what would occur. "I merely point out an opportunity for us both to rid ourselves of… What did you call them… a filthy and forsaken lot of animals? The level of crime moving up the tiers is increasing. It is time we cleansed ourselves of those that do not have enough skill to be of use to the upper tiers." He waved his hands in dismissal, as though changing his mind. He lightened his tone. "What am I thinking? No… We should not. Why people might hold you accountable for such an act." He shook his head. "I fear I fell into a bit of whimsical fantasy. It is hardly a proper plan." He sighed with exasperation. "I just don't know when another chance might present itself…"

"I can seal them without detection," Lady Caterine offered.

"Could you?" He looked a bit amazed, but inwardly he felt like the angler setting his hook. "I don't know… It would have to be our secret." He tapped his lip thoughtfully.

She moved to him, a bit of hopeful familiarity emerging as she laid a hand upon his robe. "I can keep secrets, Luthian," she murmured.

She gazed up at him for a long hopeful minute. Luthian sighed inwardly. Some sacrifices had to be made when one was attempting to keep one's hands clean. He bent his head to let his lips hover just above hers.

"Then let me send you on your way," his soft words for her ears alone. He laid his lips against hers, revolted at the cold, fish -like kiss she attempted to return. "I will see you as soon as you have finished. We can… share other secrets," he promised.

She nodded happily and turned, hurrying from the room to order her least favorite mages sent to seal the storehouse.

Luthian wiped his mouth on the back of his hand as soon as the door shut. Thankfully, he would not be keeping that promise. The woman kissed worse than a virgin.

He turned back toward his desk, seeing Severent step from the side door. "Is the plan still as we discussed, milord?" He was dressed in drab grays and browns. Luthian knew that if he walked the lower tiers, he would likely never notice the man. Here in his office filled with rich tones, he stood out.

"Yes, all is in place as we discussed. The occupants of the trench will have only one way out. Through panic or storm, we should see the population diminish greatly." Luthian chuckled. "And the current level of dedication in our Trench Lord means I will likely lose him as well. Pity… the man had a head for business."

Severent nodded and glanced at the door, then back at Luthian. "And the woman?"

Luthian did not hesitate. "As soon as the last wall is in place… kill her."

## Chapter Five

Levielle moved quickly down the tier. The driving rain pelted him, already beginning to soak through his cloak. He was not a sea goer - his military experience was on land. However, he had seen the worried looks as the naval officers left earlier to move the fleet to a more secure harbor. He had known by their hushed tones that there was something different about this storm; now he had the High Minister's confirmation. Shaking his head, he concentrated on the mission ahead. High Minister be damned, he was going to get people out of the trench.

Deeper puddles soaked his boots as he splashed through them near the third tier. What orders could he give now? The men would have some family on some of the tiers, including the trench. Apparently, he thought, the High Minister must have also seen an uprising from troops in order to place them in harm's way.

Grimacing at his own internal thoughts, he pushed his way through groups that were helping each other on the fifth tier. Everyone seemed to sense that this storm was going to be one of unforeseen power. Servants were actually nailing their shutters closed in addition to merely closing them. Everyone was scrambling to gather in any lose objects to protect them from the rain as well as the increasing wind.

He almost started barking orders at some of the

people in the tiers. Many were set to the tasks they needed to complete, but others wandered, trying to find a place in the chaos. Nevertheless, he had his own orders from the High Minister, and his idea of what needed to be accomplished quickly. Therefore, he shook his head in dismay and prayed for the best.

The tiers did not always lend themselves to a speedy travel path on the best of days, and right now, it was beginning to become utter chaos. Guards were helping the best they could on the upper tiers. Some inhabitants were already hunkered down, with the warmth of hearth behind them, looking out their windows at their neighbors scrambling to get goods under cover.

The casual attitude of the people already inside reminded him that many would not care if those of the lower tiers perished due to trampling or drowning as they tried to save what little they had. He shook his head clear of these grim thoughts, crossing the fourth tier gate as he did.

As he crossed into the third tier, nicer shops had boarded up their windows. Thankfully, it appeared as though they had also assisted more of their neighbors securing windows and doors. Levielle could see the streets were almost empty. The few windows not boarded gave him an opportunity to see that the occupants were preparing inside as well. The women were setting out candles and rations. The men were preparing their rain gear and tools in case something broke.

The rain fell harder, and the road was practically a stream. Levielle finally caught a glimpse of the bay when he rounded the gate into the second tier. The few remaining ships bobbed and swayed heavily from side to side in the increasing wind.

As the clouds darkened, he finally made it to a lieutenant that was directing some people as his men stood guard at the gate. Almost blinded by the rain driven into his face, the young officer started to direct Levielle away before realizing his rank. The man snapped to attention and saluted smartly.

"Lieutenant! How many men do you have at the gate to the first tier?" he shouted above the ongoing din of wind, rain and people. Standing there, he wished he would have grabbed some warmer clothing, but he set himself to ignore the cold, pushing it to the side.

"Sir! We have a normal guard squad there. Six men total. They are there as ordered b-"

"Call them down here. Send runners to the rest of the posts. We need to make sure that as many people survive as possible; direct them to the storehouses quickly, before the stone mages seal them against the storm. I have been told this storm is going to be a behemoth! He turned to make his way down the rest of the way to the trench. When he looked back at the man, he had not moved - a group of men in rain gear was distracting him.

"Get these people to the storehouses and safety!" Levielle repeated, sharper this time.

"But, sir!" The man stammered a moment before quickly shutting his mouth. Levielle spun on his heel and took the few steps back to plant himself in front of the junior officer. He was not used to having his orders questioned.

"I'm positive that my order was not lost to the wind, lieutenant!" Levielle growled with authority. "This is an order from your general! Now, make it happen or I will throw you in a dungeon cell myself!"

The man only nodded, fear showing on his face and in his eyes; he knew as well as Levielle did that the prison was likely flooded. Levielle moved away before the man could say more; he had an army to get to and a trench to save. His footfalls splashed through puddles that brought chilling rain to above his knees as he moved quickly toward the barracks.

Once there, he ducked in the door without hesitation, dropping his cowl and pausing just a moment to savor being out of the rain. The men within were between watches or working on paperwork from their shift, but the man on the door recognized him immediately and came to attention.

"General! We were not expecting your presence today." Even caught by surprise the guard's tones were well-schooled and measured.

Levielle paid little attention to the man. There was no time for civilities. "Soldier, I need you to gather all the men and materials you have and bring them to the testing ring on the third tier." He moved past the man as he spoke, expecting him to follow and listen. The main common room was before him, about half-full of soldiers playing dice or sleeping away their off hours.

The soldier behind him cleared his throat and spoke

loudly. "Attention!"

A flurry of activity met this announcement; Levielle was proud that the men under his command moved with such swiftness. Only the sound of rain and wind could heard after the din of shuffling feet died down. He cleared his throat once he was sure he had their attention.

"This is an evacuation notice of all men in uniform. We are moving all equipment and personnel to the testing ring on the third tier. You are also hereby ordered to assist in the movement of all civilians that can fit into that ring as well. The storm mages expect a massive wave, perhaps several, to strike the city within the next two hours; as such, lives will be lost if any of us, or the occupants of the lower tiers, remain here. Am I clear?" Levielle spoke loud and true for every ear to hear him. The response was short and curt.

"Sir… Yes… Sir!" The voices rang out in unison. The room went silent once more.

"You have your orders. Dismissed!" He stood with his hands clasped behind his back, watching as the once quiet men moved in a frenzy. Leisure items and clothing were stowed, men yelled to one another. Occupants of the floors above began tossing things down to the first level. They were preparing for evacuation with adequate efficiency. Moving toward the entrance, the general hurried to exit. He had one last stop before he could follow his men to the ring. The warning had to be carried to the trench too.

Tossing his cowl back over his head, he began

running to the nearest ramp down to the trench – there were three where goods would brought up from the harbor and one in from the plains to the first tier. He slowed as he saw the mass of people surrounding the nearest ramp's archway. It was no longer an opening, but a stone wall. Even as a military man who had seen the carnage of the battlefield, he was shocked and sickened.

Bits of clothing stuck out of the rock - a hand here, an arm there. As he watched, a hand clutched at the air before it slowly turned to stone. This could only be the work of a stone mage. They had thrown up a wall to keep the inhabitants of the trench *in the trench!* They had no regard for the fact that they caught innocent travelers in the forming of the wall as they tried to escape to higher ground. This was the High Minister's doing. Levielle could feel it in his bones and his fists tightened at his sides in anger at the injustice.

People shouted, trying to claw and free those trapped within the stone even though the general could see it was a futile attempt. Looking on in near shock, Levielle finally broke free of the horrible spell that locked his gaze to the newly formed stone. He moved through the mass of people to find two of the soldiers that were guarding there.

"We need hammers!" Looking to his right he saw a couple of men approaching with tools. Hurriedly, he motioned them to the wall, "Break it down! We need to get to those on the other side!" The men nodded as they began their work, chipping at the hard stone.

Turning to the guards and group of people, he

shouted above the rain and clanging of hammers and chisels. "Everyone else, move to the training ring! It's for your safety!" Motioning up the stairs as he spoke. A loud murmur spread through the crowd as some immediately moved toward the upper tiers.

"You have to go, now!"

Pushing one of the guards out of the way, people began to move up the ramp at once. Levielle stood by the men with the hammers. Finding a spare leaning against the wall, he took it up. He grunted when the first swing landed on the hard rock face. He was seeing the horrible result of Luthian's plan - the horror that would take place in the trenches - and it angered him. All those lives, families, children, washed away by the storm. Luthian was turning a bad situation into one of opportunity to rid himself of the inhabitants of the trench.

He swung again, the hammer digging at the stone.

He heard an audible gasp from the people on the tier above, as if all the air had been sucked out of their lungs at one time. He looked up to see shock… no terror… on the faces that looked toward the sea. Then someone screamed and another voice joined theirs until everyone was screaming, pushing and shoving to go up, to flee, to escape. It was bedlam. He felt the wave rather than saw it. Tremors pulsed through the ground as it thundered into the harbor. The screams of people around Levielle went unanswered. He could hear the shouts of those trapped on the other side, clawing at the wall, trying to climb for freedom. His arms burned as he made rapid strikes at the stone face, but he kept up it up in a now futile attempt to save the inhabitants of the trench. His hammer was raised when the wall of water breached over the stone and silenced the screams on both sides of the wall.

## Chapter Six

Caterine could hardly contain herself. She'd had a private meeting with the High Minister! She was giddy from the mere thought of what they had planned together. They were now a team - partners. The rain tried to dampen her spirits, but it was unsuccessful. She had changed into simple gray robes and tied her hair back. The matching gray cloak had a deep cowl, hiding her face from any discerning eye. In any case, the gray matched the day and the stone surroundings, so she would be invisible while she accomplished her assignment for Luthian. She sighed. He had asked her to address him by his given name. They were going to be close. This task was just the beginning of their work together.

She felt no repugnance at what she was assigned to do. She had no love of the constant begging, manipulation and sometimes-direct thievery of those without magic. She was not concerned about the loss of tradesmen, for most with any decent skill where on a higher tier as a hand, a servant, or had enough magic to open their own shop. No, she had one goal in mind and that was pleasing the High Minister. Luthian's kiss still lingered on her pallid lips. She could feel his strong grip on her shoulders.

She ducked around people scurrying to prepare for the storm as she reviewed the meeting and the High

Minister in her mind. She had never thought him interested in her; his taste seemed to linger on those with exotic looks or a great deal of power, and she could hardly compete with the priestess mage Lady Morana in either of these. His unexpectedly expressed interest made her giddy with what they could accomplish together! She had no doubt that her role in his life would be in the background, of course, but she was content with this. Perhaps he would even bond with her, at least long enough to have a child. A boy with all of his looks and their combined strength. She would name him Rynath after his famous great grandfather.

She made her way through the streets. Water poured down rain gutters and into the street, running swiftly to the grates that led down into the sewers. Despite a flow system to help with run-off, the street was still deep enough in water that in places it swamped over the tops of her boots. The wind blew wildly and she had to hold the cowl down to keep it on her head. The fourth tier was absent of all but the miserable guards who took shelter under eaves near their posts.

She descended onto the third tier. Here there was a little more activity; merchants were securing their stalls and wares. Farmers sought shelter for their wagons, brought in to sell goods directly to the townsfolk and now left vulnerable to the unprecedented weather. Some people, like herself, hurried through the streets to wherever they were seeking shelter from the storm. She was pleased with her choice of cloak as she blended in with the few hurrying about the streets. No one would recognize her for the stone mage sent by the High Minister to deal with the Trench Lord and his riff-raff.

On the second tier, she moved to the far entrance. She saw Lady Aldemar and her group of bleeding hearts working to find places for people indoors, the group of silver and gold mages easy to distinguish in their healers' cloaks. She tucked her own cloak tighter around her and bent forward to hide her face from the woman. There was another the stone mage would not mind taking down a peg; Caterine had been glad when Lady Aldemar stepped down from the council, but her influence had not diminished. The healer had ears on the council, and she had pull within the city. With Luthian's help, perhaps a plan could be laid and the meddling wretch removed permanently. Caterine gave a snort of derision as she descended to the first tier.

Her detour worked out in her favor; she arrived at the farthest entrance to the trench, and it would let her move right around the tier. There was a steady stream of individuals making their way up out of the trench. They were mostly miners at this entrance, the dust and soot running down their bodies as they were met by the storm. It they were not needed for mining the medure they would be some of the most disgusting of the trench inhabitants; Caterine abhorred filth.

The stone mage found a spot near the entrance where she had a clear view of the opening. She stood with her back tightly pressed against a house, hidden in the dark, storm-filled shadows. It gave her a bit of respite from the wind and rain so she could see better.

She concentrated on the rock of the ramp. Most did not know that the spell to move stone was not actually movement of rock. It was really the replicating of the small specks of material the stone mages learned to see. Once the small elements were in her view, she began to whisper the words of replication, her hands moving before her like a sculptor on a clay wheel.

She almost lost the concentration of the small stone elements when she heard the horrified cry of those still on the ramp who were engulfed by the building of her wall, but she pressed onward, smiling inwardly. That was one occupant of the trench would not have to face drowning. Her mouth upturned further as she continued, mindless of those scrambling over the growing wall. She did not pause when the scream of a woman caught in the growing stone drew attention from those on the first tier. People raced to try to help those still coming over the growing barrier. pulling on the woman's arm as the rest of her body was slowly engulfed by the slithering stone. By the time it arched over slightly to prevent anyone else from climbing it, the woman's screams had stopped. The stone slowly formed over her face, creating an open-mouthed sculpture on the wall, her hand the only thing left not covered in white creeping stone.

Caterine was swift to melt into the horrified crowd once the wall was finished. The sound of chaos from the trench erupting from the other side brought an evil grin to the stone mage's face. Hidden by the cowl, she made her way through the throngs of bodies milling about at the ramp. Once free of the press, she hurried to the second entrance before word could spread from the first.

The spell now came quicker to her hands, as if remembering what she had just done; this stone wall rose up in mere seconds, taking three more souls into it. She did not bother to wait for their screams to cease. She built on. The wasteful, 'magic-less' bags of flesh in the trench would be washed away in a torrent of rain, waves and filth.

It would be just as she and Luthian planned. He would be so proud of her work. She knew that few mages were capable of dispelling her work even if they were called to the trench; certainly the mages she had sent within were lesser mages that would not have the time or capacity to undo the wall. Lady Aldemar had the skill in magic to dispel such powerful spells, but it was not her sphere and would take time. In addition, Luthian had assured her that no movement between the tiers was to be allowed. It was unlikely the Lady could make her way down here in time.

The next wall did not entomb anyone. There was less movement from this ramp. It made sense - the door from the trench up onto the plains was not far. She was fearful of being spotted, so her movement to the final entrance took time. Once she felt sure that no one was looking her way, she slipped down the tier to the final entrance.

If he were not already on an upper tier, this would be where the Trench Lord would emerge. In the time she worked with him to seal over the sewage canal, she had realized that the people in the trench were truly the man's first priority. She rather suspected, that much like a captain, he would go down with his ship. She wished she could see the horrified man's face when he realized that the rest of the denizens had only one way out.

Caterine took a little more time on this wall, enjoying her thoughts of what would occur when the wave swept into the harbor and up the sewage canal. The milling bodies, debris, and filth of the sewers would ensure that even if the trench occupants lived through the wave, they would die from infected wounds. She formed the wall carefully, making sure it was far stronger. She smiled as it closed over the entrance.

She turned and hurried to the stairs to the second tier. She eyed the press of people there attempting to move up a level; the first tier had grown crowded even before she sealed the trench. She remembered Luthian's words that none would be allowed to climb tiers, suddenly realizing that this would include herself. She cursed inwardly. Now what was she to do? She could take shelter in a tavern, but they would all be full of the rabble from the first tier. As she hesitated in thought, she felt a hand on her elbow and looked up to see a most horrid looking man. His face was pockmarked and hard. He wore no cloak or cowl, his long hair plastered about his face.

"I have been sent to help you leave this tier, milady." The man's voice was rasping and unpleasant. "Lord Luthian did not wish you trapped here."

Caterine gave a deep sigh of relief. Luthian had cared enough to send someone who could get her back to him! She smiled at the man, despite his appearance as more a thug than a servant of the High Minister.

"I am most grateful." She let him lead her around the corner and they made their way swiftly to an area of the wall that was obscured from the street's view. There was a rope hanging down over a deep puddle that had accumulated in a sinkhole at the base of the wall. She looked up in alarm. "I do not know how to climb."

"Do not worry milady, just put your hands on the rope; when I give a signal, another will pull you up. You just hang tightly to the rope and walk up the wall. I will be here to catch you if you slip." The man's voice was a harsh whisper.

Caterine was hesitant about her ability, but she was looking forward to sitting down with a glass of wine and recounting her efficient dispatching of her assignment with Luthian. She stepped into the puddle, even though the water ran up and over her boot tops. She followed the servant's direction and took hold of the rope.

"Like this?"

"Exactly like that," came the voice in her ear. She glanced to her right about to say something else when she heard the screams and then saw the massive wall of water cresting over the rocks on the far side of the harbor.

"Oh gods!' she exclaimed and began trying to scramble up the rope. She felt a strange pain in her throat and let go of the rope to put a hand to her neck. Warm blood spilled over it and she heard the grating voice as she sank to her knees.

"No time for niceties then," he hissed.

Her eyes blinked as she watched the man jump up and catch the rope. His feet were the last thing she saw as she slumped to the ground. Whether it was the knife that slit her throat or the water in the deep puddle that drowned her, no one would ever know. Unfortunately, a life with Luthian was not in her future.

## Chapter Seven

The rain grew from a shower to a torrent in the time it took Alador reached his home. As he burst through the door a servant appeared to assist him, but he brushed them aside. He had no time to take off his cloak.

He looked back at the man and snapped, "Prepare for the coming storm, quickly! It will be severe this day."

Not waiting for a response, he hurried along to his study. The room greeted him with its usual warmth, both from the fire and the comfort of the various books and documents. However, the dark gray cast from the day and its rain gave it an ominous feeling through the windows. He placed his fingers in the eyes of the skull on the shelf and opened the door to the small secret room that contained the black spell book. He sighed heavily to see it still there, a reminder of the evil once committed by his ancestor using its dark magic. Perhaps today he could do some good with its power.

He frantically scanned through page after page of spells, but nothing jumped out at him that would help. He was desperate. He didn't have the power or the knowledge to stop this storm. He muttered to himself, reading the various names, but none really met his need to save the city or even deflect the storm.

"Alador?" The soft voice called out from the doorway. Startled, he looked over to see Nemara standing there. She wore simple clothing, a soft, golden, floor length gown with dark brown lace at the neck, cuffs, and hem.

She glanced around the room in surprise. "I didn't know this room existed. Hiding somethi…" She cut off short, looking at the black spell book as Alador shut it.

"It's nothing. Just a spell book." He waved his hand casually, and moved toward her.

She nodded, but kept her eyes locked on the book for a moment before her gaze snapped to him. "You know, if you wanted to make it cold and damp, couldn't you have waited for another day?" she teased, but then frowned, wrapping her arms about herself.

Alador smiled, but it vanished in a moment. "Nemara, this storm is unnaturally large. I must try to mitigate its impact on the city, but I don't know if…" He trailed off, his mind racing with possible spells to use. Even Renamaum's memories didn't bring anything to the forefront that could be useful.

Nemara looked at him curiously before stepping closer to place her hand on his cheek. She directed his eyes to hers. "What do you need?" she asked, her voice full of concern.

"Honestly… a storm mage, but Luthian may not be able to get them to me in time."

He huffed, moving them both out of the way of the door that swung shut with barely a whisper. He pulled at her hand to exit the study.

"I have seen it… The trench and the first tier will

be wiped out from the coming surge."

"Are you sure?" There was a touch of panic in her voice.

"Renamaum has seen a storm like this in the past. His memories keep urging me to run." Alador ran his hand through his wet hair. "It is hard for me to fathom such a force... something a dragon would run from." His hand ran absently through his hair again as he stood in the doorway of the study - as though somehow, the action would clear his thoughts. "And my uncle seems to think I can stop it. How can I stop it?" This time when his hand went toward his hair he noticed it was shaking and stopped it in front of his face to stare at it in disbelief.

Nemara took his hand in hers. "Let me help," she urged. "What is your plan?"

"I had hoped to find something in the spell book, perhaps an incantation to magnify my powers, but I didn't." He squeezed her hand. It felt good to be grounded by her presence. "I am headed back to the outlook on the third tier. From there I can see the storm clearly and do my best to lessen its impact."

"I will change and come with you. I can bind us to the wall, so the storm doesn't take us away. Creating brambles and woods is a specialty of mine, after all." She tried to make light of her power and the situation to calm him.

They started to move in sync, training taking over for them both. The seriousness of the situation took over. She kissed him lightly on the cheek and vanished from sight as Alador moved to the entryway.

He waited for her to return, considering changing into his own leathers. He missed the comfort of his oiled armor. He mused to himself how it was that he could end up missing something he had not particularly enjoyed in the first place. But he knew he needed the greater freedom of movement that robes provided today.

His inner dialogue stopped when he saw Nemara hurry down the stairs. She was now a warrior, her hair tied back to keep it from her face, leathers molded to her body like a glove. She was both wholly feminine and wholly practical. Her sword at one side and a pack on the other provided the last bit of evidence that she had taken the situation seriously. She found her black cloak in a closet and put it on, pulling up the cowl.

He shook his head, pulling his thoughts back to the emergency at hand. "Shall we?" he motioned to the door. Smirking as though she had read his thoughts, she opened the door to be greeted by the howl of wind and force of the driving wall of rain.

"Don't mind if I do, milord." Her tone playfully mocked him as they both stepped outside.

Without another a word, they made their way past the residents of the city, who were scurrying about, preparing for the coming storm. The streets were a mess of people scrambling to get out of the rain and shouting imprecations at each other and the storm. Fighting the people was like wading through the ocean surf itself. A few times, Nemara and Alador were separated but managed to find one another in the breaks of the crowd. They dodged carts and foot traffic, civilians and guards, until they made it down to the third tier and the outlook.

The darkness they faced once they reached the wall was terrifying. Both of them were at a loss for words as they looked upon the tempest. Lightning dance over the surface of the black wall of clouds, the angry sea swirling green and gray below. The storm extended to the left and right as far as the eye could see. This storm was bigger than anything Alador had ever seen – larger even the snow storm he built with Rena's help. The top edge of it was creeping up and would soon block out the sun. Silverport stood at the very edge of this storm's gaping maw.

Movement to his right caused him to look over at Nemara, who was digging in her pack to fish out seeds and begin manipulating them with magic.

The cold wind clawed at them both as Alador began to concentrate, looking toward the ocean. He could feel the surge of the sea. Closing his eyes, he took a deep breath and let his soul drift out to submerge in the ocean under the storm. The water was seething as the storm approached. As before, the power of the sea pushed the sand and silt from the bottom to swirl about him. He was startled to see a fuzzy image of Nemara beside him in this out-of-body state. He was relieved it was her and not the incarnate of Dethara as he had encountered in the past.

He shook his head and returned to his corporeal state on the wall, concentrating on drawing his power from the world around him. Raising a hand, he opened his eyes and began trying to focus on the air stones about him and control them.

Pushing and pulling, he could barely get a handle on them. They did not behave as he had come to expect, and seemed to work against him. The storm front was almost upon them, the sky darkening to almost a twilight haze. He closed his eyes again, mage-sight showing him the vast power that stretched beyond. He toed the edge of the precipice wall.

Could he manifest enough magic to harness this beast of a storm? If he did, could he control such power? If he could not, what would happen to him? Panic and fear filled him. What if he couldn't save the city? What would happen to the egg? The Blackguard? The city? The people? All the possible outcomes rushed to his head.

With a slight whimper, he dropped his hands to his sides. He opened his eyes to see Nemara had completed her work. They each stood with their back against a huge tree, roots anchored firmly in the stone of the outlook and its wall. Around their feet grew brambles which held them securely in place and against the trees. She looked at him intently as the lower branches from the trees reached down to wrap their arms around them as if they were a mother holding a child to their breasts.

"What's wrong?" she yelled above the wind's howl.

The barrier she had grown around each of them was a tough wooden plant that reminded him of ones he used to build forts with in Smallbrook. Thoughts of Smallbrook - family, home, Mesiande - all rushed to his mind, and he fought to push them back.

"I can't do it, Nemara. I... I... don't have the

power. It's too strong!" he admitted, his fear overtaking him. Renamaum's memories were becoming almost overwhelming, urging him to fly. Closing his eyes, the sound of the angry tempest loomed over them, growling and screeching.

"You can do it. Give in," Nemara whispered in his ear, or was it Rena? He could hear it as clear as a bell struck on a summer day. Her words rang, shaking him to his core. "You need to give in to this. Use me as a conduit if you must."

In his mind's eye, he moved toward her and held her close. He could sense her magic, her power, knowing that she was Nemara *and* Rena. He winced at the first touch, wondering what Rena had really given to Nemara.

As her power circled around him, she screamed, "Give in, Alador!"

In a moment, he twisted their essence to fall into the magical ocean before them. A rush of power much like he had felt when he manifested in the ocean before greeted him, unlimited and unfathomable power. It coursed through him as though it was living lightning. It craved to be used, harnessed, unleashed. In the real world Nemara reached over and took his hand, gripping it tightly. Power coursed through her as well, as they joined. She stiffened as if being shocked, soft cries muffled against the storm's rage.

All at once Alador felt the sea tugging and pulling back away from him and Nemara. It was receding under the storm.

Opening his real eyes, he saw the bay empty of

water, the sea heaving back – leaving the ships anchored there sitting like toy boats in any empty tub.

An enormous wave, a wave of gigantic proportions, was growing up off the ocean floor and into the storm clouds above.

Alador's free arm sprung up, a ball of lightning forming in his hand. But this was no offensive spell; it screamed with a soundless voice, turning from white to a blackish purple. It clawed at reality, desiring to be released, Alador hardly noticed as it fought against him. This magic was palpable in his fingertips, stronger than what he had shared with Rena.

Releasing the power from his hand, a beam sliced through the oncoming storm. It split the clouds in two, but it did nothing to mitigate the massive wave that broke and burst over the rocks of the harbor's edge to come rushing into the bay over the sandy beach.

Drawing upon the storm's own energy, Alador continued to dump power into the spell. The skin upon his hand began to turn raw as if it were too close to a fire. It splintered and cracked, the feeling of rain hitting it almost unbearable. But the wave continued to rush forward, towering over the trench and the first tier.

He stole a glance over to Nemara; her gaze was transfixed upon the wave that was bearing down on the city. But as he looked closer, Alador could see her gaze was glassy. She was soaked from head to toe in her leathers, but it was her hair that made him pause. Streaks of white coursed through the normal dark red. Being a conduit for Alador's magic was more than she could handle. The magic may have had the essence of Rena, but the woman beside him did not have the dragon's strength.

Panic struck through Alador like the power of the wave descending on them. It was clear to him that he had to choose: either continue to use her to channel the magic and likely kill her to save countless lives inside the city, or sacrifice them all and save his friend. He looked back upon the storm and the merciless wave as it met the ships in the harbor and splintered them into kindling with the force of its impact. The howling wind and driving rain seemed to mock his failure. How could he have thought he could stop this?

The internal struggle only lasted for a moment; his split attention was all the power needed to wrest itself out of his hands. What control he had over it was lost. A screaming ball of power shot into the sky, engulfed by the oncoming cloud wall. Alador caught Nemara as her spell-cast trees and brambles withered to dust around them and she crumpled to the ground. He collapsed with her, pulling her into his lap and cradling her in his arms, trying to protect her from the onslaught of the driving rain.

The enormous wave crashed against the sea wall, overwhelming the tiers and shaking the ground beneath them. It threw up a spray that drenched the outlook where they huddled. He could hear the agonizing screams of the dying below.

"Nemara!" He cried.

She did not respond.

*Chapter Eight*

Sordith felt a great sense of relief when the bronze mages showed up to help seal the storerooms and mines. He had already recalled the miners in anticipation of the mages' arrival; he could not leave the workers down there if the trench was going to flood. He refused to lose that many good men and women when he had the time to recall as many as could hear the warning bells. If they were not out by the time the mages got to their hole, then they would have to ride out the storm behind a solid wall. Some would panic because they had family topside, but in the end, it would probably be one of the safest spots to weather this storm. He assigned one of his men to each mage to show them the tunnels to be sealed and sent them on their way.

Fortunately, the water had not breached the slopes into the storerooms or the mines yet. With the four bronze mages going from door to door, opening to opening, and placing a firm stone wall over each, they should be secure. He finally left them and his men once he was satisfied this action would safeguard the city's treasures from any storm or ocean damage. He once more hoped that Alador was being dramatic and that while the harbor might be in danger, the trench would not.

Keelee was at the far end of the trench. He sent a runner down to inform her to move the children up to the second tier. She had a head start, and the children all knew her from her regular visits to bring them food and blankets. Sordith knew Keelee had friends on the second and third tiers that would shelter the orphans, giving him peace of mind so that he could concentrate on the rest of the migration of the trench populace to the first tier or above.

The Trench Lord sent Auries a message to move her girls up a tier as well. He knew they would not mind; in such rain, the taverns and inns would be full. Business would be booming and most of the owners were not too particular in letting a newcomer from another tier ply their trade to satisfy his or her customers.

He had had little time for Auries since she threw perfume at him. It crossed his mind that after the storm, he would have to see about mending that bridge. She had always been special to him, it was just that Keelee now possessed his heart.

Sordith stepped out of the mining area and was surprised to find people milling about and the general sound of panic. He grabbed a miner close to him by the arm. "What is going on? Why are you people still down here?"

"Som'un put up a wall, Lords'p." The miner stammered, wide-eyed. "People saying every ramp be closed."

"What?" Sordith hissed, truly shocked. "No, he wouldn't have done that." he mumbled under his breath. Luthian could not be that callous.

Sordith pushed through the milling and panicked

people to cross the bridge to the nearest ramp. The city had run-off troughs that naturally spilled into the trench. He had made sure to keep rainwater from flooding the areas of occupation when they covered the actual sewage canal to create these sloughs. Despite this preventive step, the troughs were like rushing rivers overflowing at their banks onto the walkway and into the surrounding homes and shops. The water was pouring down so hard from the upper tiers that the sloughs were like funnels, sending the water down in torrents and creating standing water everywhere, rising almost to his knees in places. He had to fight to get past some areas. So far, the sewage trench itself had not overflowed, but the grates allowing water into it were not keeping up. Soon, the refuse and garbage from the five tiers would be flowing over the trench and its inhabitants.

Sordith could not see the ramp through the rain and press of bodies. The wind was now whipping projectiles through the air - pieces of cloth, debris and wood. He saw a man on the edge of the ramp get hit by what looked like a flying awning, ripped from a storefront on one of the upper tiers. The pole attached to the fabric struck him so hard he was thrown from the ramp and down onto the harbor walkway below. A woman screamed and tried her best to fight her way back down the ramp to the man, who must have been her husband.

Sordith shook his head. He had to get these people moving.

"Let me through," he demanded, elbowing and shoving the mass on the ramp aside.

Slowly, as people recognized their Lord, they parted to let him through.

When Sordith got to the top, he was horrified at what rose up in front of him. Not only was there a thick stone wall, but there were bodies embedded in it. He slowly reached out to touch a hand that extended from it and found the flesh still warm beneath his fingers. He cursed under his breath; this was the work of a stone mage who had no humanity left in them. They had sealed the passing people in stone. He prayed the poor sod had not suffered. He turned to look down into the panicked faces of his people. How could he fight this? He had no magic to rip down the wall. The water was rising with the tide, already at least a foot deep at the bottom of the ramp.

He had no choice. He had to send them onto the plains and hope that this wave his brother predicted would not rise to such a level. Every eye was on him and a sense of dread filled him, as he looked over the men and women, some holding children.

"Make for the outer exit to the lands of our people," he commanded loudly over the howling wind. "If you can, get up onto the bridge. At the least, make for the garrison. It might give you some protection."

He had not asked Levielle, but he knew the general would never turn the people away. He was too honorable a man for that.

He stood on the ramp as the people turned, pressing and shoving to make for the one ramp left up onto the plains. He could only pray that Luthian had not had that sealed as well.

"Move quickly, but take care with the children," he warned. "Don't let your loved ones get trampled."

He picked up a small child as it passed him and handed it over to the parent who already had two teens and a wife in tow. "Quickly now!" he urged.

Sordith had not told them of the wave. Most thought they were seeking protection from the wind and rising water. He did not dare tell them now. People would die in the panic.

When the press had moved off enough that he could elbow his way around the trench, he set out for the far end. If he found one of his men, he gave the order to evacuate onto the plains. He kept shouting for them to all make for the exit as he moved. Fortunately, it was on the other side of the trench and while it bottle necked as he passed it, he still was able to force his way on the opposite side.

He continued down the tier, re-routing those he could. He reassured them there was time, but to move quickly. He shouted orders and urged people not to push, but most were not listening. He had never realized before how many people were part of his holdings. Seeing them all in the main pathways of the trench, moving to the one exit left to them, made him very grateful the main sewer canal was covered. He was certain more than one would have found themselves floundering in the depths of the vile liquid.

The crowd dispersed a bit, and after several minutes of sloshing through what had developed into a fast flowing stream on the walkway, he found himself outside Auries' house. He called in through the open door. There was no answer. The room stood a good six inches deep in water, rugs soaked and drapes whipping in the wind. Sordith breathed a sigh of relief to know his friend had received his message, and hopefully was safely on the first tier, rather than being in the press across the trench. He tried to pull the door closed, but the water inundating the house from the walkway prevented him from it. He finally gave up and moved on. There were more pressing matters than soggy rugs.

As he moved his way around the trench, the press became less. People at this end must have realized they were blocked in earlier. Most likely, the first ramp down had been the first to be walled up.

He thought he heard muffled crying below the sound of the driving rain and the howling wind near an alcove where some merchant had stored his boxed goods for later retrieval. He spotted a piece of material and shifted a box. In the shelter of the small dugout alcove a little girl was huddled, filthy, wet, and sobbing.

Sordith knelt down and put out a hand. He called to her, raising his voice above the din of the storm, but still trying to sound gentle. The child could not have been more than three.

"Come here, sweetheart."

She stared at him with large, brown, almond-shaped eyes. She was barely visible in the filtered light of the storm. Slowly she moved forward.

The storm took that moment to send a streak of

lightning cracking across the sky, followed by a boom of thunder that seemed to rock the very ground beneath their feet.

The child shrieked and drew back into her cave of boxes.

Sordith tried again. "Come on, sweetheart. You can't stay here."

Her fear of being left alone was stronger than her fear of the storm. When she tentatively moved forward again, he grabbed her and swept her up into his arms.

"It will be okay. You and I will be just fine," he assured her, rubbing her back. He hoped he was not lying to the child. She clung to him - her arms so tightly around his neck that he was certain he could have let go of her and she would not have lost her grip.

Sordith made his way to the last ramp, which was empty. He would not rest easy until he checked the cave where he originally sent Keelee though. He was able to run now, dodging items that rolled and tossed in the wind. He splashed through the standing water and held the child close, covering her head with one strong hand.

When he reached the cave and stepped within, he pushed the water and loose hair from his eyes. He knelt and did the same for the child he had put down in the shelter of the cave's mouth.

"Wait here, little one," he said, tucking wet red hair behind her ear.

He moved swiftly into the cave's depths, the slight ramp making for dry stone beneath his feet.

"Keelee?" he shouted out. "Keelee, are you here?"

He saw a flickering light ahead.

"Yes!" Her voice was shrill and held an edge of panic.

He heard her running steps before she launched herself out of the semi-darkness into his arms.

He hugged her to him, both in fear and relief. "What are you still doing here?"

He pushed her away from him to search her face. Those emerald eyes were large and he could tell she was frightened.

"The wind got so strong that the children were afraid. The older children and I were helping them across to the ramp and up to safety when a wall went up. I didn't know what to do, so I brought them back here."

"Oh Gods, how many are still in here?" He attempted to look past her. From where he stood, he could only see a couple.

"There are only six left. We got the rest out." She searched his face. "We can stay here, in the high part of the cave, yes?"

"I... I don't know Keelee. Alador said there was a wave coming. Larger than any of us has ever seen. The tide is high and already lapping up the steps of the trench." Sordith pulled her back to him and hugged her tightly. "I left a child at the entrance; I will return shortly, I can't leave her there."

He looked at the frightened, exhausted children he could see with a sinking heart. How would he get them out? Staying here was not an option. He squeezed Keelee's hands and ran back the way he came.

The short distance took a mere minute for him to reach the bend where the cave opened to the trench. The child stood where he left her, watching the rain and mud pour from the plains on this side of the trench and descend like a chunky waterfall over the mouth of the cave.

He swooped the little girl up, and started to turn, when he heard a faint call over the wind and rushing rain.

"Anyone down there?"

Sordith put her back down and stepped through the vertical stream of mud and water. There, peering down over the wall was a guardsman, a rope dangling inches from his face down the trench wall. Sordith waved to him as he shouted back.

"I have about half a dozen children." He attempted to shout back as he held up five fingers. He shrugged back through the wall of muddy water to grab the little one he had found in the alcove.

Sordith swiftly tied the rope around her. "Hang on as tight as you can," he shouted in her ear, then tugged the rope. He did not wait for her to reach the top. Once he was sure she was being lifted, he sprinted back for Keelee and the others. He knew they were running out of time.

Sordith ran into the cave, honing in on the flickering light Keelee created to give comfort to the children. Water was beginning to seep from the roof of the cave. Small pools were showing where the cracks above had given the water access. All of a sudden, the idea of a cave-in was added to his fears.

He grabbed up the first child he reached as he shouted to Keelee urgently. "Quick! There are ropes! We have to get them out!"

He did not wait, turning to run back to the mouth of the cave. By the time he returned, there were more ropes. He secured the child he carried, and sent her up. As he finished, Keelee emerged with the others. One by one, he sent them up. Finally, he got to Keelee. He wiped the mud out of his eyes and swiftly pulled a rope around her.

"Time for you to go, love," he shouted over the din of the gushing water and mud.

He just began to tie the knot when he heard the screams from the tiers above. He say Keelee's eyes grow wide as she stood before the mud flow, while the sound of a million men running filled the air. "We're going to die," she breathed and reached out for him.

He flung the rope around Keelee and frantically tied the rope around her waist with shaky hands.

"Go!" he shouted. He tugged on the rope and hoped the gods gave the guardsman on the other end courage to stand his ground and pull.

She screamed as her feet were lifted off the ground. She grasped at him to try to keep from leaving him behind. The guard was frantically pulling on the rope.

"I will be right behind you," Sordith promised.

The ground began to shake as the enormous wave curled and hit the seafloor to come rushing in at an incredible speed. The roaring sound of water filled his ears and he leaped for another rope, not taking the time to secure it.

Sordith had begun to pull himself up hand-over-hand when the rushing wall of water and debris slammed into them. He clung to the rope desperately in the torrent of swirling water. He felt underwater projectiles of debris strike him, and almost lost his grip when something hit his side so hard he knew it must have broken ribs.

He heard Keelee scream and looked around madly for her. He barely caught sight of her being swept down the trench in the rushing current of water before it curved from his sight. Sordith looked up one last time, muttered a quick prayer, and then let go of the rope.

Sordith struggled to reach Keelee. The water was powerful, but the debris in it was the more imminent danger. He had been hit so many times in a short few moments that he was already feeling like he had been in the practice ring with Owen for an afternoon and come out wanting.

He got lucky when Keelee's rope snagged on one of the ship's masts that had broken up. It slowed her drift away from him. Unfortunately, the mast began to roll, and quickly pulled the young woman under. As she came up, thrashing and gasping for air, Sordith was swept by her and grabbed her in his arms. With one hand around Keelee, he pulled a dagger and cut her free of the rope he had tied around her only minutes before.

The wave continued to push them. He saw part of a hull of one of the ships roll up behind her, driven toward them by the powerful wave. He dropped his dagger and grasped Keelee as tightly as he could, kicking his feet to turn them. He wanted it to be his back that struck the floating hull rather than hers. She screamed when she saw the debris bearing down on them. It crashed against his back, and he almost lost his hold on her. The hull rolled out of sight behind them and they were swept around the last corner of the trench.

The end of the trench was a mass of jagged rocks. The city was built on a cliff-face and once the trench reached far enough to take in the sewage, the diggers and mages had just stopped.

Sordith swiftly considered their choices. Swimming against the current was not an option - the water was moving too rapidly. The initial wave that hit the rock face would create a rebound wave. Hopefully, it would be enough to slow them down. Maybe they could get a purchase on that rocky slope and move up from there.

Keelee screamed again when a body popped up from the depths beside them - a woman with her face bashed in. Her long hair was tangled with seaweed and her gown threatened to wrap its folds around them. He did not have time to console Keelee. If he did not think of a plan quickly, it might be their fate as well. As the water carried them to the jagged wall, Sordith pulled a second dagger in an attempt to try to hook anything on the trench's smooth wall to slow them down. The surf took that moment to push them forward and his hand was rammed into the rock face, the dagger falling from his grip.

As he predicted, the initial wave hit the wall and

created a rebound wave. Water ebbed and flowed as it found no way to move forward. Sordith realized the trench was inundated; there would be no escape that way. If they could keep their heads above water, they could get out on the landside of the trench. They had to find a way to get on this rocky outcrop. Twice they were pulled under by the agitation of the waves. Once Sordith was slammed against the rock wall so hard, that for a moment he could only gasp in shock and pain.

Eventually, the power of the wave ebbed, as did the water coming from the first tier. If they were to escape, it had to be now. If they did not make it up the slope or find a way to anchor themselves, the water would change its course and carry them back down the deep passages toward the harbor. The tide would not remain high for too much longer. Fearing that they would be swept to sea, he looked about wildly. He saw a small flat ledge that might hold Keelee.

"You have to let go of me, Keelee," he shouted to the nearly hysterical woman.

"No!" She clutched him tighter around the neck. Her eyes were wild and glazed in shock.

"Keelee, let go! If you don't let go we are both going to die!"

His harsh tone seemed to reach her through her shock, and she loosened her nearly choking hold around his neck.

"I am going to push you up onto that ledge." His words were nearly inaudible to his own ears and so he motioned pushing her up.

Keelee followed his eyes to the ledge then nodded when she realized what he meant to do. They both worked their way over to the rocky outcrop. Keelee was hampered by her wet skirt; it was weighing her down and would keep him from lifting her up to safety. He pulled his last dagger and, holding her as tightly as he could against the rock face just below the ledge, reached down and slit her skirt off her dress. He had to tug hard at the waist to rip it off. She went under in the process and came up sputtering and spitting, gasping for air. He dropped his last dagger as she thrashed, but she was now free of the weight that held her down.

Sordith frantically felt around for anything to press against with his foot. Finally, finding purchase, he held her waist and thrust her up. His exhausted muscles burned with the effort, and the pain in the side that had been hit with something in the initial wave made him grit his teeth. It took two tries, but finally Keelee pulled herself up onto the narrow ledge.

Sordith now struggled to stay afloat. He was exhausted, and if it were not for Keelee he might have given up. She reached down a hand, and the need to live coursed through him. He worked his way to the corner. Fortunately, years of climbing sewers and walls as a street urchin served him now. His fingers slipped more than once, but finally he was able to pull himself up onto another small outcrop on the rock face that connected to the plains. He flopped to the ground wearily taking a few deep breaths – well, as deep as he could with the ribs he felt shattered on his left side.

Despite the lack of ocean water here, there was no shortage of rain and wind. It was not as strong as he suspected it was up on the tiers, though; they were somewhat sheltered here from the brunt of the storm.

With a groan, he forced himself up and turned around. The water was still milling beneath him, a slurry of garbage, sewage, debris, mud, and bodies. He realized he could not quite get his hand out to Keelee on her ledge.

He motioned and called, "You have to jump."

He had to give her credit, despite the terror on her face she nodded and carefully pushed herself up to her feet, using the wall to creep up. He watched helplessly as she almost slipped on the slick stone back into the filth beneath them.

"Catch me," she hollered over the roar of the wind. "Don't let me fall."

She leaped forward and he snatched wildly at her. He managed to grasp a hand and an arm and pulled backward as hard as he could. She landed on top of him. They both groaned in an exhale of breath.

They laid there for a moment, their combined rapid breathing and exhaustion making movement impossible. Sordith knew they could not stay here, there was no shelter from the fury of the storm. It had rolled ashore with the wave and brought all its force, throwing lightning bolts across the sky in rapid succession.

It felt like the end of the world.

He pushed Keelee off him and helped her up.

Sordith searched the cliff face they were currently sheltered against. His keen eyes observed an area where water was rushing in and disappearing. He motioned for her to wait and moved along the rocky wall. Finding an opening a little above his head, he struggled up onto a rock, his body cramping and pain-ridden with every move. There below him was a cave. It did not look to be much of a cave, but from where he stood, he could see it was above the waterline.

"It's a cave," he hollered, the wind whipping his words away.

He motioned her to him and gingerly pulled her onto the rock where he stood, his body screaming at the effort. He dropped down into the hole first. The impact of a mere ten feet took his breath away. He had been right; while there was a small stream rushing off into the depths of the cave, there was also a large sandy ledge well above it. He motioned Keelee to come down. She dropped into his arms and he went down on his butt in the sand, but they were out of the wind and driving rain. They both were covered in mud and sewage. Sordith pushed the hair out of Keelee's eyes and smiled at her. It was just so good to be alive.

"Milady, you look like shite," he said between painful breaths.

"And you as well, Milord." To prove her point she literally removed a turd caught in the folds of his shirt and tossed it to one side.

He chuckled and leaned forward to kiss her, but stopped mid-lean with a painful groan.

"Sordith…" she said with fear in her eyes.

"I'll be alright," he assured her. "It only hurts when I breathe."

Instead of leaning, he scooted over to put his arms around her. He had no way to light a fire nor to keep her warm. She shivered in his arms from the cold and wet. As he sat there in the dim light, anger began to seethe within him. He had been betrayed. He was certain it was Luthian's doing, but until he had proof, he should not act. Still, he would have retribution for those in the trench. He would find that proof, and whoever was responsible, he would personally ensure they felt every death and ounce of fear that the trench denizens had faced today.

Water poured around them, and the wind howled across the openings in the rock, creating a musical edge to the violence above. Sordith kept Keelee close, watching the small river sink into the black cavern below them. He would have to come back here one day and see what was down there besides water. He kissed the top of Keelee's head absently, murmuring reassurances. His last thought before sleep claimed him was envisioning the many ways he would exact payment from the murderers who sealed the trench, and those who ordered it done.

## Chapter Nine

"RUN! WAVE!"

Levielle felt the wave before he saw it. Tremors pulsed through the ground as it thundered into the harbor. The screams of people around him went unanswered. He could hear the shouts of those trapped on the other side, clawing at the wall, trying to climb for freedom.

The mass of water swept through the first tier without hesitation, rushing through the city streets, consuming everything not bolted down. The grinding and scraping of material and the rumble of moving water had him watching in shock as it inundated the city's lower levels. As he stood dumbfounded, his arm holding the hammer went slack, dropping the tool down to his side.

He felt hands grabbing at his arm, snapping him back into the moment. The men that were with him pulled at him. He was hardly able to hear them above the noisy din of this storm.

They ran as a group toward the nearest stonework building. They pounded at the door, shouting to be let in, clawing at the rough woodwork. Levielle, still carrying the hammer he had at the wall, moved to the front of the small group of men and gave the lock on the door a resounding blow. The door swung open.

The home was dark and abandoned. He and the others quickly moved inside and barricaded the doorway, shoving whatever furniture the occupants had against it.

But the door had barely been blockaded before the wave struck. The door was blown open by the mass of rushing water. Men and furniture swirled in the room as it quickly filled. One man was swept under the staircase and could not escape before the surge filled the room, the powerful force trapping him against the wall and drowning him.

Levielle managed to catch the railing on the stairs to the upper level when the water began pouring into the room. He dropped the hammer and threw out his other hand. One by one the men caught his lifeline. The railing groaned, but thankfully held.

"Quickly! Up the stairs!" His words could barely be heard above the rushing waters and driving rain.

They all struggled to hold on and pull themselves up the stairs. The water continued to rise at an alarming rate. Levielle pulled men up and pushed them past him toward the upper floor.

They splashed and scrambled their way up the stairs, wet boots against the smooth wood of the well-worn stairs caused them to slip and nearly fall through the railing and off the side into the ferocity of the swirling pool in the main room.

Catching himself, Levielle clambered up behind them. A primal fear filled him as the rushing wall of water flowed, and only decades of training and discipline allowed him to keep an upper hand as he struggled up the stairs.

By the time he reached the second floor, the men

had already began scrambling up a ladder that led to the roof. The building groaned as the weight of the water threatened to take it from its foundation. The floor creaked as the pillars downstairs were being pounded by water and debris. Reaching the ladder at the heels of the men, there was shouting outside. Levielle couldn't understand what was being said. Soon a loud thump greeted his ears as the roof itself gave way, water pouring in from a gaping hole and slicking the rungs of the ladder. The men above him began to pull themselves out.

When it came his turn, Levielle gripped the top of the roof, but his hand slipped off of the slick tile. The rain and wind made it difficult to find purchase on the edge. Levielle cursed softly as he reached back up again, and this time a hand grasped his to help him up. Finally, he was out. Levielle clapped the man that assisted him on the back. Looking up he saw multiple weighted ropes being lowered down from the next tier. The first man was already being raised up when another rope coiled down. The wind fought them to pull the ropes away, but the weight seemed to help counter that.

"Go! They'll hoist you up, I'll follow in a moment!" Levielle shouted over the din.

The man nodded emphatically before beginning the relatively short ascent. Looking about finally, Levielle was horrified to see the devastation that had been caused by the first wave. From here he could see the debris on the first tier. Everything not nailed down, and much that was, had been wiped out by the force. Even as the wind whipped the surface into a froth, he could make out floating wood, cloth, food, and bodies – many, many bodies. He shuddered for a moment as he realized it could have been his fate too.

The closed off ramps meant there were many souls who didn't even get a chance to hide or escape from the trench. Those that might have managed to live through the first wave would most likely die in the successive waves – many nearly as powerful as the first – as the sea continued to heave and pound against the walled ramps. The trench inhabitants would likely all eventually be drowned by the ocean surf if they hadn't already. Shaking his head, he focused back at the situation at hand.

Levielle grasped the rope tightly and began to walk up the wall when his turn came. The wind howled and buffeted him against the wall as if warning him of the impending doom he was facing. He fought to keep hold, as the men above kept a firm grip on the coarse rope and worked hard to pull him up as quickly as possible. No one knew what the storm might throw at them next.

Soon, the man above him was pulled over the edge onto the second tier, and not long after, Levielle emerged to a small round of applause. Exhaustion rolled over him as he crawled into a sitting position. Someone offered him water, which he took and drank thankfully. Even though the rain still fell in sheets, he needed that drink.

A man helped him to his feet and assisted in moving him toward a covered building, out of the rain. As he stood inside, he could see that others had been saved. However, in his opinion the numbers of saved, compared to those lost, was paltry.

"General…" A young soldier stood before him and saluted smartly.

Levielle hadn't noticed the man approach. He was so exhausted from his fight to escape he had not been paying attention. He shook the feeling off. He could not afford to be tired. He noted the rank of the man and the fact that he was soaked to the core.

"Report, lieutenant."

"We are saving as many as we can, but it's difficult. When the wave hit, it stopped our efforts." His tone was sullen. "Some of my men did not survive."

The general had caught his breath and began to take command. "We've all lost people today, lieutenant." Levielle placed a hand on the man's shoulder. "Carry on; we need to save as many as we can. We need to move the survivors up to the training circle. Bring as much food as you can find. I don't want to add starving to our challenges in keeping our residents safe."

The man nodded and saluted before moving to his tasks.

Still soaked, Levielle found a nearby chair and sat down, his eyes heavy with the desire to sleep. Processing what he had seen already today, he was just glad Nakyra was home and out of harm's way. The horror of what Luthian had managed to do terrified him. It was at that moment that he knew Luthian had to die.

*******************

The rain was so heavy that the men usually posted outside the Blackguard caverns could not be seen. Alador scooped up Nemara and strode for the cave entrance. The wind was too strong now to try to get her up two tiers. She was dressed in the garb of the men within, so he counted on the High Master to assist them.

He glanced down at Nemara; her face was pale, and even though the rain had plastered her hair to her head he could see the distinctive streak of white in her darker tresses. He cursed inwardly; he should have known better. Henrick had told him magic always cost. He should have listened, but in the heat of the moment he convinced himself Nemara could channel with him as Rena did. He could save the city… He really had no idea what Rena gave, or didn't give, to Nemara. He never should have risked her life.

He stepped into the recess of the cave. Sandbags had been placed at the entrance to keep the standing water from the tier at bay. As he glanced backward through the rain, the tier walls were like waterfalls at every drain spout.

The two guards greeted him with hands on their swords. "Sorry milord, the Blackguard is not accepting any but fellow guardsmen. The caverns are struggling against the amount of rain themselves."

"I am Alador Guldalian and I will come in. You will send a runner to the High Master informing him of my arrival." He adjusted Nemara in his arms; she was still unconscious and that worried him.

The guardsman blinked, eyeing the two sodden

souls before him. After hearing Alador's full name, he thought better of rejecting him, nodding to send his younger companion at the entrance through the door and down the hall.

As they waited he tried to make amends without breaking his orders to keep immigrants from the tiers at bay. "Here, set her down." The man swept his cloak off and laid it against a wall out of the blowing rain. "What happened to her?"

Alador was about to tell the truth of the situation when he realized that after his uncle's reaction, that might not be wise. "Debris hit her in the head," he murmured. He laid her down on the cloak and smoothed her hair out of her eyes.

"What were you doing out in this madness?" The guard looked toward the entrance of the cave. Between the cascade of flowing water, the wind and the actual rain falling, you could not see more than a few feet beyond the wall.

"Trying to help." Alador flatly stated.

He stayed crouched beside her. He did not bother with a drying spell for himself. When he was done here, he would be going back out. However, he did cast the cantrip over Nemara. He did not want her chilled on top of whatever he had done to her.

"Did you see? Were there many people hurt in the quake?" The man asked, moving to the entrance and trying to peer out.

"It wasn't a quake." Alador looked over. "It was a wave."

"A wave? The whole ground shook, how can that be a wave?" The man peered more intently but the ocean was lost in a gray shroud.

"It was a very large one." Alador answered. "I think it breached the first tier."

The man at the entrance let out a low whistle. "I did not think that possible. Are you certain?"

"Fairly certain…" Alador had been about to say more when Nemara stirred.

"Ala… lador…" Her eyes fluttered open.

"Shhhh, I am right here. I am taking you to the Blackguard healers' quarters." Alador took her hand and squeezed it to reassure her.

"Did you stop it?" Her worried question hung between them for a long moment.

"No...no, I was unable to stop it," he admitted softly.

"Why is it so bright? It hurts." She closed her eyes and frowned. "Even when my eyes are closed it is so bright."

"Bright?" Alador looked around the dark, dismal opening. "It is not bright, Nemara. Can… you see me?"

She turned her head to his voice and opened her eyes. "No? All I see is light."

Alador cursed inwardly. He stood up and paced toward the door. "I am taking her down now." He wasn't going to wait any longer.

"Not until we get the order from the High Master," the guard stated firmly.

Alador drew lightning to his hand without even thinking. "I am taking her down right now to the healers' quarter. You can let me go peacefully or you can dance in lightning." he hissed, the level of dangerous tension rose immediately between the two.

Nemara sneezed and reached out her hand. "Alador?"

The guard moved between them. He knew the mage would not loose his power with the woman behind him. "Whoa now, we don't need any trouble here. You may be one of the magi, but you are also one of us. It won't be but a minute or so more I am sure."

Alador let the power fade from his hand as he eyed the man. "I am going to pick up Nemara and head for that door. It had damn well better be open for me when I get to it or by the gods I swear…"

The door opened and the High Master eyed Alador. "Threatening my men already, mage?" He shook his head in disappointment.

He had men with him as he stepped forward and a healer rushed past them both to Nemara's side.

"She needs a healer." Alador defended, his face flushed with his anger and distress over what he had done to Nemara.

"And she will get the attention she needs. Now, how about you and I go to my office and have a…" The High Master Bariton had barely started talking before Alador overrode him.

"There isn't time. A wave hit the city. I know it

was at least as high as the first tier. People need help and the army is likely inundated as well," Alador moved forward, urgently explaining. "If ever the Blackguard was needed by this city, it is now." He eyed the taller man. "And… it is time that they were seen in a positive light."

The High Master's eyes narrowed. "Are you certain?" He glanced out at the gray veil between him and the city.

"Absolutely." Alador stated. "There isn't time to waste."

The High Master turned to one of the men Alador knew only as an instructor. "Sound the alarm. I want every available guard down on the tiers and into the trench to help anywhere, and anyone, they can." The High Master turned to another hovering guard. "Open all the cells and classrooms. We may be damp, but the caverns are safe from the wind." Both men snapped salutes and Alador turned to go help the healer with Nemara.

Bariton caught his arm. "Change into a uniform, for now you are Blackguard and not a privileged mage. I want you with me."

Alador pointed to Nemara. "But I need to…"

"Let the healers do their work – it is their special gift. Your abilities can be better used helping the people of Silverport." Bariton's tone brooked no argument, and Alador responded properly without even thinking.

Alador stepped away from everyone and muttered the spell to transform his gear. His rain drenched robes were replaced by shining black leather. His sword hung at his side. He swept his hair back and secured it.

He could already hear the bells ringing inside the caverns through the opened door. He watched as two men helped lift Nemara onto a makeshift stretcher and disappear into the caverns with her.

Bariton turned to one of his officers. "Lieutenant, as the guards appear, break them into groups of ten. They are to help secure the city, bringing the injured and anyone without shelter here. Make sure each man is equipped with a sturdy weighted rope; I image they will be pulling people from tier to tier in some cases." Bariton looked over at Alador. "The second lieutenant and I will be out on the tiers above, assessing the damage - likely the second tier to start."

Alador looked around for the second lieutenant that Bariton spoke of, but realized Bariton was looking at him.

"Wait? What? When did I get promoted?"

"About ten seconds ago. Display your rank on your uniform as required," the High Master ordered.

Alador passed a hand over his right sleeve to materialize the insignia of a Second Lieutenant. He took a moment to admire the blazing crossed swords before Bariton called him back to the present.

"With me, Second Lieutenant." Bariton strode out into the wind and rain, disappearing behind the waterfall cascading over the entrance.

Alador ducked out as well and was caught by the wind and slammed into the wall. "Shite," he murmured, as the wind pressed him into the stone.

He looked forward and saw that Bariton was working his way along the wall toward the third-tier buildings. Alador began to follow him, fighting against the gale. He could not see more than ten feet in front of him. The rain was hitting the wall at almost a horizontal slant. The wind was so vicious it felt as if it tore the air from his lungs.

When they got to the walkway from the caverns out to the edge of the city, the damage just in front of them was astounding. Many of the roofs were made of overlapping half-circle clay tiles, durable and effective under normal circumstances. These were not anywhere near normal circumstances. He could see more than one roof where the tiles were flapping like wings on a bird and other places where they had peeled away completely. Shutters had come loose and were banging wildly and yet he couldn't hear them over the wind. Rain catch barrels were rolling unchecked along the tiers. Awnings, boxes, boards, tiles, papers, smaller carts, and limp bodies were all being propelled along the walkways of the tiers by the gale.

The two men made their way to the buildings along the third tier and stuck to their walls, trying to avoid the flying debris. Bariton dashed across the walkway to the tier edge, a place somewhat sheltered by the buildings on either side of them. Alador panted with the exertion of just staying on his feet as he joined Bariton. Both men stared in horrified fascination at the scene below them. Whatever waves had hit prior to their arrival finished the initial devastation. The water was slowly making its way off the first tier. Debris was pooling in the ramps down to the trench. Alador could not even see the ramps down.

The lands beyond the trench were also saturated. Though the initial wave had passed over the city, additional smaller surges of water kept moving the flood inland. People could be seen attempting to stay upright and above the fast-moving water Children were held up on the shoulders of the adults. Those that had made it to the bridge up to the third tier stood at the edges much as the High Master and Alador did, mouths open in shock.

"It is completely under water." Alador shouted over the wind and rain. "Do you think the Trench Lord got them all out?"

"By the gods, I surely hope so." Bariton grabbed Alador's arm. "Let's get down there." He indicated the closest stairs to the second tier.

They made their way, buffeted by stinging water and howling winds, to the second tier stairwell. Four guards were at the gate, huddled in the lee of it from the storm as they guarded the tier path. Recognizing Bariton they waived him through; orders were to not let people up, but no one said anything about going down.

The second tier was a mass of swarming bodies, each seeking shelter. The panic was palpable as the two made their way to the ramps down to the first tier. Here the guards were pulling people up and passing them on to others who were helping them find a spot. There was no shelter to be found as they moved through the crowds. Every house that could open and take in people seemed to have done so. The people of Silverport who had survived the wave were now at the mercy of the full fury of the storm.

Bariton grabbed a young man who seemed to be directing rescues. "How can the Blackguard help?" he shouted.

"Best to ask the General, he is in the third house down to the right." The man shouted back. Bariton gave a nod and tugged Alador with him.

Alador dashed water from his face and moved to keep up with the High Master. He stopped in horror when a shutter broke free, the wood peeling back in pieces and flying into the crowds. People were screaming and pushing, trying to work their way into the lee of buildings. There was a press to move up a tier and Alador could see the General's guards holding them at bay with swords. They would not hold out much longer by the mood of the gathered survivors.

He hadn't realized he had stopped until Bariton grabbed his arm and pulled him forward. He nodded and continued to follow the High Master. Bariton pounded at the door and must have been asked to identify himself, though Alador hadn't been able to hear anything above the din.

The door opened and both men practically fell into the building with relief. They were shown into a room where General Levielle was standing. The man's face was pale but resolute. As they were shown into the room, Levielle abruptly stopped pacing. Both Alador and Bariton saluted the General.

Levielle recognized the two immediately. He strode to stand toe-to-toe with Alador, his rage just held in check. "Did you know?"

Alador took a step back at the look on Levielle's face. "Did I know… what? About the wave? I am the one that gave Sordith and Luthian warning, if that is what you mean?" He was shocked. He could never remember a time when Levielle had not been in good temper and very centered.

Levielle took one step forward. He was taller than Alador and he knew the proximity would make him more imposing. His tone and posture looked calm, but was anything but. "You didn't answer the question, Guardsman," he growled. "I asked if you knew." Levielle's tone held a deadly edge to it.

High Master Bariton wedged his way between them. "General, I probably want to know the answer to whatever you're asking, but you might want to take a moment and clarify... what it is he knew?" His tone was placating, but held a question as well. He wanted to know what the general was after too.

Levielle looked to Bariton and frowned. Setting his jaw, he spoke at Alador, but did not look at him. "Did you know of your uncle's plan to seal the trench level?" His body tensed for the response. His gaze locked on Bariton before him.

Bariton stared agape at Levielle, stunned by the words. He turned to look at Alador as well. The huge pools they saw on the first tier… The standing water… They were not caused by the debris backing up on the ramps to the trench?

Now both ranking men glared down at him. Alador felt his heart turn over. "Seal the trench? What you are talking about? Did he try to put a block at the harbor entrance to prevent the wave?"

A grim, cruel smile grew over Levielle's face. "Oh, Alador… No…" Stepping around Bariton, Levielle placed himself once more directly before the young mage. "He had stone mages seal the trench from the upper tiers," his smile dropped as he relived the horror, "trapping the unfortunate in the stone and in the trench as the wave struck."

Alador shook his head in disbelief. "No. No, I know he is a power seeking despot, but not even he would sink that low. You must be wrong." Alador shook his head at Levielle's revelation. "There are miners… women... children. He couldn't have done that. There must be another explanation." Despite his desire to see Luthian unseated as High Minister, the one thing that Alador had learned from his uncle was that you didn't waste resources. Even if the man was heartless enough to kill women and children, he was certain that he would not wish to lose the miners that brought in the city's medure and other wealth.

"I spoke with your uncle just before the wave struck." Levielle gazed unblinking toward Alador. "He wanted me to move the army either to the plains, or to the training ring, and ordered me *not* go into the trench." The pain in his words could be heard.

"Yes, to get the army out of the winds, we spoke of

this." Alador nodded, not seeing how this meant that Luthian had sealed the trench.

"No, Alador, he specifically ordered me to not enter the trench. The High Minister stated he would send bronze mages to..." he chewed on the last word for a moment longer, "...assist." After a moment of silence that lay between them, Levielle moved back into the room once again, looking for something.

No… No… It couldn't be true. What had Luthian done? Where was Sordith? Alador thought in a moment of panic. His half-brother would have been down there in the trench until the last moment.

Bariton coughed to ease the tension, clearly accepting Alador's shocked look as confirmation that the young man had not known. "General, we can ponder the intricacies of motives and fault later. We have people out in this storm," he gently reminded the man. "The caverns will be out of the winds and direct rain," he offered. "Our dining hall is quite large and the men can bunk together to open up some cells for families with children. I have a full healers' quarter. How do you want to evacuate this tier?" The High Master was turning over command of the Blackguard to the General with his words.

Levielle once more stood still. He looked toward the wall that he faced and breathed deeply. He didn't say anything for a moment and then spoke with a command. "Get as many people off this tier as you can and into the caverns. They are to take as much food as possible, but as little else as necessary. We need as much room as we can get for people, not things. Second tier only. Those on third tier should be able to recover in time on their own. Make sure all innkeepers on the second and third tier know that this is an emergency and they will need to keep every door and bed open for the night."

"As you command, sir." Bariton snapped a salute and turned on his heel.

Alador turned to leave as well. "I can move amongst the inns and identify the injured to be taken to the caverns," he murmured. He would have the opportunity to look for Sordith and Keelee as he helped move the walking wounded to the healers in the caverns. He stole a last look at Levielle, whose back was still turned to him before moving to follow the High Master of the Blackguard.

"Master Guldalian." Levielle called, his back still turned. He waited only a moment before speaking again. The rage seeped from his tone. "If I find out you knew of the High Minister's actions, I will personally make sure you are slowly lowered, hog-tied, into the bay."

Alador paused when he heard his formal name. Levielle's heavy words were followed by a tense silence before Alador answered, "Understood."

## Chapter Ten

Alador's stomach growled, and he was once more reminded of his empty belly and his seemingly permanent state of exhaustion. The storm had kept the day a dim gray, but now nightfall was bringing an even darker tone. He told himself for the umpteenth time that he needed to check on Nemara, but he kept on working. The task seemed endless.

The last hour or so he had been helping move the dead to a wagon; once full they were taken to a pile on the plains. They were attempting to identify everyone before the nature mages and fire mages disposed of the bodies in funeral pyres.

The first tier had taken a hard hit, mostly those milling about from the trench prior to its being sealed off. He had seen firsthand the walls of stone and body parts that had blocked those seeking higher ground. He just could not believe Luthian would do such a thing. Surely it was beyond even his darkest thoughts to murder people in such a vile way.

At first, it seemed like the hours crawled by slowly. One by one they were able to get the survivors from both the first tier and the third tier bridge into the caverns. The Blackguard made a line of men to help those with small children make their way up and across the third tier. Some with housing on the first tier chose to stay to salvage what they could.

Alador was taking a breath in the lee of a building on the second tier. From there, he could see the trench. Little was left – it was hardly more than a ditch of mottled water and debris. The tide turned mid-day and with it, the water level allowed for drainage to begin. But, the water coming off the upper tiers seemed to be keeping the trench full.

The rain had lessened to nothing more than an annoying drizzle that showed no sign of letting up. A couple of hours ago Alador watched the storm spin off multiple tornadoes which moved rapidly across the plain and away from the city inland, leaving nothing behind except thick rain clouds and torn up channels in the muddy soil.

There had been neither sign nor word of Sordith or Keelee from those he assisted. He was praying to the gods that he had simply missed them in the weather and chaos. He tried to picture them somewhere safe, warming themselves by a fire, but failed. He knew if his brother had lived, he would have been in the thick of the clean-up. He let out a deep sigh – Sordith had most likely died in the trench with his people.

He could see the bodies floating in the trench. For a time, he used his dragon-sight to try and locate Sordith in the water of the harbor, but he gave that up. He saw too many things he wished he hadn't – dead mothers with their dead children clasped tightly to their breasts; mangled and crushed bodies; and partial bodies that made his stomach roll and heave. All that were not eventually washed out to sea would have to be collected and brought to the plains for disposal so disease and infection would be kept at bay.

He turned his eyes toward the plains. It too was dotted with the bodies of people who tried that route to escape the wave. Those would not have to be moved. They had already found their final resting place.

Two Blackguards walked by carrying a makeshift stretcher cobbled together from a wooden door. There were two bodies on it – a man face down dressed in leathers and a woman with dark hair beneath him. Alador snapped to attention, his adrenaline kicking in. He pushed off the wall and ran to the men.

"Stop! Let me see!" he said in a panicked voice. It couldn't be… please… he silently prayed.

The men, stopped almost happy to be relieved of moving their heavy burden any further.

Alador gently lifted the man's head and turned his face so he could see… Was it Sordith and Keelee beneath him? He almost cried when he saw that it was not either of them, just some other unfortunate souls.

"Do you know them, Sir?" one of the guards asked.

"No…" Alador said as he stepped back. "No… I thought I might, but I don't."

He felt tears welling up and turned to hide them as he went back to lean against the building. He was just so tired. He was losing control. When he leaned up against the building he realized his knees were weak and his hands were shaking. Once again, he told himself he should go check on Nemara.

A voice brought him out of his thoughts. "High Master requests your presence in the caverns, Sir."

The guardsman looked young and Alador smiled grimly at the thought. He had been young once, before he had been forced to grow up too quickly.

"I am to take over whatever you are doing," the young man added.

Alador nodded. "I am gathering dead and helping stragglers up out of the weather. Good luck." Alador turned and stepped back out into the rain. It stung as it hit his chilled cheeks. The weights that were his feet plodded forward in resistance to the lessening wind. As he made it up onto the third tier, the rain came to a stop. He looked up and there above him was blue sky. He made his way to the overlook as the wind began to die down further. Was it finally over?

Standing on the overlook, he could see the last part of the cloud bank forming into one final funnel cloud to escape across the plain. He looked to his right to see people peeking out of their homes and businesses. Everyone had noticed when the rain stopped and the wind had died down to a mere breeze.

A woman stepped up to him, another member of the Blackguard, but one he did not recall. "Is it over?" She looked at the sky uncertainty.

"No." Alador stated watching the air stones. They still held that strange erratic element in the tornado which was rapidly leaving. "It is just moving away."

"Will it come back?" she asked with a touch of fear in her voice.

"I hope not." Alador turned to go report to the High Master.

"Me too, Lieutenant."

For a second, Alador wasn't sure who she was talking to, then remembered his on the spot promotion, and the insignia on his sleeve. He wasn't even sure he was technically in the Blackguard, but then again, he never had officially left it.

He ducked into the cavern. He had never seen it so full. The press of warm, wet bodies left a humid feel to the cave's tunnels as he made his way through to the High Master's office. There was a low rumble of voices that echoed throughout the cavern like the buzz of bees in a massive hive.

He was waved through into Bariton's private quarters. The door shut behind him as he cast a drying spell to ease the movement of his leathers and help with the chill that permeated his body.

"Have you stopped since we left General Levielle?" Bariton voice barked out the question as soon as he entered the room.

"No," Alador admitted. "I have been working while trying to find Sordith and Keelee, but there is no sign of either of them." Alador sank wearily into the chair Bariton indicated. The High Master went to a side table and poured them both a stiff drink.

He did not speak until he handed Alador the glass. He leaned against his desk in front of the beleaguered mage, eyeing him. "Sordith is a man with a quick mind. Who knows, he could have had some bronze mage wall him in. We have bigger problems."

"Besides the aftermath of a storm like none we have ever seen?" Alador took a long drink; the warm burning was welcome for a change. He closed his eyes, just resting in the sensation of the fortifying liquid.

Bariton sat in a chair angled toward him and sipped from his own glass. He leaned in and spoke in a low tone. "There are whispers going through the caverns that the high mages tried to kill everyone below the second tier."

Alador paused with his hand halfway to his mouth, staring into the amber liquid. He looked toward the closed door. Shadows were cast under it as people passed back and forth, but it didn't look like anyone was loitering outside trying to listen in. All the same, Alador lowered his voice as well when he answered, "I'm not sure it isn't truth more than rumor. I saw the wall with people stuck in the stone blockade."

"If it is truth, the upper tiers may very well find themselves in a civil war."

Alador ran a weary hand over his face. "The lower tiers would just lose. If Luthian holds the army and the highly skilled mages to his favor, we have no chance of cleansing the greed and hubris from the upper tiers." He could not help yawning.

"Yes, well, I would welcome a suggestion that might calm the people down." Bariton drained his glass and set it aside.

Alador sat for a moment deep in thought. If Luthian had ordered the sealing of the trench… If Sordith and Keelee had lost their lives because of Luthian's orders… But he couldn't take on his uncle right now. If he was to be successful in bringing down Luthian, and the evil ways of the ruling body, then he needed to plan… He needed help… He had to wait, bide his time, until he would have a real chance of success.

"Let rumors loose that it was stone mages that had an axe to grind. I am sure Luthian has a couple that are in his way." Alador also drained his glass. "Better that a couple of mages die than three tiers worth of citizens." He stood up and stretched. "If the rumor is out before the citizens start making their way home to mount repairs, we might not have a riot."

"You realize that I am not able to stand up to any order Luthian may give for this garrison." Bariton rose as well.

"Neither is Levielle. I will find out if my uncle did this. If he did, I will be the one that will need to deal with him."

"Can you?" Bariton took a step closer and looked Alador in the eye. "Could you kill your own kin?"

There was not even a pause before Alador answered. "Definitely."

Bariton held his gaze for a moment before turning away. "Then we will get together and plan when you know for certain. I will get that rumor started. Guards passing the news loudly enough to be overheard should do the trick." He picked up their glasses and went to the board and refilled them.

Alador was pleased to hear Bariton would still be with him when he challenged Luthian. He would need men like the High Master, especially if Sordith was gone. He cleared his throat of the lump that appeared at the thought of losing his half-brother.

"One more to fortify you, Lieutenant." Bariton brought the glass over to Alador. "I hear Nemara is awake."

Alador smiled for the first time in hours. "That is good news. I will see her before I rest. Did they say how she was?"

He took the glass gratefully. Already the warmth of the alcohol's burn was easing its way through his exhausted form.

"I do not know lad, I only heard she was awake and asking for you." Bariton held up his glass. "To the people who died this day, may they be avenged swiftly and thoroughly.

Alador could drink to that. Their glasses clinked and then Alador drained his in one go. He walked to the table and set the glass down. "Anything else before I go to check on Nemara?"

"Not that can't wait until you have eaten and had some rest." Bariton walked with Alador to his door in the cavern wall. "You are ordered to bed for at least six hours."

"Yes, High Master." Alador saluted the man and then left him. He picked his way swiftly through people huddled against walls and milling about down to the healers' area. Once there he made his way swiftly to Nemara's side.

Nemara must have been able to see him for her head tracked his movement to her. "How are you, Nemara?"

Nemara frowned. "Better, though everything still seems very over-lit. Bright light actually hurts." As if by signal, she closed her eyes with a slight sigh of relief.

"I am so sorry. I should have let you go earlier." He took her hand. "I was mistaken in assuming you had the same abilities as Rena." He hooked a stool with his foot and pulled it over to sit down. "I would never have hurt you on purpose."

She opened her eyes and raised his hand to her lips to kiss his fingers. "You did what you needed to do. You couldn't help it if I wasn't as strong as your last partner." Though she was tired, she sounded more herself. "The healer said that I should stay the night. My vision is clearing up with the compresses they are applying. I should be able to see well enough to get around by tomorrow."

"Well then, you should follow their advice." Alador brushed her hair back from her forehead and tucked a stray lock behind her ear. He was so relieved to have her recovering. He had managed to save her.

"I won't complain and I'll be good if you will go check on the egg," she whispered. "It needs to be rotated," her tone all but begged this of him.

Alador sometimes swore she laid the egg the way she mothered it. He wished he knew how much Rena had imprinted on Nemara for her to retrieve the egg and care for it. Obviously, Rena had not fully transferred herself to Nemara as Renamaum had to him, but it was equally obvious that something had been done.

"I will go as soon as we are done here. I could use a hot soak and a few hours of sleep."

Nemara licked her pert lips. "Is it bad? I heard the wave was enormous."

"It's bad."

"People died, didn't they?" she whispered her question with a touch of sadness and regret.

"Quite a few." Alador looked down studying her small hand in his. He toyed with her fingers and stroked the back of her hand gently as his mind flooded with images from the first day of clean-up. "I think there would have been losses no matter what we did. They are greater than they should have been. A mage, or mages, walled the first tier closed so no one could move up from the trench. Even so, a lot of those that did come up were contained to the first tier and it also got hit hard." His voice broke when he once more contemplated the death of Sordith and Keelee. He had not realized how close he had become to his half-brother in such a short time.

"Are Keelee and Sordith all right?" Nemara grasped his hand tighter. Her eyes opened wider in question. She winced slightly at the bright light.

"I honestly don't know. I never saw them." Alador squeezed her hand back. "You know he is the type that would have stayed there until he had everyone out. If they walled it off before the wave hit, it is likely that he was in the trench."

Nemara let a tear slip down her cheek. "I am so sorry, Alador." She rolled to her side toward him and pulled him forward into her arms.

He lowered his head to the edge of the bed, and she kissed his hair and pet his head as he let the tears finally escape. She hovered over him whispering gentle encouragement as he sobbed quietly under her soft embrace. She cradled his head in her arms and let her own tears fall.

Eventually, he was too exhausted to even cry anymore. He raised his head and she pulled the sheet up to wipe the tears from his cheeks. He thumbed the ones she had shed from her eyes.

"Is the water receding yet?" She asked to change the subject.

"It is moving slowly. The culverts are sending water into the trench like geysers. With the walkways walled up, there is nowhere for the standing water on the tier to go in those recesses." Alador reached out and put a hand on her face tenderly. "Get some rest. I will go check on the egg."

Nemara nodded and let go of his hand as Alador

rose.

"I will be back in the morning to check on you," offered the mage. "You do what the healers tell you until then."

Nemara laughed lightly. "Yes, because you have been so good at that yourself. Pot calling the pan sooted."

"Yes, but I am doing what you have asked and so you must return the favor." Alador chided gently.

"Okay, I didn't plan on rushing off anywhere." She ran a hand to push her hair out of her face. Alador saw the telltale streak of white but said nothing. If she didn't already know, she would find out soon enough.

"I will see you then." He leaned down and put a gentle kiss on her forehead. He would have liked to crawl in bed with her and just be comforted by her embrace until he fell into oblivion. But he couldn't. He had to see to the egg and all the rest of the things that needed his attention. He turned and strode away. He had things to do and he didn't have much energy left to do them.

## Chapter Eleven

Jon waited in the antechamber. All praetors and priests had been summoned by the High Priestess. They all were milling around the outer chamber awaiting entry and the arrival of Lady Morana.

The upper openings of the temple created the illusion of a tiered city, but on a normal day this visual effect also created a gentle whistling like the sound of flutes. It was usually a soothing background noise, but today with the high winds of the storm, which seemed to blanket the whole continent, it was more like a hundred flutes all screaming a different tune. It was difficult to hear anyone, so everyone's voice was raised, creating an overpowering din..

Silence descended as the door opened and they were all ushered into the inner room of the High Priestess' audience chambers. Jon hung to the back, picking a place against the wall of the chamber. If someone made her angry, the last place he wanted to be was in the front of the target of her ire.

Lady Morana beckoned them to come forward. Jon mused at how the rest of them looked as hesitant as he felt; she had not been in a good mood of late. They all shuffled forward slowly – none of them wanting to be the focal point of her glare. He had to give the woman credit, she had her claws sunk deeply into all of them. He hung back in the shadows so she would not catch sight of him from where she was on the onyx platform.

She stood in front of her ornate throne, her jet-black robe glistening, with the intricate bead work on the stand up collar which framed her pale face and her dark hair piled up in braids on her head. She swept her hands in front of her to indicate the whole room and recited a spell which dropped the sound of the wind's effect on the temple to a low hum and amplified her own voice so she could be heard clearly throughout the room.

"As you all know we are experiencing a severe storm across the continent. We are needed by Silverport and the villages north and south of the city for five hundred leagues. Our capital was at the forefront when the storm first came ashore. I am told there was an enormous wave, which caught many unprepared. People are injured and dying, and it is our duty to help the injured to healers where we can, and ease the suffering of those who cannot be healed.

"I need every priest, praetor and those that have been trained in the rites ready to leave here as soon as the storm wanes enough to make lexital travel possible. You will need to send the lexital back from your assignments so they can ferry another." She was all business. Morana usually had a silkiness to her voice, a persuasive tone to build trust with those she commanded, but not today.

A murmur broke out in the enclave as people took in her words. Some were from coastal villages, so the shock and concern for their family and friends was evident. Jon suddenly had a moment of inspiration. He could endear himself to the High Priestess with one or two small suggestions.

"Milady, if I may?" He stepped forward into the light, and as he spoke people moved away from him a bit. It made him smile inwardly because he knew it was not out of politeness, but rather that no one wanted to associate themselves with him if his words brought anger from Lady Morana.

"Yes, Praetor?" She moved on the dais to face him directly.

"With it raining as it is, burnings will be difficult unless we suddenly have a beautiful day on the far side of this storm. I suggest we put the dragons to a test." Jon stood perfectly still. His face was schooled with its usual lack of emotion.

"And what sort of test did you have in mind for my dark beauties?" She did not scowl, but her eyebrows knit together as she questioned him.

He knew it was a warning. She had been building her dragon flight for years. She had not revealed them to anyone other than her followers. No one knew their numbers or strength. She would be hesitant to allow her power to be known.

"Let the dead be piled and send the dragons to fetch the corpses to bring here. They can be properly placed in the crypts." In Jon's role as spy for Alador he had found out that she was amassing the bodies of the dead under the temple. He had not discerned the purpose yet, but by suggesting this action he hoped to gain entry to the bowels of the temple and learn her plan.

He inwardly felt accomplishment, though it did not show on his face, when she smiled with delight.

"That is an excellent and thoughtful idea." Her voice was a purr, sounding more like her usual self. "The far villages will know their kin have been properly seen to, and we can ensure that the dragons will follow my commands to the letter." She moved down from the dais to the main floor and approached Jon. Those gathered bowed and parted further, allowing her to pass.

Jon did not move as she approached and put her fingers under his chin. She was pure Lerdenian by birth, and taller than him, so as she lifted his chin he looked up into her dark eyes. Their gaze was almost hypnotic.

"You are the one called Jon?"

She knew damned well what his name was. He had felt her eyes on him almost daily since he arrived months ago. He had always been on his guard not to let her see anything that would put his loyalty in question.

"Yes, High Priestess. I live but to serve Dethara," he murmured.

Around him the whispered echo of *live to serve* was uttered from the other members of her following.

"It is as it should be, Jon. As such, you will stay here and coordinate the gathering of the bodies the dragons bring and see to their proper interment into the crypts." She dropped his chin and turned to glide back onto the dais.

She turned and stood with her hands folded in front of her. "Here is my full command," her voice ran out once again over the gathering. "All will be sent out.

Once you have done what you can at a coastal village, work your way inland toward the temple. Order the dead to be piled, that Dethara's own dragons can recover them to lay beneath the temple. Impress upon the living that this is an honor afforded to few."

Morana looked around making eye contact as the murmur of agreement rippled through the room. When her gaze reached Jon, he merely dipped his head in acknowledgment.

"You will need to take a full plague kit, as I am told dead and broken bodies abound which will pollute the water and the air." She looked around at the eager group. It was rare so many were allowed out of the temple at the same time. "Good. I know some of you will want to check on your home village or city. Leave the name of the city you wish to start at with Jon. There is no room for doubling up; this will be a challenging endeavor for all concerned. So, if one claims a city, then you must choose another." She looked out over the crowd. "Gather your supplies and move quickly now." With a wave of her hand, she dismissed them all.

Jon almost panicked as people immediately flooded around him, throwing out the names of towns and villages.

He put up a hand and yelled, "Silence!"

The shock on the faces closest to him was almost amusing. He had taken time over the past few months to build a reputation as a soft-spoken man.

"Let us take this out of the High Priestess' chamber. We will do this in an orderly fashion. We have time; the storm is still too strong for the lexital. I will get paper to take note of who is dispatched where. Form a line outside in the waiting chamber. I will be ready in less than an hour."

He sent a servant running for quill and paper. As soon as he felt suitably organized, he sat down at a small table where a line had already started to form. One by one, he took down the names of coastal villages and towns he had never heard of. He was surprised at how easily they were accepting him as one appointed by Lady Morana as a leader.

It took almost three hours to register where everyone was going. He had ensured that Silverport had a number of members headed to aid them. It was a big city with a harbor, and the trench was at sea level. He almost wrote his own name down for the tiered city of his best friend Alador, but he knew his command from the High Priestess had been for him to remain here, and in truth this was where Alador needed him to be, too.

When the last priest had left the table, Jon rose wearily and stretched. He had seven pages of names and locations. He carefully approached the priest who guarded the door between the outer audience chamber and the inner.

"I have the lists the High Priestess commanded. If I may beg a moment of her time, I would like to know what she desires of me now," Jon stated in a low and somber tone.

The guard nodded and opened the door a small bit, whispering to someone standing on the other side. He had to give Morana credit, she was very careful. How else could you manage a plethora of death mages and devotees? He waited for over twenty minutes before the door opened to admit him.

Jon strode in with the list in hand. He dropped to one knee before the priestess, waiting until she recognized him. He caught a glimpse of her small feet as she approached him down the onyx steps from the dais where she had been sitting when he entered.

"Rise, Jon," she said softly.

Jon did as he was bid and smiled up at the lovely woman. There was no denying she was the most beautiful woman he had ever seen. It was why, when he first started having dreams of her, he thought she was Dethara herself. He realized he was staring and broke his gaze. He knew that attention always pleased her, but it hadn't been an action with intent by him. She truly was mesmerizing.

"I have finished the list, milady. I will get them to the scribes to encode in a more organized and proper fashion. Everyone is readying for departure when the lexitals can fly." He gave the stoic report with his head bowed and his eyes on his feet.

"Very good. You could have just left word." She continued to stand in front of him. "So, tell me what it is that you really wished to say, Praetor."

Jon swallowed. "Milady, may I be so bold as to suggest something that, perhaps, you have already considered?"

"Go on," she coaxed.

Jon cleared his throat and set his sights to work his way into favor with his High Priestess. "Could this not be an opportunity for the black flight to feed without restraint or criticism, and thereby taste mortal flesh?" His offer was soft and carefully worded.

"Usually, my advisers warn against them tasting mortal flesh for fear they will turn on their keepers." Morana voice held the edge of interest.

"That is why this is an opportunity." Jon ventured a look up into her eyes. He needed to see her reaction in order to gauge his ability to convince her of his sincerity. "We all know that the taste and smell of meat is different in a body left lying, than in a fresh kill. Teach them to eat the dead on the battlefield. They will be terrifying to your enemies both in their very presence, and then seen gulping down bodies. Their appearance at a battle will create quite the effect on a soldier's resolve. Our enemies do not need to know that they only have been taught to eat the dead."

Morana began to pace, her long, black velvet robe trailing behind her giving the appearance of floating. "I have need of these bodies in the crypt, but your idea has merit." She continued to walk and think.

"Perhaps only the bodies that are not whole," Jon amended his suggestion. "While I do not understand what is going on in the crypt, I have seen enough to know you prefer those interred to be whole of limb." He pulled his eyes away from her and nailed them to the floor. He just put it all together. His heart dropped and he quickly tried to hide his reaction. *She was making an army – an army of undead!*

"What is amiss, Jon?" The question was suddenly hard in contrast to her soft manner.

"Nothing Lady Morana." He glanced up and tried to look sickened, which was not difficult. The idea of an army of undead at her command made his own blood run cold. "It is just the thought of feeding mortals to dragons brought a bit of squeamishness." He quickly attempted to focus her on the ones being eaten and not the ones being set aside. "It cannot be a pretty sight."

Morana walked back to stand in front of him. She took his chin in her hand again. He could feel her black painted nails bite into his flesh – not painfully, but possessively. "Perhaps it is time for you to rise to Priest, Jon. You have a quick mind and an even manner." She stared into his eyes. He felt he might drown in their dark pools. "See this done properly and you will rise in my service." She released him and started the climb back up the dais. When she got to the top, she turned back toward him. "Sort those that are not whole and send them to Senon, who runs the caves. Tell him it is my will that the dragons feed upon the dead to forestall disease and to teach them the taste of our enemies."

Inwardly, Jon breathed a sigh of relief. "Of course, High Priestess… immediately."

Jon bowed low and then turned and strode from the room. His heart was pounding with the realization that Morana was forming an army, an army of undead. How could she possibly raise so many? Where would she keep them as she turned them? Or would she try to do it in a single ceremony? Turning one took an enormous effort for a death mage and usually could not be held for very long. What had she learned that he did not know? It seemed he would be spending many hours in the library as soon as this business of mass death was finished.

## Chapter Twelve

Before Alador could do anything, he had to find something to eat. He felt if he didn't he was going to collapse. He had consumed nothing since prior to the storm. His magic drained him and his dragon-self was gnawing at his gut. His mind could not help but reflect on Henrick and his enormous appetite. Alador felt he could rival his father, and his dragon-self, in his need to feed at this moment.

It was too crowded to use the amulet to teleport himself home – there were watching eyes everywhere. He decided as much as he promised Nemara to check on the egg, it could wait a half hour more until he filled his belly. He headed toward the cavern kitchens.

When he arrived at the dining hall there was a multi-layered line out the door and down the corridor. He walked on past and went to the back entry to the kitchen. He and Jon had found this once after a particularly strenuous day and they had helped themselves to an apple pie sitting on a cooling rack.

This time the kitchen was abuzz with cooks, helpers and the massive clean-up crew. The minute the aroma of the food hit him, the beast within him was unleashed. The closest thing was a prep table full of vegetables. He grabbed a handful and gobbled them down, hardly taking the time to swallow, much less chew.

Just past that someone was stirring a pot of soup with savory potatoes and hunks of meat bobbing in its bubbling broth. He pushed the man aside and started ladling up a bowl.

"Hey! What the…" the cook protested. "Who do you think you are." The man tried to elbow him aside.

Everyone in the busy kitchen turned at the man's protest to stare at the Blackguard who was raiding their kitchen.

Another veritable mountain of a man strode forward. In truth, he was too tall, and way too broad, for either race in the city. Alador had a fleeting thought that he might be a troll from some foreign island captured by Luthian and set to work here in the caverns.

"Out of my kitchen!" the troll man shouted as he grabbed Alador at the collar and by his sword belt from behind. He started toward the door to eject him.

"Master Chef…" one of the dishwashers called, "Don't… Please." The young man ran forward and put a restraining hand on the troll's arm. "That there is Lord Alador. The one what shattered the Testing Dome. I overheard the High Master sayin' 'e done 'is best to stop the wave. Ain't 'is fault 'e couldn't."

The troll stopped. Alador hung in his grip, the bowl of soup still in his hand.

"Well, I suppose that does make a difference." The man mountain released Alador who stood licking his lips with a glazed expression on his face.

The troll took an empty tray to one of the prep-tables and scooped all but a thigh and leg of a turkey they were chopping up off the table. He placed the tray to one side and then physically moved Alador to the table. Pulling up a stool, he plopped Alador down on it.

"Don't move!" he ordered. "We'll bring you something to eat."

Alador did not wait. He immediately dove for the turkey leg and started devouring it.

A succession of dishes was brought to him by various cooks and helpers over the next hour. His servers exclaimed at how much, and how quickly, the slender young mage ate, but he was totally focused on getting the food into him and ignored them.

At the stroke of the hour, the troll man came back to the table. He folded his arms across his broad chest and looked down his long nose at Alador as the young man shoved yet another huge hunk of bread and sausage in his mouth.

"I must admit I appreciate the compliment that you have eaten everything we have set before you, but frankly, you need to leave. I could feed a troop of foot soldiers with what we have fed you so far."

Alador swallowed and smiled at the man. "I will replenish the stores from my home," he offered the cook. "I greatly appreciate your hospitality." Alador rose to his feet. He was satiated enough that he could take time finding a quiet place where he could use the amulet to get home and check on the egg.

He rubbed his greasy hands on the towel some helper had given him earlier. He stuck out his hand to the cook, his disappearing in the troll's huge hand.

As he turned, he picked up a chicken leg and waved it at the kitchen crew. "Thank you all and keep up the good work."

\*\*\*\*\*\*\*\*\*\*\*\*\*\*\*\*\*\*\*\*\*\*\*\*\*\*\*\*\*\*\*\*\*\*\*\*\*\*\*\*\*\*\*\*\*\*\*

As soon as Alador found a place where he could use his amulet to transport him home, he pulled it loose, focusing on his bedroom and casting the spell. Manifesting at the foot of the bed, he breathed a sigh of relief. Alador always feared that someone was going to move things about and he would appear with a chest for a foot - or worse.

Using a simple cantrip he changed into a simple robe, tied at the waist. He strode into the bathing room and was relieved to see the egg still sitting as he had left it, partially submerged in its rocky nest in the large pool.

He undid the robe and hung it on the wall. Stepping into the water, he made his way over to the egg. The water was slightly cool, and Alador's dragon-self complimented him on the fact that it had not cooled too much to damage the hatchling, but was not hot enough to change the gender of the egg; his dragon memories had shown him that keeping it cooler guaranteed it would be a female.

To Alador, the water was comfortingly warm after hours of cold driving rain. He carefully turned the egg over as he had seen Nemara do a hundred times. He ran his hand over the sapphire scales and fingered the silver lining. The shell was beautiful.

"What manner of creature are you, I wonder?" he murmured to the egg.

The egg lurched, falling sideways toward him. Alador laughed and sat on the ledge, sitting the egg on his lap. "Don't be in such a hurry little one, the world is a very unkind place for some." He smiled at the egg. He did not care what came out of it. It was the only part he had of Rena.

"When this storm is over, I am going to take you to see your Grandmother. She is a nice dragon, for the most part. She can teach you everything you need to know about being a dragon. Most importantly, you will be safe there until things here are done." He sighed and carefully laid the egg back in its stone nest.

He moved across the deep pool and hopped up to the side. He carefully lit the small burner near the pool. It took a few tries as his fingers were wet, and it didn't occur to him that he could just remove the water from them till the third try. He shook his head at how easy it was to use magic and yet, he often forgot he had the ability. His thoughts led him to Sordith as he laid some meraweed on the burner. Sinking back down into the water, he let tears fill his eyes.

So many had died today, was Sordith among them? Had he lost his brother? Those he could trust were few in Silverport, he could count them on one hand - Nemara, Bariton and Levielle so far. The sheer impact of the storm and the damage it had done to property and goods was but one level of damage.

His thoughts led him to his uncle. Could Luthian

have walled off the trench? Did he detest the lower class so much that he would murder them en mass? It countered his politics completely, especially his teachings around the use of resources. There were so many unanswered questions. The smoke from the meraweed began to fill the chamber and Alador laid back and closed his eyes. It had been a long day, and he was exhausted.

*************************************************

*Alador drifted into a dreamlike state. He smiled as he stared down at the ocean from the council tier. A little voice called out, 'papa' and he turned. There, on the green lawn of the tier, sat a little girl. She was about seven years old and was holding a glowing bloodstone in her hand. She had taken such delight in the fact she could make it glow. Alador remembered when Henrick came yearly to test him and he could not get a spark out of it.*

*Alador didn't feel confused that she had called him papa. It seemed right for some reason. He moved to her and knelt.*

*"You are getting very good at that Latiera."*

*He scrutinized the child. She had long white hair and the most amazing sapphire eyes. She was Daezun for the most part, but you could see the Lerdenian influence in the angles of her face.*

"I learned something new today from Grandmother." She slowly stood up, her blue smock clearly showing that she was not one to avoid dirt or act the proper young princess. "Watch me."

"I am watching, princess." Alador smiled. "Let me see what you can do."

Latiera grinned and closed her eyes, opening both hands before her. One filled with water and the other fire. Alador stared in disbelief. A water mage could not handle fire, and usually the reverse was true as well.

"Where did you learn to do that?"

Latiera giggled. "I figured it out all by myself. Grandmother calls water and Grandfather calls fire. They both have been teaching me, since my sphere has not been revealed."

Alador's vision suddenly shifted. The top tier was engulfed in a raging fire. It was so real he could feel the intense heat. Latiera screamed and he threw up a protective shield.

"Daddy?" the child said in a questioning voice. She reached out her little hand and touched his face. He was instantly pulled back to *the present.*

*He dropped the shield surrounding them and put his hand over hers to douse the fire with a great deal of water.*

*"Are you okay, Daddy?" she stood peering into his eyes.*

*"I'm fine, little one." He would talk to Henrick about his vision; he also needed to find out how such a young mage could call dual spheres. For now, he took the young girl – his daughter! – by the shoulders and asked, "What has Grandfather told you about using fire?" He was trying to be gentle with his reprimand and did not want to step on her excitement.*

*Latiera's face fell into a pout. "I was just showing you."*

*He could hear her disappointment.*

*"Sweetheart, the fact that you can do that is amazing. I can't even do that." He lifted her chin to look her in the eyes. "This time was fine, but you said you had been practicing. Have you been in the practice room?"*

*"No," she admitted.*

*"When you use spells that could damage things, you may not practice anywhere but in the*

room. I will make sure that your escorts know to let you enter alone." He looked up and around to spot her personal guard. The guard nodded that he had heard.

"Really?" She threw her arms around his neck; on his toes as he had been, he was set off balance and they both collapsed into a heap.

Alador was laughing at her excitement. "So, has either of them made you wet and dry dirt a million times?"

"No, why would I do that? It has no purpose." She laid on his chest looking at him with those great big eyes.

"Your grandfather would not let me do anything else with magic until I could fill the dirt with water and pull it once again." Alador winked at her. "I think he likes you more than me."

"He does," she sighed, "I am cuter than you."

Alador chuckled. "That you are, princess, that you are."

\*\*\*\*\*\*\*\*\*\*\*\*\*\*\*\*\*\*\*\*\*\*\*\*\*\*\*\*\*\*\*\*\*\*\*\*\*\*

Alador was startled out of his dream. He looked around, uncertain what woke him, when he realized the egg was bobbing next to him. Had he seen this hatchling's face? He pulled the egg over and when he did, he realized there was no other explanation.

"So, welcome to the world, princess," he rubbed a scale with his thumb, trying to share the happiness the dream had brought to him. "Latiera... It is a fine name. If you are the girl in my dreams, well then, that shall be your name."

He realized he had tarried too long in the comfort of steam and meraweed's intoxicating effects. He carefully put the egg back into the nest and then put a couple of the rocks a bit higher so it would quit bobbing or rolling out of its safe confines.

He pulled himself wearily out of the pool and dried off. He put on the robe and went to the bell pull in his bedroom. His gentle tug was all that was needed. The door opened and his personal attendant, Radney, stepped through it.

"You have a need, Lord Alador?" His soft question held a hint of deliberate mischief; he still refused to drop the Lord title.

Alador sighed. At least the man had honored his request to be called Alador and not Guldalian. "I need to be up at first light, and I fear I will not wake on my own. I need you to come wake me with breakfast."

"Of course, Lord Alador." He bowed low and waited to see if there was anything else.

"That is all, thank you."

He watched as Radney pulled the door shut, then turned and flopped into his bed. It was the thing he needed most. Yet sleep did not find him for a long while; his mind was filled with images of a seven-year-old mage that could hold fire and water at the same time.

*Chapter Thirteen*

Alador had only just left his bed when he received a summons from the High Minister. He wasn't sure he was ready to face his uncle just yet, but at the same time, he had appearances to keep. He changed into robes more fitting the council tier and was soon headed up the stairs to the highest level of the city.

The morning fog hung like a shroud over the tiers. The rain and winds had ceased, but the sound of dripping water reminded one of the catastrophe of the night before. The sounds from the city were muted and did not have the usual clamor of a busy morning. There was one new sound, the sound of pain. At times, it was far away and muffled, other times close and loudly demanding. Pain of injury... pain of loss... pain of devastation...

He showed his pass to the guard mindlessly, a routine done hundreds of times. This time, much to his surprise, the guard stopped and redirected him.

"High Minister Guldalian requests you join him in the council chambers," instructed the guard.

It was rare that he got to sit in on council, but this morning he was sure it was to discuss the storm. He swiftly strode to the council area of the final tier. He was not sure he wanted to sit in on any of the accusations that were bound to be thrown about.

As he approached the council doors, the sound of

angry voices increased his hesitation; although he could not make out individual words, he knew they were not pleasant. He paused and nodded to the guard, one he had run into on the tier many times before; Blackguard tended to be the main contingent for guarding the council tier.

"How long have they been sounding like a hornet's nest?" Alador inquired.

The guard looked at the door and back at Alador. "Since the doors closed, Lord Guldalian."

Alador grimaced and drew a couple of deep breaths before he nodded to the man to open the door. He slipped into the room, hoping they wouldn't notice him for a few minutes so he could assess the major points of contention.

"There is no mage that would dare wall off the trench like that without your order!" The mage speaking was from Nemara's sphere, the green tones of his robe reflecting his status as a high-level nature mage.

"Apparently, there is…or was." Luthian put both hands out palm up before him. "I swear I had no hand in this."

While Alador wanted his uncle removed from power, he also knew the city would be devastated by a power struggle in the wake of the disaster. His eyes darted around the table and he was surprised to see Lady Caterine was not present. She was always jumping aboard on one side or the other.

"I assure you that we have the culprit, we just can't question her." Luthian pointed to the empty chair. "Lady Caterine was found dead, but not by the storm's blow. She clearly had been murdered."

"How convenient," muttered Lady Aldemar. She led the healing spheres and she was usually quiet in council.

"High Minister, if I may?" Alador called from where he stood.

Luthian turned to him, looking rather relieved to see him. He nodded for Alador to approach and he stepped aside so the young mage could address the whole room.

"I was shocked, as I am sure all of you were, to find the trench blocked off." As much as Alador hated it, he had to defend his uncle until he found out the truth of this matter. He had to at least give them all time to plan the High Minister's overthrow. An overthrow with a chance of success. "Ask yourself 'Why?' Why would the High Minister do such a thing? Would he not be wasting valuable resources?" Alador hated referring to people as if they were so much property, to be used as such, but that was how the higher tiers saw them. He had to speak the language of the mage-born. "There is not a single resident above the third tier who would work the mines. The loss of the miners is going to be a devastating blow to the city. Add to this, our current Trench Lord, a man of business and learning, also seems to have been lost in the storm. Another resource wasted."

Alador spoke slowly, moving his eyes about the table as his uncle had taught him. He took in who was following him and who discounted him before the words left his mouth. "I submit to you that this was a plot to remove the non-magic citizens from the city." He had already heard Luthian trying to lay the blame at Lady Caterine's feet and opted to follow in that vein; she was dead and could no longer be harmed. "We all know how vocal Lady Caterine has been about the filth and stench of the trench. It is not surprising, therefore, to consider that she may have done this on her own."

He could feel Luthian's eyes boring into him. He was hoping that his uncle's trust in him had just increased, because if it turned out that Luthian had killed Sordith in the attempt to cleanse the city, Alador was going to want someone to pay as well.

"I would think this honored council would be planning how to help the city recover, not casting blame when a culprit was quite obviously found in the act and murdered," Alador added, since no one had spoken for the moment.

"The mage has valid points. Our healers are overrun. The number of dead to be dealt with is heart wrenching." Lady Aldemar nodded her approval to Alador.

Luthian, always the master manipulator, stepped up beside Alador. "Alador is right. We have larger matters to pursue." He looked at his nephew. "I understand that you worked alongside the Blackguard last night. Can you give us a quick assessment of what needs to be dealt with right now?"

Alador glanced at his uncle, clearly surprised at the man's deference to him. He was not used to public praise from the High Minister.

Before he could speak, another mage stood up – a

fire mage. "Should we not get Commander Levielle in to give us a status report? He is our military leader, and I believe in charge of the clean up."

Luthian was ready to object when Lord Daybrooke, a mage Alador had seen many times in the company of Lady Aldemar, interceded. "I heard Lord Alador battled the storm's elements throughout the day and into the night. How many of you ventured out yesterday to help?" the elder healer mage demanded in an accusing voice, glancing around the table. "Did any of you offer up your halls to bed down those evacuating to the upper tiers? Let us hear what Lord Alador has to say. He has earned a right to speak at the council."

Alador's eyes moved quickly to assess his uncle, though he made no physical move otherwise, keeping his hands clasped behind him as he waited for the council to speak. Being allowed to speak, or even being on the council, would have great advantages for him. He wasn't sure how one made it to the council, though every sphere was represented except death. He had never seen a death mage at the few council meetings he had been privileged to attend.

Luthian, to his credit, never batted an eye. In fact, there was an edge of satisfaction to his posture that Alador did not understand. "I quite agree, Lord Daybrooke. He has more than earned the right to speak and a place on the council." Luthian drew himself up. "All in favor of granting Alador Guldalian a council seat?"

Alador almost gasped out loud at the nomination.

He was even more surprised when most of the council's hands rose to confirm his placement.

This was a boon. He would know more of the mages' plans in the future. He would never have thought it possible. Even though he was a Guldalian by birth, he was a half-breed. He glanced at his uncle, who was practically preening. Why would he want him on the council?

"Welcome to the council, Lord Alador. I think calling you by your first name will stop any confusion of our surnames." Luthian grinned mischievously at him.

That was fine by Alador. He felt uncomfortable every time he was called Lord, let alone Guldalian.

"Thank you, I am truly honored by the council's faith in me," he murmured. He moved around to one of the two open chairs at the table.

As he was about to sit down, Lady Aldemar spoke up. "Before we continue, can you give us an assessment of the damage from your viewpoint?" Her words held no censure, and were almost welcoming.

"Well, as you already stated, milady, there are many injured. Between the flying debris, the panicking crowds and the wave itself, even the Blackguard caverns are overrun with those needing healing." He clasped his hands in front of him as he considered what the council truly needed to know.

"The trench has not drained enough to assess the damage to the storehouses and mines. Hopefully, the mages assigned to assist in this were able to put walls up for safety." He looked about the table solemnly. Some were taking notes. Luthian had sat down and was also scribing as Alador spoke. "In addition, the walls need taken down that were erected to trap those escaping from the trench. This action alone will help greatly in the draining of the upper tiers."

Alador continued when no one spoke. "It is likely that the deep mines are flooded despite the attempts to stop the waves from entering. I understand that air flow shafts were established on the plains surrounding the city; those have likely filled in based on water movement I saw." Alador swiped a hand over his face as he sought to recall details.

"The first tier took a great deal of damage from the initial wave, but all tiers have buildings in need of repair – some minor, some extensive. I am sure if we inspected this fine hall," he looked around at the amazing mosaics and tapestries, "there are repairs to be made even here. You are going to need every surviving citizen willing to swing a hammer."

"You are quite observant for a mage," a red robed mage commented.

"Yes, well, a benefit from being initially trained as a guardsman. You have to notice details if you are going into battle," Alador acknowledged.

"What else can you recommend, Lord Alador?" Luthian asked steering the conversation back to the storm and away from battles, real or imagined.

This took Alador a second to answer as the shock of hearing himself addressed as Lord by his uncle threw his thinking off. "I would suggest mass funeral pyres. We have already started to gather the dead and move them to the plains. There are too many dead to build individual platforms. I would employ all those who honor Dethara to see to these rituals and burning. This should take precedence over everything else other than healing, since leaving the dead untended would add illness and possibly plague to our list of damages."

His voice grew in confidence as he continued. "You will need every craftsman who has a skill with clay to begin making roof tiles. I would suggest a tax-free status for any craftsman who will donate his or her time. There have to be clean up details set for each tier. We must cleanse the buildings, walks, ramps, and bridges of all filth brought in from the sea and trench, or down from the overflowing tier sloughs. Lastly, I would send the garbage carts around both morning and night until all the debris is cleared." Alador paused, "I cannot think of anything else at this time." He looked about the table to see if this was enough.

"What of the water still in the trench?" asked a man in silver robes.

"I will see to the drying of the trench." He had realized as the man spoke that he could force the water out if he started at the far end. "If there are any masters of stone, I could use their help to open the sealed storerooms to check that the city supplies and storage areas are still intact and usable." Alador frowned as he realized he might have kept the wave from the trench. If he had done that, how many more lives could have been saved then his failed attempt to stop the storm itself? Guilt built in his heart as he realized he had misdirected his attentions.

Luthian stood up. The council was now focused on recovery. Alador was quick to note that given the conversation when he entered, it was probably more comfortable to keep their focus off the matter of the walled off trench.

"Given this very detailed account of our city's needs, here is what I submit for the council's approval." Luthian waited to continue until all eyes were on him. "The healing spheres will be headed by Lady Aldemar as usual. We will offer all such mages and those with basic healing skills to assist the wounded, and provide what supplies we may for their use."

He took note of the nods of approval but continued. "Lord Daybrooke, I put you in charge of gathering craftsmen with the appropriate skills to assist the city in rebuilding. We can offer them sixty days with no taxes in return for their service."

Lord Daybrooke nodded in agreement.

"The stone sphere will help with the removal of any barriers to supplies and movement." He hurried past this statement and on to the next.

"I will inform the black sphere of our needs, and my sphere will work with them in the disposal of the dead."

"I will take Lord Alador around the city and see to any additional needs. The blue sphere is more than capable of helping to dry the trench and clean the city without him." Luthian looked to Alador and he slowly nodded in agreement.

"All in favor?" Luthian called.

Every hand in the circle went up. Alador was pleased to see the council was eager to assist the city. Perhaps they were not all arrogant and useless. Could there actually be some decent attributes in the ruling mage class?

Luthian stood up. "Then we all have work to do. Those that were not assigned specific duties, speak to your spheres and listen to their voices as to how you may help. We are concluded for today. We will meet again in the morning."

Notes were rolled and stowed away. Some members formed small groups, making plans as they exited the hall. A couple hurried out of the chambers to duties they had left hanging to attend the meeting in the first place. Many others stopped on their way out to offer their thanks for Alador's service and congratulations on his new position. Alador for his part nodded and smiled, but did not say much.

When the last of them were going out the door, he looked to see Luthian still at his seat making notes. Alador picked up the wine glass that had been filled for each council seat and took a deep drink.

"Well played, Uncle." He toasted the man.

"I do not know what you mean. If anything, the salute should go to you. Probably one of the youngest to make council in our history." Luthian laid the quill down and looked up at him.

"And the only half-breed," Alador added.

"Indeed," Luthian smiled, "and the only half-breed."

"Did you do it?" Alador walked to the end of the table where Luthian still sat.

Luthian picked up his own chalice. "Did I do what?"

"Did you order the trench sealed?" Alador's intent gaze was not veiled. He really wanted to know the answer.

Luthian took a long drink and slowly lowered his glass. "That would have hardly been in my best interests, as you pointed out."

Alador shook his head. "There is wise and then there is expedient. Did you choose opportunity over wisdom, Uncle?"

Luthian looked at him, his face blank as he answered, "I did not."

Alador had not been watching his uncle's face. He had been watching his eyes. Even as Luthian lifted the glass to take the second drink, Alador knew he was lying. Anger surged and it was all Alador could do to contain himself.

"I am relieved to hear that. I would hate to have to kill you for being a despicable bastard," Alador answered just as evenly.

"I am a despicable bastard," Luthian conceded. He toasted Alador. "Though… you are always welcome to try."

Alador did not miss his tone. It was the same tone

Luthian used with Henrick. He was pushing his line of safety. Perhaps, truth had ceased to be the weapon of choice. Alador clenched his fists to steady himself. As much as he hated it, it was time to lie. Yes, the game had escalated and lying was the only route to take.

He nodded to his uncle, hands clenched behind his back. "I will keep that in mind, Uncle."

*Chapter Fourteen*

Sordith woke first. He ached all over and was almost afraid to move. In any case, Keelee was lying huddled against his side, the arm he had wrapped under and around her as fast asleep as she was. It was going to be painful to move once he woke her.

He lay quietly assessing his own injuries. He was as sure now as he had been when he fell into an exhausted sleep that he had broken ribs on his left side. He could not take a deep breath, and even a shallow breath caused him minor pain. He also realized even in the dim light that he was only able to see out of one eye. When he raised his hand to his head, he could feel the lump on his forehead and the swollen eye. Hopefully, the eye was just bruised and not permanently damaged. He moved his legs, and though it hurt his side to do it, it did not seem as though there were anything wrong with the legs themselves. However, when he moved the leg closest to Keelee, she moaned in her sleep.

The rain appeared to have stopped, or at least it was not gushing through the hole above them. Instead, there was a faint light through the hole. The day had dawned.

"Keelee?" he said softly to her. "Keelee, love…"

She moaned again in her sleep and curled tighter against him, if that was possible.

"Keelee…" he smoothed her hair back away from

her face.

She didn't appear to have more than scratches on her face, neck and what he could see of her shoulders. He ran his free hand over her head. There was a lump on the back of it the size of an egg. Now he was worried. Did she have a concussion?

When he started to free himself from her so he could have a better look at her, she cried out in pain.

He pulled his arm from beneath her. He winced as the first needles of pain began to occur in his otherwise useless arm. He clenched his fist and let go repeatedly to try to rush through the process. Painfully, he pulled himself into a sitting position, gritting his teeth and rubbing his arm as it sent shooting pains from his finger tips to his shoulder. When it was finally awake and he could feel sensations with both hands he ran them over her sides, but received no response.

He started to pull his legs up to kneel beside her and she cried out again. It was her legs. He tried to investigate, but the dim light from the hole above was cast too far above their heads for him to see decently. He felt with his hands and became worried when they felt sticky. He raised one above his head into the filtered light. His hand was covered with blood.

"Keelee…" he pleaded. "My love… Can you hear me?" He leaned over her and kissed her gently on the forehead. "Please wake up. I need your help."

Her eyes fluttered open and though she did not seem to be able to focus on him she whispered, "Sordith…"

"Yes, my love… I am here, love." He was so happy to hear her voice.

"Are we dead?" she asked groggily.

"I don't think so. If we were, I think we would be in a lot less pain." He smiled down at her and leaning forward again, he kissed her. "Can you make me some light, so I can assess the damage?" he coaxed.

"I'll try…" The hand that was laying on the sand opened and a small ball of light sat in her palm.

It was enough for him to see what was paining her. The front of her legs where he felt earlier were scratched but otherwise undamaged, but the back of her left leg had a piece of wood the width of a broadsword sticking out of it. She was lucky it was not long or she could not have been able to get through the hole and down here last night.

Sordith whipped off his belt and made a tourniquet around her thigh. She screamed in pain and her voice echoed around and down through the cave for minutes before it died.

"Thirsty…" she panted after the pain had subsided.

The drizzle from the opening's edge was filthy and unfit to drink. He stumbled around the cave for a few minutes until he followed the sound of running water to a spring bubbling through the rock wall and falling into the cave depths below them.

He cupped his hands and tasted the water. It was fresh, and he thanked the gods that looked favorably upon them. He removed his leather gauntlet and, squeezing one end shut, he filled it with water and took it back to Keelee.

She drank with desperation, and he let her. He knew she had lost a lot of blood, and he still would have to put her through further pain removing the wooden spear, cleaning her wound and wrapping it before he could spare any thought to getting them out of the cave.

He took his dagger to the long sleeve of what was left of her gown. He removed it at the shoulder and took the material to the spring to wash it as clean as possible, setting it aside to use as a bandage. "Roll over on your stomach for me," he instructed her gently. "And try not to move. This is going to hurt." He braced her leg between his knees, probing gently around the edges of the wound. She screamed, and a part of him died inside, but his hands remained steady. Finally he shook his head with a growl; there was no way to know exactly how much damage the wood had done without removing the piece, and he just couldn't risk it without a healer nearby. He gently tied the sleeve around her calf, lightly but firmly securing the wood and protecting the wound from any further debris getting into it. Then he loosened the tourniquet so that blood would flow and the nerves would not be cut off; she wouldn't be able to walk on it otherwise.

She cried and begged for more water. He brought another gauntlet full and sat holding her head as she drank. He waited until she was finished, and seemed to be a bit more awake and focused on him, then broke the news to her. "It's not good," he explained. "You're going to have to be extra careful not to bump it, but we don't have any choice."

She nodded solemnly, then smirked at him and raised her bare arm, waving it lazily in his face. "If you had wanted me naked, all you had to do as ask."

He smiled and she giggled. He tried to lean over and kiss her, but the pain in his side made him groan.

She took the hand he held the crushed gauntlet in and gently kissed his fingers. "How are we going to get out of here?"

"Can you keep that light burning?" Each time she had screamed, the light in her palm went out. He needed to know before he formulated a plan.

"I think so…" She lifted her hand and the light shone brighter. "I'm feeling a little stronger now."

"Then lay here for a little while and gather more of your strength. I need to check on something." He smoothed her brow and rose to his feet. He took the glowing orb from her hand and went to check out the plan that had been formulating in his head since he found the spring. The dripping foul water suggested that even if he could get her up to the rock above, the plains were going to infect the wound further.

He went to the spring at the wall of the cave. He held the orb out over the edge of their sandy beach and looked for where the water fell. As he suspected from the sound, there was a pool below, only about six feet down. He could slide down the rock face and catch Keelee when she slid down. He walked along the edge and saw that the spring water flowed unchecked from the pool, carving a path in the rock. He followed the stream as far as he could from the ledge above, then lay on the ledge and hung over as far as safely possible, grunting as the pain of the effort shot through him. The stream appeared to run down the center of a huge tunnel. The rock floor even appeared to be flat.

Sordith rushed back to Keelee.

"How about a dip in a lovely pool to clear your head and clean you off?" He reached down and handed her the orb. Before she could even answer he helped her up. They both groaned with the effort and then laughed. It was good to just be alive.

Sordith held her up against his right side and helped her to the edge of the ledge where he sat her down.

"I'll go first and then you can slide down on your better side. I'll catch you." He grinned. "Or if not that, at least I'll break your fall."

He slid down the rock face and landed harder than he would have liked at the bottom. Even though the drop was just a matter of a foot or two, it took his breath away. He stood with his back against the rock wall until he could breathe regularly again. Then he pushed away and turned to look up at Keelee.

"Just a short drop. Remember, be careful not to bump your bad leg! and then we'll have a nice lounge in the pool." He held his hands up toward her as high as he could without it sending shooting pains through his side.

She tossed him the orb and he set it down by his feet, then she slid down into his arms. He kept her from hitting the floor and she kissed his neck in thanks. Sordith carried her over to the pool and just walked in, clothes and all, setting her down on a natural ledge where she could rest her legs.

"It's cold," she hissed as the water covered her lap.

"But clean and fresh."

The water around her wound immediately blossomed dark red before his anxious eyes, but after a moment it cleared some, and he figured getting it clean probably outweighed any further harm.

He unbuckled his leather tunic and slipped it off. There was all sorts of mud and filth caked to the surface of his torso. He knelt beside her and started to splash water over his skin. The water ran off him in a brown slurry.

"Oh Sordith," she leaned forward and ran her hand over his chest. "It must hurt so badly." His torso was a mass of bruises.

"I'll live." He grinned at her. "Isn't it great to be able to say that?"

He took off his leather britches and washed himself thoroughly, after which he rinsed the leathers and then wiggled his way back into them.

"You look worse than a woman getting into a corset," she giggled, releasing some of her pain and tension at his expense.

Once dressed he helped her out of her top and rubbed her down. He dipped what was left of her dress over and over in the water until when he squeezed it the water ran clean. Then he helped her back into it, as she gazed wistfully at her filthy pantaloons. "I wish…" she started, and he cut her off with a kiss.

"I know. But I just don't want to risk dislodging the spear. At least they're cleaner, now. "You ready to see where the stream leads us?"

"Ready when you are. Let's just stay behind our filth. I might want another drink of water."

He helped her up and hugged her to his good side.

The stream ran down the middle of a huge tunnel. They were both amazed at the size of it; it must have stretched up at least thirty feet above their heads. The floor and sides were smooth, even smoother than any rock work you could do with a chisel. When they came upon a vein of onyx in the rock wall, they stopped to take a rest and inspect it closer.

Keelee ran her hand over it. "It's almost like it has been melted."

Sordith stood out away from it as Keelee sat on the floor of the rock tunnel. It was less trouble to stay on his feet than to sit and stand with his broken ribs. He followed the vein with his eyes over their heads and down the other side. He could not see the other side clearly, it was hidden in the shadows. Keelee's orb only showed them about thirty feet in each direction and the tunnel was a little more than that across.

"It's so uniform. Almost as if someone embedded it in the rock on purpose."

He took the orb and stepped across the stream which had now grown to about a foot wide and same deep.

He walked a bit past the onyx arch.

"Hey, don't get too far away," Keelee called. "You're leaving me in the dark and I don't have the energy to conjure another orb."

A moment later the orb winked out as if snuffed.

"Sordith!" she called in a worried voice from the dark. "Damn it, Sordith! Come back here."

She started to struggle to her feet when she heard a shout. She felt her way along the wall in the pitch black of the tunnel.

"Sordith?"

She was frightened now, and suddenly the tunnel seemed blacker and colder than it had been moments ago when Sordith was at her side with the orb. She stopped and tried to conjure another orb, but it fizzled in her hand and popped out leaving her in total darkness again.

"Sordith? Answer me please…" she begged.

Tears were springing to her eyes when she saw the orb break back into view.

"Keelee, you have to see this!" Sordith said in an almost reverent whisper. He stepped over the stream, handed her the orb and scooped her up in his arms in spite of the hiss of his breath as he sucked in air to stop himself from hollering out loud at the pain in his side. "You aren't going to believe this."

Keelee almost hit him for scaring her so, but thought better of it considering his condition and the fact that he was holding her. Instead, she bit his ear.

"Owww… What was that for?" he yelped. He stopped and looked down at her.

"For leaving me in the dark!" She did strike him on the shoulder this time. "And worrying me."

He brought his lips to hers and silenced her with a kiss. "I'm sorry, but wait until you see."

There was a cavern off the main tunnel on this side that she had not been able to see from her place against the far wall. That was why the light went out; Sordith had ducked in here.

"Hold the orb up and don't be scared," Sordith warned.

She held it up and he took a few more tentative steps forward.

Despite his warning, she wasn't prepared and let loose a small scream, much like she heard earlier from Sordith when he disappeared.

They were standing in front of a huge dragon's skeleton. The head pointed directly at them. The teeth in it massive maw were easily as tall as they were. It was laying on its stomach with its head on its fore paws like some gigantic dog.

Sordith walked her around the head and back toward its side. One wing was folded up against the side of the cavern, but the other was stretched out, creating a kind of tented framework across the breadth of the cave.

"I have heard stories all my life about there being tunnels and dragon caves under the city, but I always thought they was legends, with no basis in real fact. Why would dragons live under Silverport?" Sordith asked rhetorically as he walked under the wing and back toward the tail.

No wonder he had not answered her call. Seeing this, she would have ignored her too. It was magnificent. She ran her hand along one of the bones as Sordith passed. It was smooth as glass.

"He must have been incredible in his time," she exclaimed.

"Or she," Sordith suggested. "The stories say that at one point man and dragon lived as friends."

"Wouldn't that be marvelous?" Keelee asked. "To be able to consider one of these magnificent creatures a friend?"

"Indeed, it would."

Sordith hated to leave, but he felt the weariness of his injuries, and Keelee was shivering in his arms. He needed to get them some help, and he wouldn't find it among dragon bones. One day, he promised himself… One day he would return.


After what Sordith estimated was another couple of hours they came to the end of the tunnel. It had dwindled to only about fifteen feet tall by the time they came to the rock wall.

He and Keelee had about reached the end of their endurance. He leaned against the rock pile blocking the tunnel and cursed. The stream flowed right under it, but there was no opening. He had dunked himself checking.

The stream ran through a series of cracks in the pile of rocks.

He put his right shoulder against one of the smaller rocks as he stood in the stream, the cold water flowing over his boot tops. The rock did not budge.

He pushed again, harder.

Keelee was sitting against the rock wall and she squealed in surprise.

"What?" he asked.

"There!" she pointed. "The rock right above the one you pushed. I can see daylight!"

He backed away and sure enough there was a crack where you could see light. He pulled out his knife and used it as a pick to pry the smaller rock free. He could see out, or more correctly, in. The stream dumped into one of the well rooms on the first tier of Silverport. He had been in this room many times, in fact, and had drunk from this well!

"We're home!" he called to Keelee as he pried away another rock.

Sordith only had to remove five rocks, the last being the biggest and most difficult. He actually put his shoulder against it and pushed it into the well on the other side.

It was not really a well, more like a deep pool – a catch basin for the stream. When it ran over, a series of troughs filled barrels to be transported along the first tier. Each tier had a well like this, and it made Sordith wonder if they were all connected to dragon caves. The old stories were true.

He lifted Keelee one last time and helped her over the boulders at the base of the blocked tunnel. Then he followed her.

Sordith stood as open mouthed as Keelee when they emerged onto the first tier. The tier was totally abandoned. The second tier did not look much better, and they could just see that the garrison roof on the third tier was gone. There wasn't a tent left standing that was intact. There was still about a foot of standing water on the first tier that they had to slosh through on their way up.

The damage to the first tier was almost incomprehensible. There was not a home or shop left with its roof in place. Shutters had been ripped from their hinges, and there was standing water in most of the buildings they passed.

The rock walls were still blocking the ramps. Keelee shuddered and cried at the sight of them.

"I hope the miners got to high ground before the trench was sealed off." His words were soft and laced with grief at the sight before him.

He could see the Silver Guardsman were gathering up the dead from the plain. Those would be either garrison dead or his own people. Grief hit him so hard that tears fell silently down his cheeks. He had sent them up onto the plain in hopes they could get to the bridge. It was clear that many didn't make it.

Sordith held Keelee close as they carefully made their way along the first tier and up to the second. More than once, one of them saw something they wished they had not – a partial body or a child who had been crushed in the stampede to get to higher ground. The walk down the length of the second tier seemed endless. Finally, they made it to the bridge to the third tier.

Sordith looked at Keelee and they both smiled. There were some people on this level and it looked as though they were cleaning up.

"We'll find you a healer," Sordith stated as he moved forward.

"And a gown," Keelee added, feeling self-conscious about her lack of attire.

Sordith looked down at the trench. It was still full of water though it was no longer even with the plains above it. He could see areas of wall that had slid in. The trench would not be reopening any time soon. He hoped the manor had survived. They did not stop on the way up. It was a detour and he needed to get Keelee to a healer.

The sound of rebuilding was already ringing through the city, a drum without rhythm as they made their way onto the third tier. The damage about Sordith and Keelee appeared to be just from the wind. Urchins were running throughout the city gathering roof tiles that had not broken. Sordith smiled when he watched one given a trading token for the pile of tiles in his arms. He had done the same when younger. Though the storm he remembered did not have a wave, it had torn loose a good number of tiles.

They saw a crowd and Sordith steered them to it. He hoped to find help for Keelee. However, when he drew closer, what he saw was Luthian speaking. His hand went for his sword, grasping at air in reflex for a weapon lost.

"Stay here," he whispered angrily to Keelee.

"Now is not the time, Sordith, please do nothing today." She looked pointedly at his sword belt wrapped as a tourniquet around her leg.

He kissed her forehead. "That bastard killed and injured hundreds. I still have a dagger." He motioned for her to stay and started moving through the crowd, stalking the High Minister.

"Today is a sad day for us all," Luthian called out loudly. "We have found the evil mind that would do such a thing. In fact, it appears that one of you fine people put an end to her before the council could."

Lady Caterine's body was being held up by two guardsmen. It looked battered and barely recognizable.

As Luthian was speaking, Sordith made his way quietly toward the group protecting Luthian. No one would think anything of the Trench Lord moving into his inner circle.

Alador saw Sordith. He almost cried out before he caught the glint of the dagger in his brother's hand. Sordith started to move closer to get within reach of the High Minister. He was taking full advantage of the attention that the High Minister had secured by his speech.

"No charges will be pressed for the death of this mage. She deserved her fate for the atrocity she committed." The crowd's approval masked any sounds Sordith made.

"High Minister, I suspect the Trench Lord saw to the matter, and look, here he is." Alador called loudly.

If Sordith could have punched Alador in the face in that moment, he would have. He glowered at Luthian as the High Minister spotted him in the crowd. Luthian tipped his head at the gaze and gave a look of puzzlement before he called out loudly, arms open in welcome.

"Our Trench Lord lives!"

People began cheering and suddenly Sordith had Alador's arm grasping him so tightly around his ribs that he hissed in pain. The dagger fell from his hand. He tried to push back to Luthian, but Alador pulled him aside. Any chance of killing Luthian was now gone. Alador's words had made him an instant hero and there would be no convincing the populace in that moment that the real enemy was Luthian. One thing for certain, Alador and he were going to have words. There may even be a few fists to emphasize his points.

"Come with me, brother," Alador whispered in his ear. "You are in need a healer and I see Keelee would be happy to see one too." Alador heard the hiss of pain, and having known broken ribs himself, he knew a bit of pressure would give him an advantage over his larger and stronger brother.

"I will kill him," Sordith growled under his breath.

"And I will assist you in the deed, but later – now is not the time."

Alador smiled at the crowd surrounding them. "We must get the Trench Lord and his woman to the healer," he announced in a loud voice.

Sordith was immediately lifted, as was Keelee, and carried to a relatively undamaged home in the middle of the third tier. Out front stood Auries directing her girls in the art of administering healing to the injured.

She saw him coming and hurried to his side, all past issues forgotten when she saw his mangled face and heard the groan as they put him down on her doorstep.

"Bring him in," she instructed. "Put him in the bed in the room to the right."

"Auries," he called as they took him past her. "Keelee… Please help her. Her leg," he added quickly as he was dragged out of sight and into the room Auries indicated.

Auries looked at Keelee as she was brought forward and shook her head. "Damn you, Sordith," she mumbled under her breath. "Put her in the room at the end of the hall."

## Chapter Fifteen

Sordith woke to the delicious smell of roasted prang. His stomach growled before he even opened his eyes.

"Did you say something, brother?" Alador asked in a teasing voice. He was surprised when Sordith opened his eye. "Hey, you're awake."

Sordith tilted his head so he could see Alador at his bedside through his one good eye. He spied the tray sitting across his brother's knees. "Is that the remains of a full hindquarter?"

"I have been working hard," Alador spoke around a mouthful of meat.

"Give me some." Sordith held out his hand and his stomach growled again in anticipation.

Alador carved off a slice with his knife and was about to hand it to Sordith when Auries walked in.

"Stop!" She scowled at them and crossed her arms over her chest.

Sordith smiled – this was the Auries he remembered.

Alador halted mid-air, the prang hanging from the point of his dagger.

"He hasn't had solid food for over two days. I don't want him throwing up with broken ribs and undoing the healing I have accomplished so far." She turned and called back up the hall. "Betra?"

A young girl who couldn't have been more than 12 turns old came rushing to her side. "Yes, milady?"

"Fetch me a tray with a bowl of soup, bread and some clean water... Our Trench Lord is finally awake."

"Yes, milady." The child hurried off to prepare the tray.

"Milady?" Sordith smiled at her. "You have come up in the world, my sweet."

Auries came to the edge of the bed and frowned at Alador's hand still holding the offering. "Take that away," she huffed.

She set about fluffing Sordith's pillow and adjusting his covers, then took a jug from the bedside table to pour some liquid into a cup. She held his head and offered him the drink. "A lot has changed since we thought you were lost in the storm."

He took a sip of her offering and grimaced at the bitter taste. Why did her healing concoctions always taste so vile?

"Drink!" she ordered.

He gulped as she poured. Two big swallows and the evil stuff was down. He just hoped he could keep it there until he was able to spoon in some soup over it.

"Keelee?" he asked. She was his first thought after his stomach and the shock of Auries arrival.

"She's in the room down the hall," Alador volunteered. "She and Auries have become close friends." He winked at the woman standing over his brother.

Sordith looked from Alador to his former lover. Keelee and Auries had been talking? Best friends? Oh, this just was not right, and could not be good for him.

"Friends?" he asked. The last time he spoke of Keelee with Auries she had thrown a perfume bottle at his head and ordered him out of her quarters.

"She is a… unique… young lady," Auries said under a hooded gaze.

She put the cup back on the side table.

"I must see her." Sordith started to rise, but two sets of hands forced him back down onto his bed.

"Not until that potion takes effect and you have eaten. If you can keep your food down, then I will allow Lord Alador to help you down the hall to say hello, but I warn you," her tone grew stern, "only a few minutes. She has lost a lot of blood, and she needs rest more than anything else right now."

Sordith reached out and captured his former lover's hand as she continued to fuss over the arrangement of his blankets. "Thank you, Auries." He lifted her hand to his lips and kissed her knuckles.

She gave him a grudging smile, but anything she might have said was interrupted by the arrival of the tray.

"Thank you, Betra." She took the tray from the child, and the youngster slipped back out of the room.

Alador helped his brother sit up and propped the pillow up against the wall behind him at the head of the bed.

Auries set the tray down on his lap. "Eat… I will be back to check on you later." She turned toward Alador. "The slop bucket is under the bed if he needs it for either end." She swept up her skirts and left the room.

For a few moments the room was silent as Sordith dove unhesitatingly into the soup and bread. He hadn't been this hungry since he was an orphan in the trench trying to make it on his own!

While Sordith ate, Alador sat back and marveled at the strength, and run of good luck, that had saved his brother. Keelee had not been able to sleep when they first arrived at the make-shift healer's clinic. As exhausted as she was, Auries had had trouble finding a potion that would relieve the pain in the injured leg. Sordith was out cold, unable to comfort Keelee, so Alador sat by bedside listening to her tell of their near brush with death and their escape through the caves below the city.

He realized what she was talking about long before she revealed the discovery of the dragon skeleton. Renamaum had deep seated memories of those caves, and they bubbled to the top when Keelee started to describe them. If only something had triggered the memory prior to the storm, Alador could have opened them up to shelter the populace. But, perhaps there was a reason Renamaum had not revealed them. Perhaps Alador's dragon-self had other plans.

They spoke quietly out of respect for the other patients, but when he heard of where the tunnel came out, he swore her to secrecy and excused himself. He hurried down to the well and closed their entry back up, taking his time and making sure the rocks were set exactly as they had been in the past. He did not want anyone else knowing of the tunnels' existence just yet.

Uninterrupted by conversation, it did not take Sordith long to finish off the soup and bread. Alador took the tray from him and sat it on top of his own, on the floor.

"You ready to go see Keelee? She has been asking about you." He offered his brother his arm to rise.

Sordith took it and stood, pausing to be sure he was steady enough on his feet.

Alador was so happy to have his brother back. The thought of his death had haunted him the past two days. They had not spoken of the flood yet, but he was anxious to explain to him, as he had to Keelee, what he believed had happened and who was responsible for the trench being walled up.

He turned to Sordith, but his vision was filled with a fist. He hit the floor. It took a moment for his head to clear, before he managed to put up a staying hand toward his brother.

"Wait," he stated firmly. Feeling something moving about his mouth besides blood, he spit. There on the floor was a tooth. "Dammit Sordith! And, I think you broke my nose too," he managed to squeak out.

"Good!" Sordith snarled down. "Stand up and let me see to the rest of your teeth."

Alador knew at that moment that he had better not get up just yet. He had no doubt where this was coming from. Sordith thought he had known about Luthian's walling off the ramps.

"How about we save this until we get to my home and I explain. If you still want to punch me out, well then you can have your go." Alador formed a cloth in his hand and pressed it to his bleeding nose. He slid the bone into place, cursing as he did so.

"Deal." Sordith put a hand down to help him up.

Alador was a bit hesitant in taking it. "I didn't know," he gave as a short apology. He winced at his nasal tone.

Sordith helped him to his feel, but grimaced at the effort.

Alador walked over to the side table, fumbled off the lid on the jug of healing potion and poured himself a shot. He downed it and stood for a moment sniffing.

"Feel better?" he asked Sordith sarcastically.

"Much!" The Trench Lord turned and headed out the door and up the hall, with Alador following in his wake.

He entered the room just in time to see Sordith lean over Keelee and kiss her. "How do you feel?" his brother asked with genuine concern.

"Tired, but I think part of that is Auries' potions. She has been controlling the pain while I heal."

"She can be moved to Lord Alador's home tomorrow," Auries said from the doorway. She must have seen them headed down the hall and followed. "We need the room here for the more seriously injured."

"I have already arranged for the men to transport you both tomorrow morning," Alador said between snuffles. His voice was sounding a little less nasal to his ears as the potion took effect. Whatever Auries had concocted to heal Sordith's ribs was doing a fast job of healing his broken nose.

"We can go home to my manor," Sordith objected.

"Not yet," Alador said. "You both need care and my home has already been repaired by the staff."

Sordith realized that probably meant his home was damaged to a lesser or greater degree – probably the latter – since his home was in between the trench and the first tier. Even his brief glimpses had shown that not much had been spared on those two levels of the city.

Sordith looked at Keelee, and then at Alador. Keelee had been his younger brother's bed servant. He was not going to take her into his home without first claiming her permanently, and totally, as his.

"We will go, but under one condition," he looked at Keelee and gave her his best smile. "Keelee, I want us to be wed - now. This very moment. I came so close to losing you; I don't want anything to ever take you away from me again. We will have a formal wedding when things are more settled, but for now, I need to know you are mine."

Keelee reached out and grasped his hand. "I am yours and ever will be, milord." She smiled at him and pulled him down toward her for a kiss.

"Will you do the hand-fasting?" Sordith asked of his brother as he raised his eyes from her.

"It would be my pleasure." Alador had only seen one hand-fasting since he had become a high mage. He hoped he remembered what was done. The fact he was performing the rite for Keelee barely even registered as he materialized a long, blue, velvet ribbon in his hand.

Auries stepped up quickly and removed a ring from her finger. "I know it is used, and worn in the past by a whore, but it is offered with love to you both," she said in all sincerity. She could not doubt how much Sordith and Keelee loved each other, and was that not what you wanted for someone you loved, for them to be loved too?

Keelee nodded to Sordith, and he took the ring from Auries. "Thank you." He slipped it on Keelee's finger.

Auries stepped back and started to leave.

"Stay, please," Keelee called.

Auries looked toward Sordith for approval.

"Please, you are one of my closest friends." He beamed with his current happiness, both for his bride and his mended friendship with Auries. She smiled and settled in on the other side of the bed.

Alador moved from the foot of the bed to where the two sat, hands clasped. He wrapped the ribbon around their hands and up over their wrists, securing them gently together. He placed his hand on their joined hands.

"With this hand-fasting we secure the hearts of Sordith, Trench Lord of Silverport and Keelee, hereby to be known as wife of Sordith, the Trench Lord of Silverport, together for their lifetime. Let all know that they are one in body, soul and love."

"One in body, soul and love," Sordith and Keelee repeated in unison.

Sordith bent over and gently kissed her. Keelee closed her eyes with the kiss and did not open them as he pulled away.

"Keelee?" he questioned, almost verging on panic.

Auries reached across the bed and felt the pulse at her neck. "She sleeps. It is not your lack of masculine attraction, it is the potion," she assured him.

Sordith pulled the ribbon from around their hands, rolled it and placed it on her pillow.

"Back to bed with you." Auries shooed him out the door. "You need your rest as well."

*Chapter Sixteen*

Alador appeared in his library holding the traveling amulet in his hand. He had sent one of the children who were running errands and messages home ahead of him and asked Radney to lay the fire in the study and prepare a room for Sordith and Keelee's arrival.

The fire was already working at taking the chill out of the library. Henrick's magic had always kept the fire burning brightly, but Alador was forced to import the wood for his fires, being a water mage. The cost was high to have it all either carted in from the forests beyond the plain or brought in by barge through the harbor and up the tiers. However, Alador noted that Radney was his usual efficient self and obviously used household money to purchase scrap wood gathered after the storm by the locals. They were pedaling it to any who passed at the bridges from tier to tier. It smoked and streamed from the water captured in it, until Alador put out his hand and drew the water from it in a cascade that fell through the grate and evaporated in a puff of steam. The fire leaped into a new, stronger life as the wood dried, and the room immediately took on a nice woodsy aroma.

He snuffed, which reminded him of his still healing nose. He made his way to the desk and dug out a healing potion. He downed it and closed his eyes. Relief flooded through his pounding head and jaw. He put a tongue where his tooth should have been. He would have to see to a spell to replace it. Fortunately, it had not been a front tooth.

Alador knew his brother was angry at him for stopping his assassination attempt on Luthian. But the High Minister was good at playing a crowd, and at every tier he had spoken on he had been well received. He stopped Sordith because he had not wanted Luthian to die a martyr's death. The man deserved to die as the bastard he was, not as the loving benefactor he was pretending to be to the surviving tier inhabitants. Alador knew Luthian was responsible for the walling of the ramps from the trench. He all but admitted it when they met after the council. Even though Lady Caterine had done the actual deed, Alador knew his uncle had given the order. It had taken a twisted mind to give that command. The horror of their death masks in the stone walls would haunt him for a very long time.

He stepped to the table between the two chairs where Radney had thoughtfully placed a tray, three glasses and a carafe of smalgut. He poured himself a glass and collapsed into a chair. Sordith and Keelee would be here soon. Alador had arranged with Bariton to have an escort transport them by wagon; he still did not trust his uncle to not try and assassinate the Trench Lord.

He ran over his last conversation with Luthian when he returned to calm him after delivering his brother and Keelee to Auries for healing.

He knew his uncle saw the dagger in Sordith's hand and the look of murder in his eyes. "Lord Guldalian," he said as he slid to a halt at his side, "I have taken the

Trench Lord and his partner to the healer. He was overwrought by his near-death experience. He had not heard the news of Lady Caterine's evil deed." Alador looked into the older mage's eyes. "I fear the look he gave you was founded in misunderstanding of the true culprit responsible for this horrendous crime." Alador pressed his point. "The Trench Lord is a well-respected man. You will need him to reestablish the trench."

"Surely, he could not think I was involved," Luthian said for the benefit of those who might overhear their conversation. "We have Lady Caterine's body and the obvious connection between her sphere's powers and where she was found." Luthian frowned.

Alador knew while those words implied his innocence, Luthian was even now considering his next move. He hoped the High Minister would choose to follow his suggestion and not just remove the Trench Lord.

"I believe given his experience, he may just be fueled by the trauma he witnessed. We are good friends," Alador added. He continued hands palm forward and arms out. "Let me secure him to our cause and calm him down. A healer's touch, good drink, a bath, and some food in a safe location should do him well."

Luthian conceded. "Very well. I will continue here; you see the man shored up. I will not tolerate dissension when the people need unity."

In this, Alador agreed with his uncle. The people of the city did not need an uprising at that moment. He nodded at the High Minister and merged into the crowd to head back to Sordith's side. He breathed a sigh of relief. He knew his brother was angry and did not have the full picture.

Alador rubbed his face, took a sip of his smalgut and wondered just how to present the full picture to Sordith once he arrived. He stood and pulled the bell cord by the fireplace. Radney came almost immediately.

"Get a message to Lady Aldemar and to General Levielle to join me for a meal. Ensure they know it is urgent." He ordered quickly. "The Trench Lord and his wife will arrive shortly. Have you finished preparing their room?"

"Yes, Lord Alador."

Alador was so lucky to have Radney at the helm of his household. The man may not have possessed magic, but he worked miracles.

"We will need a full meal for five," he added, "and enough smalgut to put Sordith and I both beneath the table. The General will probably drink with us, as well."

"Right away, milord."

Someone pulled the bell at the door. Radney started toward it to answer.

"You see to the meal, Radney, I will get the door," Alador offered, knowing it would be Sordith and Keelee.

Sordith had helped Keelee from the wagon and was shutting the blanket around her, murmuring words that Alador could not make out.

"Thank you," Alador said to the escort as they dispersed. He handed up a slip to the civilian wagon driver who had been pressed into service to transport his brother and his new sister-in-law.

Sordith gathered Keelee to his side and they limped in.

"You said we would discuss the walling of the trench when I arrived." They followed Alador to the study. "Start explaining," Sordith said, as he eased Keelee down on the couch and turned toward his younger brother.

Alador closed the door to the study behind them. He leaned against it and pinned Sordith with a solid gaze.

"First, no I did not know what Luthian was up to. Secondly, I agree that the man had a part in it." Alador took a guarded breath under the look his brother was boring into him. "Next, yes, the High Minister needs to die. However, if you had succeeded just then you would have made him a martyr."

"I didn't care. He would be dead. Problem solved," spat Sordith as he moved to the fire. He picked up the poker and started to take his aggression out on the wood. He jabbed at it as if he were stabbing a dagger into a victim.

"I am trying to ensure he is replaced by someone who cares more about the city and its residents then he does." Alador pleaded.

"You mean, you are trying to become the next High Minister. A feckin' half-breed with no real anchor in Lerdenian ways," Sordith snarled still not looking toward his brother.

Alador winced, "Yes, meaning me." He pushed off from the door and came closer to the fire and his irritated brother. Whether that was a wise move or not, he was not sure. "The only person I admit would do better is Lady Aldemar. Perhaps she should be the next High Minister. If she can get away, we will know soon enough." Alador took the chance and reached out to his Sordith. He placed a hand on his shoulder. "Brother, I would never hurt or kill your people."

Sordith stood and turned toward Alador. He wanted to see his eyes. "Even if it made you the next in line?"

Alador's hand dropped. "Especially if it made me next in line. I have more regard for life than that. Those were your people, your friends, the ones you protected and watched over. I am not a cad that uses or hurts family in such a manner."

Sordith replaced the poker in its holder. He let out a sigh and turned back to Alador.

"Promise me, Luthian will die."

"I promise, Luthian will die." Alador let out the breath he had been holding when Sordith turned away with the poker. He had been preparing himself for another punch just in case.

"Now, let's get you both up to my room and into the bath." Alador paused. His bath was ready, but the egg was there. He decided a show of trust was needed and after a long moment exhaled his breath. "Just… don't touch the dragon's egg."

Keelee came off the couch in an instant. "You have a dragon's egg?" she nearly squealed her words.

"Yes, it is Rena's. I must ask you both to promise me you won't touch it. Nemara and I are caring for it."

"But we can look, right? we can look at it?" Keelee was practically bouncing with excitement.

Sordith was just staring at Alador with a slack-jawed expression. Meanwhile, Keelee moved to Alador and grasped both his hands, her blanket falling away.

"I promise... I am so excited..." she looked to Sordith and when he did not chime in she kicked him in the shin. "We promise we will not touch it... Right?"

"Owww... yes, of course, we will not touch it." Sordith managed to exclaim.

"Alright. I am going with you to ensure it is all in order." He led them out of the library and upstairs.

"Through here," he said when he got to the bath's door, "and remember, no touching!"

He opened the door and stepped into the room. The egg was out of its nest again. It was bobbing on its side in the warm water. "Dammit, it won't stay in the nest." He moved to the shorter side of the tub and carefully pulled the egg to him."

"Yes... eggs do that I suppose," Sordith managed to murmur sarcastically.

"My knowledge of eggs is limited to fowl, but I can tell you that no bird I watched over ever had an egg that continually moved out of the straw." Alador carefully set the egg in its rock nest.

"Maybe the problem is the 'nest' is not comfortable straw, but rock." Sordith plucked a stone from the nest and inspected it.

Alador reached over, took the stone away and replaced it, moving it twice before he was satisfied it was seated properly in the ring.

When Alador looked up Keelee had peeled out of her dress and was already getting into the bath. He quickly turned away.

"Keelee, love, perhaps you could have waited until Alador had left the room?" Sordith scowled at his wife.

"Why? He has seen it before."

Sordith ran his hand over his face and inwardly complimented himself on securing Keelee as his wife prior to taking his little brother up on his offer to come stay with him.

Keelee happily made her way to the egg, marveling at it. "It is such a beautiful color."

The two men looked at each other in awkwardness. Alador coughed politely. He placed his hand in the water and raise the temperature just enough to make the pair comfortable and not upset the egg.

"I will leave you two to clean up." He fled the room.

Once out of the bathing room and the unsettling company of his brother's nude wife he gathered his thoughts. They both needed something to wear.

He carefully pictured Keelee and formed a dress over her in his mind's eye. It was a deep green to match her eyes, the fabric crossing her breasts but most of her midriff exposed. The skirt was slit slightly to allow her movement and not hinder her still bandaged leg, but otherwise clung to her body. Smiling, Alador whispered the words and the gown appeared on the bed.

He knew Sordith was more comfortable in leather. He created a matching shirt for Keelee's dress. Then he formed the leather vest and pants as he had seen Sordith wear several times. Using Renamaum's dragon greed for shiny things, he pictured and then called for Sordith's flame like swords from wherever they were hidden or lost. They now lay on the bed beside Keelee's dress. He looked at the two outfits on the bed and was satisfied.

He went back to the door, being careful not to look at the pool directly. "You two need anything else?"

"No, we are very good," Keelee called.

"I will have food and drink waiting when you come back to the library." Alador turned to leave them.

"Alador," Sordith called.

"Yes?" He turned to look directly at the man.

"I am not sorry I hit you." Sordith stated firmly.

Alador wasn't sure what to say to that. He shut the door and left them to the bath.

## Chapter Seventeen

Keelee swept into the library, her face filled with the vibrancy of a hot bath and her excitement. The dress fit her exactly as Alador had imagined, and he smiled as Sordith followed her in with the matching green shirt.

"Alador, I simply must know how you got it?" She moved to him, mindless of General Levielle standing at the fireplace, and Alador's eyes narrowed at her careless statement as he looked pointedly at General Levielle, who had turned from his gazing into the flames at the exuberant voice of a woman.

"Why, magic, of course." The tension in his voice did not match the playful words, a fact not lost on the watching General.

"Oooh." To her credit, her hands went over her mouth at her near slip of his secret.

Sordith flashed Alador a look of apology and shrugged helplessly. Alador moved around the desk and poured a glass of wine for Keelee and a stiffer drink for Sordith. He handed each their drinks and indicated the chairs by the fire. "Feel free to rest, we merely are waiting for Lady Aldemar and then we will go into dinner; she shouldn't be long.

Sordith walked over drink in one hand, his other arm going out to clasp the General's. "Good to see you survived, General. I hope your losses were minimal?"

"Mmm," Levielle grunted shortly, but he grasped Sordith's arm with a comfortable grip. As he released it, he looked about the room to those gathered around, letting out a heavy sigh, then he moved to a more comfortable position next to Sordith's side. "Hopefully the same for the Trench? You were safe, it seems." Alador watched the exchange with the careful eyes of the battle-trained, noting that the general was dressed in a simple brown tunic and black pants – a sharp contrast to Alador's mage robes, and even the elegant clothing he had conjured for his brother and sister-in-law. He wondered briefly if it was a calculated statement, but decided that it probably had more to do with the hard work Levielle had dragged himself away from to be present at this gathering.

"No," Sordith was answering, "I have no idea how we survived. The wave hit as we were climbing out to the first tier. Then, it was swirling angry waters and a swiftly approaching wall of rock." Sordith words were almost to himself, his eyes far away as he spoke.

Levielle did not seem to notice, looking toward Alador and Keelee. "Then you are lucky to be alive." Clearing his throat, he spoke a bit softer. "You would have thought we could have saved more lives."

"Yes, well. Bastards walk among the best of us. I would have had them all out, but maybe it makes no difference. They were all taking refuge on the first tier anyway." Sordith's gaze sharpened, his attention coming back to the here and now..

"Quite." It was Levielle's turn to gaze off into the

distance. "I was shocked to see the gates were blocked, walled off by stone."

"Yes, well I was on the other side of that wall. The trench's occupants were terrified, like cornered cattle. Many were hurt or injured just by the pushing and shoving." Sordith stated, taking a sip from his glass.

Alador coughed politely. "There are two others in the room, gentlemen. Perhaps we could have an inclusive conversation?" Alador had placed himself out of sword and fist reach just in case.

Levielle smiled, more a slight tightening of the lips than anything. "Just a small conversation about the events earlier this week. My apologies." He took the first step forward, his movement comfortable.

"Levielle, I asked you here not as a council member, mage or Blackguard. I am speaking as your friend." Alador took a deep breath. "You are no longer safe in Silverport."

To this, Levielle chuckled. "Oh? Was I ever safe in Silverport?" A bemused look crosses his features as he crossed his arms.

"It is not a time for jokes." Alador looked at him with genuine concern. "Luthian will not allow you to live long, knowing you were asked to block the tiers." "And where exactly do you expect me to run off to?" the general shot back with a slight growl. "He asked me to protect them, to keep people from becoming a mob running up the tiers, and to keep order." He shook his head mournfully. "Nothing more."

"Approach him head on and tell him you serve the

council no matter the cost. Ask to take the army to the coast and other outlying villages to help the people of Lerdenia." Alador insisted. "Take Nakyra with you before she becomes leverage."

Sordith nodded, "I would not put it past him to place a threat upon your wife. He seems to prefer an upper hand if he feels his control has slipped." Sordith took a long sip of his drink, then moved back over to refill it. Keelee had curled up in the corner of the couch and was just listening to the men.

"I don't expect him to let go of such an obvious token of control." Levielle admitted evenly. "But to go with the army was my original plan anyway. Nakyra was to be delivered out to one of the less affected coastal towns." He paused a moment before speaking again. "Besides, as far as the High Minister knows, I am completely loyal to his designs."

"Good," Alador stated. "Lady Aldemar will be here any minute. Do we tell her of what he has done?" Alador looked between the two men, both rulers of Lerdenia in their own spheres of control.

"What does it gain us to tell her?" Levielle asked with a heavy tone.

"I am considering her as a replacement for the High Minister of the city. She is well received by all, seems to have a level head, and she saw through Luthian a long time ago." Alador counted out the reasons on his fingers."

Sordith nodded. "She would be a fine choice." He moved over and sat with Keelee. "I have never heard a bad word spoken of her. And I hear a lot of bad words," he added with a chuckle.

"A mage for a mage? Seems like a choice that is obvious and will only last as long as Lady Aldemar remains uncorrupted." Levielle crossed his arms and planted a foot heavily.

"What do you suggest, then? The mages would never accept a non-mage." Alador tipped his head, his curious expression focused on the General.

"Change the rules then." Levielle shrugged. "But you are correct, it would be difficult to see another being accepted. Getting back to the point, however, what purpose does it serve to tell her now?" he asked, his tone calculated and slow.

"I think we will need her to spread the rumors of Luthian's involvement. Between her and Sordith, the rumor should take hold." Alador stated the beginning of his plan. "Right now, Luthian is the noble benefactor; we need to get him out of that position."

"Hmm. An interesting approach. That rumor being what?" Levielle tapped his finger on his lips before stroking his goatee.

Sordith spoke from where he was on the couch. "That Luthian actually put Lady Caterine, the bronze mage, up to her foul actions."

"Oh? Could the populace not see through that lie already?" Levielle asked coldly. "Perhaps it is because I saw it first hand, but one rogue mage could not have done that much damage without help."

"Although I suspect you are a mage, the fact that

you keep it hidden has left you unused to what can be done if you're willing to spend a lot of power, general." Alador looked at him seriously. "If stone had been my sphere, I could have done it alone. Start at one end, move swiftly to the other." He was not bragging; it had become simple fact to him.

"In addition, sometimes people will believe a lie when they wish it to be true. They see what they hope to see." Sordith added, running a hand over his face. He still held his drink in one hand but he laid his arms across his leg, hunching over to stare at the floor. "In my case, it is what I do not want to believe."

"I never claimed to be without magic." Levielle retorted to Alador with a small smirk. "But still, if that is a rumor you believe will spread like wildfire and turn the populace against the High Minister, then I would not want to stop you, not in the least." His tone was one of dark humor; something was very fitting about the means to an end here.

"If I am to leave Silverport on an errand of peace, the High Minister will still know where I am and what I am up to. It is not difficult to send a man with a knife to see to my end in a tent." Levielle laid out logically.

"I was thinking more of Lady Nakyra. Surely you can separate her under a veil of deception so only you and those you send to guard her will know where she is." Alador had not thought about a sent assassin. It was not unreasonable to consider that Luthian might try to just send such a man. This train of thought was interrupted as Radney stepped through to announce their final visitor.

"Lady Aldemar has arrived and dinner is ready, Lord Alador."

The lady in question stepped over the threshold to the library. She looked exhausted, and her usual silver robes had been exchanged for a straight gray smock. Alador moved to her right away and took her hand.

"Thank you for coming. I would not have sent if it were not urgent." He looked her up and down and turned to introduce her to the others. He knew that she and the General kept company now and then, but she wouldn't know Keelee and he wasn't sure as to Sordith.

"May I introduce Lady Aldemar. And there before you is the General, the Trench Lord, and his wife, Keelee."

"Lady Aldemar." Levielle bowed a bit, his tone lowered and softened. Levielle stood back up to his normal height, keeping his watchful stance and watching the healing mage carefully with his hands clasped firmly behind his back as Alador continued.

"I know we have much to discuss, but I am doubting any of you have eaten properly since the wave hit. Let us have a meal together and speak there." Before she could protest, he escorted the lady to his dining room. He left it to the rest to follow. After all, they had been through his manor before.

Sordith saw Keelee properly seated before taking a seat himself. Alador did the same for Lady Aldemar, leaving the general to fend for himself.

Waiting for the other gentlemen to take their seats, Levielle took one of the open chairs near Alador.

Keeping an eye on Lady Aldemar, he continued to listen.

Alador waited until Radney had directed the dishes onto the table. There were roasted game hens, tubers, fresh hot bread, and a few other delicacies. It was better than he usually ate, but he didn't know the preferences of his guests. Sordith was busy filling his plate and Keelee was setting a few tidbits on her own. Lady Aldemar seemed unwilling to add anything to her dish. .When the servants withdrew and the door shut behind them, Alador finally chose to speak.

"I am just going to be blunt. There is no way to broach this but to lay it out. If I have been wrong in trusting each of you, well I am sure this will represent my last meal." His words had the desired effect as they all looked at him. "I am going to kill my uncle." There he had said it. It strangely didn't feel wrong to do so. It was actually a bit of a relief.

"Well shite man! Why didn't you just let me do it?" Sordith exclaimed throwing a bird leg down onto his plate..

"I didn't want him to die a martyr, as I have told you. He needs to fall from grace before I can act." Alador explained. He looked about the table nervously.

Levielle kept quiet, watching the reactions of all of them before speaking up as he calmly took parts of dishes and loaded up his own plate. "And your plan is what, exactly?

Lady Aldemar finally added a few bites of vegetables and some bread onto her plate. She did not speak, but she was watching Alador closely. She picked at the bread as Alador continued.

"Well, it will start when you pull the army out to help the various villages. You will let Luthian know that by working with the Blackguard, and with no present threat, the city should be good hands with Bariton's command," he said to Levielle.

Alador took a breath and rambled out the rest. "Lady Aldemar will pull all mages she trusts down to the fourth tier and hold a line between there and the third tier; the Blackguard will assist. Then I and a few hand-picked guards will assault the top tier with the help of dragons, to ensure that the mages supporting Luthian are hewn down. While that is occurring, I will face my uncle." Everyone was staring at him open mouthed; he remained silent till one of them spoke.

Levielle wiped his mouth, a bit of sauce from one of the dishes catching against there. "That sounds like a good plan, one that is well thought out and could be executed well. However, even though it sounds good on paper, what are the safeguards for this action?" Levielle's tone was one of command and experience.

"In addition, what makes you think I would sanction killing him?" Lady Aldemar asked quietly.

"My lady, I remember the day of the challenge, when you were a bit afraid of him." Sordith pointed out.

"That doesn't mean I can sanction killing him. I am a healer for the gods' sake." She said, wringing her napkin.

"And how do you get the dragons?" Keelee added with a glimmer of excitement.

"Safeguards? I don't understand." He could only handle one answer at a time. He took a bite of hen and waited for Levielle to answer.

"Safeguards meaning if you fail, this coup fails, and we all are tortured and perish beside you. What is your backup plan to make sure this succeeds?" Levielle took a bite of his own hen, his gaze never leaving Alador.

"The red dragon, Keensight, will personally remove him if I fail." Alador stated softly. "I have no doubt in my mind of this."

"Why would one of the dragons care about our petty squabbles?" Levielle demanded, looking rather curiously at Alador. "Why should we trust it to do what we need?"

"May I ask how you came to align with dragons?" Lady Aldemar interjected.

Alador took a deep breath. It was all on the line or fail before he started. He began his tale from the harvesting of the bloodstone to the fall of the bloodmines and Rena.

"That is where the egg came from, isn't it. You saved it when Rena died." Keelee's words were soft and admiring.

"Nemara did." Alador stated quietly.

Lady Aldemar sat back in her chair. "Unbelievable."

"Yes, but true!" countered Keelee, "Sordith and I both have seen it. It is beautiful."

"Alador, I don't mean to take the wind out of your

sails, but if you challenge the seat of the High Minister's power, the council will expect you to take the station." Levielle's voice became more and more emotionally charged. "If you turn it down, it will be seen as a weakness to be exploited."

"Surely not. I was hoping Lady Aldemar could take such a seat." He glanced at the lady in question.

"Oh goodness me, no. I have no desire to lead those malicious, backstabbing bastards." Lady Aldemar exclaimed.

Alador stared at her in disbelief, not only that she would refuse but that she had just used such strong language. He had never heard her utter an unkind word before tonight.

Levielle simply chuckled and took another bite of his food. As he chewed, he watched the interaction between the others.

Meanwhile, Sordith had been glowering at Keelee's exuberance. "I don't know if I like the idea of these dragons of yours. They could do a lot of harm to the city." Sordith pointed out. "As for taking Luthian's place, Levielle is right."

Lady Aldemar shook her head in agreement. "Yes, if you overcome Luthian and his dogs, most of the city will expect you to don the mantle of High Minister."

Alador sat quietly, taking this all in. He had really been hoping to escape Keensight's plotting.

"Not going according to plan already?" Levielle spoke up after watching Alador sitting in exasperation for a while.. He reached for a roll on the table and began to butter it.

## Chapter Eighteen

Luthian sat back from his desk with a sigh. A casual observer would have seen a map of Cliffview, a large Lerdenian city with a fourth tier, but a closer look would have shown a record of his current activities. After the assault on the stables, he had realized his organization was not as spy-proof as he had assumed, and moved to a less-obvious system, with misleading titles. He still suspected that his nephew had been involved in that particular disaster; the obvious use of magic, including lightning, pointed at the boy. Then the fall of the bloodmine coming so soon after, with the blue and silver tabards, was a coincidence he could not ignore. After all, he didn't believe in coincidences.

The bloodmine would be re-established in time, but for the moment he had been unable to procure eggs. Lady Morana was still miffed with him and was not answering his correspondence, even though she had dispatched dragons and members of her sphere to deal with the dead. He disliked her ignoring him, and one day soon he would remind her she was not the ruler of the country despite her rise in popularity.

The storm had provided him with the opportunity to remove some of the scum and low life of the city. It had been a risky move, but the population seemed to have settled down and accepted that Lady Caterine acted of her own accord. It helped that she had not hidden her disdain for the lower tiers. Those that knew her were not surprised and fed into his accusation that she was responsible.

However, something was still off. He stared at the map for a long time. He couldn't ignore it. His nephew was somehow playing the game so well that he could not track Alador's movements. It was time he gained some control of the boy. He added a new circle and connected it to Alador's. It was time to bring his little lady love in for a visit. If anything could hold that boy's loyalty, it would be leverage over someone he loved. He just hoped the girl was still important to the boy.

Luthian got up and poured a glass of wine, then moved to the servant's pull and rang for assistance. When the young man stepped in, Luthian smiled at him warmly. It was good to keep the servants uneasy, and never being able to predict the High Minister's mood was but one tool that he used.

"Fetch Severent to attend me as soon as he can," Luthian drawled out.

"Yes, milord," the door was closed quickly.

It didn't bother Luthian that they didn't want to remain in the room any longer than they had to. Truthfully, he preferred it that way. He carefully folded his activity map and secured it in his desk. Turning to the other missives of the day, he began to read through the various city reports.

A knock came at the door and Luthian looked up in surprise. Surely, the man had not been located that quickly?

"Come!"

The door opened and the doorman stepped through. "Milord, General Levielle is here to see you. Should I have him wait or can he attend you now."

Luthian took a deep breath. The general was a problem he had yet to deal with and it piqued his curiosity as to why the man would come seeking him out. "Show him in."

Levielle strode into the room confidently. He looked worn and ragged, someone overworked for the past couple of days, but his stance told a very different story. His energy had a driven quality to it, his boots still muddy, tunic still showing sweat and stains from the day.

"High Minister." Levielle addressed Luthian with a curt bow. "I thank you for seeing me on such short notice."

Luthian did not rise. "Of course, General. I am glad to see you hale and whole. I have had reports your men were working hard to help shore up and repair the trench as the water recedes." Luthian eyed the man with deep scrutiny. This was not a man he could underestimate. He had been on the fifth tier longer than Luthian and only rumors were available as to his skills demonstrated at his testing. It was a strange situation. No one seemed to quite remember it, other than that it had occurred.

"What brings you to my chambers? You rarely seek my advice or counsel," Luthian pointed out. "Please have a seat."

"My men have been working double time to try and recover following the storm, wave, and that damn mage that put up those walls," he sighed out in disgust. "She… what was her name again?" he prompted, his tone curious as he stepped forward and took the chair across from Luthian's.

"You speak of Lady Caterine. I will be sure to put a couple extra slips into the budget for a bonus for your men. I have even seen them up on rooftops helping to re-tile." Luthian attempted to move the man away from the topic of sealing the trench. He had asked the general to assist him first, and he doubted that Levielle had forgotten their conversation.

"I appreciate the gesture, High Minister, and I'm sure the men will appreciate it too after such hard work." His tone was measured, but not taken off guard. "Yes, Lady Caterine. Any idea why she might have wanted to seal off the trench?"

Luthian put a look of genuine concern on his face. "Why General… your guess would be as good as mine, I assure you." His cold eyes didn't mirror his expression, and he watched the man with an intensity he had not shown in a long while.

Levielle responded with a practiced metered tone. "I see… well, while the rest of the populace may take that scapegoat as a real and quantifiable solution, we both know the truth of the situation."

Levielle was so oddly calm looking, not at all concerned about the fact that he was sitting before a man that could easily wipe him off the face of the earth without much trouble. Or could he? Luthian began to second guess himself. He knew so little about the general.

Luthian had feared this. The General had connected the pretty clear dots from their own conversation. He would have to be dealt with.

"I see. Well, being a general, you are aware the truth of any situation is told from the perspective of the one in control." Luthian sat back, his hands steepled as he eyed the man. "Any other perspective could have, shall we say, lasting consequences."

"Doesn't it always? It seems that I'm an easy target then. Removal of my person would make it much simpler to keep something like that quiet." A cold smile was drawn across Levielle's features and he leaned lazily back in his chair, comfortably crossing his legs. "However, I don't plan on telling anyone of it, High Minister."

"Oh, how interesting." Luthian leaned forward watching the man closely. "And what is to your benefit, other than your life, to hold your tongue?" Was the man more loyal than he had given him credit for? In some ways, he wondered if this man weren't Alador's father. They had that same strange sense of morality unusual in the tiered cities.

"While I may not agree with your means, you typically have a point to the things you do." He met Luthian's gaze. "Understand that my loyalty lies with the council. I do not need to rock the boat as I would only crash into the rocks that is the council's will. Besides, the army reports to me not out of duty, but from respect -

respect that can be far more easily lost than it was earned."

"So, are you here in hopes that this confession of loyalty will earn you a long life, or do you seek something else, General?"

Luthian wasn't stupid. He understood quite well the man's meaning. He also knew with the same surety that if this man ever saw that he would not crash upon rocks with his knowledge, he would reveal it in a heartbeat. He could not foresee such an opportunity with the well-controlled council, but then he had never thought the bloodmines would fall either.

"Not at all, I am simply telling you what I know and informing my High Minister that I am marching the army along the coast to grant aid to nearby towns and villages that were affected from the storm." Levielle remained smiling that cold smile. "My life could be snuffed out by you at any point, but I'm still valuable to you, something that is not easily replaced."

"What of protection of the city, and the help needed here?" Luthian pondered the idea. The army responding would make the council look good, and given the damage to the city, he was sure the rural areas could use the help. "Are you dispatching units differing directions?"

"Leave the planning to me, High Minister. The various forces will depend on what areas report the most damage. I have scouts moving to the towns and villages up and down the coast to ascertain what aid is needed." He uncrossed his legs and straightened a bit in his chair. "As for the protection of the city, you have some of the city guard still at your disposal, as well as the Blackguard to enforce the law." The report rolled off his tongue quickly.

"Then you have my permission. I have no doubt the council will agree as well. Such help will bolster the feelings of the populace who often feel abandoned in such situations." Luthian nodded. "It is a fine idea, and given the circumstances, likely a smart move on your part."

"Thank you, High Minister. I had assumed you would see this path as the most reasonable." Levielle rose and bowed politely. "With your permission, I shall take my leave and continue preparations."

"As you will." Luthian rose. "May the Gods speed your path to those that need it most."

His words were polite, but they both knew there was no real feeling to the sentiment. Besides, if the man had an 'accident' far from Silverport, the powers that be were less likely to be blamed for it.

With a quick nod, Levielle turned on his heel and made his way to the door. He paused there for a moment, as if to say something, but instead opened the door, exited and quietly closed it behind him.

Luthian sat back down slowly. Having the army out helping repair would be good for the country. It was smart thinking on Levielle's part given that the knowledge he held was dangerous to him. However, the High Minister decided that the General's wife, Nakyra, would become his house guest after the man left. It never hurt to ensure that the man had a reason to make sure his loyalty was as deep as he had declared.

Severent arrived about a half hour later. Luthian was deep in compiling the list of damages as various cities with a scrier could report in. He looked up with relief when the man was announced. More that it gave a break from the menial tasks he was completing then the man himself. Luthian smiled coldly, so many people wanting to be at the top of the ladder, not realizing that the top of the ladder was boring work for the most part.

He beckoned the man closer as the door was closed behind him by a servant. "Ah, the man I wished to see. I have two tasks, no make that three, that I need from you and those you manage."

"I am here to serve, High Minister." The pock-faced man, his faded red hair tied back severely, bowed low.

"The young lady you mentioned from Smallbrook, do you remember reporting on her?" Luthian stood and went to refill his glass that had set empty for some time now.

"I never forget a report once it has been completed, milord." Severent raised an eyebrow as if Luthian should know that.

"Yes, Yes… Well, I wish you to extend her an invitation to reside as my guest this winter." Levielle capped the decanter.

"Am I to assume refusal is not an option for the young woman in question?" Severent smiled coldly.

"It is not. However, she is to arrive untouched." Luthian didn't like the look on the man's face.

"Of course, High Minister." The man's grin faltered slightly. "What else is it that you require?"

"I need one of your men to move out in the company of General Levielle. He is moving the army to help the populace in the surrounding areas. I want reports on his action and if the opportunity arises to arrange an accident… well, let us say that I would not be heartbroken."

"You want him removed?" Severent shifted with a somewhat predatory air.

It had always made Luthian a bit uncomfortable. Fortunately, Severent had a price and Luthian had been happy to pay it. "For now, only if an accident is viable." He stressed the word accident. "Reports will suffice until then."

"And the last task, High Minister?" Severent was not one for small talk.

"I wish a similar invitation for the winter to be extended to Levielle's wife after the army departs. Only, I don't want anyone else in the city to know of it." Luthian didn't know how Severent got around with no one noticing him, but he knew that if it were required, Severent would ensure that the lady was delivered without anyone being the wiser.

"These are matters easily seen to." Severent almost sounded as if he was complaining.

"Yes, well then consider yourself overpaid." Luthian said in a dismissive tone.

Severent nodded, turned and strode out the door. Luthian realized he didn't know where the man went when he left. He was notified by simply sending a homing pigeon he provided the Minister. One day, he might need to know more about the man. He thought for a moment. Maybe not, some rocks were best left unturned.

## Chapter Nineteen

The troll cook and his head-baker sat on the wall of the outlook smoking their pipes. They had started preparing breakfast in the kitchen far before dawn broke. Now they were resting as the first wave of Blackguard, and immigrants sheltered in the cavern, ate.

"I swear, Troll, they have to do the city clean-up faster," Gralin said after he exhaled. Smoke curled up above his head.

Calling the troll-cook, *Troll*, was not in any way derogatory. In fact, the baker considered the cook one of his closest friends. However, troll language was very guttural, not something a human could easily wrap their tongue around. Also, troll names usually took at least a minute to say since they was always based on lineage. Their names were not something quick you could yell across the kitchen in an emergency. Therefore, everyone called Troll by his species name, and he was good with it. No one understood where he came from; he had simply gotten off one of the great trading ships one day and he had not seen fit to enlighten them.

"I never had so many folks to bake for. We got to get them city folks out and back on the tiers where they belong." Gralin sucked on his pipe so hard he made the packed tobacco glow red in the bowl. "They eat the bread as fast as I can bake it."

Troll grinned and smacked the baker on the back with a meaty hand. The baker almost fell off the wall. "You ought to be happy. Folks likin' your bread and such."

"That's not the point," Gralin pulled his pipe from his mouth and pointed at the cavern's entrance. "The point is that I used to bake in the morning and then go lounging in the pub and dittlin' with the fair ladies, but no more. Now I finish bakin' in the morning, they eat, and then before lunch I bake again, and before supper… again!"

Troll thumped the baker soundly on the shoulder. "The ladies won't forget you," he laughed as he puffed on his pipe. "I heard the first tier was getting cleaned up enough that they may let the folks back in soon."

Gralin looked over the edge of the outlook toward the plain. You could barely see it from the outlook, but Troll's words were true. Over the last few days they had watched the piles of the dead grow out on the grassy field. Luckily, the wind had been such that the stench from the dead had been blowing inland rather than up the tiers.

As they sat discussing the state of the cavern's populace, and the ladies Gralin missed, the folks who had been first to eat started to emerge on the platform the outlook created. It was going to be a beautifully clear day, and the sun was already warming the stone. Mothers with their children came first. The mothers set up a perimeter along the wall of the outlook, partially for the safety of the children, but also to keep the young ones from seeing any dead.

The kids were not interested in anything, but the joy of freedom from the confines of the cave. They were full of breakfast and energy from the monotony of being cooped up for days. They ran in big circles chasing each other, like dogs scenting for their hunting master.

The next ones to come out to bask in the sun were the elderly who were too infirm to assist in the clean-up. Most of the civilian men, and the whole of the Blackguard, would go out immediately and continue the clearing and restoration of the tiers.

Troll crossed his legs and thumped his pipe out on the bottom of his boot. He was finished and it was mostly ash. It was time to go in and see that the pots and platters were filled for the second wave they had to feed. Then they would start to prepare the food to be served for lunch.

The baker rose and stretched his arms up high to get the kinks out of his back. Lifting tray after tray of bread and rolls was tiring work. They both headed toward the entrance and back to work.

"Mama… Look…" a child called, their shrill voice rising over the others as they squealed and played. "Big birds!"

Gralin and Troll turned to see the child pointing out to sea.

The baker shaded his eyes with his hand and peered over the tops of the children's heads. He could see what looked like five giant birds flying toward them with the sun at their backs. They were just silhouettes. But, he could easily see those creatures were not 'big birds.' They were dragons!

"Dragons!" Gralin shouted. "Into the cavern!"

The mothers cried out in alarm. They had never seen dragons in their lifetime. The stories they had all been told were of the Dragon Wars… Fire… Destruction… and Death. They corralled their charges and started ushering them back into the cave as Troll, Gralin and several of the elderly stood mesmerized watching the dragons wing toward them.

They were easily discernible from a big bird now. There were five flying in a 'V' formation and the lead dragon was enormous. It was black as obsidian. At first the people watching from the outlook thought its coat of scales were shining in the morning sun, but they soon realized as it drew closer that it wore a suit of armor. Its head was encased in a helmet of silver with a bridge of metal running down its muzzle for protection of that vulnerable area of its body. Its chest was also encased in armor, and that piece rose to form a saddle on its back, where a death mage all dressed in black rode, with his hair and robe flapping in the wind like two smaller wings over the dragon's shoulders.

When they were over the plain, and close enough that Gralin could see the color of the large dragon's red eyes, the beast gave out a mighty roar and circled the dead piled deep on the grass. The other four dragons, as if instructed by the largest of their group, sailed down and landed by the pile of the dead, the mages riding them sliding from their backs and leading them closer.

Troll and Gralin could tell by the humans' body language that they were appalled by the sheer numbers to be disposed of. As the largest made lazy circles over the other four on the ground, the beasts stretched out their long necks and seemed to inspect the pile. What they were looking for could not be determined by those on the outlook.

After a few moments, each of the four dragons picked up a body in its clawed feet and sprang into the air, winging their way back the direction they flew in from originally.

"Do you think they're going to eat them?" Gralin asked Troll.

"Of course, they are!" one elderly man said as he stood leaning on his cane at the wall. "I heard my father talk of the horrors of the war... Men swallowed whole by those vicious beasts."

The large dragon who had been circling overhead ignored the dead. Once the four seemed to be on their way, the large black armored giant turned toward the city. It thrust its powerful wings down to gain altitude. It swooped so closely past the outlook that those still standing there ducked and felt the air from its wings.

They watched it rise. It was headed toward the fifth tier.


Luthian heard the roar of the dragon as it announced its arrival in his garden courtyard. His servants seemed to appear from every doorway, their eyes wide in their fearful faces. He waved them back to their work, but he conjured a shield before he stepped out onto the porch of his home.

Mattis, one of Lady Morana's priests, slid from the dragon's back and stood with his arms crossed, buried in his sleeves. "I come to report that Her Highness, Priestess Morana has dispatched her black dragon flight and her followers to assist with the proper disposal of the dead."

Luthian had been to the bloodmines. He had seen dragons, but never one like the one standing behind Mattis. The dragons in the mines were pathetic compared to this magnificent ebony monster. It was at least four times the size of any in the mines, and its gaze was intelligent and appraising. It eyed him over the head of its rider.

"Tell Lady Morana that the High Minister of Silverport thanks her for her concern and assistance." He was sure her choice to send aid was not out of generosity; she always had a second purpose to what she did. His eyes returned to the dragon greedily. He would have liked to approach the dragon and even stroke its sleek black scaled neck, but he knew from the mine visits that they could be disagreeable creatures. Where the ones in the mines were chained down, this one was free, without even a harness for the rider to give it direction.

"How many dragons did you bring?" he asked. Alador had been correct, Lady Morana was collecting dragons. Maybe he needed to start listening more to what his nephew was saying. After all, the boy had proven he could play the game. Luthian's mind flitted back to the dragon. How many was the question and what was she training them to do?

"We have five who will be working Silverport," Mattis answered. The large black took that moment to nudge its partner in the shoulder as if reminding him that they did have orders to carry out for their priestess.

"And did Lady Morana dispatch others to the coastal cities?" Luthian asked. What was her purpose here? Why were the priests not just giving rites to the piles? So many questions raced through his mind. He usually prepared for everything. He was not prepared for this.

"Others have been sent to aid up and down the coast," Mattis confirmed. He appeared uncomfortable with the High Minister's questions. Whether he had been told by Lady Morana to keep their numbers secret or whether he was just not one to talk, he turned at this point and mounted his dragon.

"We will be making trips throughout the daylight hours. We have already found the dead piled on the plain. I would suggest you start a new pile further inland, so the clean-up is not hampered by the arrival and departure of the dragons."

"I will see that it is done." Luthian stepped back from the enormous beast as it started to walk toward the overhang of his garden.

It walked to the edge and hopped up on the wall. It stretched out its neck and let out a powerful roar that hurt Luthian's ears., then spread its wings and dropped over the edge.

Luthian rushed to the wall to see the monster spiral down to the plains below. It sailed over the pile of the dead and without stopping reached down and grasped two bodies, one in each taloned paw, and with a mighty thrust of its wings headed toward the rising sun.

Luthian tapped his lips, hands flattened against each other. He had to find out more about Lady Morana's control over these beasts. He had to learn how to control his own flight of dragons.

## Chapter Twenty

Amaum sat upon the tall peak of a mountain, his grief still coursing through him. He had not realized how important Rena was to him. That she had died for some mortal did not make sense to him. How could she love a mortal more than her own kin? There were so many questions that the young dragon had, and there was no one to answer them. Well, no one but Alador. Had the mage somehow bewitched his sister to such loyalty?

His father had chosen the mortal for his Geas. Why hadn't he chosen his own son? When they had been afforded the opportunity to meet his sire briefly, there had been no sense of giving his son this responsibility other than to help Alador. Helping Alador had killed his sister, it was as simple as that.

He sensed the presence of another dragon and looked off into the distance. It was his dam. He kicked off into the air to land somewhere with room for them both. He only saw his mother when she was seeking him; feeling like he needed to be independent now, he did not go to her other than to bring her a gift for her mound of treasure.

Pruatra landed with a light touch that seemed impossible for a dragon so large, yet he had never known his mother to shake ground when she landed. He bowed low, both to his dam herself and her station. She had been the flight leader's mate and was afforded proper respect amongst those that remained of the blue dragon council.

"Amaum, I have been searching for you for days." Pruatra flicked her tail with irritation. "You have not been to your cave in weeks by the looks of the entrance."

"My cave is properly guarded, mother." Amaum stated with an edge of youthful pride.

"It is not like you to leave it so long." Pruatra said gently.

"I have not felt like returning." Amaum admitted, ruffling his wings slightly.

"Because of Rena?" she pressed.

"Amongst other things." Amaum snapped his response and a slight guttural growl followed it.

"Talk to me Amaum. You cannot sort such things in your own mind." Pruatra pointed out. "The mind plays tricks when the emotions are high."

"There is nothing to sort. My sire chose a mortal for his task. He ordered us to assist the man and now Rena is dead." Steam billowed from the young male's nostrils. His tail slammed into the ground.

"Amaum, you could not have done Alador's task. It must be done within the mortal city and its guiding council. Dragons have tried to stop the blood-mining of our young, and only died for the effort." Pruatra's gentle words did nothing to ease his anger.

"Then the gods should lift the prohibition against harming them except in defense." Amaum snarled. "Let us burn their little mountains down."

"Our purpose has always been…" Pruatra began.

"Our purpose ended when they betrayed our blood for their own power." Amaum roared with frustration. "Dragons have attacked before." He finally said after his forefeet hit the ground once more.

"The Daezun have never betrayed their oaths. We will continue to protect and honor them." Pruatra rose, her chest puffing as she drew her full weight before the smaller dragon. "We will continue to help Alador," she stated firmly.

"Keensight was allowed to attack that village!" Amaum wanted that freedom, to act in his anger and tear apart those that had led to Rena's useless death.

"Keensight will pay for his actions before the gods. His path is not yours. It is not mine. I gave my mate my word I would help Alador." Pruatra counseled. "And I will keep it."

"You prefer him over your own daughter." Amaum snarled. "I didn't give my word. I will not help the human again."

"Amaum, I trust my mate and his magic to see things as they should be. Alador will unite the isle in time." she assured her son. "It has been foreseen that such a mortal would rise up for a very long time."

"Then what? We serve the mortals as we once did?" Amaum shook his great head. "I will not be a slave."

Pruatra sighed deeply, and Amaum did not miss the irritated flick of her tail. But he was grown now, she could not use her powers as his dam to insist upon his compliance. He was not helping the half-breed again.

"If you remember your history, dragons were revered and cared for. We were never slaves." Pruatra pointed out. "If anything, they were more our servants then we theirs."

"Until they figured out they could steal our power." Amaum knew his history just fine. He knew that the mages had betrayed dragons and separated the isle beyond hope.

"Alador has already seen one mine closed. With the betrayal of the black fight known, those with clutches are keeping them well hidden. Finding our eggs will be a great challenge now; I do not think that such a place will return."

Pruatra was helping guide one poor blue fledgling. Its wings had been so damaged during its imprisonment in the bloodmines that it would never fly. She had helped the young male find a cave in the sea, and assisted him in creating the pressure needed for a dry place to rest. He could live his days beneath the sea. In time, his body would adapt to undersea life. He would just need to rise for air now and then.

"You didn't want to help Alador either." Amaum tried one last desperate time to sway his mother from her course.

"Yes, well if someone doesn't help him with your father's geas and assist him with his magic, the young mage could kill us all, dragon and human alike. It is in my best interest to see him fully trained." She shook her wedged head. "I do not claim to understand your father's gifting of his powers as if Alador were a son. I am grateful that he still gifted you as well. Personally, you are acting like a spoiled fledgling who didn't get his way."

"MY SISTER DIED," roared the young male.

Then Pruatra did something she had never done before - she attacked her son. The older dragon lunged forward and caught the young male in the chest. He was not prepared, and she was able to bowl him over. Her talons dug into his throat, and he struggled beneath her weight before finally going still and looking away.

"She was MY DAUGHTER." Pruatra snarled down at him. "Don't you ever act as if I have forgotten again, or I will send you to your father's care. Am I very clear, Amaum?"

Her muzzle was against the side of his head. She was nearly double his size, and despite his male bravado he could not move her. Amaum laid there stunned. His mother had never treated him with aggression before, and he truly did not know how to react.

"You will answer me, Amaum." She demanded, her sharp talons digging deeper.

Amaum whimpered before answering. "Yes, Dam," he called up softly.

She let him go and shook out her wings. "When you have quit feeling sorry for yourself and can become the male I expect of you, come find me." She looked down were he still cowered before her. "There is more at stake than your sister or Alador. I expect a male of my line to rise to his potential. There will be no more talk of this. You will support the boy or I will personally see to it that you never leave the sea again."

Amaum wasn't sure how she could do that, but he also had not thought her capable of dropping him as if he were nothing more than a fledgling. He huffed out steam as if to save some small part of his ego.

"Yes, Mother," he stated softly.

Pruatra took off, clearly still angered. He had pushed too far. He rose to his feet, shaking his wings to make sure they were unharmed. He decided that maybe caring for his cave was not such a bad idea right now. He knew one thing. He never wanted to see his Dam that angry again.

## Chapter Twenty-One

The body hit the courtyard head first, the sound much like dropping a melon on the rock pavement. Jon had become immune to the implications of the noise by the tenth body. He still looked away as they hit the ground, but that was to ensure no body fluids splattered into his face. The red bricks of the small outdoor area were now darkened even further by such escapes of fluids. He moved to the body quickly to ascertain its condition. This one was intact – not missing any appendages.

"Move this one into the crypt," he directed.

The young acolyte looked at Jon with concern as his fellow acolyte hastened to collect the body. "We keep adding bodies like this, we are going to run out of room."

"The High Priestess keeps a stone mage in her service. You will never run out of room." Jon sounded bored. "Now move it before another drops."

His command was obeyed immediately, one of the benefits of being trained and recently raised to a priest's status by Lady Morana. He was grateful for this, as he had seen some of the tasks the acolytes were given and he much preferred his status and duties as they were.

He scanned the sky for another black dragon. The bodies had been coming in regularly all afternoon. Despite the morbidity of their task, the blacks were amazing to watch in flight. The gliding of a fully extended wing drew the eye and sometimes Jon wondered if some magic was in play that left mortals with that continued sense of awe.

Jon was startled out of his thoughts by a strong push against his back. He stumbled forward and turned around with a smile.

"Nightmare, we have talked about this. Eventually you are going to be big enough to fling me across the yard. You need to stop doing that."

Despite his words, the usually reserved priest moved to the dragon and stroked its muzzle with affection.

"But it's fun!" Nightmare's somewhat guttural speech had only recently cleared enough that Jon did not have to decipher it. The dragon grinned.

The acolytes moving the body hustled past the dragon, giving it a wide berth.

Jon shook his head, but couldn't blame them. A dragon grinning could be really quite frightening if you were not familiar with their expressions. He cuffed the dragon lightly and the dragon's tail started playfully wagging back and forth at the end.

"Don't do it," Jon warned.

The dragon was just about to pounce upon him, something Jon would have been unable to stop, when another body hit the ground behind the priest. Nightmare bumbled around him to sniff the corpse.

"You people are falling from the sky." Nightmare looked up at the sky as if searching for another falling corpse. "I do not think they should try to fly."

Jon chuckled. "We are bringing in the dead from the last storm."

"Why?" Nightmare looked at him in confusion.

"The High Priestess is helping put the dead to rest by moving them on to Dethara or other Gods." Jon explained.

"Why?" Nightmare tipped his head almost upside down as he looked at his friend.

Jon groaned inwardly. It seemed like 'why' and 'what for' had become the dragon's favorite questions of late.

"Do you remember when we spoke of the Goddess and her purpose?" Jon knew he was going to have to be thorough when the black fledgling was in this mood.

"Yes, she created the black dragons. We are her children." The fledgling puffed up proudly.

"Yes, but she is also the guide to the dead, ensuring they pass to the God or Goddess that they most honored in life." Jon explained. "So, since there are so many beyond healing from the storm, she is assisting the cities and villages with proper burial rites after the storm."

"Do dragons have burial rites?" Nightmare tipped his head the other way. It was rather comical despite the seriousness of the conversation.

The priest pondered for a moment. "I honestly do not know the answer to that. You are the first dragon I have ever spoken too. You will have to ask one of the elders of your flight."

"Oh no, they go on and on and on and on and on and on…"

Jon jumped in. "I get the idea, but even so, elders often have great wisdom. Give them the time and they will share what you wish to know." He remembered the elders of the village he had been born in. As a middlin, he had felt much the same as Nightmare with regard to the long winded explanations from his elders. However, unlike the rest of the middlins, he had quickly learned they did not wish to hear his thoughts or questions.

"Maybe later." Nightmare said with a great huff of air, causing Jon's hair around his face to dance in its wake. "I am hungry. Let's go eat."

"I cannot leave this area until the sun has set." Jon shook his head, Nightmare was such a middlin despite being a dragon.

"I am hungry now." The dragon pressed his nose to Jon's chest and honestly looked like he was pouting.

"Then go hunt. You fly well enough now."

"Hunt? Why would I hunt when you feed me?" Black wings ruffled with irritation.

"I am no longer going to do that," Jon stated flatly.

"What? I will starve." Nightmare wheezed out his nostrils in shock.

Jon laughed. "You will not starve, you are a hunter by nature. Your flying is under control." Jon put his hands on either side of the dragon's snout. "You are old enough to feed yourself. In fact, I have obviously spoiled you far too long."

Nightmare drew up as high as he could. With his neck stretched out in such a manner, he could look down at Jon's head.

"You are serious. You are not going to feed me? Even if I wait 'til the sun has set?"

Jon looked up. One of the first lessons the flight master had taught him was never back down from the dragon who bonded with you. He clasped his hands behind him. "I am no longer going to feed you. This is correct."

"I thought you were my friend." The dragon lowered and turned his head so they were eye to eye, his expression rather pathetic.

"I am. You are old enough to take care of yourself." Jon tried to assure the dragon with a gentle pat on its neck.

"Fine." Nightmare frowned and snorted smoke over Jon in what could only be interpreted as a huff. He took two faltering steps before he leaped into the sky. He flapped his wings a bit harder than needed and wobbled off.

Jon realized as the dragon flew off that he should have cut that string a bit sooner. He had not thought about it because feeding the slick black reptile had never been an issue with his duties until today. He looked over at the body that had hit the ground to see the returned acolytes staring in awe.

"You have work to do, stop your gawking," he snapped. "Get this body down into the crypts."

As the acolytes scrambled to do as they were told, he watched as they grabbed the bloodied corpse by arms and legs to haul it down. When the last dragon came in for the night, another priest would be administering the rites for those received into the crypts. A different priest would say the rites over the those delivered to the flight master.

Lady Morana had accepted his suggestion on how to ensure that the dragons knew the taste of mortal flesh and were not appalled by it. He had so far resisted feeding the dead to Nightmare, but he knew one day Morana would test the fledgling and if he refused to eat, she would feed him to the older flight members. She had no patience for a dragon that did not bow to her wishes. How she had convinced them all that she was the true flight leader he did not know. He had seen the flight leader of the black dragons reluctantly obey her every whim. What hold did she have on them?

It was close to dark when the last dragon laid its load gently on the ground, unlike many others, and flew to the caves. He was relieved to set off for his own food and then rest. He passed through the temple heading for the door to the stairs that led to the dragon' caves. He still shared a cave with Nightmare, but he was fairly certain this would not last much longer with the young fledgling learning to hunt and fight. He had to wonder how many meals the dragon had turned to an acid reduced blob?

"Priest, a moment if you will?" Morana's silky purr was unmistakable.

Jon turned slowly and went down to one knee, "My time is yours, Priestess Morana."

"Rise and be recognized."

He looked up to see a kind smile on her face, which he quickly noticed did not reach her eyes. He decided caution was warranted. He clasped his hands before him and waited.

"Were we able to add any abundance to the crypts?" She moved closer to him, her steps oddly silent.

"We did, milady." Jon's tone was polite and measured, but he made sure to maintain eye contact. He saw the High Priestess much like he saw Nightmare; this was someone that you dare not back down from outside of proper respect. "May I ask why we are collecting the intact bodies?" He made sure to keep any speculation or accusation out of his voice. He did not want her knowing he was wise to her plan. He wanted her to trust him enough to reveal it to him. Though he had scoured the library every free moment he had since he discovered her plan to raise an army of undead, he had not found the spell that would allow such a massive undertaking.

"You interest me. Come, we will take a glass of wine and I will tell you why we do not burn them." She turned, expecting him to follow, and glided to her personal rooms.

Jon was quick to fall into step behind her. He preferred her in front of him versus behind him.

She had him close the door as he followed her into her chambers. She moved to the wine table and poured them each a glass, then held out one for him. He took it, careful not to touch her. He was not ready for that move yet.

They both sat on her couch, Jon upright and formal in contrast to the way she draped herself at the other end facing him.

"Jon, tell me where you come from." She eyed him, raising her glass of wine to wet her lips.

"I was with the Blackguard of the High Minister." Jon glanced her way, then back into his own wine glass. It felt as if she was looking right through him.

"Remind me why you left?"

He could feel her deep gaze without even looking at her. "I was assigned to the bloodmines. If you remember, I brought Nightmare to you. I thought it best to disappear with the rest of the dead."

"Disappear?" she coaxed.

"The dragons that assaulted the mines that night took the dead. I think they ate them. The only body left behind in the enclave was that of the large Black from your flight." Jon finally glanced at her. "My loyalty to Dethara and you were my priority. Nightmare was my priority." He hoped this would satisfy her curiosity and pushed to change the subject.

"Why do we keep the dead?" he pressed. His usual stoic way of talking had slipped in the face of what was going on.

She shifted and studied him closely. "I want you to focus just on the well of power within you. Tell me what you find."

Her instruction was a bit confusing, as Jon could not see how this would connect to his question. He thought she was just evading - it until he focused on the well of power within him, something he had not done for some time. He was surprised with what he found.

"It is greater than it was, as if almost overflowing." His surprise echoed even in Jon's voice.

"We have created a pool of necrotic power to draw from. This adds to what Dethara gives us freely. Here, we are stronger. No attack upon the temple will succeed as long as we keep the well."

Jon blinked back his many questions. Right now, he needed to focus. Finally, he picked the one question he felt safest asking.

"To keep the power of death here, the rites would have to be foregone. That would leave such souls trapped in Dethara's realm." He looked at her with great concern on his face.

"I thought you smarter than most, thank you for the confirmation." She sipped her wine, letting the pregnant silence build. "They are trapped in Dethara's realm. I came across a spell from an ancient tome that will allow me to reanimate them into an army at my command."

Jon had expected as much, but hearing her confess it stunned him. He took a drink to buy him time. "Milady, with all due respect, what could possibly necessitate such a force? The country is well guarded by the army, and even the Blackguard if needed."

"There is a time coming when those forces will be raised against us or against the island itself. Until then, the souls serve the one with the spell. Until I enact the spell, they make for that strong pool of necromancy to help increase our following's power and access to the power that death brings when life departs." Morana smiled, the cold evil within her reflected in the intensity of her gaze.

"Do you have a problem with this, priest?"

Jon held the horror of what she was doing to the souls committed to the crypts tightly to his breast. "I do not." He finally managed. "I just am surprised that such things are possible."

"Good, then tonight I will ensure that the temple knows I have chosen you as my praetor. I have not chosen one since I was forced to kill the last."

Morana stood and took his drink from his hand. He could not disguise the shake of it.

"You look exhausted. Go and get your rest Jon. Report to me first thing in the morning."

Jon rose to his feet, his mind reeling from what he had learned. "Yes, Milady."

"Don't disappoint me. I would hate to kill a second praetor so soon." Her caution lay between them until he finally nodded.

Jon left her rooms as fast as he could. Everything he suspected about the High Priestess was true. He wasn't sure if she was serving Dethara or herself. However, he was smart enough not to rile her to commit a second murder of a faithful.

*Chapter Twenty-Two*

Alador carefully shifted the egg into a water-filled container that he had fashioned so he could slip his hand in beside the egg to warm the water. He would tie it to the horn of the lexital saddle to keep it close. Alador had an inner knowledge, which he attributed to Renamaum, that he could not travel by spell without damaging the dragon in the egg.

With the arrival of the black dragons, it was imperative to get the egg out of the city. If they were to get close enough, there was a possibility they might smell it and come to investigate. He was grateful that the enormous black monster that flew over earlier did not detect it. Now more than ever, he had to get the egg to Pruatra. However, breaking it away from Nemara, even though she saw the danger too, was becoming a challenge.

"What if she destroys it?" Nemara wrung her hands and looked at Alador with fear in her eyes.

"It is Rena's egg," he said softly. He reached up and stroked Nemara's cheek with his fingertips. "I cannot see her destroying it unless it hatches into some kind of abomination." Alador carefully tied the bag which held the container. "If it is mine by magic, and not some other mate she had, then it could be defective in some way. Messing with magic can end badly, a fact I have learned the hard way." He cupped her cheek in his hand and thumbed off the tear that threatened to fall from her eye.

Nemara could still not see clearly, though thankfully she was no longer completely blind. The healer said it would heal in time. Alador felt horrible that he had not foreseen the effects of drawing power from another mortal.

"Some other mate…?" Nemara's voice trembled. "So you did consider her a mate?" Her eyes met his.

"No, it was a slip of the tongue. I will not lie to you. I loved her. However, it was not the love one would have in a bonded mate." Alador reassured her gently. He leaned in and kissed her lightly on the lips. "My relationship with you is about as close to having a mate as I have ever come." He tipped up her chin and held her gaze, her eyes darting left and right as if seeking something in his. He gave her another reassuring kiss and released his grip. The black dragons were absent for the moment; he really had to leave. "I do not feel that I can truly have a mate until I have completed this geas."

She reached out and clasped his free hand. "What if it never ends?"

"I have seen its end - I know what I must do." Alador held up the sack tightly in his other hand. "I need to get this to Pruatra so it is not caught in any miscalculation on my part."

"What if she blames you for Rena's death?"

Nemara's grip grew tighter on his hand. Once again, Alador wondered how much of Rena lived on in Nemara.

"It is a chance we have to take, Nemara. There is nowhere else to hide the egg." Alador raised his hand and pushed a strand of hair out of her eyes with a tender touch. "I feel this as deeply as you feel about its safety."

She leaned up against Alador's chest. "Promise me you will do everything you can to keep it safe."

He stroked her hair and kissed the top of her head. "I promise, Nemara. But, the ultimate decision must be made by Pruatra. I feel instinctively that she will know what to do."

Nemara sighed deeply and then stepped back.

He shifted the hand that the bag was in; the tie strings were cutting into his hand. "I will be back as soon as I can."

Alador turned from her and walked away. He needed the egg out of the city. He never had trusted Luthian, but now he was even more concerned. Not only had he seen the huge black dragon land in his uncle's courtyard, but Luthian's move earlier to procure him a position of power on the council didn't make sense to him. His uncle had not done that because he valued Alador's views - he had something else planned.

Alador quickly made his way to a stable close by, where he had reserved a lexital. He tied the bag securely to the saddle horn, than placed himself in the crook of the lexital's neck. He stroked the feathered neck raised before him, then gently prodded the bird with his foot, signaling for it to take off. Flying was a cold way to travel, but it was beautiful. He let himself relax and just enjoy the view as they soared over the changing landscape. Regularly he checked around him to make sure there were no black dragons in sight, and then he would lean down to check the temperature of the egg's water and reheat it if needed.

Finally, the coastline near Pruatra's cave appeared. Alador turned the bird to find the clifftop where he had fallen when Henrick brought him here to let Renamaum have closure with his family. How close he had come to dying that day still caused a shiver to run down his spine.

He knew the way to the entrance of the cave as well as Renamaum did. He spiraled down until he found the ledge at the opening and landed, then gratefully slid off the lexital's thick neck. The position on the bird was not one he was accustom to, so he stood bowlegged in pain for a few moments before he managed to shake it off by walking around the lexital a few times.

Once he was steadier on his feet, he carefully untied the bag. He released the lexital and the bird took off immediately. They always returned to their home. Like the birds that migrated each year through the Daezun territories, they always found their way. He would find his own way home via the traveling amulet he carried.

Alador picked up the bag and carefully looked over the edge of the rocky ledge. He found a place where he could levitate down to the water. He did not want to jump for fear of hurting the egg.

He would need to swim in order to get into the underground sea cave Pruatra called home. The egg needed to stay at the same temperature and not chill any further or there would be a chance of harming or even killing the dragon within it. He heated the bag once more, then formed an air bubble around his head, slipping into the sea. The egg weighed him down, but that turned out for the good, because the underwater cave was much deeper than he remembered from his previous visit within Renamaum. Then again… He had seen it through Renamaum's eyes and the dragon was vastly larger than Alador was as a human. It grew darker as he dove deeper, and he was forced to form a light in his free hand as he descended.

He swam to the entrance and proceeded inside. When he saw light above him, he slowed, dropping his own light. He did not want to startle Pruatra if she was sleeping. The large blue dragon was bound to be angry with him, at some level. There was no sense giving her additional cause to steam him to death. He poked his head up carefully. The air bubble popped as he did so.

The dragon was on top of her mound of treasure and seaweed. Her welcome was more of a growl than speech. "You have one moment to explain this intrusion before I see that you never appear anywhere uninvited again."

"I have Rena's egg." He stood in the shoulder-deep water and held up the sack it was housed in as proof.

The dragon's head rose from her paws, and even on that reptilian face he could see her surprise. "Rena laid an egg?" Pruatra's long neck reached out to sniff.

Alador walked out of the water and up onto the sandy beach in front of the dragon. He untied the leather sack and carefully withdrew the egg.

Pruatra lumbered to where he stood and tentatively sniffed at it. "It doesn't smell right." She looked at him intently.

"I know, Pruatra, I... see... the thing is…" How did he explain this to a towering dragon who could probably fit his entire body into her mouth? "Rena and I… We danced on the wings of power."

"You danced with power? With my daughter?! With Rena?!" The dragon drew up over him. He had known she was large, but right this moment, she seemed enormous.

"We did not know this would happen!" He held the egg to him to protect it. "She was as surprised as I," Alador blurted out.

"Let me have the egg," Pruatra demanded, extending a paw.

Alador dipped his hand in the water of the container and gave the egg a reassuring pat, then withdrew it and held it up to the dragoness. It was the last piece of Rena and no matter what it was… he wanted to keep it alive.

Pruatra took the egg in her talons and carefully sniffed it. "It is alive. I do not know of this ever occurring. It could be…," her voice trailed off.

Alador looked up at her. Tears glistened in his eyes. "I know." Whether it would turn out to be dragon like

Rena, or by some twist human like him, he had grown to love it. He realized in leaving it in the care of this dragon, that he hoped and prayed it would survive and be something he and Nemara could love.

Pruatra took the egg and put it in the dry nest. She swiftly manifested water around it and then set to warming it. "It will be a girl, it has been too cold."

Alador smiled to himself. He had instinctively known this, but it was nice to have confirmation. His keeping the water cooler had kept the gender female.

"I want to help raise it…" Alador began.

"Indeed you shall." The huge female glared down her muzzle at him. "It is your hatchling and therefore as Rena is gone, your responsibility." Pruatra lowered her head to bring her muzzle nose-to-nose with him. "Assuming it remains viable... I have no idea what will come from this egg."

He put a hand to her muzzle. "Please Pruatra, if it can be saved, save it."

"I will do this, but not for you." She eyed him coldly. "I will do it for Rena."

Alador let out a heavy sigh. He had not realized how much he had been holding in for fear she would reject his plea.

"Thank you Pruatra. I wanted to warn you too, and have you spread the word, that the black dragon flight is out and sailing the skies along the coast to the north and south of Silverport for many leagues."

The dragon curled back her lips in disgust and

hissed. "What brings their kind from their hiding place at the temple?"

"We had a large storm that killed people and unroofed many homes. They are helping to collect the dead and assist with the passage of many souls to their chosen gods."

"Indeed…" Pruatra hmphed. "The storm has taken its toll across the land. Many dragons and Daezun villages fared much the same." She shook her wedged head.

"Daezun villages?" Alador said in surprise. "I saw the tornadoes spin off from it, but I thought they would dissipate before they got very far inland. They crossed the whole Great Isle?" Alador had not considered how far inland the storm would go.

"What do you care? You will make another in the year to come." Her disapproval was dripping from her words.

"Wait… What? What do you mean I will make another?" Alador was stunned by this accusation.

"You did not think you could change the weather for a full turn and not pay the price of interfering with the natural order of the seasons?" Pruatra eyed him as if he were a small one. "By the gods, you did," she gasped sadly. Why had she let him learn the way of the air stones?

"I… just… I thought the cost was to me. The power I used. The spell I cast?" Alador was stammering. "R-rena never said a word about causing some later storm."

Pruatra shook her great head. "I was as much a fool as you are now. I should have seen what you were attempting. Rena was in love, and I knew it! She was helping you do something that had never been done before, because she wanted so desperately to please you. How could such a young dragon possibly know how big a mess you were capable of creating once you were let loose? Foolish dragoness, putting faith in a mortal."

Alador was horrified. He had never considered that casting Luthian's spell would cost the isle as a whole. Luthian had to know. He was the reigning mage. How could he have not known? It did explain his calmness in the face of it; Alador realized that Luthian had been expecting this outcome, or something very similar to it. He had been so casual. Had his plot upon the trench gone all the way back to when he had Alador start casting the spell? Was there some way Luthian knew that the wave would come, or had he just adapted his plans once he knew the magnitude of the storm? Anger flushed through the young mage.

"It is never a good moment when one realizes they have been manipulated to do great harm." Pruatra's tone became more of one teaching. "You must remember that magic always has a cost. Most of the time, it is small, but sometimes, it is so great that even death of the mage has occurred.

"Why mages and not dragons?" Alador asked - his words terse. He honestly thought the reason he could channel so much magic and not be harmed, was because he possessed Renamaum's essence.

"Dragons are connected to the spiritual plane. We can walk with gods if we choose, though the gods frown upon it except at the time the fledglings pass into adulthood. Then the fledgling is brought before them to receive their magic and their blessings," Pruatra explained. "Mortals are earthbound. They live, they die, and nothing is left of them once they pass."

Alador could have taken issue with this statement. Mortals did not leave magic behind in their bloodstones, but they did leave their children and perhaps a hoard, though small by dragon standards. Personally, Alador hoped to leave behind whatever was in that egg as his legacy. That brought his mind back around to his family.

"Do you know if my home village of Smallbrook was hit?" He realized in spite of everything he had done to protect his village and his family, they might have been harmed by his spell.

"You should go and see. I stayed within and have not left the sea but a few times." Pruatra's nostrils flared. "I will care for the egg." She leaned down and rolled it over gently in its watery nest. "Go find your kin, but be sure to check back with me regularly, or you will not meet a warm welcome when you arrive again."

"How long until it hatches?" He glanced at the blue egg. Its silver edges glimmered with the water's magnification.

"It will be some time. I do not know exactly, as I do not know when it was laid or how your mortality will affect it." She nuzzled the egg again.

"I will check back." He leaned over and placed a hand on the shell. "It seems to like getting out of its nest," he warned. "Though, your nest looks a bit more restraining than the one I built."

Pruatra turned one large eye to look at him. "That is a good sign. It seeks. Now go," she commanded. "And if you are diligent in your paternal duties you will find a warm welcome here, or at least as warm as my watery cave allows."

Alador nodded and slipped back into the depths. He had to see his family and make sure his village was all right. He did not want to believe he was the cause, as Pruatra stated. How could he live with himself knowing he was responsible for all the death and destruction from the storm? He knew one thing… this was a secret he would never tell to Sordith.

## Chapter Twenty-Three

Alador appeared in the coal room of his mother's house. Alarm filled him as he carefully opened the door; the roof was gone off his mother's home. He could hear muffled voices in the distance. He carefully moved into the house itself. Debris lay everywhere. He was horrified, knowing that this destruction was his own fault. He had worked so hard to negotiate so Smallbrook would be spared all this, and in the end it had not mattered.

The outer walls seemed to have held, but pieces of the second level were totally missing. His mother was crying at the table as he moved slowly down the hall, careful that no one outside the family would know he was there. . He checked but did not see anyone except Tentret, Dorien and his mother, so he quietly stepped into view.

Dorien was the first to see him. He rose from the bench where he had been comforting their mother.

"Did your storm mage do this?" His anger was unrestrained and Alador took a step back.

How was he going to handle this? He could not tell anyone this was the result of his magic… his doing… his fault.

"It is not my storm mage, brother, it is Luthian's; but yes, this is the work of the storm mage." Alador watched his brother closely. He could not misstep here. "Is ours the only damaged?"

"Far from it," his brother snorted. "The village is in total disarray, with most homes and buildings in similar condition. The smithy seems to be the only one that made it through untouched - too much metal holding things down there." Dorien's fists were clenched and his face did not hide his anger.

Alador never wanted to hurt anyone, and he knew that the blizzard that he had created caused hardships for the Daezun. He would not be easily forgiven if they found out. The guilt he felt kept him sobered as he looked about. His mother's kitchen, her pride and joy, was all but destroyed.

"The storm struck Silverport as well. It did a massive amount of damage to the city and its people." Alador's vision swam with the memories of those that had died. The bodies and wanton destruction strewn about him in the city. Pruatra's revelation that he was the cause of all that, and this, was just starting to sink in. He struggled to find his voice again.

"Why would Luthian's storm mage create a storm that hurt his own city?" Dorien looked puzzled.

"It was a backlash from the storm created last winter," he confessed, though he did not take it so far as to say it was his fault. "Was anyone in the village hurt?" His tone was pleading. Inwardly, he pushed down the guilt of his actions. The look on Dorien's face sent a bolt of fear through Alador.

"There were several injuries and there is one still missing," The reply was measured and softly spoken. Dorien's reaction had changed at the mention of the injured. He moved around the table to stand in front of his mage brother.

"Who?" Alador's heart sank as he worried who it might be. His sister was not here. Could that be the reason for his mother's tears, rather than the state of her home? Questions rapidly fired in his mind as he waited for Dorien's response.

Dorien put a hand on his brother's arm. "No one has been able to find Mesiande since the storm hit the village. We have looked everywhere. There is no sign. I am so sorry, brother. I know she was dear to you."

Alador's mind went numb at the realization that Mesiande was gone. He could barely process the thought.

"She's… gone?" He looked up into Dorien's gaze, searching for something – an indication there was still hope. Some area they had not searched. There was none.

He forced his mind to focus and push aside all the memories that flew through it. He could not deal with this loss now. He would find her body and lay it to rest later. He promised himself that.

However, seeing this destruction, knowing what he knew now about the storm and his involvement in it, crystallized his desire to overthrow Luthian. Now was the time – not later! He needed to make sure he could rally the Daezun to his cause. What better fuel to use than the damage done here by the High Minister's Storm Mage?

His eyes filled with tears, but he wiped them away as the anger and his determination built. Luthian would never, ever, force him to create another storm. He would never force him to do *anything* again. "I need to discuss something with you, brother."

"It might have to wait," Dorien answered. "If you cannot see it, I am a bit busy right now." He waved his hands about, indicating the chaos around them.

"It is of utmost importance," Alador pressed.

The look on his younger brother's face gave the older man pause. Dorien looked about, searching to be sure there were no peering eyes through what was left of the windows. "Speak."

Alador cleared his throat, forcing the last bit of guilt from his thoughts. "We need to mobilize the Daezun people to help tear down Luthian from power. Nothing like this and the destruction of the lower tiers at Silverport must ever happen again."

"You want us to go to war? We cannot attack this despot." Dorien ran a hand through his hair. "How do you expect me to convince the elders of all the Daezun that war is the best course at a time like this? The village is rubble!" Dorien's eyes squinted at the thought. His disbelief was mirrored on Tentret and his mother's faces.

"It must be done now. You are respected among the Daezun. You must convince them that if they don't, war will find them first and crush all without question." Alador's tone was now one of business.

He knew what Luthian planned to do. The High Minister no longer hid his hatred toward the Daezun people. Power was what he craved, and having any group of people not following his dictates was never going to allow him complete control of the isle.

Alanis had stopped crying and sat watching her sons speak of death and war. Tentret had gotten out paper and was drawing the two men who now stood an arm's length away from each other. If Dorien agreed, it was going to be a moment of history.

"Luthian is preparing to strike against the Daezun people and enslave anyone that gets in his way." Alador's mother made a sound of alarm, and when he glanced at her, he saw her hands covering her mouth. The fear on his mother's face said all that needed to be said.

Dorien stared at him, trying to comprehend the immensity of what his brother was saying. "Enslave? There have never been slaves on the isle!"

"I know, but that will not stop Luthian," Alador said with conviction.

"He will not be alone, brother," Dorien reasoned. "His fellow mages will follow him. What can we do against people of their kind?"

"We can fight alongside dragons," Alador announced.

"We have not called upon the pact between dragon and Daezun since the Great War. I am not sure the dragons will even honor it!" Dorien began to pace in front of Alador. "If I go to the elders with this, I am going to need a dragon willing to stand at my side." The door scraped open, askew from a loose hinge. Henrick stepped into the room and carefully replaced the door. He needed to lift it to make it close.

"That can be arranged." Henrick was filthy. He must have been out helping search or cleaning up.

Alador could not help but smile; it was so good to see his father. It was a rare sight these days. He missed him, and his wise counsel in dealing with Luthian. Alador advanced and pulled his father into a rough hug.

Henrick patted his son's back, but then slipped free. "It seems I have come at an opportune time. I have been dealing with the consequences of magic for hours and thought my sweet love might feed me." Henrick looked at Alanis, his affection clear upon his face. "Please continue."

Alanis jumped up and began to find food that had been tossed around the room by the storm, but remained edible. The plate began to fill with bread, fruit and cheese. Dorien looked between the two men, his anxiety clear. He lowered his voice.

"So how do you provide a dragon?" Dorien asked with genuine interest.

Alador looked to Henrick. Henrick nodded – it was time

"Dorien, technically, you have been speaking to dragons." Alador crossed his arms. He scowled at Henrick when Alanis placed a tray in front of his father and the impossible man began to wolf down the bread, making it impossible for him to add to the conversation or help explain.

Dorien pulled a chair over and sank into it beside his brother and Henrick. He needed the support for his legs, which had weakened as all this had been piled upon him. "What do you mean technically?" Dorien now looked genuinely overwhelmed.

"Well, I'm what is called a pseudo-dragon these days and Henrick... well... he's... "Alador waved his hand toward Henrick, as the statement continued to hang in the air. Henrick, who had a mouthful of bread, continued to chew. "...Father, please."

Henrick swallowed, cleared his throat and said, "I know you will find this difficult to believe, but I am a red dragon. I chose this form to train Alador for what was to come. My dragon kin believe him to be the 'Dragonsworn.'"

Dorien's gaze shifted from man to man in disbelief. Tentret was making sounds of awe, and the men all turned when Alanis dropped a bowl. Henrick beat Alador to his mother's side.

"Don't be alarmed, my dear. Our love is real." He pulled Alanis into his arms to reassure her.

"He speaks the truth maman." Alador stated, as he stopped just short of his mother. His outstretched arm fell to his side as he looked about the room at the others gathered here. "The man formerly known as Henrick was an evil person. He was my father, but he was replaced shortly after my birth by the Henrick we know and grew up with - this red dragon." He knew the shock of this would take some time to sink in. He knew he had needed time to absorb it, but at least they knew the truth now.

"I will stand, in my dragon form, at your side when you meet with the village council, Dorien." Henrick announced.

Tentret had resumed frantically drawing. "I am not missing that, Dorien. I will stand with you so I can draw it later."

"We will need not only Smallbrook, but all the Daezun nation for this action," Alador insisted.

"That is a tall order, but with a dragon at my side…" Dorien stood and looked at Henrick. Alador could see his brother trying to picture the man they all knew as his father in dragon form. "The elders will honor my request since the winter was as bad as I predicted it would be based on your warning. Plus, the dragons did come dig refuges underground." He rubbed his chin as he began to pace. "Maybe it will be easier to convince them then I first thought." Dorien stopped his pacing. "Dragons, speaking at my side. Who would have thought it?"

"It's not as strange as you make it out to be, brother. Isn't that right, Henrick?" Alador's gaze settled onto Henrick as Dorien stopped pacing. His lips forming a bemused smile. "The dragons are only one part of the force, correct Henrick?"

"Don't ask me, lad. It is your plan and you have not told me the details of it." Henrick had led Alanis to the table and had her sit with him. He draped one arm over her protectively, shoving bread into his mouth with the other hand. "I can affirm the dragon's commitment to see the man unseated."

"Do you two just…have an open dialogue with the dragons?" Dorien looked at the two in amazement.

Both men answered together simultaneously, "Yes."

Finally looking over at Dorien, Alador spoke to

him again. "I need an answer, a confident answer to all this, Dorien. Will you help?"

"You just told me you're half a dragon... My mother's lover is a dragon in disguise... That people mean to enslave us... That dragons will help us." Dorien looked at him, his confident tone gone. "It is a bit much to take in all at once."

"The world rarely allows for you to take it much slower," Alador replied. "But moving before Luthian does will save us all, dragon and Daezun alike. We need to do that."

Henrick looked up from where he had been whispering to Alanis. "As much as I hate to say so, the boy is right. I will speak with the Dragon Council as soon as we have spoken with your village elders."

Dorien slowly stood up. "The People will honor the pact that was made by the gods to partner with the dragons and keep them safe. On this, you have my word." He moved to Alador. "When and how do you want us to support the removal of this tyrant?"

"As quickly as the Daezun can muster forces; it should be soon before he can bring war down upon you. I am hoping for a month. Will that be enough time to muster and get the army to Silverport?"

"It will be if we use the gift the gods gave us during the Great War. We can travel to the very gates of the city without the High Minister knowing we are there." Dorien stated confidently. He laughed at the questioning look on Alador's face. "You didn't stay here long enough as an adult, brother. There were further secrets to learn than how to bed a woman properly."

## Chapter Twenty-Four

Levielle fastened the last clasp of his armor with a sense of satisfaction, the worn leather strap folding into place as though it had a memory of its own. While many of his station might prefer regal, shining armor, and in fact he did have a formal set on display in his home, he vastly preferred his plate and chain. He felt that his deceptively simple day-to-day armor made him more approachable to the average soldier; although finely made, its obvious wear clearly showed that he was a commander who led from the thick of battle.

With one final shake to settle everything, he swirled his regal blue cape about his shoulders with satisfaction; now there was one piece of ornamentation he *did* enjoy! Still chuckling, he stepped outside into the bright day.

His ears were immediately assaulted by the noise of the camp and the repair work being done all over the city; between the two he could barely hear the crunch of his boots against the gravel as he strode toward the tent where his command was housed. Men saluted smartly as he moved past them, but he merely waved them down and continued on his way. Finally, making his way to the center of camp, he entered the tent.

The table at the center was a large rectangle, built more for function than form, surrounded by a few chairs. Side tables covered in wine goblets, half eaten food, scrolls, and parchment lying about cluttered the periphery of the tent. He smiled and gave a soft sigh; it was good to be in a more simple place.

"Good to be back," he muttered quietly to himself.

"Hello?" A voice called out from behind a fabric wall. A man stepped out and immediately saluted upon seeing who was in the tent. "Sir! I apologize, I was not expecting…"

Levielle waved at the man. "Save it, corporal, I did not give notice. I have orders to give and not a lot of time to do it." His tone was gruff; with tensions in the city rising, it would be good to get away again. He looked forward equally to not being drenched in the politics and to not waxing the behinds of those that saw themselves as the powerful.

"Yes, sir. What orders to you have for your men?" The corporal relaxed a bit, his uniform ruffled and dirty, Levielle assumed from assisting in the relief effort of the city. While Levielle always had a great appreciation of keeping a camp, and by extension the men, groomed and well-cared for, this was anything but a normal campaign.

Moving to the table, he unfurled a nearby large piece of parchment. The map of the island was drawn in relatively good detail. The Daezun villages and settlements dotted the center of the isle and coasts. Taking some weights and placing them on corners of the map, he looked up to the other man.

"Get the commanders in here, we'll need to discuss a plan of action in order to move forward with the relief effort." Levielle remained hunched over the table, supporting himself by his outstretched arms.

"Sir, with all due respect, the city has a relief effort underway from the Blackguard and citizens within."

"Yes, but the rest of the affected cities and villages will not have fared so well. Gather the commanders, son."

With a quick nod, the man was off. Levielle hung his head down and shook it slowly. He knew the meeting was going to be one of resistance and distress The men had just finished helping those that remained and mourning those lost. Moving them would not be the most popular task, but he knew it was not only the only way to keep Luthian from taking his head, but also about making sure the people outside the city knew that someone had their best interests at heart.

===\*\*\*===

A meaty fist fell upon the table as wine goblets flew aside, along with a small plate of cheese. The clatter caused some of the servants to startle; the yelling that came next had them running for cover.

"This is nothing but a political farce, General!" the man's voice thundered.

Many moved back from the man in question. Levielle stood at the end of the table, his back turned away from the group sitting there as he studied a map of the coast that hung on the wall. His hands were behind his back as he turned with a sigh.

He had expected this reaction from some of the men; none would really want to leave their families and homes when they were in need.

"I understand, Colonel... Really I do..." Levielle spoke softly, he was not about to raise his voice to assert his position. They knew the ranking well, and he had earned his. "The High Minister sees this as a way to get the vote of confidence from the people outside the city. Anyone with his rank is not going to let a good crisis go to waste."

"I'm not some dog he can whip to go where he pleases! We're just going to be helping the enemy anyway!" The shouts from the colonel were not easily masked by the tent at large. Levielle knew the men immediately outside would be discussing what they could hear through the thin tent wall, and word traveled fast in the camp.

"We are going to help our own and just our own. Now..." Levielle took a step toward the table and leaned onto it, his arms straightened, "...keep your voice down, colonel, or you'll be the dog I'm whipping around." His voice was lowered and the tone let the man know he had stepped too far.

Looking around and realizing he was the center of attention and all eyes were on him, the colonel shrank back into his seat.

"Apologies, General." he muttered quietly under his breath.

Levielle finally relaxed. He knew all these men were on edge from the recent storm, as well as the relief effort that was underway in the city. They were tired and worn, but asking a bit more was not going to kill them. At least it was not war out there.

"I want the men ready to march by the end of tomorrow. We leave at first light the following morning. We will make our way down the coastline, stopping at the few villages and trading posts along the way." He moved back to the map, giving a small pause before pointing to the known villages. "We can hit these few before seeing how Clavenport handled the edge of the storm. Make sure your divisions bring tools and wood for repair; send some into the forest to fell trees for lumber if you have to." He turned back to the men, none of whom looked particularly eager to take on the task. Levielle sighed. "I know this isn't the job you all wanted to do. Frankly, I'd like to get out there and do some fighting, or anything other than being the High Minister's latest political champion."

A few chuckles came out of that statement. He was turning them around a little, and while he could command them to go march off the edge of the world, a disgruntled force was the last thing he wanted.

"Let the men know that the High Minister has promised double pay when we get back. He's been pleased with the work the men have done to take care of the city, not to mention the extra mile being taken here to assist with the villages in need." Levielle smiled and turned to lean on the table once again.

The men straightened at this announcement. Double pay would go very nicely for extra goods, or extra time at the brothel for the army. Inwardly he sighed; the fact he had made that promise put Luthian in an interesting place. He had promised to pay them extra, though; Levielle was only taking liberties with how much.

"I expect reports by mid-morning telling me how we are progressing on preparations." Levielle took up a goblet and raised it briefly before taking a sip. "Dismissed."

===***===

Levielle found his way to his tent, heaving a heavy sigh before sitting down on the edge of his bed. While a nice quality, he never enjoyed the lavish accommodations that some generals enjoyed. Unbuckling his armor quickly, he draped it over the mannequin that held it. He sat back down to take off his boots, enjoying the freedom his feet felt being let loose from their leather prison.

Flopping backward, he watched the dancing shadows cast from a nearby torch. The sound of men moving, working, singing, laughing all filled his tent as his eyes finally closed.

Hopefully, Nakyra was safe - away from the greasy clutches of Luthian. He had planned her departure meticulously. The lexital had been rented under one of his lieutenant's names, heading to a vacation spot they enjoyed and hoped to retire to one day. She would be comfortable reading and being in the forest until it was safe for her to join him. A smile crept over his face at the idea of retiring at such a location. His last thoughts before sleep hovered around Alador, hoping the boy played his hand well. Otherwise his retirement was going to be much more bloody than he desired.

## Chapter Twenty-Five

Jon looked up when he heard the soft footsteps. He had known she was coming; Nightmare bristled far before Jon could hear her. It gave him time to prepare himself for what he must do next. He would take no pleasure in it, and yet, he knew it was the only way he could accomplish his own ends.

"I have come to check on your progress, Praetor."

Lady Morana's attire was reserved. She often wore simple black robes while in the temple. Still... they hugged her figure in a way that made you very aware of her beauty.

Jon simply nodded. "He is growing quickly and is very smart."

The black dragon was now the size of a full flight lexital and able to fully understand Jon, though he still took what the human said literally and asked repeatedly 'why.'

Nightmare puffed himself up with pride, and ruffled his wings, showing off for the High Priestess.

Morana nodded. "How are his hunting skills coming along?" She moved to Nightmare and held out her hand. The dragon slowly lowered his head until the top of his muzzle was against it.

Jon frowned when she touched Nightmare. The dragon was too young to understand the woman's motives, but he had to allow this light bonding between them or risk losing his position. He moved to stand next to the High Priestess. "I no longer have to feed him. He gets only treats for training." The young dragon had been feeding himself for some time now, and seemed to be growing by leaps and bounds because of it.

"He is truly beautiful," she murmured as she ran her hand up between the dragon's eyes, bringing a rumble from the black's chest.

"You are well matched." It was all Jon could do to keep the contempt out of his voice.

It was not a lie, unfortunately. The High Priestess's raven-black hair shone every bit as much as Nightmare's polished scales. Her lined eyes seemed large like the dragon's, as well.

Morana smiled and looked over at Jon. "I have to wonder if your admiration is more for the dragon than the woman."

Jon allowed a slight smile to curve his lips. "Cannot a man admire both?" He reached up and stroked Nightmare's neck. His touch generated a deeper rumbling response from the young dragon and put him very close to the priestess. "May I be frank, Lady Morana?"

"You may." She turned slightly to face him.

Jon took a breath to prepare himself. "You are not admired as much as you could and should be. Why do you dance on the strings of the leaders of the Great Isle when you could lead it all? You are smart, beautiful, and so talented in magic." Jon dropped his hand from the dragon and dared to take the priestess' hand in his own.

"You are the chosen of our Goddess. You should be revered and loved." He watched her eyes closely, seeing the pupils dilate as he hoped.

Morana did not pull her hand away as she looked up at the slightly taller mage. "What would you do differently, Praetor?"

Jon felt no threat here, and his dragon remained calm between them. He boldly pushed some hair back from her eyes. When she did not admonish him, he leaned forward and kissed her with all the tenderness he could muster. When she returned the kiss, he smiled within; some people were so predictable.

He pulled away with a soft smile on his face, mostly because it had not been as revolting as he thought it might be. He had never lain with a woman, finding their games unappealing, but now he needed to play his hand. He was not just seeking to help Alador protect all the dragons, he also coveted the High Priestess' position.

Her eyes remained closed for a moment. "I see." She opened them and surveyed him and the dragon. "Perhaps you should have dinner with me tonight. We can discuss matters of the temple, and then you can show me how much reverence you really have."

"I would be delighted." He released her hand to stroke Nightmare's head. "I am sure the dragon can find other amusements for the evening."

"No," she said as she reached up to pet the dragon again, her fingers gently brushing past Jon's. "Bring Nightmare. I have prepared a treat for him; it is time he was introduced to the taste of mortal flesh. You will meet me in the prayer circle in half an hourglass." She looked at the dragon. "Does he not speak?"

"I believe he is overcome by your presence." Jon said stalling for time to think.

Morana reached up and stroked the dragon again.

Jon was not ready for this… Nightmare was not ready for this… And, he knew this was more than a treat for the dragon, this was a test.

"Are you sure he is not too young?" he asked hoping for a reprieve.

"He is of the size all others have been prior to tasting the sweetness of mortal flesh." She eyed him. "Is there some reason you want to avoid this, Praetor? The suggestion that the Black flight feast on the dead was yours. Do you not remember?"

She seemed almost to taunt him. Her voice held an edge that Jon knew well. He dared not refuse her.

"No, I just don't want him to like it and eat me. He is still young and might not discern the difference between living and dead." Jon looked at Nightmare. The dragon was unusually silent. He softened his voice at the end with affection. It was the last emotion he felt like displaying. "We will be there, my lady."

Morana nodded and turned, her robes sweeping the area clean as they spun about her. The two, dragon and man, watched until she was out of sight, neither speaking. When she turned the corner below them, Nightmare swung his wedged head so one bright eye could gaze into Jon's.

"What is a mortal?

"I am a mortal. She means people, like me." Jon was tense. He had never wanted to have this conversation with the youngling. He had purposely kept the dragon away from the others while they fed on the pieces of the dead from the storm.

"I thought you said dragons are supposed to protect the ones like you." Nightmare's confusion was visible, his individual scales were more prominent, unlike his former slick appearance of contentment under Lady Morana and Jon's attention.

"I did." Jon took a deep breath and hoped that Nightmare was old enough to understand this. "Sometimes... sometimes you must do something wrong for the greater good. I have not yet earned a position that would entitle me to the mantle of High Priest. We are going to have to do this. You are going to have to eat mortal flesh."

"Why?" The dragon's favorite question lay between them.

"She will kill us both if you do not," Jon explained.

"So, our lives are more important than this mortal?" Nightmare twisted his head upside down to look Jon over.

"You won't be killing anyone. You will be eating those killed by the storm."

The young dragon's long neck arched back and his lip curled up in disgust. "Like those dropped in the courtyard?"

"Exactly," Jon confirmed.

The dragon began to sway his massive head back and forth. "Nope… No… They smell revolting."

"If you don't, she will kill us. We must think of our preservation first. We cannot protect if we are dead." Jon laid a hand beneath the dragon's jaw, pulling his head down. "I need you to do this."

"What if they taste as bad as they smell?" The dragon grimaced, making him more terrifying to look at.

"Try not to chew much and just choke it down." Jon hoped they tasted bad to Nightmare. He would be less likely to look for more.

"I will do this for you." The dragon conceded. "It is not pleasing."

"No," Jon admitted. "It is not pleasing to me either. I will meet you at the path below."

He patted Nightmare on the shoulder as the dragon passed him to leap from the cave opening. His wings sprung apart a little late making it more of a fall to flight then a lift.



Jon strode into the clearing, his robes as black as the dragons mingling and growling about them. His stride was confident. He took note of the circle of dragons before he approached Morana.

"Where is Nightmare, Jon?" Morana demanded.

"I sent him flying before I came down from the caves. I am sure he just got distracted. He is very young after all." The priest put his hands behind him. He appeared far more relaxed than he was on the inside. He was not sure that the violation of what he had been teaching the young dragon would not override their last conversation.

"If he does not answer my call, his loyalty is in question." Morana nuzzled another young dragon beside her and turned to look at the priest.

Jon just shrugged as if unconcerned. The priestess slowly turned, calling a strange word. The dragons made a circle around the two of them. Nightmare glided in, followed closely by a very young dragon, not even fully winged. Jon's dragon landed, but the young one bumbled in out of the air and collapsed unceremoniously on the ground not far from the group. Nightmare nuzzled the fledgling affectionately and they both lumbered over to the priestess.

"It is time, Jon." Morana said firmly. "If he does not obey my command, I will have him put down."

"What would you have him do?" Jon asked in a formal way. "He is still very young. You will need to make your intention clear," Jon stated in as drab a voice as he could command. He tried to appear bored with what would soon take place before him.

"Aniata, bring the treat," Morana commanded.

A young woman dressed in the red robes of an acolyte appeared from around the bushes. Jon watched as she eyed the dragons while moving around them pushing a large cart filled with dismembered body parts of the dead. She was accompanied by a huge hound with an ebony coat. It seemed to herd her forward.

She was fearful, as she should have been. The other dragons had already acquired a taste for the dead. They eyed her cart and their long purple tongues licked their lips. Some leaned in to sniff, and drool fell from their giant maws as they hungered to relieve her of her burden. Her feet appeared weighed down as she moved slowly to Morana and knelt, her eyes to the ground.

"Milady…" Her soft voice was barely audible. The dog sat down beside Morana.

"Aniata… rise." Morana demanded.

Aniata moved to stand and as she did so she gave the dog a worried look.

Morana's eyes followed the young woman's to the dog. "Oh yes, you have done well Vicktor. You may go." The dog transformed into an old man before Jon's eyes.

He had not known this was possible. What kind of Black Arts was this? The priestess obviously commanded minions beyond the scope of her death mage members. Or, could this be a death mage with spells beyond his knowledge? The man was clothed in the black robes of his sphere when he turned from dog to man.

"I live to serve, milady," Vicktor answered. The man bowed low and left them.

Aniata's gaze followed the old man's departure. Only when he left the clearing did she look slowly back to Morana.

"Now to business. Push the cart forward to Nightmare." The priestess commanded.

This was the test. Jon silently prayed that his young dragon would eat, and also stop before he thought to eat the girl. Nightmare must show restraint, but also obedience.

The other dragons in the flight who were present fell back away from Nightmare. Aniata slowly advanced on the young dragon pushing her cart of rotting appendages, the blood oozing through the bottom to leave a trail across the stones of the prayer circle.

When she halted, Nightmare dipped his head toward the cart. Jon could hear the intake of breath and he caught the dragon's eye as it lifted its lips to snarl at the offering. He shook his head in warning.

To his credit, Nightmare opened his huge maw and buried his face in the cart. When he came up, he had an arm and a foot sticking out of his mouth. He tilted back his head and like a large bird eating a fish that is too big, he literally swallowed the mouth full in two large gulps.

Jon smiled encouragement. The dragon's scales had taken on an unusual texture. They honestly looked like they were raising from his body like hackles on a dog.

Nightmare continued to lower his head, fill his huge jaws and tilt back to swallow. He was taking Jon's instructions seriously and not chewing more than he had to.

Jon hid the disgust he felt at what was done here. He needed Morana to believe that he was as callous and cold as she was. Nightmare was efficient and had the cart empty in four large mouthfuls.

Aniata stood shivering in front of the young dragon when he was finished. Lady Morana let her stand there for several minutes to test the dragon's resolve. When Nightmare made no move against the acolyte the priestess waved her away.

"You may go, Aniata," she said, with what Jon thought was a bit of disappointment in her voice.

The young girl turned and left as swiftly as she could push the cart without turning it over.

"May I see to Nightmare before I join you for dinner?" Jon asked Morana. "I would like to make sure he is clean before returning to our cave." He looked toward the dragon. The beast's muzzle and chest were dripping in blood and he stank of the dead.

"Of course, but hurry. I wouldn't want to delay dinner long." Morana dismissed the other dragons with a wave of her hand, and turning, headed for her quarters.

Jon patted Nightmare's shoulder to get him moving. His hand came away sticky with blood. When the dragon threw back his head each time, the blood had dripped from his maw onto his long neck and shoulders.

"Come," he commanded.

The dragon followed him out of the prayer circle back toward the dragon area and the pool where Jon and he often spent time quietly talking. They had a hidden spot on the backside of the pool in a grove of aspen trees, and he led the dragon to it.

The moment they were out of sight and sound of the other members of the black flight, Nightmare halted and, sides heaving, vomited up the contents of his stomach. Jon barely had time to move to one side.

He looked at the mess and scratched his head. They would have to bury it somewhere it would never be found.

"You said I had to eat it," Nightmare declared, his scales starting to smooth out. "You didn't say I had to keep it down."

## Chapter Twenty-Six

Levielle braced his hands on the table in front of him in the command center. He was studying a map of the area indicating the locations of the surrounding villages along the coast.

"FIRE!" someone hollered off in the distance.

He immediately moved to the tent flap, flipped it back and stepped out. He scanned the camp. Off in the distance he could see that a tent, maybe two, were in flames. Most likely sparks from one of the camp's cookfires. He turned to his guards.

"Nolin... Edard... go check that out and report back to me as soon as it is extinguished and the damage is assessed."

The guards nodded and trotted off toward the fire.

Levielle watched for a few minutes longer, his hands on his hips. Men were already setting up a bucket-line from the nearby stream to the tents. Confident that the fire would not spread throughout the camp, the general ducked his head and went back into his tent.

What he found there shocked and surprised him. The intruders had come in through a slit in the tents back wall. There were three in all. Dressed in black, masked and all armed.

Levielle instinctively pulled his sword with one hand and his dagger with the other. His first thought was to back out, but as he took a step backward, he heard the rustle of the tent flap as someone entered behind him. He turned just in time to raise his sword and prevent the fourth man from decapitating him. He struggled and threw the lighter built man back away from him. The man fell against the table hitting his head and collapsed unconscious to the floor.

Levielle crossed swords with another who moved forward. They were all thrusting and forcing him into the middle of their circle. He parried and sliced at his assailants. They returned his strikes with counter thrusts. The three worried him like a pack of dogs cornering a lone cat. The man behind him sliced and he felt excruciating pain as the blade passed through his tunic and found the flesh of his lower back.

Hollering for help was not an option with the commotion from the fire. No doubt that was exactly what these devils had planned all along. The one he was facing lunged toward him and managed to nick his sword arm. The man behind him continued to feint in and out. If the general was not careful, the man would hamstring him and he would go down only to have his head lopped off by one of the other assassins. They continued to circle him trying to find an opening.

Levielle took a deep breath. He had not been in a situation this dire since his testing so many years ago. As he did then, he pulled on the inner power that few knew about, and none remembered he possessed.

He waited for the three to fall back to circle him again. He dropped his weapons. There was no use for them now. He thrust his palms together and hissing out an incantation he had not used in decades. He forced his hands apart. A glistening ebony orb appeared and before his attackers could even take another breath, he brought his hands back together with force. The clap was ear splitting and the power burst through the room lifting the tent to flutter a moment, only held down by its stakes. The men encircling him exploded into a black dust that dissipated on the wind, created by his power, like dandelion fluff on a summer breeze.

Levielle looked quickly around. The first man he struck still lay on the floor by the table. The release of the general's power had not been aimed at him. In fact, the commander purposely left him unharmed so he might question him.

He pulled a rope lose that held back the flaps separating the sleeping area of the tent from the meeting area and went to tie the man before he awoke.

He started to pull the man to his feet and secure him in the closest chair, instead the man rolled away from him and threw up a hand flinging a fountain of fire at the general.

Levielle reacted instinctively. He foiled the man by throwing up a protective shield. The fire snuffed out, back to the attacker's hand.

"Underestimating your mark, that's going to be seen poorly by your employer." Levielle tsked as his sword instantly appeared in his hand and came up under the man's chin. "Keep your hands where I can see them."

He indicated the chair with a nod of his head. The

man stood up and went to sit. Levielle raised his sword and deftly slit the cord which held the mask to the man's face. It fell away. The general's eye widened in surprise when he discovered the man was not a man, but a woman, perhaps forty turns old.

"Well played," the woman complimented in a voice that told him she knew her attack had earned her execution.

Levielle could not take his eyes from her. He could have sworn he knew her. No... Not really her, perhaps her mother, or her aunt, because the woman looked exactly like his dear friend Lady Aldemar when he met her so many years ago in her youth.

Levielle finally found his voice. "You learn a trick or two as you work your way up the ranks." Levielle shrugged, almost casually, but he did not let down his guard. "Who are you?"

"I am afraid I cannot answer that question, milord." She bowed her head.

"Guards, attend me." Levielle's voice boomed, his eyes never leaving the woman. He hoped the guards had returned.

They rushed in at his call and looked absolutely, startled at the woman standing at the end of Levielle's sword.

"Watch her," he ordered his guards. "She is of the Fire Sphere so do not let her hands leave her sides."

He stepped to the trunk at the end of his bed and withdrew a pair of gloves. These were specially made to prevent the casting of spells by mages. He tossed the gloves to the nearest guard. "Glove her. Then tie her to that post." He indicated the main post of his tent.

The guardsman did not treat her gently. Though they did not see the remains of the other assailants, they could see the tipped furniture and the numerous swords on the carpeted tent floor. They had no tolerance for anyone assaulting their commander, woman or not. They searched her for further weapons and when they raised her sleeves to check for hidden daggers, Levielle saw the Death Rune on her forearm.

He walked over and examined it closer as the guardsmen slipped the gloves on her and secured her to the post. His men turned for further instructions. They were ready to assist in the questioning of the intruder.

"Leave us. Gather four more men and post them in a perimeter around this tent. I do not want to be disturbed"

Levielle still had not broken his hardened gaze from her.

The guards reluctantly left. They would have liked to stay for the questioning, but they would not disobey their commander's orders.

Once the tent flap closed behind the guards, Levielle turned back on the young woman. "There is no use in your staying quiet. I have a pretty good idea of who sent you. Tell me your name and confirm your employer. Perhaps I will be able to find you a place in a dungeon rather than death at the end of a rope."

"The confession of my name means nothing now.

Trust me, General, you could not do anything to me that would outweigh what my employer will do when he finds out we have failed," the young woman answered matter-of-factually. "I am called Ruby."

Her name was appropriate. She glared at him through ruby eyes. Her hair had come lose as the guardsmen searched and tied her, now its chestnut mass nearly fell to her waist.

"Speak his name. Tell me who sent you." The general requested.

"I do not think Severent Payne anticipated this outcome," she smiled at him.

It was hard for him to concentrate when her voice, her hair… so many things reminded him of Lady Aldemar's.

"Severent?" He asked.

"The one who sent me," she confessed. "I do not know who employs him."

"I do…" Levielle squinted his eyes in anger. It was the High Minister behind this attempt at his life.

"What proof do you need to bring back to prove my death?"

"Your hair," she stated.

"My hair, that's it?" He blinked, looking back at the youth. His features betrayed what he was thinking at that very moment. Disappointment. "And, if I just give you a portion of my hair to report back?"

"The master said that the mage could tell by the hair if you were truly alive or dead." She turned to look at him. Her ruby eyes were mesmerizing. "You would obviously not be dead."

He could not help himself, Levielle grinned. "Obviously not. We are at a bit of an impasse."

"We are. I am afraid failure was not an option for this assignment." She looked down at the rune on her arm. "I go back, I die. If I do not return the Death Rune flares and I die… That is provided you don't kill me first."

"What was your reward for a completed job?"

She sneered at him. "My reward was to live until the next assignment. I am part of Severent's death squad. I have been under his control since I can remember. My life is simple… I do as I am told or I die."

There were so many questions Levielle wanted to ask. Where did the young woman come from? How did she come to be under the control of Severent? Did she have any knowledge of Lady Aldemar? Was she related in any way? However, the first order of business was to get her free so she could answer those questions sometime in the future.

"How would you like to be free of that sentence? Hmm?" He asked searching her gaze. "I take some blood, maybe a bit of something from you, send it back to your master, and make a threat. You go free and live out your life." Levielle mused, watching her carefully for any shift in her actions or tone.

The woman stiffened. "Just kill me." She closed her eyes. "It will be easier for all of us. Severent has twenty more like me – slaves to his orders."

"You place me in a difficult position. You remind me of a friend and I would like to help you. I could have the rune removed and send a message that you are dead. Killed in the line of duty, we might say. That would be better for you, wouldn't you say?"

"You can't do that. The rune marks the soul." She still had her eyes closed in quiet desperation.

"I would hope not. Look at me, Ruby." His tone was commanding, but gentle at the same time. "Look at me." He waited until he could see her gaze. To look into her eyes and have her understand what truth he was holding deep inside. "I can do this for you."

She smiled for the first time, and she looks so much like his young love, Lady Aldemar. "I guess I have nothing to lose," she breathed out. "I never tried to cut it out because the master said it would be there imprinted on my very soul. I believed him," she admitted. "You will send it to him?" She actually looked a bit excited about that.

"Oh, I plan to Ruby. I plan to. Along with your clothing soaked in some blood." Levielle smiled at her excitement.

He watched her as he called out for the medic. When the man arrived, he asked, "How difficult would it be to remove the mark from her arm?" He indicated the rune.

"It is a tattoo, we would have to go down to a layer beneath the skin." The medic stated. "It will be painful."

Levielle looked at Ruby with a bit of a sullen gaze. "Well, it's better than dying. Give her something for the pain and remove the mark. Do not destroy it, deliver it to me along with her jacket. Soak it in her blood."

"Soak it in her blood, Sir?" The medic looked confused and a bit alarmed. He eyed the general attempting to verify he had heard right.

"From the arm wound," Levielle explained tossing his hand in the air with frustration at the man for not following his line of thinking. "If I'm going to tell someone I killed an assassin, I need to make it look believable." He picked up his dagger off the floor and slit the ropes that held her to the pole. "Take her," he ordered.

It was a half-hour glass later that the medic brought the piece of skin and the blood-soaked jacket. "She managed fairly well considering how deep we had to go to get the last traces of it. Fortunately, it did not penetrate the actual muscle." He held out the items the general had requested.

Giving a wide grin, Levielle looked up from his field desk that held his work on it. "Good… Thank you… You may place them on the table there." He motioned with a quill toward the nearby table. The medic did as he was told and left.

Levielle took a piece of parchment out...

He picked up the quill, dipped it in the inkwell, and began his letter…

*"High Minister…"*

*Chapter Twenty-Seven*

Alador reluctantly dragged himself up the tiers to attend Luthian. He was looking forward to his uncle's trip to check on the other cities affected by the storm. During his absence, Alador intended to complete the list of things he needed to push through for his plan to overthrow Luthian's rule.

He entered the office not bothering to hide his exhaustion. Every one of the Blackguard was pulling double duty to keep order and help with repairs. He looked at his uncle through a heavy-lidded gaze and noticed immediately that he was riled. This meant the younger mage was in for a bad day; his uncle often took such emotions out on those closest to him. He cringed as Luthian fixed a cold and angry look upon him.

"It is about time you got here. I sent for you over thirty minutes ago," he barked.

Alador did not bother to defend himself, snapping back "Some of us have been on the streets trying to help, not sitting in a gilded office making decisions based on reports."

"Watch your tongue, Alador, unless you wish it removed," Luthian snarled.

"Yes, can't live too dangerously these days," Alador smirked. "My abject apology, Uncle. May I ask what has you in such a pleasant mood this morning?" The young mage flopped down in a chair before his uncle's desk. He was too tired and too fed up to play games.

"General Levielle," Luthian spit, flailing the parchment in his hand. He rose from his chair. "He had the audacity to accuse me of trying to have him assassinated. Listen to this…"

*"High Minister,*

*As much as I know you wanted your assassin to succeed, she failed. If you want me silenced for good, you might lower yourself to do it personally. If there are other vipers that you plan to cast against me, I will take off their heads one by one.*

*As a token of my appreciation for you revealing your intentions toward me, please accept the Death Rune I carved from your assassin's arm, along with the coat she wore, soaked in her blood.*

*Ever the people's servant,*
*Levielle"*

Luthian paced as he read, then spun around to look at Alador, waving the parchment. "The brazen lack of faith in the man shall not be borne."

"Are you upset that he killed your assassin, or that he dared to send you a piece of the woman?" Alador met his uncle's gaze evenly, and his words were calm. He did not rise or look away, his hands clasped in his lap.

Luthian stopped his grandstanding and stood for a long moment staring down at Alador. "You are pushing my familial allowances."

"Uncle, I have worked with you long enough to know that nothing you do is simple. If you had risked sharing something with the General and he refused you, or did not concur, the most logical course would be to kill him." Alador appeared to relax, leaning back and crossing his legs. He was not yet willing to confront his uncle physically, but he was not going to play along with Luthian's charade any longer either. He knew exactly how vile his uncle was after he had not denied his actions prior to the storm.

He gazed down at his clasped hands in apparent indifference. "The army pulled out when we needed them most. There is a reason that one or the other of you did not want the two of you in the same place." Even though Alador knew Levielle had gone to request permission to assist the seaside villages, he was not going to share that knowledge.

Luthian flung the parchment down on his desk and returned to his chair. "You are too discerning for my tastes at times."

Alador grinned. "Apple to close to the tree?"

"Yes, and I am not used to it from any but Henrick." Luthian admitted. He closed the box that held the piece of skin and the jacket and removed it from his desk to the floor at his feet.

"The fall will come soon. I wish you to bring winter early," Luthian said, blatantly changing the subject. He pushed the general's letter to one side and made a show of studying some notes on top of the pile on his desk. "It needs to be heavier this winter. I did not see much impact from my spies with what we attempted last year."

"I will not cast any more major weather changing spells." Alador unclasped his hands and sat up straighter. His refusal to do as ordered might bring on an attack by his uncle.

Luthian looked up and pinned him with a calculating gaze. "Our agreement for your place, your privilege, was that you would cast the spells I require."

"Except, you nullified that arrangement when you failed to share with me that those spells would cause this storm." Alador stood and put both hands on his uncle's desk and leaned over. "You lied to me deliberately, and don't tell me you didn't know. I knew there was something wrong with that storm the moment I touched it." Alador straightened. "I am done casting weather spells. You want me to do more? This city could not handle anything stronger than what we just withstood."

Luthian leaned back. He did not admit his knowledge in so many words. Like always, his uncle slithered around the subject. "Further uniting the isle was worth the risks we took."

"Korpen shit!" Alador hissed. "You're not out to unite the isle. You want to rule the entire island like some King or Emperor from the tales the elders speak, and you don't care who you kill to do it. Lady Caterine danced to seal the trench for you. The guard kept the city residents from moving up the tiers on your orders. Who do you think you are hiding this from?"

"So, that is how it is going to be, hmmmm?" Luthian appeared too calm, and it worried Alador. The older mage rose and slowly went to the bell pull.

Alador turned to keep him in front of him. What was his uncle doing? He had expected a much more heated discussion then what had just occurred.

A servant entered. "Yes, Lord Guldalian?"

"Have Leonard bring down our guest," Luthian commanded.

"Yes, my lord." The servant scurried away.

Luthian turned back to Alador. "You see Alador, I knew this day would come. You have too much of your father's damn sense of right and wrong. What the two of you fail to understand is that only works if you make the rules." Luthian shrugged as he drawled on. "However in this case, my dear nephew, you do not make the rules. I do."

Alador's guard was up and he was watching Luthian's every move.

"You will cast the spells I require," Luthian commanded again.

"I won't." Alador tried to stay firm, but he knew he was missing something. He felt like he was in a chess game and Luthian was two moves ahead of him, yet he could not see it.

"Ohhh, but you will." Luthian's cold smile brought chills down Alador's spine. "I have brought you a gift. Your gratitude will exceed your love for the people."

"I can't see how any gift would compel me to cast your spells." Alador's defense sounded weak even to himself.

The door opened and Alador turned. There was Mesiande. He sucked air in surprise. She was alive. She had not died in the storm. Relief flushed through him. He wanted to run to her. Catch her up in his arms and spin her around the room laughing with the joy of having her back. However, his eyes fell on her guards and he knew instinctively he must not show how much he cared. The situation was already out of hand just having her here.

Mesiande walked right past him, her eyes glazed in a look of euphoria. She went straight to Luthian's side and dropped a demure curtsy.

"What did you do to her?" Alador hissed, his fists balled up with anger at his sides. He wanted to rush to her, grab her, drag her from this horrid place.

"She is a rather spirited young thing. Like a good lexital, I fear I had to break her of some of her habits." Luthian moved a lock of hair tenderly from her face and tucked it behind her ear. Mesiande didn't flinch, murmur or even move. "I can see your attraction. I myself love a feisty frolic, but I fear it just wouldn't do for my purposes in this case." His words slithered over Alador like a snake that had made its way into his bed.

"Now turn around, my sweet, and say hello to your dear, dear friend," Luthian oozed. He took Mesi's shoulders in his hands and gently turned her.

The young mage wanted to yell at his uncle to take his filthy hands off her, but he held his tongue. Not now… he cautioned himself. Not yet…

"Hello Alador." Her words were somewhat monotonous, and there was no reaction to him on her face.

"Uncle, taking the will of another is outlawed by the council – your council," Alador spat, seething.

"Well, yes… but we are not really talking about lawful things now, are we?" Luthian still had his hands on Mesiande's shoulders, standing behind her and smiling pure malevolence at Alador. "The best thing is you cannot tell anyone, for I assure you that her life would be one of misery and service of the lowest nature if you utter a single word." He gave his nephew a calculating smile. "However, do as I wish, and she remains an honored guest in my home. She will have pretty clothes, the best food, and she will remain untouched by anyone."

"Foul, but well played, Uncle." Alador stated. "Let's call it what it is. She will be your prisoner."

"Well yes, but she will be one you can visit." Luthian pointed out with a satisfied grin. He had Alador in his grip and he knew it.

"It is hardly a visit if she is a puppet with no will or voice of her own," snarled the younger mage.

"Ah, see this is where we negotiate. As long as you do everything I request, I will release her will, but you will not be able to see her without guards present. If you take her, the link I have created within her will allow me to kill her." Luthian appeared very pleased with himself. "If you wish to meet with her alone to sample her sweet charms, well then my spell will leave her as she is now."

"That is rape, High Minister." Alador's anger was building and he no longer could hide it. He clenched and unclenched his hands.

"Call it what you will, the offer is there." Luthian leaned forward and lifted a lock of Mesi's hair. He sniffed it and taunted Alador. "Sweet…" he breathed.

Alador literally shivered with anger. His dragon-self threatened to overrun his good sense. He mentally pounded the emotions into submission. He took several deep breaths and tried to get the picture of Luthian's vile innuendos about Mesi's fate out of his mind.

"I will cast your spells when the seasons change," he acquiesced. Until the plan was enacted Alador had to do anything the man before him wished in order to keep Mesi safe.

"Now there, I knew you would see reason." Luthian looked quite satisfied with himself. He squeezed Mesiande's shoulder and turned her, pointing her toward her guards. "Child, return to your room."

"Yes, my lord." Mesiande left without giving Alador a second glance.

His heart wrenched at the sight of this demure vision of his young and feisty friend. Despite his efforts, he had not protected her from Luthian's grasp.

"There is no doubt in my mind any longer… I hate you, High Minister."

Luthian gave a mock bow. "Why thank you, Lord Guldalian. I do not need you to like me. I only need you to obey my commands. I hope now my position is quite clear."

"Careful, Uncle," He quoted one of the many sayings Luthian had drilled into him. "Overconfidence has gotten many a mage killed."

"Yes, but I will not be one of them. I plan my moves far in advance." Luthian stated with more seriousness. "You played your game well, but you have lost."

## Chapter Twenty-Eight

Alador paced in his library, his footfalls almost shaking the floor with their impact. He could think of no way to release Mesiande from the control of Luthian's spell. He could try a counter spell, but if there was a trap built into it, he could find himself in the same state. There was no choice - they had to move up the attack. He could not go to the council tier for a month and do Luthian's bidding and tasks while Mesiande was his prisoner.

Nemara appeared, leaning in the doorway. She squinted to see him better. When she saw his face, she moved closer. "Did she eat it?" Her voice held all the horror of her thoughts.

"No…" Alador pulled her into his arms. She had misinterpreted his pacing. "Pruatra agreed to see it hatched," he assured her with a squeeze and a kiss on the cheek.

Nemara pulled back and her face showed her confusion. "Then what is amiss?"

How did you tell a lover, that your other lover was in danger? Alador ran a hand through his hair, pulling it loose from its tie. He just laid it bare. "Luthian has Mesiande."

"Oh Gods!" Nemara's hands went to her mouth.

"Nemara, I can't leave her there." Alador looked at her, pleading for her to understand. "I have to kill him, and quickly - before he can act."

"Of course you can't leave her with him," Nemara put her hand on his arm, "but it needs to be planned. Let's just move up our timeline."

"He has used black magic to control her. She is totally at his mercy. Every minute she is there…" Alador could not express how much the situation appalled him. His anguish oozed from every aspect of his being.

"It will do her no good if you rush in unprepared," Nemara warned him. "You have told me repeatedly that his overthrow must be meticulously planned." She cupped his cheek with her hand, drawing his eyes to her. "You cannot barge in. Your death will only leave her open to whatever abuse he wishes."

Alador did not want to listen. He wanted to rage in and kill his uncle with daggers of ice and drown him in chilling saltwater, but deep down, he knew that he should heed Nemara's counsel. "You're right," he breathed.

"Go… see to the progress your brother has made with organizing the Daezun. Speak with your dragons. I will go to the High Master Bariton and ease him into a tighter timeline," she offered.

Alador wrapped his arms around her and kissed her on the forehead. "Thank you."

He stepped back from her and pulled out the traveling amulet Henrick had given him, fingering it with fondness. It had become very useful over the last two turns. Now, it was a critical tool.

He focused on the coal room in his mother's home.

When he arrived, he carefully opened the door and was relieved to see a new roof on the house. The village way was to have all hands work on one roof, and then move on to the next. It was an efficient process.

The house was quiet, but the sound of building echoed through the village. They would all be out working. He moved into the next room to see that Maman's kitchen was not only rebuilt but improved. Alador had no doubt that between his brothers and Henrick, it had been a focal point. He decided to prepare a meal for them to eat when they arrived home for the day.

He stood for a moment staring at the banked fire and realized he had no idea how to cook. All his life, meals had been provided. Fortunately, he did know how to roast meat over a campfire. Unfortunately, a careful look through his mother's kitchen found no fresh meat, although there were plenty of tubers and fruit. Finally, he found some cheese and decided to lay out fruit, bread and cheese on a tray. He started to slice everything.

He just finished setting the table and placing the tray when the bell rang to end the workday. It was not much longer before his mother hurried into the house, anxious to start preparing dinner. She saw the table set and the tray Alador had laid out. Her face lit up when she spotted him by the cutting board. He noted she had thinned over the summer, but her welcoming smile reassured him of her health.

"Alador, twice so soon? I am so happy to see you." She practically ran around the table and pounced on him with a big opened arm hug. "What do you think of the kitchen? I love it. I can't wait to be able to start my storing up. Well, what is left to store up. Storm took a lot of harvest." She rattled on without seeming to take a breath. "What am I going on about? You are here."

Alador could not help himself, he laughed and squeezed her shoulders. "You need to take a breath, Maman."

"Yes, I do. Henrick is always telling me that." She punched his arm. "You knew he was a dragon all that time and you didn't tell me! Seems to me something your mother should know."

Alador flinched; she had not held back her solid punch. "Look how you reacted, Maman! but I am here for more serious matters."

"More serious than my housemate is a dragon?" She searched his face and sobered immediately as the pain in his eyes registered. "What has happened?"

"Mesiande wasn't lost to the storm. The High Minister of Lerdenia stole her from the village." Tears filled his eyes.

He had anticipated his mother's distress, but her reaction was far beyond his predictions. "Korpen shite he did!" Her hands went to her waist and she glared at her son with misplaced anger. "What you doin' about it?"

"That is why I am here, Maman." He took a breath as the door opened and decided to wait until everyone was there.

Maman took control of Henrick, Dorien and

Tentret, as they entered. All noted her commanding tone and quickly did as they were told, sinking down in their chairs around the table.

His mother stood at the foot, hands on her hips and continuing to give orders. "Okay now, you all listen up. That nasty man, the High Minister, has our Mesi. Henrick, you are going to go eat him right now."

Alador stopped in the middle of silently greeting Henrick and his brothers and turned toward his mother in shock. "Maman, if the High Minister is eaten by a dragon, the divide between mortals and dragons will only grow."

"We forgave that big red beast that flamed our homes," she poked at the air for emphasis.

Both Alador and Henrick winced. That was one thing they would never tell her - that the same dragon she now abided with in her home was the one who attacked the village. Some things were better left unsaid.

"The Lerdenians are not the forgiving sort, Alanis," Henrick replied softly. He looked at Alador with sympathy. "This changes little, though I imagine in your heart it changes much."

"We can't leave her there, Henrick. You know what he is capable of and what he has done before." Alador threw the man a pleading look.

"Agreed! It is for leverage over you, correct?" Henrick's face was hard. Gone was the jovial mage he usually projected.

"Yes," Alador hesitated as to how to proceed. He

needed to keep in mind that no one knew of his involvement in creating the storm that had decimated the village. "He wants me to cast the spells that the storm mage has refused him."

"Ah, I see." Henrick answered knowingly. He looked over at Dorien. "Can we move it along faster?"

"I don't know, Henrick. It is a lot to do, making preparations and still trying to get repairs done before winter comes." Dorien sounded very unsure.

"We will move it faster." Alanis decreed, still towering over them at the foot of the table.

"Alanis, dear…" Henrick tried to reason with her.

"Don't you 'Alanis dear' me! This village is still led by the women, though we let the men think they are leading it," she boldly declared. "When I share that this despot has Mesiande, the women will rise up and insist that we move immediately."

"Maman, we have other people to coordinate. 'Immediately' will not let me put things in place to ensure the least loss of life." Alador tried to explain.

"That is your Mesi he has," his mother firmly stated. "We attack in a fortnight, with or without your fancy mages." She plopped down in her chair and glared at Henrick. "Or dragons."

"A fortnight will work," Henrick offered, trying to placate the angry Daezun woman.

Dorien did not look as certain as their mother did. Regardless, they spent the rest of the cold meal planning the attack to remove Luthian from power. Alador just hoped he did not lose Mesiande in the crossfire.

By the time they were finished, Alador was on his way to see Sordith, and Henrick was planning on reporting the situation to Rheagos.

*Chapter Twenty-Nine*

Alador did not risk using the traveling amulet to appear at Sordith's manor. His brother's home had been gutted by the wave, and he had no idea of a safe location to arrive without the possibility of injury. Instead, he went home and then moved quickly down the tiers.

People were still talking about the storm and the dragons that were taking the dead. Luthian had been forced to send out criers to calm the populace and tell them the dead were being taken to Dethara's temple for their final rites. Even so, if the many conversations he heard bits and pieces of were to be believed, no one had a recent memory of dragons helping Silverport.

As he entered the trench, he once more observed the damage and realized it would be a long time before the area was functional. Miners were still shoring up walls and moving dirt despite the many days they had been working.

Alador made his way to the trench hall steps. Many of the imposing statues had been overturned or destroyed. It was an improvement in his opinion; they had been rather morbid in their focus.

He rapidly ascended and entered the hall looking for Sordith. The sounds of hammering and movement could be heard from the doorway.

"Sordith?" he called. He did not want to be

mistaken for an intruder.

He heard a faint call back and moved toward his brother's receiving room and office. Here, the repairs were finished. New doors had been installed, and Sordith's weapons were on the wall. There were a few empty spaces, hopefully due to cleaning and not misplacement. Sordith was rather finicky about that collection.

Since the room had needed repair, it seemed the Trench Lord had decided on a full renovation, sparing no expense. Instead of the previous stone floor, there were red rugs. They complimented the strange red desk with its unusual water stain patterns that only seemed to add to it. His brother had arranged to have everything else done in hues of gray and black. It was impressive.

Sordith sauntered in. He had clearly been giving a hand with the repairs, as he was not in armor and his hair was filled with sawdust and…what appeared to be a piece of seaweed.

"I didn't expect to see you so soon, Alador. Everything all right?" Sordith opened his bottom drawer, pulled out a bottle of smalgut and poured them both a stiff shot.

"No…" Alador paused, "Luthian has Mesiande." He didn't bother to soften the news.

"Shite!" Sordith handed over the shot of alcohol. "You might need this more than I do."

Alador tossed it back, grimacing as he set the small glass down. "The timetable is being moved up."

Sordith indicated for him to sit and plopped down in the chair behind his desk. "Afraid he will act before you can?"

"I am afraid of what he will do to her. He has already taken her will." Alador scrubbed his face with his hand. It had been a very long day. "Like that stone that Veaneth, the Stable Lord, possessed."

"It might be better that way," his brother offered. "Maybe she won't remember anything."

"I can hope so." Alador exhaled a deep sigh and looked up. "You ready for the plan?"

"One moment." Sordith opened an upper drawer and took out parchment and quill. "Alright… Let us hear this plan and see if I concur."

"Dorien is going to move the Daezun force right onto the plain in a fortnight. I need you to join up with him and lead them through the city, securing each tier as you go."

"Wait!" Sordith looked up from the parchment and pointed the quill at his brother. "How are the Daezun coming? Horse? Cart? Marching? Did you take into consideration the dragons of Morana are still flying over the city? They will spot them coming and might even attack if Luthian can get the Death Priestess to order them to."

"We do not have to worry about them being spotted. It will be a surprise arrival."

Sordith frowned at him. "I do not like surprises when planning an assault on a mage-fortified city."

"You will have to trust me on this Sordith. It is a Daezun secret, and one I am sworn not to share. It is the one thing I cannot share with a Lerdenian." He looked apologetic as he studied the glass in his hands. "Trust me," he repeated. "Just be on the edge of the plain to meet them."

Sordith huffed his disapproval of secrets between them, but lowered his quill back to the parchment and scribbled a note.

Alador continued. "Bariton will pull his men to the third tier, so this should go quietly. Levielle's army is gone, but any leftover guards will have to be silenced." He waited for his brother to take notes.

"Easy enough… me and my boys can move quietly through the city before they are expected and make sure those that might give cry are too drunk, or too dead, to care." Sordith stated with confidence.

The mage looked at his brother and sighed. "The idea is to offer the people something better, Sordith, not the status quo. We need to do this with as few casualties as possible."

"Of course…" Sordith acquiesced with a nod of his head.

"Don't patronize me. I might just decide to freeze your arse to your chair and let you sit out the battle." Alador's warning held an edge of seriousness.

"And here you said you wanted to limit death." the Trench Lord teased.

"Oh, it wouldn't kill you. I would leave you thawed enough to breathe," Alador smirked.

"Whoa… You are such a spoil sport." Sordith winked at Alador.

Alador frowned. "Let's be serious for a moment?" They really did not have time for this foolish banter.

"You want to be serious, brother?" Sordith leaned forward, picked up his glass and threw back the rest of its contents. "A man you wouldn't let me kill has eliminated a good third of the trench, if not more…" His smile had turned into a frown that heavily creased his brow. "My home was destroyed by an unnatural storm…" Sordith was building up steam. If he had been a dragon his nostrils would have been smoking. "The trench itself is looking at a couple more weeks before it becomes remotely habitable, but I am certain its occupants will be forced into it sooner." Sordith shot to his feet. He slammed the glass so hard on the desktop the bottom broke out of it. "AND, I am about to make an impulsive young man 'King,' because the populace would never accept me." He leaned over the desk and glared at Alador. "Serious will get someone killed."

Alador took a gulp of air because in that last moment of ire, he realized if Sordith knew the truth of the storm and who started it, it would be him the Trench Lord would want beneath his blade. "Sorry I asked," he managed to mutter.

Sordith pulled himself up and set back down. He took several deep breaths and then picked up his quill. "Shall we continue?"

The young mage sought to refocus the man. "I need you, my brother Dorien, and Bariton to hold the line at the gates to the fourth tier. Let the people flee down if they choose, but I need you to coordinate forces that have never worked together."

"Wait! Wait… Wait…" With each repetition, his voice grew deeper and harder. Sordith pinned him with a stare. "When do I get to the top tier to kill Luthian?"

"You don't."

It just hung there.

"I don't?" One eyebrow shot up.

"No."

"Unacceptable!" Sordith threw down the quill. "I demand satisfaction."

"I know my geas will not be fulfilled if Luthian is killed by any other than a Daezun hand." Alador firmly stated. He had known deep down this was true, but could he convince his brother? "You, my dear Trench Lord, are not Daezun."

"I don't give a shite about your geas. He killed my people. I must be the one to kill Luthian." Sordith stated very firmly.

"How about a compromise?" Alador offered.

"I fail to see a satisfying compromise." Sordith let his quill drop again, leaned back and crossed his arms in rebellion.

"First one to him gets to kill him." Alador offered. Really, the goal was to see Luthian dead, so motivating Sordith could hardly hurt his cause.

"Hardly fair, as I assume you have some plan to be at the top." Sordith pointed out dryly.

"Yes, but you are better than I am," Alador offered as consolation.

"Well, there is that." Sordith picked up the quill eyeing Alador. "First man to him," he stated for verification.

"First man to him," Alador agreed.

"I will coordinate with Bariton. You are certain this Dorien will arrive on time?" Sordith pressed. "I normally don't work with the unknown."

"I am betting my life on it," Alador stated firmly.

"You are betting all our lives on it," Sordith reminded him, sobering them both once more. "I will be honest, letting an army of Daezun in our gates goes against everything I have learned and believed."

They sat silently for a few moments. Sordith rose, and after finding a new glass, he poured them both another shot.

"To change," he held up his glass and saluted.

"To change," Alador echoed and their glasses clinked with the final nail. Their path was set.

## Chapter Thirty

Keensight waited in the large cavern for the rest of the flight leaders; this would be their first meeting since shortly after Renamaum's death. Some wanted to honor Renamaum's quest to reunite the island. Others resisted, insisting the blue flight leader was betrayed by those he sought to help. Unfortunately, in his anger, Keensight had been the leader of that side of the great debate. A big sigh rumbled up with a bit of smoke. He had been so wrong.

Over the years of taking on a mortal form, he had learned that people in general were good. Everyone, just like dragons, had flaws. It was not the populace that was the problem - it was the overall tone of their leadership. By ranking people by their magical skills, the country had become one of elitism. Only the privileged benefited as the rest of those in the country tried to carve out enough slips for small comforts. The only class that had it easy was the fourth and fifth tiers. He had liked that comfort as well, as he lived among them. However, unlike many of the elite, he made an effort to help those in need whenever possible.

Helping others in need... It had been a foreign concept when he was younger. Renamaum had tried to show him the way so many times, but Keensight knew he chose not to listen. The mortals killed his mate and stole their egg. He waited until it should have hatched and even years after, but he knew the hatchling was lost to him. He never saw a dragon that could possibly have been his and Alkalay's. He rolled the name over in his mind. He could not remember the last time he spoke it.

He wondered if any of the flight leaders would even answer his call. He took a deep breath and considered what he would say. He would have an uphill battle unless Rheagos appeared. The problem was the great golden dragon did not wake often these days. He often slumbered for turn after turn before he finally made an appearance. Keensight did not know if his call had been strong enough to reach the senior dragon's consciousness.

Keensight reviewed the last few days. The Daezun were very welcoming at each village he and Dorien visited. However, they were making very slow progress with regard to Alador's deadline. The dragon finally had to convince Dorien to either ride on his back or let him take them with a travel spell. The young man was more horrified of the thought of flying than magic. By the third casting of the spell, the man had quit throwing up. Keensight rumbled with laughter.

A sound broke him out of his reverie and he looked up to see Amaum. He was surprised for a moment, then realized that no other older blue dragon must have challenged the young male for command of the flight. As such, he had inherited his father's right to attend the council. Keensight watched as Amaum drew himself up to appear larger and walked toward him. He saw something in the fledgling's… no young adult's…eyes. There was a hardened edge the big red dragon had once held himself when he was young and arrogant. He wondered where Amaum would stand, after Rena's death.

He dipped his head in acknowledgment of the young dragon's equal rank. Amaum returned the gesture, but only as much as was required. Keensight suspected that this blue dragon was going to be his first hurdle. Before he could begin to work on him, a large green dragon strode into the cavern.

"Ivy, it has been long since I have seen you. How have you been, or more importantly, where have you been?" Keensight was pleased to see the dragon. She was older than he was and he had always found her charming.

"I have been on the main continent. More room to breed and the interference of mortals is easily dealt with." She smiled at him. "We eat them there."

That did not bode well for his cause. "Let me introduce Renamaum's son, Amaum." Keensight stepped aside so she could see the younger dragon clearly.

To his credit, Amaum stepped forward, extending his wings and dipping his head deeply. "May your wings be ever filled and the turns treat you with grace."

Ivy's toothy grin showed the edges of sharpened fangs. "Ah, a charmer like your father. I always regretted not taking a flight with him before he chose Pruatra."

"I am sure you would have danced with skill equal to my mother's." Amaum smiled at her in answer, becoming a bit more comfortable.

Before they could continue, one by one the other

leaders appeared. Naturally, after finding that the Black Flight had been the instigators of locating and stealing the other flight's eggs, they were not present. Frankly, Keensight had not asked them. However, every other color was represented but gold. No doubt, Rheagos still slept soundly in his cave.

Keensight let out a sigh of relief once all of them arrived. He roared a call for order as the dragons greeted old friends and new ones.

When they quieted down, he began to speak. "Many turns ago, this council separated for the last time over the argument of the worthiness of those who had once been tasked to work with us. The Great War separated those who shared our land with us into two distinct people – Mages, who betrayed us for power, and The People, who fought at our side. Over time, The People have found their own place, continuing to honor the pact. Lerdenia, the tiered cities of mages, has continued to violate the rights of dragons, stealing our young and killing our mates."

There was a rumble across the hall. Keensight caught a glimpse of Amaum out of the corner of his eye. He was very serious and watching all the dragons present. The large red dragon brought his full attention back to the dragons in the great circle. Many were displeased to have the argument brought up again.

"If I remember right, was it not you who led the division suggesting their extermination?" Ivy asked. Her welcoming tones fell to a hardened accusation.

"It was," Keensight admitted. "I even went to the Gods and was given permission to seek my revenge, but only after I had lived among them for a year."

"So now you have called us back to help you take your revenge?" Silverbell eyed Keensight with disapproval.

"No, I have changed..." he took a deep breath, "I have changed my position."

This created a huge uproar among the many flights represented. Strangely, it appeared that Silverbell was going to align with him on the matter.

A deafening roar sounded from the entrance of the cave. All the dragons spun toward the opening as one, except Amaum. Their wings shot out, and their chins touched the ground. It only took Amaum a moment to follow suit. A huge gold dragon lumbered into the cavern, at least twice the size of the largest among them. Keensight remained where he was, in Rheagos' place on the large rock ledge a few feet above the others.

The golden dragon drew himself up until his head nearly touched the stalactites hanging above them. "Since when do we start a council when I am not present?"

Keensight bravely raised his head, though even he feared Rheagos, whose fire was so pure it flamed blue before moving to the oranges and yellows. "I am sorry, Sire, you have slept a great deal these days and..."

"So, you thought you could just proceed without me?" The dragons fell back as Rheagos approached the ledge.

Keensight found himself stammering. How did you tell the patriarch of all dragons that he was getting old and was rarely around? "I did not wish to disturb you, Sire."

Rheagos stood waiting and finally harrumphed. "Well…"

"Well what, my Great Lord?" Keensight could feel his heart thumping in his own chest. The stink of his fear filled his nostrils and he knew none of the others were likely to miss it.

"Get off my ledge so I can relax. I am not getting any younger." Rheagos' words were followed by a short flash of blue flame.

Keensight scrambled off the ledge to make room for the gold dragon. He was more than happy to relinquish the position to the older male. As Rheagos was settling into his higher seat in the cavern, everyone else formed a circle around him.

"Now, Keensight, what is this uproar about? I have not been disturbed in ages." Rheagos booming voice made the bones of the other dragons vibrate like drums. "Wait!" The leader raised a paw. "Where is the Black Flight leader?"

"He was not invited, Great Lord." Keensight followed this with a quick explanation before the golden dragon chose to roast him for not including all the flight leaders, "We discovered the Black Flight were the ones who were revealing the location of the other flight's nests and stealing the eggs for Lerdenia's bloodmine."

Rheagos rose and shot blue flames toward the ceiling in anger. "Our own kind turned on us?" He roared in disbelief and pain. "How was this discovered?" Keensight could tell the Great Lord did not wish to believe this atrocity.

"Milord, it was the dragonsworn. He has appeared and it is time to see him seated above the mages of Lerdenia." Keensight stated respectfully.

"Has it been that long already? How many turns have passed?" It was a rhetorical question and no one, much less Keensight, chose to point out that the golden leader had been slumbering for ages. Rheagos scratched his muzzle and a great scale of gold clattered to the ground. He eased himself down. "Black flight running rogue... dragonsworn..."

Keensight was very aware that all eyes were on him. His announcement of the dragonsworn had not been made prior to their leader's appearance.

Smallstone, named for his unusually small size, bravely stepped forward. No one wanted to go into detail about the Black Flights' betrayal, but he was willing to pursue the topic of the dragonsworn. "How can Keensight know for sure that this dragonsworn is real and not just some manifestation of his hope?"

"Because he carries the powers of my father," Amaum offered.

"Wait, who said that?" Rheagos demanded.

"I did," Amaum squeaked. He stepped out to where Rheagos could see him.

"Who by fire and stone are you?" Rheagos leaned off the ledge, stretched his long neck out and sniffed him.

"I am Amaum, hatched of Renamaum and Pruatra." The young dragon managed to hold himself still. Keensight could not have been prouder of him at that moment.

"Ah yes, sad day when Renamaum died. Noble dragon that one." Rheagos tipped his head slightly, a great copper eye looking at the young dragon. "This mortal has your father's power, you say? Are you certain?"

"He was able to bring back my father's spirit and form so we could meet our sire. I am certain." Amaum said, drawing up a little and demonstrating his confidence in the matter.

"I see. A geas stone then." Rheagos murmured. "Haven't seen one of those in an eon." The great dragon turned his gaze on the red dragon.

Keensight felt his heart skip a beat when Rheagos fixed his huge copper eyes on him. He made sure not to look away, though instinct suggested that he do so.

"What does the dragonsworn need of the flights?" Rheagos demanded.

"He seeks to replace the leading despot. To do that, the dragons will need to assist in the assault on the city." Keensight looked over to the other flight leaders. "Regardless of how you feel, this is our time. Those that want revenge can breathe down upon the mages resisting. Those that want to help the dragonsworn can work with me and the chosen few that will go after their leader."

Keensight had only, in that moment, realized that all the dragons would be satisfied regardless of their motives. "I only ask that you do not assault those that are helping the dragonsworn win the day."

"Bow your head if you do not wish to help the chosen in his quest to renew the oath once broken by the Lerdenians." Rheagos commanded.

Keensight did not know the motives of some, but none dropped their head to the ground. He breathed a sigh of relief. What could have been hours of debate had been thwarted by the arrival of Rheagos.

"The dragon flights will assist you. I command that all dragon flights send some of their battle capable dragons to this endeavor. I expect each of you to lead your flights." Rheagos commanded.

The bugling of each of the dragons brought tears to Keensight's eyes. He had not seen them united since before the death of Renamaum. In spite of what he had done to divide the dragon flights, now he felt as though he had succeeded in reuniting them. He threw back his head and roared, even though his flight had no members left to answer. He promised himself he would fight with the ferocity of three dragons.

As soon as they all settled down, Rheagos sent them off. Amaum was the first to scurry away. Keensight was of a mind to follow him when their leader called him back. He turned and padded over to the large gold dragon.

"I am here, Sire." Keensight lowered his gaze in respect.

"I have a very serious question to put to you." Rheagos looked exhausted - as if the meeting had taken every bit of energy he possessed to get through it - but his copper eyes sparkled as he asked, "Do you wish to challenge me to lead all the flights - to be their ruler?" Rheagos' question caught Keensight off guard.

"Of course not, I would not wish to find an early grave." Keensight uttered with a bit of shock.

"Oh, do not give me that. I am old and slow in the air. A young buck like you could out maneuver me." Rheagos scoffed.

Keensight found amusement in being called a young buck; he had not been of an age to be called 'young' for many turns. "Yet old enough to respect the wisdom that age brings," he offered.

"I was hoping you would say that." The large golden stretched his wings and then folded them tighter to his sides.

Rheagos' triumphant tone made Keensight's heart sink. If he was honest with himself, he secretly did wish to lead the flights and his banter was merely to placate their current ruler.

The golden dragon's eyes looked heavy, as he said, "I will want weekly reports until this matter is settled. I expect you to deliver them personally. Now get." Rheagos head sank to the floor of his ledge. "I need a nap."

Keensight did not need a second command. He too scurried out of the council cave.

Rheagos smiled as the tail of the red dragon disappeared around the bend. He had chosen his successor well. Now... now, it was time to train him.

*Chapter Thirty-One*

Jon returned to Nightmare's cave from a long day of serving Morana. His office as praetor required he be at her side. Add to that being her current lover and well, breaks were few and far between. Morana was a skilled lover and had taught him many things, but even with that, her presence had become cloying.

He now had rooms in the temple proper, but he felt safer in Nightmare's cave. There were those threatened by his rise to power and the fact that Morana did not hide the identity of her lover. Between the two, he did not wish to find a dagger protruding from any part of his body, or worst yet, find himself in Dethara's care too soon.

Nightmare had not returned from wherever he bumbled off to for the evening. Jon was content with that. He told Morana he needed to return to his rooms to study and meditate then made a quick exit. Her good-byes were longer than a Daezun middlin courtship.

He sat in the cool evening air, his back against the cave wall, and just let himself exist for a time. As the night grew darker, Nightmare returned. He landed without finesse, the dim lightstones of the cave making 'nightmarish' silhouettes.

"You are here!" He shuffled over and nuzzled Jon. The young mage had more than one acid hole in many of his robes due to these affectionate greetings.

"I am here most nights," Jon pointed out in his bored monotone. The timbre of his voice had become habit over time.

"Yes, but it is important tonight." Nightmare tucked his wings close and plopped down beside Jon. It was not really laying down. He just suddenly was not on his feet.

"And why is it important tonight?" Jon asked only half-paying attention.

Nightmare often told him that his presence was important. Then as if it never occurred to him that his day was not important in the scheme of things, he would lay out in detail everything he did and practiced. The elders of the flight had begun to teach the young dragon, taking a great deal of the burden off Jon.

"I heard something I think you should know," the dragon declared. He nodded his head to add emphasis.

Jon waited a moment or two and then finally asked. "What is it that I should know?" He grinned because the dragon always needed some kind of verbal response to continue.

"Dragons are going to attack your people," Nightmare declared as if giving Jon a beautiful stone for his meager hoard.

"Wait! What?" Jon sat up straighter and turned toward the dragon. Nightmare had his full attention.

"Dragons are going to attack your people," the black restated, as if Jon had not heard it the first time.

"Yes, yes I heard that. The black flight is going to attack people?" Jon had heard nothing of this.

"ALL the dragons." Nightmare emphasized and watched for Jon's reaction. "I thought this was bad based on what you told me about dragons and mortals."

"All of them? Do you know where?" Jon's mind was racing.

"Yes, the flight leader said a place called Silverport." Nightmare aimlessly picked at a scale loosening on his leg.

"Tell me everything," Jon demanded.

"Okay," Nightmare closed his eyes in an effort to remember *everything*. "Blacksaber said; 'I have called you all together for the King has spoken.' Everyone grew very still. It seems the King speaking is a big deal. He said that he was looking for volunteers to help him attack Silverport. Many raised a wing. He then warned them this was a conflict of loyalty. Wings dropped. Morana was not to know of this attack, Blacksaber said. If she knew, she may demand the flight not attack and then we would be disobeying the King. Destruction rose to his full height and demanded to know the King's..."

Jon interrupted. "Can you summarize rather than giving me every word and action?"

Nightmare looked indignant. "You said tell you everything."

"Yes, well, I didn't realize how much *everything* was going to be." Jon sighed. "Let us go with the main points of Blacksaber's words."

"Well you should have said so." Nightmare huffed with indignation.

"I know," Jon offered in a soothing tone. "Tell me just what the flight leader shared."

"Fine." The growing dragon laid his head on Jon's lap. "The King was angry with the Black Flight and said that the dragons must support someone called a dragonsworn. He said, now was the time for dragons to rise up and support a ruler that reveres dragons. Morana does not revere dragons," Nightmare huffed, "she uses them, which suited Blacksaber for the time being. However, the King's demands might be dangerous to this arrangement between black dragons and Dethara's temple.

"He then chose five to go with him... soon. He did not disclose when they would go, but they are going." Nightmare raised his head and looked into Jon's eyes. "Can I go with them? I want to watch."

"It is best you don't, my friend." Jon rubbed the young dragon's snout as he contemplated what he just heard. He had not known there was a dragon king, let alone that Morana did not have control of the flight as she thought.

"Why?" Nightmare tilted his head and brought it close so his eye was only a couple of inches from Jon's.

It created a visual disturbance to have one eye so large before two. It always made Jon's stomach uneasy. "I don't want you caught in a crossfire."

"I would stay far away, just close enough I could see." The dragon did not move his head.

Jon gently pushed the muzzle a bit further from his face to relieve the effect. He was also trying to prevent any snorted acid hitting his skin if Nightmare went into a huff. "If Morana finds out, you are not large enough to defend yourself."

"She is little like you," Nightmare insisted. Since he started training with the Black Flight adults, his confidence had grown.

"She is stronger in magic then both of us. Sometimes size is deceptive," Jon instructed and scratched the dragon affectionately under the chin. He was so young and still innocent. "Do not underestimate a small and seemingly helpless adversary."

"So, she is large due to magic?" Nightmare pressed, trying his best to understand Jon's reluctance.

"Yes." The mage was still trying to process the onslaught of information. Morana only had the dragons' loyalty because it suited them. He made note to be prepared for the day it did not suit them. He had truly thought she had 'control' of the Black Flight.

Then there was the dragonsworn… Had Alador earned that title among the flights when he released the bloodmine dragons?

"You won't tell Morana will you?" The dragon asked abruptly, a look of concern creasing its brow all the way down into its muzzle ridges.

Nightmare's sudden question jolted Jon from his musings. "I will not tell Morana," he promised.

"Oh good… I don't want to get in trouble with Blacksaber for sharing dragon secrets."

"I will never break your confidences, Nightmare, as long as you tell me that the information is a secret," Jon sincerely promised.

"It is a secret," Nightmare whispered even though their conversation thus far had been at a normal volume.

Jon laughed. "I had already gathered that."

If Alador was making his move, he was not about to tell Morana. He did not want the same division of loyalty that the Black Flight now faced. No… silence was beneficial, as well as an honoring of his bond with Nightmare.

Nightmare shifted and laid his forehead against Jon's. The young dragon rumbled contentedly – the vibration was soothing against Jon's brow. It was something the dragon often did when seeking affection.

They sat that way for some time, love emanating from the dragon. It was a palpable sensation when the dragon touched him this way and Jon never wanted to interrupt it. It was the only time in his life that he felt absolute acceptance.

*Chapter Thirty-Two*

Alador felt a sudden pull on his very soul. He moved to the balcony overlooking the city and saw a dragon winging away in the distance. It had been either Amaum or Pruatra, which meant…the egg! It must be the egg.

He turned to where Luthian was working on the damage reports from around the city; Alador's task had been writing letters of response, detailing the aid that would be given. Sordith's report in particular had not been good. Some of the air vents on the plains had been filled with water, flooding the deeper mines.

"My Lord, I need to see to a matter of personal concern. May I depart the rest of the afternoon?" His words were respectful and held none of the animosity that he was feeling.

Luthian looked over, eyebrow raising. "You know I prefer to have you nearby."

"I understand, and I understand the reasons why. A dear friend of mine is ill, however, and I wish to look into her care and health." Alador turned to face his uncle, his hands grasped before him to stop them from shaking.

"I see." Luthian thought for a moment and then looked over to where he had set Mesiande with a book. "I will allow this. I will see you in the morning."

Alador inwardly breathed a sigh of relief. "First thing, High Minister," he promised.

He took his leave, only giving a side long look at Mesiande. Luthian had been treating her as a great doll. If she recalled any of this, he was certain she would never wish to remain as his queen. Though he still had great love for Mesiande, he had decided that it would be best for everyone if Nemara were queen, and mother of Latiera. Well, if Latiera had survived her own creation.

Thinking of the future put a little more bounce in his step. He noted on his way home that he was being followed by one of Luthian's hounds. He grinned, slowing to conjure a horizontal wall of water; then, before the man had a chance to look up, it cascaded down, knocking the spy off his feet.

Alador took the hysterics of those splashed and the confusion of the man on the ground as a chance to slip his spy. He ducked into a small recess in a servant access and activated the traveling stone, envisioning the underwater entrance to Pruatra's cave. This seemed like the safest choice, as he figured she would be somewhere within tending to the hatchling.

The materialization into water was shocking, much like diving into a deep cold pool on a hot summer day. He quickly moved up to the edge, pushing his hair back from his eyes, and pulled himself up.

Pruatra looked over at him. "Took you long enough." She sniffed at something in her talons, then looked back to him.

"I came as quickly as I could disentangle myself from the High Minister's web." He cast a drying spell so his robes were not weighing him down. "Is she here?"

Pruatra's expression softened, and she held out a small blue hatchling. Its scales were a light blue on the edges, and grew darker as they neared the body. The small fins at her face were almost laughable, more like butterfly wings, but they framed the deep sapphire eyes beautifully.

"May I hold her?" he asked, his reverence for the beautiful creature in his eyes and tone.

"Of course, she is partially yours." Pruatra carefully held out a talon.

He lifted the little dragon up and she opened her eyes. She turned her head to stare at him. "Hello Latiera, welcome to the world."

"Latiera? Why this name? I have never heard it." Pruatra eyed the man with curiosity.

"She told me." Alador simply said.

"She told you? How did this occur?"

"I was taking a bath next to her and I fell asleep. She came to me in a dream." Alador smiled and rubbed the top of the hatchling's head.

All of the sudden, Latiera began contorting about in his arms. Her body began to change and it was all he could do to hang on to her.

"Pruatra, what is happening? Is she dying?" Alador gasped out, his alarm palpable as he struggled to keep hands on the changing shape.

"I don't know. I have never seen a hatchling do that. Soothe her as best you can." Pruatra encouraged. Alador looked up at her and saw the fear in her eyes as well.

They both stared at the thrashing, swelling dragon in confusion. Pruatra realized what was happening first. "She is changing shapes."

"Are hatchlings supposed to do that?" Alador looked more closely. Pruatra was right.

"No. But then she is not wholly a dragon, so I do not know what such a mixture on the wings of power might bring." The dragon nuzzled the shifting infant in Alador's hands.

They both stared until the process was done. When at last she stopped whimpering and moving, a small naked baby with a clear Lerdenian look lay in his arms.

"Well, that explains that, I guess." Alador tried to let out the stress that had built up within him to see his child flailing in such a manner.

"I fail to see what it explains." Pruatra was staring at the child as if it had grown a second head.

"She wasn't a dragon in my dream," he elaborated.

"Yes, well she can't stay here like that. The chances of her becoming chilled or falling into the water are too great." Pruatra drew her head up imperiously.

"I agree. Nemara will be excited to see her. Any chance of stopping her changing like that without harming her?"

Pruatra sniffed the baby who reached up to touch

the dragon's muzzle. "Your guess is as good as mine, Alador. We both are dealing with a creature that I have no memory of ever having existed."

Alador pulled off his cloak and wrapped it around the baby to keep her warm. "I see. Well here I go again, onto paths heretofore unknown. I will be comfortable when the day becomes routine."

Pruatra laughed, bringing a scowl to Latiera's small face. "You would die of boredom," she predicted.

"It would be nice…for awhile." He paused. "Will you be at the attack?"

"I will be, as will Amaum.'

"Is he still angry?" Alador wanted to make sure he wasn't going to have an angry dragon on his back.

Pruatra sighed, more of a deep rumble to the mage. "He nurtures anger like Keensight once did.'

"I am so sorry Pruatra. We all lost that day." Alador laid a hand on her muzzle. "I will ensure that Rena is never forgotten."

Pruatra nuzzled the bundle in his arms. "*She* will ensure that Rena is never forgotten - as long as you can help her reach adulthood."

There was a long silence. "I will take her home to Nemara now. Do you think it is safe to travel with magic?"

The blue dragon sniffed Latiera again. "I cannot say for certain; there are definite elements I cannot sense in her.

"Then let's hope I don't kill her. I have no other way to take her back." He should have thought of that. "Thank you for all you have done, Pruatra." The dragon nodded.

He pulled out the amulet and envisioned his bedroom. Ever since he told her of his dream, Nemara had been nesting; there was already clothing for a baby and blankets galore. He appeared and immediately checked the baby, heaving a sigh of relief when she giggled as he unwrapped her. He moved to the bell pull after flipping the cloak back over the small infant.

Radney did not take long to appear. "It is difficult, Lord Alador, to know where you are in this house. How may I serve?"

"Fetch Lady Nemara, even if you have to send a runner looking for her. It is urgent." Alador stated.

"She is in the library. Should I escort her?" Radney raised a brow, trying to discern what could be urgent, but then his face melted into a roguish grin. "Or not?"

Alador chuckled at his manservant's assumptions. "She is in no need of escort."

They both grinned at one another as Radney left. He took the baby up once more, this time without the cloak. He looked at his favorite cloak and realized that it would need washing.

Grimacing at the mess, he took her into the bath and pulled out a pail of water. He had just finished cleaning her up the only way he knew how, dipping her in and out of the pail, and was wrapping a blanket around Latiera when Nemara rushed in. She saw the blanket and her face lit with excitement. "She is here? Let me have her! You're doing that wrong." She gently took the baby out of his hands. "Did you name her?" She flipped back the cover that hid the child's face. "Oooh Alador, she is beautiful." The infant looked up at Nemara with those great big eyes.

"Yes, her name is Latiera, and she is beautiful, but there is a problem." Alador put a hand on Nemara's arm. "We have to keep her covered when out of this room. It seems she can shift shapes to a hatchling dragon."

Nemara stared down at the baby in amazement. "I have never heard of an infant having that much magic?"

"Neither had Pruatra. It will take some time to ensure it doesn't happen randomly." Alador admitted. "How do we feed her?"

"I will hire a wet nurse. Until then, a cloth soaked in teben milk will have to do." Her authority on the matter was clear.

"How do you know this stuff?"

Nemara smiled. "I, unlike you, paid attention while I lived with the Daezun."

Alador took her hand. "This means you won't be fighting." He cleared his throat. It was as clear of a command as he dare give the impetuous woman.

"I may. I dare anyone to come in here. I will down them before they are even aware that they have found us." Nemara clutched the baby protectively. It was as if it were her own.

"I am sure you will, my dear woman." He grinned

wickedly. "I pity the poor guardsman that wanders in searching for the enemy.

*Chapter Thirty-Three*

The army of hundreds of Daezun had convened at the cave entrance in the mountains above Dorien's home. Dorien and the elders of each village had made their way to the front of the well-provisioned assemblage. They estimated the journey might take over a week, and they had to be on time.

The blacksmith was not the most senior in the gathering of leaders. However, because he had called them all to arms with the help of the red dragon, and because he did possess the physique of a bull, each of the other elders bowed to him.

"Shall we proceed?" Dorien waved a hand toward the cave.

This had once been a dragon cave, eons ago. It was deserted now, but lent itself well to the starting point for the army's journey to Silverport, and their battle to support the dragonsworn.

With torches in hand, they led their men and women into the massive cave. The floor had been rubbed smooth as glass from the many years a dragon family lived here. The main cave had many smaller tunnels, which curled off into darkness and no doubt led to other sub-caves.

Dorien moved slowly toward the back wall, scaling a large earthen mound well over twice his height. He wondered if this had been the place the nest rested, or if it had been where the hoard of the resident dragon was once piled and on display. In any case, he made it to the top, closely followed by the handful of village elders leading the Daezun complement.

The young man reached for the huge dragon horn slung across his back. It came easily out of its sheath, its ivory glistening in the torch light, its carved runes worn by age. The elders during the Great War were told by the golden dragon who gave it to them that it was one of the horns of the original golden dragons. The dragon leader instilled in it magic the Daezun would not normally be able to access. Everyone in the forefront of this gathering had heard the tale, but none had ever heard the horn or seen its magic called upon.

It was so heavy Dorien had to hold it with both hands. He hesitated. The oldest elder of all the villages came to his side and laid a hand on his arm.

"It is time, Dorien. Let us rout these elitist mages once and for all. Let us be the ones who help bring the balance of magic between dragon and mortal back to the land."

Dorien took in a deep breath and raised the horn to his mouth, blowing as hard as he could. The horn did not produce the sound of any instrument anyone had ever heard. Instead, it emitted the mighty roar of a dragon.

Everywhere the sound hit… everywhere it bounced and ricocheted off the rock… the rock vanished. The cavern grew larger and by the third blowing of the dragon horn, the back wall of the cave was developing into a massive tunnel. A tunnel that would take them across the island and up under the plains outside of Silverport.

===***===

Sordith stood on the plain. It was fast approaching daybreak, and if Dorien did not arrive soon the assault on Silverport would take place without the help of the Daezun.

The Trench Lord paced and cursed quietly below his breath. "LATE! Damn it! I swear I'll never…"

His whispered words caught in his throat when he felt a trembling below his feet. Panic overtook him as he turned to check on the harbor. Was it another wave coming to destroy all he and his people had managed to salvage from the last one?

The sea was calm, but the tremor below his feet increased. An earthquake then! He ran back toward the city and the stone of the ramp to the first-tier in order to gain a firmer footing. Once on the ramp, he turned back toward the plain. He was amazed at what he saw.

A huge portion of the plain had disappeared and left a mighty sinkhole. Sordith had just enough time to think that it might be residual damage for the storm. Would it expose the caves he and Keelee came back to the city through?

Before his mind could question any further, the Daezun army started to bubble up out of the hole like water from a mountain spring.

Dorien had arrived.

## Chapter Thirty-Four

"Milord, Severent is here and is requesting an audience. He says it is urgent." Luthian's servant stood in front of the High Minister's desk awaiting instructions.

"Send him in," Luthian granted with a wave of his hand. He shuffled the papers on his desk into a pile as he waited for his head henchman to appear.

Severent stomped into the room with a burst of energy, but he held his tongue until the servant retreated and closed the door behind him.

"We have a problem," Severent blurted out as soon as he heard the latch click into place.

Luthian had rarely seen his trusted assassin so shaken. He rose from his desk, as he demanded, "Speak up man... What is it?"

"I believe the Daezun are on their way to attack the city," he replied, as his hand flexed involuntarily on the hilt of his sword.

Luthian went to the sideboard where he poured himself and Severent a drink. He needed time to consider this outburst. "What brings you to this conclusion?" he asked as he turned back and handed Severent a glass.

He usually did not offer the man a drink. After all, he was a servant, if a servant of a higher grade then the house staff. However, he wanted all the information Severent possessed, and in a manner where he could sift through it and plan properly. This just might be another way to deal with the Daezun, which he could use rather than starving them out. A show of superiority was always a wise tactical move and might prove a much faster solution to the problem. Luthian prided himself on being flexible with his planning.

Severent accepted the glass and followed Luthian to the two chairs by the fire. When the High Minister took a seat, the assassin had the sense not to sit without being invited. He positioned himself in front of his employer at the mantle.

"The first I got wind of something developing was from my 'eyes' in Lady Aldemar's make-shift healer's clinic."

Luthian had tasked Severent to place spies in key locations. He told the man he needed eyes everywhere. Since then Severent had called his circle of assassins and minor henchmen his 'eyes.' Luthian had not trusted Lady Aldemar for years, and he'd made a point of being sure Severent kept an 'eye' on her.

"Even though the injured from the storm have all been gathered and attended to," Severent went on, "the Lady still requested the production of spools of bandages and compresses. When my 'eye' asked for the reason, since many were being sent home from the clinic, she was told by one of the other girls that Lady Aldemar said there might be further need in the future. I think she is in league with the Daezun and preparing to assist with the wounded in the coming attack."

Luthian sipped at his drink. "Well, preparation could mean other things too. It does not seem to be something to be alarmed about. Perhaps she is just being cautious.; another storm could descend on us."

"But, milord," Severent cautioned, "that is not all." He took a swig of his drink as if to fortify himself and went on. "My 'eye' in the Blackguard says that there seems to be an escalation of training and preparation of weapons. What if the Blackguard intend to join in this attack by the Daezun? The city could be taken on two fronts."

"Seems to be?" Luthian asked. "I see no reason to worry about what 'seems to be.'" Bariton always had the Blackguard at the ready, or the High Minister would have his head. Why was his man running scared?

"And then my 'eye' in the trench has witnessed the Trench Lord and his man Owen in secreted conversation several times this past week." Severent's eyes squinted in distrust. "You know he holds no love for the members on the higher tiers of this city, especially you, milord."

"I really do not see what you are so worked up about, Severent." Luthian rose and headed back toward the sideboard for a refill on his drink. He was perfectly aware of the Trench Lord's animosity – that was the reason he was having him watched. "It is only natural that the Trench Lord and his man should have meetings."

"But this is the most important piece, milord," Severent said, "the 'eye' I have in the Daezun community sent me a message by bird today. There has been a mass exodus of adult Daezun from all the villages he has contact with."

Luthian stopped in his tracks and turned back. "Where did your 'eye' say they had gone?"

"Unknown… His note said they 'disappeared.'" Severent downed the last of his drink in one long drought.

This was a revelation. The Daezun had to be coming on foot, or those slow korpen beasts they used. They could not be here before Luthian had the opportunity to prepare a warm welcome for them. He put down the glass and went back to his desk. He almost grinned at this juicy piece of information. He had time to call in Levielle's troops and alert Morana so she could bring her dragons. This was almost more than he could have asked for. The Daezun were going to walk right into a trap he would set to take them all down.

"Severent! Position men around my mansion. I have plans to execute and I do not want them interrupted."

The man placed his glass on the mantel and gave the High Minister a slight bow. Luthian smirked and waved him away. He had taught this man how to serve and respond properly… he would teach the Daezun to do the same.

## Chapter Thirty-Five

The army's scryer ran through the camp to deliver the urgent message to the general. He wove in and out between the tents and campsites with only an occasional burst of profanity from someone he accidentally kicked dust on. He slid to a stop outside the main entrance and took a couple of breaths before he entered the tent.

The four men gathered round the table eyed him with dark scrutiny. He stammered, "Message from the High Minister, General." He handed it across, his face white and his hand shaking. He had not meant to interrupt an important meeting, but the message was urgent.

Levielle looked toward the other men around the table and smirked at the young scryer and his disheveled state. "I'm shocked it hasn't exploded into flames." Levielle waved the man a dismissal. "Get yourself some water and then return to your post, master scryer."

The young man nodded thankfully and scurried from the room.

"Hmm..." Levielle read the note slowly as he paced around the room. Finally, he crumpled the parchment and tossed it to the corner. He considered the questioning looks of the other men about the table. "It seems the High Minister is having a bit of a Daezun problem in his city."

"Daezun? Have the Blackguard revolted?" Berg was a shrewd Lieutenant and was better at reading

Levielle then the general liked.

"No, it seems that the Daezun have mounted an attack against the city and are trying to seize it." Levielle almost chuckled at the mere thought. Alador was proving to be a mage to be reckoned with. The pieces were falling into place. "We are ordered to make haste to the city, and defend the council from harm."

"I will have the word spread to prepare for immediate march." Orrin was all business. The man was the youngest in the group and from a military family; he would make a good general himself, one day.

"There is no hurry," Levielle said calmly, picking up the glass he had been drinking from and taking a leisurely sip. "We will break camp tomorrow morning and begin the march home the following day."

The three looked from one to the other. The general seemed very nonchalant about what sounded like an emergency.

"We defend the city and its inhabitants, not the council itself. The Daezun are attacking the council, very specifically." Levielle looked at the men around the table.

"How do you know this, Sir?" Orrin asked. "If the council tier is to be attacked, citizens will be caught in the crossfire. There are families of our men in that city."

"There are, and they will be unharmed." Levielle smiled toward them. "Berg, why am I not concerned?" He looked over at the man, waiting for the response that normally came correctly. Berg was older and had been with him for years.

The man stroked his iron jaw covered with a thick black and silver beard. "My instincts say you knew the attack was coming and the motivations behind it."

Orrin frowned. "Sir, are you about to commit an act of treason?"

"Committed - I helped plan it," he admitted, looking over at Orrin. "The High Minister, Luthian Guldalian, decided he didn't much care for the men, women, and children in the trench, or the families of our men. No…" He hesitated and rephrased his statement. "He decided he wanted power. What better way to deal with the unwashed masses that existed than to use a storm to wipe them out."

Levielle leaned on his knuckles over the table, the wood creaking from the shifting weight. "Our High Minister used another mage to put up the walls, and had her killed before he was found out."

The three men looked shocked. "Are you certain, Sir?" Tyloris asked. He was a big man, good at leading defense and undercover assaults.

"Positive! The High Minister told me himself. He destroyed the city, sent a hard winter on the isle, all for a grasp at power." He looked around the table, holding each of them for a moment in his hard gaze. "Have I ever lied to you before?"

"No Sir!" All three men replied without hesitation.

"General, do we tell the men of the attack? I mean... we are the defenders of Silverport." Orrin looked at Levielle clearly battling with himself over where his loyalties should lie.

"Our troops will be marching back to assist the Daezun in removing a tyrant and bringing about a rise to a much better ruler. In the meantime, I will see about taking some men back to assist in battling against the mages that are corrupt." He paused and looked at them once again, standing around the table. "How many days march are we from Silverport?"

"Three, Sir. The troops will be late to the fight. If you go, who do you wish to take charge?" Orrin's fists were clenched and his face puckered into a frown.

Looking toward the man, Levielle sighed and braced himself. "You have something to say, Orrin?"

Orrin turned to face his superior. His words were to the point and held a bit of accusation. "I do not believe a man who is committing treason by his own admission should be in charge of the army. I apologize General, but I am a man of Silverport and what you have done... strikes me as wrong."

Levielle gave a nod after a moment of consideration. "I suppose that is true." He moved around the table, opposite of Orrin, making sure not to make any sudden moves. "It does require my removal from the army, and the others around this table do get a say in that decision. With or without the army, this is taking place. So, you can call for my removal." Levielle stopped and clasped his hands behind his back, waiting for the man's response.

Orrin looked at the other two, then back. "I feel you should step down."

Berg and Tyloris shifted uncomfortably.

Tyloris spoke up. "The General has never lied to us, nor led us astray before, Orrin. I would like to have faith that his words are genuine."

Levielle waited. This was not something he could intervene in.

"Even if his words are truth, he should not commit the army to such treachery. I believe we should leave in the morning. With or without our general's consent." Orrin's insubordination brought even more discomfort to the other two.

"I am sorry General, but regardless of you commands, I believe, for the safety of the rest of us, the army should march. What if your planned coup fails? The anger will fall upon all of those that command." Orrin had calmed as he made his point clear.

"I was still planning on marching toward the city." Levielle smiled softly toward the men, making his way around the table toward Orrin. "And to your point, Lieutenant, you all are not aware of this happening. If it fails, I alone am responsible, and I will vanish into smoke." He met all their looks with reassurance. "I'm not bringing anyone down with me."

"Then will you allow us to march in the morning?" Orrin asked, clearly uncomfortable with the position he was now in.

"Of course," Levielle nodded slowly, "I will admit, I thought that you all would be more...accepting." He sighed and moved away from the table.

"Then I vote that the General does not give up his command," Tyloris stated.

"I also vote that we follow the commands of our General and trust him to lead us faithfully as he ever has," agreed Berg.

Orrin looked at them evenly. "I do not concur, but I am outvoted." He looked to Levielle. "If you play our men false, I will find you and kill you," he stated evenly. "I respect you, but this is wrong."

"It is wrong, Orrin," he agreed softly, looking out of the tent where the flaps tussled in the wind before looking to the one dissenter in his midst, "but I'm afraid there is no other way to bring about the change we need. And that is why I acted." He moved over to Orrin's side, looking down at him and gently placed a hand on his shoulder. "Trust me." He gave the shoulder of the man a squeeze and a gentle shake.

"Who will be in charge when you leave?" Orrin looked up at him; doubt was in his eyes, but he was a man of business.

"You will be, Orrin." Giving a small shake once more, Levielle let him go. "You have my full confidence."

The man was surprised, particularly after his objections, but he gave a curt nod. "Permission to order an assembly. I will not mention why, other than we are returning home." He thought of something else. "You may need to silence the scryer."

Levielle nodded. "Good point. Give the order."

Looking to the other two men, Levielle shrugged. "Anyone want to join me in causing some trouble?"

"I will." Tyloris gave a grin. "In for a trading token anyway, so might as well go the full slip."

"Any other men that may want to join in taking down a tyrant?" Levielle waited.

"I think I should stay with Orrin." Berg said. Levielle could almost see him mentally winking. The wise old soldier would keep an eye on the young newly-elevated leader of the troops.

Orrin looked at Levielle. "What do you want done with the prisoner?"

"I'll take her with me," he stated firmly. He did not want any resistance on this matter. "Tyloris, do you have another five or so men that might be willing to join us?"

"I am sure I can find some if I tell them the High Minister ordered the sealing of the trench." The man looked pleased at the idea of a real battle for a change.

"Very well, you are all dismissed." Levielle nodded.

All three men left swiftly. Orrin and Berg went to give the order for a pack up to begin. Tyloris went to gather men to travel with their general.

Levielle watched as they left, pulling out a small amulet from his pocket. He smiled down at it, giving it a slight rub. "Seems we need to travel fast, old friend."

===***===

Levielle passed the guard and knocked on the wood pole outside Ruby's tent. The camp was already readying itself for the long march ahead.

"Come," Ruby called.

Levielle ducked as he entered. "Hello, Ruby."

He was still amazed at her resemblance to Lady Aldemar. After questioning Ruby, he felt very confident she was his old friend's daughter. The young woman said she was raised in an orphanage. Severent came each year to test the children and any who showed magical talent were taken away. When she set her bed on fire during a particularly bad dream, Severent was summoned and she was taken into Luthian's private orphanage to be put with other children with powers. There they were trained at a very early age to be efficient assassins. This culling of talented orphans must have been the High Minister's first attempt at building a magical army before he thought to breed the Blackguard.

Ruby's resemblance to Lady Aldemar was uncanny. When Levielle went to see her after the surgery, while she was resting he noticed the heart shaped birthmark on her shoulder. It was identical to the one on Aldemar.

Levielle also remembered the extended stay Aldemar had with her aunt years ago up the northern coast. That time coincided with the approximate age of the young woman before him.

With all these factors in play, he had revealed to Ruby his suspicions of knowing who her mother was and where she was.

He went to the young woman and squatted before her. Ruby was stitching up holes in her clothing, and wore only a simple dressing gown. She looked up, her long hair loose only adding to the vision of the Lady of his prior affections.

"How is your arm?" he asked.

"Healing, but still uncomfortable." She pointed to the still reddened bandage where her mark of death once laid.

"Yes, well, you aren't dead," he smirked. He stood and backed away a step. "I wanted to ask, are you ready to meet your mother?" Levielle palmed the amulet, comforted by the feel of it once more in his hand. The young woman had had time to consider his revelation for several days now.

Ruby looked hesitant. "I do not think I will ever be truly ready. My mother… she may reject me. I know not why she gave me away in the first place." She looked at him evenly, her cultured tones unmistakable to any familiar with the upper tiers.

He nodded, acknowledging her concern, but smiled reassuringly. "I doubt that. I have known your mother most of my life and I have never known her to be uncaring."

Setting her sewing aside, Ruby returned a weak smile. "When are we leaving?"

"In an hour's time. We'll be there soon after." Grabbing the side pole of the tent, he looked down at Ruby. "Your mother could likely use an extra pair of hands to help with the healers, when we get there."

"You know my sphere is not in healing, milord." Her quiet words lay between them. "Fire is what I control." She held out her hand, palm up and a flame materialized. It danced around on her hand until she extinguished it by making a fist.

"You were the one who started the fire, that distracted my guards, the night you attacked me." Levielle said with conviction. That was another thing he had puzzled out, and explained why she came from behind that night. She was late to the tent – lucky for her.

"Yes, and you have powers too," she pointed out. "Severent had no idea you were a mage." She shook her head with amazement. "How have you kept it hidden?"

"Let's just say that, in a different life... I had many more secrets." Pocketing the talisman, he extended his hand before her. Pulling power to it, shadows from about the room pooled in his hand. An inky blackness filled his palm and formed a ball, pulling up into the air just above it as if liquid evaporating.

Ruby's eyes opened in surprise. "You're a Death Mage! Is that how my companions failed?" she whispered. She had wondered where they were when she woke in the tent after the attempt on his life.

"Perhaps." He admitted softly, looking at her eyes rather than the ball in his hands. He chuckled and let the shadows flow off and back onto the floor, vanishing as they did.

"I will be ready when you call for me, General." Her hands moved down her form almost seductively, and her clothes shifted into red robes. The sigil of fire appeared on the sleeves.

Levielle only watched her face. He smiled toward her, remembering the robes he wore so many years ago.

Another lifetime indeed. "I will send for you in an hour."
He opened the flap and moved outside in one motion.

===***===

Ruby was ready and appeared with the guardsman
sent to retrieve her. Her hair was tied back in a severe
style, but it only accentuated her resemblance to her
mother. He could easily picture Lady Aldemar at this age
- only their robes were a different color.

Various men were gathered, looking for blood -
specifically the High Minister's blood. They stood
silently in the tent. Placing his hand in his pocket Levielle
felt the talisman. A reminder of vast powers.

He beckoned Ruby to his side and smiled.
"Ready?" he asked quietly under his breath.

"Yes," she responded equally soft, but with an air
of excitement.

Levielle spoke up. His voice took on the
commanding tone that came with his station. "Everyone
must be connected. Form a circle and grasp a hand, wrist
or shoulder. Also, I suggest you close your eyes; this will
be... interesting... if you've never experienced it before."

Ruby placed her hand upon Levielle's arm and
closed her eyes. She was no stranger to traveling spells.
She had cast them numerous times. She smiled thinking
of how many would vomit when they arrived at their
destination.

As Levielle pushed out a small amount of power,
he could feel the energy of everyone interconnecting for
the moment, assuring him they were all touching.

"Be ready," he said, muttering the incantation as one poor soul asked, "ready for what?"

In that instant, they vanished. The tail of the tent they were in flapped in the breeze of their powerful disappearance.

Ruby felt the cool air when they arrived. She shook her head back and forth quickly to help her inner ear regain balance then opened her eyes. They were on the third tier. Everything was dark and silent. Men and women moved about. She recognized the uniform of the Blackguard and some mages in various colors of robes.

"Remain here, men. Ruby, if you will come with me?" He placed a hand at the small of her back, directing her from the crowd of dazed and moaning men. Traveling spells were often very confusing at first. Some looked at him as though he were mad.

Levielle had spotted Lady Aldemar in the crowd at the mouth of the Blackguard's caverns. She had her back to them as she addressed another mage in whispered tones. The general guided Ruby forward. When they were behind Aldemar he looked to Ruby and nodded toward her mother's back.

Ruby took a deep breath. Levielle reached out with his other hand and tapped the older healer on the shoulder. She turned.

Mother and daughter stared at each other, neither saying a word. Lady Aldemar looked at Levielle in confusion.

"In my travels, it seems I found something you lost, milady." His tone was one of softness and a bit of mischief. Taking a step back, he watched the encounter unfold.

"My child?" Lady Aldemar looked at her in shock. "Is it really you? They told me you were dead." She stepped forward, and without hesitation, pulled her into her arms. "Oh, my darling daughter."

Ruby returned the hug and responded with just one word, "mother."

Smiling toward the women embracing, Levielle spoke up after a moment. "It seems I need to find a certain Trench Lord now, but I thought it best to return this first."

Lady Aldemar nodded. She reached out with one hand and squeezed her old friend's arm. "Thank you Levielle. I will be forever in your debt."

With a small bow Levielle moved away, back toward the men who seemed to be regaining their footing.

"Exhilarating, isn't it?" He chuckled and was answered by groans of displeasure from most of them. "We've got work to do, come on."

*Chapter Thirty-Six*

Sordith jumped, pulling two of his knives in a swift reaction to the hand on his shoulder, but when he turned to fight, it was Owen.

The big man held up his hands. "Don't kill the man who came to help you," he protested.

"You were supposed to wait with the others on the third tier." Sordith hissed in anger as he sheathed his blades. He didn't like surprises, and after the sight of the Daezun arrival he would have to admit he was shaken already. Every nerve was on edge.

"I thought you might need help." His Second was not apologetic.

Owen had not been far from the Trench Lord's side since he'd been found in Aldemar's makeshift healer's clinic after the storm. It seemed the Trench Lord's 'muscle' attributed his own survival of the storm to Sordith's sending him away to help evacuate the people to the third tier; he'd actually been on the third tier when the wave hit. This had given him a bird's eye view of the event, and he shared Sordith's burning hatred of the High Minister. When Alador was not sitting at his brother's side as he healed, Sordith and Owen spent hours plotting their revenge.

Owen was already working on the Trench Lord's manor when Sordith and Keelee were released from the healers to return home. He had no family, but he had friends in the trench and had hired the surviving children Sordith always spoiled on the first tier. They almost had the manor cleared of debris by the time the Trench Lord took residence once more. Sordith saw a whole other side to his muscle as Owen arrived each morning and proved himself adept with a hammer and saw. The two men's bond grew deeper as they worked and plotted over their mid-day meals together.

Sordith shook his head, clapping the loyal man on the shoulder with a smile. "Let's go meet our new friends." He headed out on the plain to greet the growing horde of Daezun.

"Dorien?" he called in a stage whisper that could be heard over the silently moving crowd. For such a large group, they were very quiet, but Sordith reminded himself that these men and women were hunters, used to walking quietly through the woods.

"Here!" a stocky, well-built man at the front replied.

Sordith and Owen moved in closer. Loud voices on the plain would carry up the tiers, and might alert someone to the Daezun arrival.

"I am Sordith, and this is Owen. Alador sent me. We are to lead you to the third tier to join up with the Blackguard and the others who will fight on our side."

"This is my brother Tentret," Dorien said, placing a hand on the shoulder of the young man beside him. "He won't be fighting; he is here to keep a record of this event. These are the leaders and the elders of the villages who have joined us." He waved a hand over the men huddled closely behind him. "We will learn each other's names after we rid ourselves of these tyrants."

Sordith nodded. He pointed to the Blackguard's cavern on the third tier. There was a half moon, and you could see the torches which always burned at its entrance. "We are headed up there. The first tier is all but deserted; if you encounter anyone there or on the second tier they are friendly and we should warn them to stay inside. We gather on the third to make the assault on the fourth and fifth."

With those brief instructions, Sordith and Owen led the Daezun into the city, sprinting ahead onto the ramp from the trench to the first tier. The rubble from the stone wall which had blocked it during the storm was piled to either side in huge chunks. It slowed the large invading force as they made their way between the impromptu mountains of rock.

Sordith and Owen ran like prangs evading a hunter's arrow across the first tier to the ramp up to the second. They were both amazed at the silent movement of the large group of men and women behind them. They were even more shocked when they took the turn onto the second tier - there were Daezun already there and working their way up to the third tier in front of them! The villagers had brought leather-padded grappling hooks with ropes attached, and now at least half of the Daezun, with bows and swords slung over their backs, were scaling the tier walls while the other half moved along behind the two men.

Sordith and Owen grinned at each other. If the villagers were as good with a bow as Alador assured them they would be, these people were going to be a formidable enemy.

The Daezun held back on the third tier, coiling up their ropes and slinging them over their shoulders as they waited for the Lerdenians to make it to the front.

The Trench Lord arrived slightly out of breath, and Owen patted random Daezun on the back in admiration as he passed the ones who arrived before him before he slumped onto a nearby barrel. Sordith smiled at this companion. He was a fighter, not a sprinter, but he would be fine once he caught his breath.

Finally, they made their way to the front of the cavern and the greeting party that awaited them. "Bariton," Sordith held out his hand to the Master of the Blackguard.

Bariton clasped it and gave him a grin. "Looks like our Daezun friends will come in handy." He had watched them flow over the walls like the water of the recent storm. Hopefully, they would do as much damage to the fourth and fifth tiers as the wave had done to the trench and the first.

Sordith waved Dorien forward. "This is Dorien, Alador's brother. He leads the Daezun."

Bariton nodded at the man. He was built like a bull and yet, the Blackguard leader had watched him scale the wall to the third tier with ease, as if he were one of the city's rats.

Lady Aldemar stepped forward with a young lady who bore an uncanny resemblance to her. "This is my dear friend, Sordith, the Trench Lord," she told her companion. "Sordith... this is my daughter, Ruby."

Sordith looked at the healer with surprised eyes full of questions.

"I will explain later, when we have time," Aldemar added with a shy smile. "Suffice to say, she is not yours."

Sordith nodded and hoped that he lived through the battle in order to hear this tale.

"Levielle brought her to me," Aldemar said and graced the general with one of her smile.

Sordith had not seen the general in the crowd of Blackguards behind the leaders.

Levielle stepped forward and offered his hand. "I understand you are coordinating this assault."

This statement awakend the Trench Lord to his duties.

"Alador did not tell me you would be here," Sordith confessed.

"He did not know I was sent for. In fact, it was the High Minister who mistakenly assumed he could summon me to his side."

Sordith had never seen the general smile so broadly.

"Well, with this development, I would suggest that I turn over the command to you, Sir. You are far more experienced than I am in these actions." Sordith made a slight bow toward the general.

Levielle looked from one to the other of the leaders spread around him. Lady Aldemar nodded her approval, and Bariton did the same, but it was Dorien who said what all of them were feeling, "I care not who is in charge, let's just get it done!"

"Indeed," Levielle agreed. "Lady Aldemar what is the status of the mages you have gathered?"

"I have brought all of those who are with us to this level. If they remain on the fourth or fifth tiers, they are our enemies."

"Very well," the general declared. "We must be able to tell friend from foe." He raised his hand and clenched his fist. Every man and woman, whether Daezun, mage, soldier or Blackguard on the third tier, felt a slight blow of energy to their backs, as if they had been thumped resoundingly by a friendly hand. When they looked at each other's backs, where they had been blank moments before, a silver dragon was now embroidered there. The image shone in the moonlight as if enchanted. "Any who wear the dragon are friend," Levielle declared. He nodded at Dorien. "Station your best archers at the far ends of the third tier. Have them work their way up higher as the opportunities arrive. The rest of your people can make a direct assault via your handy grappling hooks."

He looked toward Bariton. "Your Blackguard must work on two fronts. Station your best trained mages down here to protect all of those on this tier and below. We'll have no more deaths below the fourth," he declared with conviction. "Send the rest up the ramps to the higher tiers to engage the enemy and protect any non-mage servants who are fleeing the fight."

He turned his attention to Lady Aldemar and Ruby. "Wreak havoc on any mage you encounter."

"And help the dragons rid the city of the fifth-tier scum," Sordith added.

"Trench Lord…" the general started to instruct.

"I am sorry, Levielle…" Sordith interrupted. "I have an appointment with Alador."

The Trench Lord turned and waved a beckoning hand to Owen. *Or more precisely, I have an appointment with the High Minister.*

## Chapter Thirty-Seven

At the first sign of attack Luthian had summoned Severent back to his side and sent an urgent message to Levielle that they were out of time. He instructed the General to bring the army at a forced march, but even as he gave the order he knew they couldn't arrive in time.

Severent stationed his men in a protective perimeter around the High Minister's manor. He personally took up a position in the lee of the garden wall, with a direct view and path to the front entrance. With four others scattered in the shadows, the front of the mansion was well covered.

There were two archers stationed on the roof. With the building two stories high, and the added height of a turret toward the back, the bowmen would have a wide area of surveillance.

The High Minister was a powerful mage, but as this battle escalated Severent could see why Luthian was concerned. He could hear shouting, sword clashes and the whine of arrows through the air. It was bedlam below the fifth tier, and headed up toward them. Even though Severent held no magical powers himself, he could feel the energy in the air. It was like another storm cascading ashore. The hair on his arms had risen, and even his scalp felt itchy.

There was a burst of flames on the tier below, and then a sound like a sheet whipping in a stiff wind. He looked up to see a huge red dragon glide over the city, followed by several other dragons. They were all raining fire down on the fourth and fifth tiers.

Severent crawled from his hiding place to the edge of the manor property and lay on his belly watching the dragons attack the top two tiers. Stone shattered and exploded around him, but not one dragon's fire hit the High Minister's mansion. It was as if it had a protective force around it, but when he reached out, he could feel nothing. Why was the leader's home being spared? He put himself in the mind of the enemy. Why would he not assault the ruler's home?

Because someone else was... One of their own was either here or coming here and they had been told to hold their fire. Most likely the human element of this battle was also being kept at bay.

Who would be the attacker? Severent had never liked or trusted the younger brother, Henrick. He was too amiable, and he reminded Severent of an actor in one of the plays you could see performed by the traveling bards on the plains during the summer.

Or could it be the nephew? Alador seemed young, but Severent knew Luthian was afraid of him on some level or he would not have needed the village girl for insurance to keep the younger mage in line.

There was an ear-splitting roar and the home just below the High Minister's was hit, exploding high into the air in a fountain of debris. Rock shrapnel rained down on Severent, and he retreated to his place behind the garden wall to wait.

Sordith watched as the Daezun scaled the wall to the fourth tier. He stopped and turned back toward Owen.

"Give me a leg up," he ordered.

Even in the pale moonlight he could see Owen's questioning look. "You ain't goin' without me," he protested.

"No, I am not," he agreed, "I just think we could make faster time their way." He waved a hand at the wall pointing out the Daezun successfully climbing up.

Owen bent his knees and cupped his hands for Sordith's boot. The Trench Lord put his foot in Owen's palms and immediately felt a surge which almost propelled him over the wall. The big man was more powerful than he'd imagined. Once on the fourth tier, Sordith quietly borrowed one of the Daezun's ropes, and with the help of the stocky owner and one of his friends, they hauled Owen up.

The Daezun were all silently working their way to station themselves at the doors of each habitat on the fourth tier for a surprise attack, but it was not to be. A cry rang out - one of the city guards had shouted an alarm before they could be silenced by the Blackguards assigned the task of dispatching them.

Bedlam swiftly ensued. Swords clashed, arrows whizzed overhead and spells were being cast like spears through the air.

A powerful light erupted on the outlook off the Blackguard's cavern. It wasn't a fire, it was more like lightning. It was shortly after that when the dragons appeared and started to attack.

As Sordith and Owen fought their way up the length of the fourth tier to the fifth, they saw a stone mage start to throw up a wall against the invading force, but a dragon flew in close and raked it down, burying the mage in the process.

Two nature mages, one wearing the silver dragon and one not, fought against each other, each wrapping their opponent in crawling vines and slinging thorny armed branches at one another.

A fire mage and a water enhanced Blackguard were dueling one-on-one on the stairs to the fourth tier. Flames were raining down on the Blackguard, who was having trouble drawing enough water from the slough to overpower the defending mage. Unfortunately for the fire mage, he was so focused on the foe he could see that he failed to notice Sordith's dagger coming. The knife caught him right through the throat and impaled him on the post behind him.

Sordith and Owen both slapped the Blackguard companionably on the back as they passed. The Trench Lord retrieved his dagger and kept on running; they were almost there.

But they were immediately stalled just topping the stairs to the fourth tier. A young blue dragon was actually on the tier, furiously digging at one of the stone mansions. Its claws ripped and tore at the stone, which flew from its paws in great chunks; whoever was in that mansion was not going to live through the assault. It head-butted the stone on the front of the building, letting loose a mighty roar as the facade began to crumble.

The dragon did not see the man who had climbed up to the roof while he was busy with the door and face of the house. The mage took advantage of this distraction by sending a bolt of lightning straight at his head. It hit the beast, knocking him off balance and sending back over the edge of the fifth tier. Sordith and Owen dropped below the wall to keep from being pushed over by the tumbling young dragon.

They were about to raise their heads when a blast of dragon fire incinerated the mage on the roof and a huge red dragon plummeted past them down the tiers after the falling young blue. The blue struck the third tier, taking a portion with him, but the red caught him in his talons before he hit the next tier. They watched as the bigger dragon took the blue to the plain and laid him down gently.

The obstruction out of their way, the two men headed up the fourth tier walk toward the stairs to the fifth tier, and on to the High Minister's mansion.

The fifth tier had not yet been reached by the human fighting force. It was eerily quiet compared to the fourth tier, where dragons swooped through the air, scorching everything they saw. But fire was not their only weapon. Some of the buildings on this tier were frozen into tombs; others had been shattered, and lay in rubble.

The mages were doing their best to defend the city, but they were losing to the more powerful dragons.

A silver dragon let out an ear-piercing roar, and the building behind them shattered into a million rock projectiles. Sordith and Owen were thrown to the ground and lay dazed for a moment.

Owen waved a fist at the beast as it circled around again. "We're on your side!" he yelled.

The dragon tipped a wing and flapped off to the other end of the tier to help another silver battling with a mage, who was levitating the debris from the broken buildings and hurling it at the dragons. Some of the stones were being caught by the dragon and thrown back, like a giant game of catch, but others were missed and came tumbling down the tiers in an avalanche. Screams rang up from the injured below.

Sordith was trying to rise when Owen grabbed his arm and pulled him to his feet.

"You alright?" he yelled. Both their hearing had been affected by the roar of the dragon and the explosion it caused.

The Trench Lord shook his head. Owen sounded far away and as though he were in a barrel. He couldn't fight the High Minister in this condition. The mansion was right at the top of the last set of stairs, then only another sprint down the walk, but Sordith motioned they should sit for a minute in the lee of the tier wall. He had to regain his balance before he could move against Luthian.

Severent shook his head. He had lost part of his hearing with that last blast. He pulled at his ears, forcing himself to swallow in an attempt to pop the bubble that seemed to have formed over his hearing.

He looked toward the archers on the roof, but they were no longer there. Either the stone projectiles from the explosion of the mansion took them out, or they had not come to the same conclusion as Severent about the house being off limits and had run away. If he lived through this and found them, he would see they never disobeyed him again.

He was still trying to get his hearing back when the Trench Lord and his lackey appeared. At first glance he thought the men were looking to take refuge with the High Minister, but then something about their approach tipped him off to the fact that these might be the ones dispatched to kill the High Minister. If they were, then his work would be easy. These men were like him, with no magic to save them.

Severent looked for his own men; there appeared to be only two left. He could see another one dead, bloody head hanging over the same wall he was hiding behind, victim of a rock from the building below. The guard Severent had stationed at the far side of the compound was gone; the wall of the mansion next door was laying where he had been crouched.

He signaled to the two remaining men that they needed to take out the Trench Lord's companion; he would handle the 'Lord' himself.

They waited until the two passed them before they attacked.

===***===

Owen, who had regained most of his hearing by now, saw them coming first. He pushed Sordith out of the way of Severent's flying blade, catching it in his own shoulder instead. The big man yanked it out and threw it back at one of the approaching enemies, but it missed its target; Owen had never been as good with a dagger as he was with a sword, and a knife wound hadn't improved his accuracy any. He drew his sword and shifted it to his left hand as the two men rushed him.

Severent was now out of hiding and descending on Sordith. The Trench Lord, hampered by his hearing loss, was operating almost solely on vision. He drew two knives and let them fly at Severent, but his aim was off; the explosion had not only taken part of his hearing, but also thrown off his balance.

Owen was hacking and slashing at the two other men as they tried to position him between them. Their intention was clear - to hamstring him and bring him down.

Sordith wanted to help, but he was having difficulty keeping Severent at bay. The man had drawn his sword and was thrusting and jabbing at the Trench Lord. Sordith turned his sword away easily enough, but could not get free to help Owen.

He heard his friend holler in pain and saw him go down. Sordith feinted back and pulled another dagger from its sheath, throwing it desperately at the man who was about to take Owen's head off. This time his aim was true, and the man went down, falling over Owen. This gave the big man time to pull his own dagger, and when the other man hauled his partner's dead body off Owen, the Trench Lord's bodyguard rose up with a roar and impaled the man with both his sword and his dagger.

Sordith didn't see the killing move, being fully occupied fending off Severent - the man was relentless. The Trench Lord had sliced him several times on the arms and abdomen, but he kept on coming. He must not have had another dagger of his own, because he jabbed at Sordith with his sword until he backed him far enough away to grab one of the fallen ones. Then, sword in one hand and knife in the other, he renewed his attack.

===***===

Owen watched the men fight, unable to rise to help. The sword swipe had taken out his right leg, and he knew he would be a cripple for the rest of his life if he survived.

The two remaining assailants circled each other, weariness showing in their movements. They were equal in size, but Severent was built slimmer, with streamlined muscles.. The better living of the Trench Lord had taken an edge off his speed, and the concussion he took from the explosion had only added to his being off-balance and slower to react.

Owen could feel his life draining away. He could not see it, but his adversary must have sliced a main artery. He was growing cold, and his vision was beginning to blur.

He dragged himself the few feet to the man he killed and withdrew the dagger. He needed to save the Trench Lord. The man was the only person the lower folks in the city could trust, and he was Owen's friend – his only real friend.

Owen caught Sordith's eye behind Severent's back. He smiled through his pain and waved the dagger.

===\*\*\*===

Sordith took a deep breath and charged at Severent. He hacked and slashed, driving the man back toward Owen.

Severent raised his sword and took the blows, but lost ground with each bone crushing whack. He did not have time to look back. He almost stumbled over Owen, and the big man raised his knife in time to catch Luthian's henchman through the back and into the heart.

Sordith pulled Severent's dead body off his friend. He fumbled with his belt and got it off to apply a tourniquet. He could not help but remember doing this just recently for Keelee. Keelee had lived, he reminded himself, tightening the belt until Owen groaned in pain.

"You're going to be alright," he said a little too loudly.

Owen shook his head. "Not this time, milord."

"Of course, you are," Sordith took the dagger from Severent's body and used it to remove the sleeve from Owen's shirt. He wrapped it tightly around the man's leg.

Owen reached out and took his hand. "Leave it. I'm as good as dead."

Sordith shook him off. "I'll not lose another friend."

"What about Luthian?" Owen asked as Sordith almost sent him into unconsciousness applying pressure to his wound.

"There is another who will take care of him," he hollered over the sound of his plugged ears and the battle around them. "I'm taking care of you."

*Chapter Thirty-Eight*

Keensight landed by the fire Alador kindled as a signal to the dragons. It was located behind the city – a direction no one ever thought of from which an attacking force might come. It wasn't far from where Sordith and Keelee had crawled out of the trench during the storm.

The rest of the flights glided in to land behind the large red dragon – blue, green, brown, silver, and gold. There were no other reds. The blues were represented by Amaum, accompanied by his mother Pruatra, and three others. The other three flights had five to six dragons each in their groups. Silverbell led the silver, Ivy the green and Smallstone the brown.

"There isn't much time," Alador said as soon as they were all gathered round. "Levielle has joined us. As with the bloodmine attack, all who are with us will be wearing the silver dragon on their backs. Bariton will have one of his storm mages send up a lightning bolt when everyone is in place. That will be your signal to attack."

Keensight moved to Alador's side and addressed the assembled group. "If you see a human with the dragon sign in trouble, go to their aid. Otherwise, concentrate your efforts on the fifth tier. That is where the most powerful and resistant mages will be."

Alador held up his hand, "But spare the mansion with the protective dome. This is the High Minister's, and he holds a valuable prisoner. I must be the one to attack his home."

Keensight did not look down at Alador, but mumbled under his breath, "unless I get to him first."

Alador knew both his father and Sordith wanted to kill Luthian, but it was his geas that needed to be met, not theirs.

"I have to hurry," Alador said. "I can't use the amulet to get through the protective shield in place over the High Minister's home. Will you take me?" He had never asked Keensight to carry him, though he knew from talking to Dorien that the dragon had invited his brother to ride.

"I will do better than that," the large red dragon said with a lopsided grin on his face. "Smallstone?" he called.

The small brown dragon trotted up to the red who had taken charge of this attack, as he had the mission to save the bloodmine dragons.

"Yes?" Smallstone answered.

"Please show Alador the back way through to the fifth tier," Keensight instructed with a wave of his wing.

"Back way?" Alador responded in surprise.

"Go with Smallstone. It is much faster and safer. Be careful my..." Keensight almost said 'son.'

Alador patted Keensight knowingly on his shoulder and smiled. "You too." When Smallstone extended a wing, the young mage accepted the invitation to mount, and they flew off toward the cliff top. Alador had nothing to hold onto but the ridge scales, which were uncomfortably poking him in the worst ways. Thankfully, however, it was a short flight.

===***===

Once Alador left, there was nothing for the dragons to do but wait for the signal from Bariton. They posted themselves along the deep shadows of the city and cliff face, waiting tensely.

Keensight sat beside Pruatra, though Amaum stationed himself lower, between a green and one of his blue flight members.

"His emotions are still running high," Keensight observed.

Pruatra snorted, ruffling her wings in agitation. "The loss of his sister has been hard for him to overcome, but he will in time. He is his father's son, and will eventually see that what Alador does, he never could do. Just as his father never could before him."

"I was just like Amaum. Renamaum was wise beyond his years. I fought him, but now I see how wrong I was," Keensight said, almost as though he could see through Amaum's eyes. "He will eventually come to accept Alador and his position as dragonsworn."

"The signal!" Ivy called out from the cliff face just above Keensight's head.

The lightning bolt streaked through the sky and crackled across the sparse clouds hanging below the half moon.

"Mind the silver dragons," Keensight intoned as a final warning. "They are our friends."

He spread his huge wings and lifted off to take part in the battle he had been waiting decades for.

===***===

Amaum was ruthless in his attack. It was as if he were taking out all his pent-up anger on the city and its mages. He swooped and swerved, tucked his wings and dove with incredible force. He could not breathe ice yet, as his mother did, but he could rip, tear, and gouge his way through the humans. He envisioned every one of his victims as Alador.

As the other dragons concentrated on the fifth tier per Keensight's instructions, Amaum dove lower and fought alongside the Daezun. His wings flapped as he treaded the air beside the fourth tier and ripped the opposing mages off the wall to chomp them and fling them out into the harbor. Amaum became what most humans thought of in a dragon. He was a killer.

A fire mage and a storm mage were standing back-to-back on a rooftop on the fourth tier. They were throwing everything they could conjure at the invading forces below them on the third tier. The fire mage was inundating the Daezun with balls of flaming liquid which exploded and danced across the stones when it hit the walk, catching everything in its path on fire - including the humans, who into flames and ran screaming; anyone they touched burst into flame too.

The storm mage had created a wind which whipped the fire mage's flame even further. The third tier was becoming a blazing inferno.

Amaum dove into the fray. His ability to summon water was not as great as his elders', but the water was not far away. He could smell it in the walls of the tiers - there were springs there on each level. He followed his nose, and when he found the source, he hovered, concentrating on pulling the water forward and onto the tier. It began to bubble forth and flow down the walk, extinguishing the flames.

However, he foolishly turned his back on the enemy to do this.

"Amaum!" Pruatra screamed, as she dove toward him.

Amaum turned just in time to see his mother hit by a blast of the fire mage's flame. She had placed herself in the path of what was meant for him. Her back exploded with the fire, burning so hot it was blue like Rheagos' flames. Her wings were engulfed in fire before she could make one more down-thrust. She plummeted toward the ground, a ball of flames.

Amaum roared in anger and followed her down as she plunged toward the harbor, her wings barely keeping her airborne. She hit the water and immediately sank. Amaum tucked his wings and dove in after her, but it was too late and her charred body drifted slowly to the bottom.

He thrust his powerful wings and exploded from the surface. As he rose he saw the fire mage had been incinerated by Keensight. The storm mage who had been his helper was scurrying over the wall onto the fifth tier. Amaum watched him dash into a house and slam the door shut – as if that would keep a dragon out!

The young blue attacked the house as if it were a living thing. He would dig out the mage and eat him alive. Nothing would keep him from dispatching revenge on these humans.

He tore and ripped at the house, his talons sinking into the stone like a knife into butter. He threw chunks off the tier, oblivious to the damage they might be doing to those below. He growled and roared, his anger beyond words.

He drew back and pounded his head into the house. It shook in his grasp, its foundation giving. He drew back again, his long neck curling with all the force he could apply, but when he opened his eyes, the mage was there before him on the roof… there was a blinding light… and then blackness.

===***===

Keensight heard Pruatra scream and saw her dive toward Amaum. He immediately perceived the danger, and would have taken the hit from the fire mage if he had only been closer. He saw her wings burst into flame, watching in stunned silence as the fire spread so quickly over them. He could do nothing to help her; she was on her way down before he could even change direction. Instead, he swooped in to dispatch the two mages on the roof, intending to flame them both. He hit the fire mage from behind while the man was still concentrating on Pruatra and Amaum, but the storm mage saw him coming and dropped down while throwing up a shield to protect himself from Keensight's flames. It was a typical fifth tier mage maneuver – protect yourself – don't worry about the other mage.

Keensight flew past and was looping around for another strafing run at the storm mage when he saw Amaum burst forth from the harbor in a fountain of water. The young blue saw the storm mage and went after him with tooth and claw.

Keensight was distracted for a moment when Silverbell flew by him and with a mighty roar blasted a house wall on the fifth tier into shards.

When he looked back toward Amaum, the young dragon was bashing his horned head into the storm mage's hiding place and making the walls rock on their foundation. He was going to help him when he saw what Amaum did not, the mage on the roof.

The man struck Amaum with a bolt of lightning which sent the young dragon flying backward and plunging down the tiers and striking the third tier before Keensight could catch him. The huge red scooped him up, cradling him in his paws as he flew the blue dragon to the plain below the Blackguard outlook and laid him down as gently as he could.

Renamaum had been like an older brother to him. Pruatra, Rena and Amaum were like family. He had lost three, he could not lose them all.

He leaned over Amaum as the battle continued to wage behind him. The young dragon had been hit in the face, and had a horrible gash ran across one eye and down almost the full length of his muzzle. Keensight mumbled healing words and leaned in closer. He whispered a sleeping spell and then breathed a searing breath across Amaum's face.

The young dragon would never see out of that eye again, but he would live to fly another day, and hopefully father other blues for his flight.

*Chapter Thirty-Nine*

Alador threw open the door to Luthian's private office. He looked about wildly for his uncle, arrow knocked and bow drawn tight. When he spotted the older man at the fire, however, he was unable to take the shot - Mesiande had been strategically placed between them. They stood facing the mantle, so Alador was unable to see her face, but Luthian's posture was relaxed, and that alone worried him.

"Oh! Alador, how nice of you to join us." Luthian did not turn, but only glanced over his shoulder. "How goes your little uprising anyway?" he asked, the words conversational but his tone dripping malice.

"You are the last to kneel." Alador stated. "It is over. Release Mesiande from your spell." He needed her to have a free will for his back-up plan to work.

"Last? Oh, my dear nephew, why do you say that?" It almost looked as if he warmed his hands next to the fire. "You act as if you have won some battle or war."

"We have taken the city, uncle. Now release Mesiande." Alador demanded. "If you are going to resist, then we should even the odds. You release her, I will put down my bow." Alador relaxed the bow as a show of faith.

Luthian finally turned, moving to Mesiande's side, caressing her face tenderly before running his fingers gently through her hair. "Let her go? Such a shame. She was one of my best guests here." Luthian sighed softly. "But I can always get back to her once I am ruling this isle. She will be my permanent property, after all."

Alador met the High Minister's gaze with a snarl, betrayal, rage and hatred oozing from him. "You will never touch her again. I have grown in skills, uncle. It will not be so easy to best me. If you manage, and leave this mansion, the dragons would like a word or two with you. Believe me when I say you would rather fall to me." The young mage needed him to let Mesi go. "Unless you are afraid?"

Pulling a strand of hair from Mesiande and smelling it with an ecstatic smile, Luthian finally moved forward from her side. "Grown in power? I'm sure, I've taught you many things. However, I am not afraid of you, or those dragons outside. I have harvested them for years, siphoned their blood, made them slaves under my control." Luthian slowly moved forward during this speech, his arms at his side, hands open.

"Let her go and I will put my weapons down." Alador demanded again, slowly drawing the bow back once more to half tension. He was watching those eyes and hands closely. Luthian always had a look in his eye when he was casting.

"Are we going to duel for the kingdom, Alador? Is that your grand plan?" Luthian laughed, putting a hand toward Mesiande. "So be it. She is free." At once Mesiande was dropped from whatever spell held her in place.

Mesiande spun to look at Alador with terror. He could see in her eyes that she had been very aware of everything Luthian commanded her to do. She ran to Alador's side. "Let's just go. Let him have his horrible kingdom."

Alador put the bow and quiver to the side. "I fear it has gone too far, Mesi. I cannot let it just end with the release of your will. Just remember me, and the day I finally bested you on the practice field." He looked at her pointedly, then back to the High Minister. "Go, Henrick waits for you." His command was firm, but his eyes never left Luthian.

Luthian just grinned, watching Alador's actions closely. "I have no sword to defend myself, good sir. It seems you have advantage over me." Luthian tsked softly. "Not a very fair duel."

Alador unbuckled and tossed his sword aside and slowly moved around the perimeter of the room. He risked a quick glance to ensure the doorway was empty; he didn't want the curious caught in any crossfire. Henrick was supposed to make sure that no one came in, but Alador was being cautious. He also used the time to gauge Luthian's first move. "Surely uncle, you know I have had many trainers besides you. Why, who knows what I have picked up." Alador pointed out.

"You know, I've considered that. I've been careful to watch and monitor your movements. Much easier to study an enemy," Luthian mused, his hands blurring into motion as those last words escaped his lips. Fireballs roared from his very fingertips.

Alador was ready, though, and they met a wall of ice, rebounding about the room without touching the older mage; that would have been too much to hope for, he supposed. He ducked across the room and dropped the wall just as he sent out a counter-strike of gleaming ice-arrows. He did not know what his uncle was doing on the other side of the wall, his form a shifting image reflected through the ice.

Luthian walked forward, a bubble of living flame surrounding him. It created waves of heat that seemed to shield him, but the licking flame lashed out to consume whatever they touched. A mocking laugh escaped his lips as the arrows were rebuffed by the shield of fire.

Alador took the advantage of the mage showing off to shift position again, and when the flames appeared to gather in the older mage's hands Luthian found himself in the midst of a deluge of water summoned from the very air. Alador immediately gathered the runoff into three solid spheres of ice, which he then hurled at the hopefully distracted mage.

In a burst of speed, Luthian dodged the dousing, his shield taking the brunt of the attack. It dissipated in a cloud of steam, momentarily obscuring Alador's view. Then his hand sprung out, and three fireballs lanced out from his fingertips, but it was too late. One of the ice balls slammed into his opposing shoulder before the other two contacted the fireballs and exploded in shards of ice.

Luthian growled loudly, letting loose a gout of flame from in front of him. Anything in the cone of flame's path erupted into flames - tables, banners, paper, it mattered not.

Alador was not concerned about the fire; he could douse whatever was close to him, and he knew that Luthian could reduce the flames as well. He focused instead on keeping in motion, not wanting to present a standing target. He lanced out lightning hoping to catch Luthian off guard, since he had only used water and pure power itself around the High Minister.

A mad cackle was heard as Luthian raised up his arm that had taken the ice orb hit, raising a weak force shield to block the lightning. Meanwhile, the flames kept licking out, finding purchase on anything they touched. "You think I didn't know about your little trick of lightning? Come now, nephew." Those words oozed with malice. "You know I'm better than THAT!"

Alador coughed from smoke and pulled the bandanna he had prepared over his mouth. He had known that things would burn; after all, Luthian was the ranking fire mage in Lerdenia. He swiftly thought of the spells of the black book. He began to incant while focusing on where Luthian turned as he moved.

The stream of fire stopped as Luthian looked round. He calmly walked toward the door to the outside. His gait was practiced and slow, sending the message to anyone watching that he owned this place, and he could take as much time as he wanted. His head swiveled around, looking for Alador. Finally spotting him, he let loose several fireballs with one hand and a wave of force with the other.

Alador finished the incantation, placing himself between Luthian and the door. A black hole appeared behind his uncle. The inside writhed with inky maleficence. Unfortunately, he could not break his concentration, and so was unable to avoid all the fireballs. The wave of the force then knocked him into the door jamb behind him.

A cruel smile crossed his uncle's features as he realized the fireballs struck home, but it quickly turned as he felt the force and eerie silence of something behind him. He glanced over his shoulder, and his body followed the turn. He gazed into the eternal darkness that was before him, aghast at what this was. He tried to back away, but was unable to fight as he was drawn toward it.

Pulling part of his robe into it, it would have grasped him if the spell had not faltered as Alador slid to the ground, the force of the blow disrupting the spell. In both horror and anger, Luthian turned back toward Alador and moved closer to him, hands up and fire dancing around his features.

"You... Are... Nothing!" Luthian spat.

Alador staggered to his feet from where he had slid to the floor. "I must be something, you look frightened Uncle. Perhaps now is the time to tell you I found the oath breaker's spell book," he taunted, moving away from the area reflexively. To prove his point, he let loose a dark cold ray. He cringed as the power moved through him; it felt wrong, as if dirty somehow.

Diverting his own spell energy, Luthian held up a hand that created a barrier of force around him, but it wasn't enough. It blocked the cold well, but the inky darkness passed through it, catching his hand and cutting into it. He yelled in pain, but his other hand was already in motion, a large fireball smashing through the building to strike the location where Alador had been. The explosion flung Luthian away from the blast center, and a small crater formed in the bookshelf, but Alador was gone.

The dark portal he had created to rid them all of the High Minister had failed, and Alador suspected that he would not get a second attempt. It was a spell that took more time, effort, and power than he had to spare twice. As if to verify his thoughts, he was hit by the wave coming off the explosion and knocked face first to the floor. He rolled quickly in case Luthian was using that distraction as a way to hit him again. His leathers had protected him from the fire, but not the force the balls carried.

Luthian was thrown a fair distance, but his force shield absorbed the brunt of the explosion. Slowly, he pushed off the rocks and wood pieces that scattered about his form. Rising to his feet, he was a bit wobbly, but made it to the outer doors and flung them open.

Alador attempted to freeze him there. A block of ice slammed down, blocking Luthian's way out. "We are not done. As you said, this is a battle for the Kingdom, and you running is not an option." Alador drew himself up despite the pain in his ribs. He let loose another dark ray at his uncle's back.

Instead of blocking it, Luthian dodged out of the way - sidestepping the misplaced shot. His hair had come loose and whipped wildly about him, giving his wide-eyed look a sense of the madman within.

"That should have killed you, half-breed!" Luthian's hands were a flurry of movement, waves of force shot along the ground, picking up burning debris - tables, chairs, paper, timbers, it mattered not. It all flew at Alador as the same gout of flame sputtered from the other hand. The flame itself growled as it came into being.

Alador was unable to douse the flame or avoid the items. He was knocked to the wall and slid down as the debris buried him with punishing blows. The fire raised blisters on his hands and face. He could smell burning hair. He knew he had to move quickly. It was all he could do to pull himself out from under the pile, only to see his uncle's boots.

Everything about him burned. Looking up, Alador saw the disheveled madman that bore down on him. His wild eyes and sadistic smile spoke everything in volumes. His hands outstretched toward Alador, one had a continuous flame, roiling in it. The other held a semi-transparent barrier of force.

His tone was unhinged as he growled out. "Any last words, you half-breed whelp?"

Alador caught the flash of blue at the door. "Yes... You forgot one thing, Uncle." He watched as an arrow sprouted from Luthian's chest. "Daezun women aren't helpless."

Blinking, a look of shock crossed the High

Minster's features as the flame and shield spells dropped. Touching the arrow with his fingertips, it became more real as he realized what happened. His blood coated the tip of the arrow. Turning around slowly, his mouth was agape, gasping for breath. He blinked to see Mesiande standing a distance away. He raised a hand toward her.

The moment his hand came up, she shot him again. It sped home, hitting him in the heart. Mesiande watched as her tormentor slid down to the floor.

Sordith appeared at that moment. "Damn it all," he spat on the floor. "You beat me to him." Realizing that Mesiande had already set another arrow waiting for Luthian's next move, he crossed to her.

"Let's just take that now, lass." He carefully led her shaking fingers to release the tension on the string.

Mesiande thrust the bow into the Trench Lord's hand and ran to Alador. She knelt beside him.

"Are you okay?

Alador had only managed to roll to his side. "I think I will be if I see a healer." The mage panted lightly to avoid a deeper breath. He coughed and blood sprayed from his mouth.

Mesiande attempted to pull him to his feet.

"Let's get you outside." She beckoned Sordith over, and they both moved to help him, placing his arms over their shoulders. As they moved forward she scolded him. "You never bested me on the practice field. I have always been the better shot."

Alador would have laughed if it didn't hurt so bad.

"I was counting on that indignation for you to prove me wrong. I brought the bow for you."

As they got to the door, he put up a finger and turned around. He would need this office soon. He doused the room with water, leaving steaming piles of books and furniture.

"Okay, now we are done," he said. He placed his arm around her shoulders and allowed her to help him outside to the waiting dragons and Blackguard.

## Chapter Forty

Sordith and Mesiande helped Alador out of the house and lowered him down on the steps. Alador looked around to see the army of dragons, Blackguard, Daezun and Lerdenians milling about. Levielle, Lady Aldemar, and Keensight moved through the crowd to his side.

It seemed as if a hundred demands and questions came at him simultaneously. He coughed again, spraying his arm with blood and the world went a bit hazy for a moment.

Lady Aldemar held up a hand as she knelt beside him. "He is hurt, give him a few minutes." She looked to Alador. "Ribs?"

The young mage nodded and winced when her gentle hands hit the first tender site. It felt to him as if every rib was broken. His breathing was labored.

Lady Aldemar whispered words of healing as she gently ran her hands over his sides. He could feel them knitting back together, which was not exactly a comfortable feeling. He sighed with relief when he could finally take a deep breath without hurting.

"That is all I can do for now without a proper bed and my healing salves." She pushed his hair, quite singed and snarled, out of his eyes.

"Help me up, Sordith." He put a hand up and took Sordith's as he was hauled to his feet.

"Reports?" He demanded. His fear was huge and while he had tasked Nemara to hide in the fifth-tier spring, he had not seen her when he moved up the tiers with Smallstone. A journey he intended to travel again once he was well.

Keensight was the first to speak. "We lost seven dragons." Alador's heart sank as he continued. "Pruatra was among them and Amaum is badly hurt."

Alador forced his feelings to the back. "Do you need any help seeing to their rituals?" Amaum had already lost so much to Alador's geas. He knew that even after he healed, there was little chance that the young dragon's anger would lessen, not with Pruatra dead. Alador forced down a lump in his throat at that thought; in her own gruff way, she had grown on him. He would mourn her later in his own way and time.

Keensight shook his head. "Each Flight is already seeing to their own. A member of the Blue flight has taken over the role of lead given the situation."

"Sordith?"

"Owen looks to have lost a leg. Lady Aldemar's people are seeing to him. Other than that, I won't know for a couple hours." Sordith's tone was grim.

Alador wiped a hand over his face. He searched out his brother. "Dorien?"

"There were losses; a battle comes with them. They were minimal compared to what could have been had the Blackguard not stood amongst us." Dorien was abrupt, but very formal in his pose and speech.

Alador looked at him, his eyes questioning whether they had lost family. Dorien seemed to know his thoughts and shook his head. Alador breathed a sigh of relief.

He turned his head, seeking out the General. "Levielle, your assessment."

"More damage to the city than I would have liked. Fifth tier will need to be totally rebuilt." Alador's heart leaped. Nemara had not been in the spring, which left the manor - he hoped.

"Sordith, will you go to my home and check on Nemara and our child?" Alador's words were soft amongst the chaos and celebration of the victors.

"Of courses." Sordith turned and then stopped to look back at Alador. "Child?"

Alador's words were pointed. "Yes, our child." Sordith knew of the egg so he hoped he would leave it at that.

Mesiande poked his arm. "You have a child?" Her face had fallen slightly. Her eyes still haunted by what had happened around her.

Keensight grinned slightly at the news there was a child. "Healthy I hope."

"Yes, very healthy." Alador managed. "He looked back at Mesiande. "I am sorry Mesi. I couldn't tell you because Luthian held your will. I hope you will be my queen and allow Nemara to remain for Latiera as she knows the people here and…"

Bariton and Levielle shifted uncomfortably. "Lad may I suggest a later time for that discussion?" the general prompted gently.

Alador looked back at those gathered around him. "Yes, your right." He looked down at Mesiande. "We can speak more later if you like."

He looked about the tier assessing what to say. There were fires still burning in the city below. "Are there any mages left who fought against us?"

Lady Aldemar's smile was victorious. "Yes, we have them held in a circle of very unhappy dragons."

"Levielle, I want them banished. Can you see that they can retrieve what they can carry and then load them onto a boat to anywhere but here?" Alador's weariness was beginning to take a hold. The dark spells he had cast had left strange sensations and a weariness like that of resisting the storm.

"Banished? Alador, I suggest that we kill them. We don't need them to assist a city that will not bow to your rule." Levielle's tone was cold.

"Would I not be as bad as Luthian if I killed them?" Alador was sick of killing.

"No," came the voices of Keensight, and Levielle. Lady Aldemar dissented with a firm, "yes."

Alador thought about this for a long moment. "Is it possible to set a geas on them that they cannot act against us?" He looked from mage to dragon.

Keensight nodded. "Yes. We can even set some very vivid images of what will happen to them if they try." Keensight lowered his great head to Alador. "I insist that they swear allegiance at the very least."

Alador nodded. "See it done." He watched as Keensight lumbered over toward a circle of dragons.

"Bariton?"

"Lost good men and women, but they fought bravely and well. The combination of skills of the army and of the magi worked as predicted." Bariton stood a little straighter. "They did not balk at working with their Daezun kin, nor the Lerdenian mages that assisted us."

"That is good to hear. We need to talk later about opening the Blackguard up to any who wish to pursue becoming a battle mage." Alador looked about for any others. His eyes fell to Lady Aldemar.

"My lady, how fared the mages who stood with us." His words were gentle as he knew that the Lady was not one for violence.

"We lost several and some have not reported in yet." Her eyes took on a filmy stare. "Fortunately, my daughter was able to fight at my side."

"Your daughter?" Alador was surprised.

The lady turned aside and beckoned a young woman to her. "This is Ruby. We were only just reunited before the battle. I have the General to thank for finding her."

Ruby stepped up and dropped her eyes before Alador. He was surprised at her deference. "It is a pleasure to meet you, Ruby," he offered.

"Thank you, Your Grace." Ruby's quiet voice could barely be heard over the gathering crowd on the council top.

"Your Grace? Please, I am Alador." He swayed slightly and Mesiande stepped up to support him.

"I thought you were now the King?" Mesiande questioned, prodding him slightly.

"He is, but it will take him a bit to get used to, I think." Levielle slapped Alador on the back, bringing a gasp of pain from the mage.

"Easy there, Levielle. Don't want to put him into bed quite yet." Bariton winked at Alador.

Keensight had lumbered back to them as Bariton spoke. "We have one thing left to do."

All of them looked at the dragon, none of them sure of what he spoke. The great dragon turned toward those gathered on the tier. He did not speak as Sordith showed up, Nemara right behind him with Latiera.

"Even better," mumbled the great dragon.

Alador pulled Nemara into his arms. "Are you both okay?"

"Yes, we took shelter in the bathing room since it is more cave than manor." She nestled close to him. Alador looked over and saw a bit of pain in Mesiande's eyes. He would have much to explain when they got a chance to sit down.

Keensight took that moment to bellow. "All hail the new King of Lerdenia, King Alador Guldalian Dragonsworn.

Many cries echoed the new title about the top of the tiers. Alador stood somewhat stunned as they continued. It was not the accolades that froze him. He felt the geas let him go and with it, a great release of pressure and pain. It was so abrupt that the world went black.

## Chapter Forty-One

Jon sat peacefully stroking Nightmare's head as the dragon lay beside him, feeling very proud of himself. He had finally located the volume which contained the incantation Morana intended to use to raise her 'army of the dead,' in her quarters. Jon was very thankful she was a heavy sleeper once she did fall asleep.

He had worked out a scenario in his head for what he would do when the time came for her ritual. He could not allow her to complete her plan, even if he had to risk death to stop her.

Nightmare's rumble of contentment was cut short when a fierce roar echoed through the dragon caverns. His head shot up at Jon's side as he immediately came to his feet.

"What is it?" Jon asked as he too rose.

The roar came again, this time louder and more frightening, with others joining in. The caves began to tremble with the sound.

"It is Blacksaber," Nightmare answered as he moved to the cave opening. "He is calling us all to join him in the crypt below the temple." Nightmare swung his wedged head toward Jon and fixed him with one eye. "Something's wrong. Blacksaber is angry about this. He planned to leave for Silverport tonight."

Jon shook his head in disbelief. "Why didn't you

tell me?" he questioned the dragon.

"You said I couldn't go," Nightmare countered, as if that made his decision not to tell Jon make sense.

"I'd better go to Morana," Jon said.

"And Blacksaber calls us all," Nightmare added.

"Be careful, my friend." Jon raised his hand and stroked the young dragon down the length of his neck.

"You too, Jon." Nightmare stepped to the edge of the cave's landing platform and dropped off to go join the others of the Black flight.

Jon took a moment to compose himself. He had confided his plan to Nightmare to make sure the young dragon did not interfere in the execution. 'Execution…' That was an appropriate choice of words. Morana's spell to raise the dead required a blood sacrifice…and Jon intended to volunteer.

\*\*\*\*\*

Jon had trouble trying to still his rapidly beating heart. He had volunteered to be the blood sacrifice for Morana's spell, and she had accepted. She would use him, and pull from the power of the dragons to raise her army of dead – and she would do it tonight. She had been informed though the scrying bowl that Luthian needed her assistance in quelling an uprising of the Daezun and perhaps some rouge mages as well. For the past half-hour Morana had been preparing him for the blood sacrifice, and she explained to Jon as she washed him with scented oils that this was what she had waited for. This was why Dethara chose her to be High Priestess. She would come to the aid of Luthian, and from this uprising a new leadership, shared between Luthian and Dethara, would arise.

Now fully anointed, Jon trailed behind her in a long black robe, into the tunnels under the temple, to the crypts below.

When they entered, the rest of the temple members had gathered and stood against the walls. The dragons, all stationed along a ledge above circling the massive crypt, roared their greeting. Jon was amazed at the lack of smell. Bodies were piled rods deep, but the decaying had been magically halted. Morana led him up a ramp, which had been left clear, to a platform with a sacrificial stone altar in the middle. This platform was surrounded by the dead.

"Here," the priestess indicated the stone.

Jon pulled himself up onto it. Before he laid down, he searched the ledge for Nightmare. When their eyes met, he gave the young dragon a reassuring smile. He did not know the full extent of the loyalty the other dragons might show Morana. He knew the flight leader was not happy about being kept back from the battle he had been told by the dragon king to attend. However, given the choice of disobeying the dragon king or Morana, he had chosen the king. Either she had a stronger hold, or the flight leader feared her more.

Jon took a deep breath and lay back on the cold stone of the altar. From what he had read, he knew the sequence of events. Morana would start the spell, drawing from the dragons' power as she spoke. This was the reason for raising and controlling the Black flight - without their power she could not have performed an incantation so large or which controlled so many souls.

Jon swallowed hard as she raised her arms and began the chant. She had not hesitated in the least when he volunteered. It was almost as though she had expected it. It made him wonder if she also expected what he had in store for her.

The dragons began to keen, something he had never heard before. He turned his head on the stone to see Nightmare. The young dragon was leaning forward, as were all his kind, with their necks outstretched toward Morana as she spoke the words. She began to sway, and their heads swayed with her.

A fog began to form and flow, creeping its way from the base of the altar out over the piles of the dead. It oozed across the battered and beaten bodies, like oil over the surface of water.

As soon as the dead were covered, it would be the time for the sacrifice. The blood from the volunteer, him, would trickle down the sides of the altar as she dismembered his body. Where it touched the fog, the mist would turn red and carry the power of the spell to animate the dead.

Jon readied himself. He had placed his hands over his chest and tucked them in his sleeves, looking ever the pious mage for his loving priestess. She had no idea, but he had conjured a dagger – a dagger especially enchanted for the purpose of killing a Death Temple High Priestess.

She drew the dagger she was carrying from its sheath and raised her hands up high above her head. She held the weapon tightly in both hands. The spell required that the death of the sacrifice come with one well-aimed blow. If it took two, the spell would dissipate and fail.

Jon drew in his breath.

Just as Morana was on the verge of plunging the dagger through Jon's heart, Nightmare roared. Morana looked up and Jon took advantage of this distraction to draw his dagger from his sleeve, plunging it into her heart.

There was a moment when Morana still stood on her feet, speared on Jon's outstretched arm with his dagger in her chest up to the hilt.

"Jon?" she breathed with surprise and then slumped over him onto the altar.

He used a quick cantrip to keep the blood from flowing off her body and into the fog. He rolled out from under her, and once he was off the altar he placed her body fully laid out on it in his place.

He watched as the fog slowly dissipated and he thanked the Goddess Dethara that he was able to stop this abomination.

It was not until he was sure there was no movement, no life, among the dead, that he thought to look up. The members of the temple were all down on one knee with their heads bent as if in prayer. He only just noticed the dragons' keening had also been silenced with the death of Morana.

His fearful eyes looked up - from Blacksaber to Nightmare, all the dragons had their wings spread and were bowing to him.

Jon addressed the assemblage. "Blacksaber... will you dispose of these bodies as befits their souls and cleanses our temple?"

The large black tucked his wings and nodded his head. "As the High Priest commands." The Black flight leader turned to Nightmare. "Take your bonded one from this place so we may cleanse it."

Nightmare sailed down and landed at Jon's side, extending a wing as an invitation for Jon to mount. Jon hesitated; he had never ridden the young dragon, and he was not sure his friend could carry him.

"I won't drop you unless you try to feed me more of that," Nightmare indicated with a wave of his wing toward the dead.

Jon smiled and climbed up on the dragon. "Not a chance," he replied, before words were forced back in his throat as Nightmare surprised him with a mighty leap into the air and a swirling flight up through the dragon corridors to the flight's cave entrances.

===\*\*\*===

The next day, Jon sat in the courtyard with Nightmare and his now loyal followers. They watched the smoke rise through the vents in the crypt to funnel out like long black snakes from the chimneys on the temple's roof. The last of the dead were being burned by the dragon flight.

The scryer hesitantly approached. "High Priest, I have a message from Silverport."

Jon held out his hand and the scryer passed it to him.

The new High Priest of the Death sphere read the one-line message.

*It is done!*
*Alador*

*Chapter Forty-Two*

Sordith stood on the new stone jetty, which bisected the harbor. The stone mages had done a splendid job constructing it, and he could not wait to put it to use, but for today it was reserved for the coronation. The tall anchoring pillars along its length each had a dark blue barrel sitting at their base where the nature mages had cultivated blooming vines. They spiraled up, dumping their profusion of blooms off their tops like the festooned, cascading locks of a beautiful woman.

At the far end where the Trench Lord stood the mages erected a trellis, and it too was covered with vines and blooms of blue and white. From the top corners pennants of blue, with the now familiar silver dragon, fluttered in the gentle sea breeze.

A lot had happened in the past two months since the battle of Silverport. That was what the people had all taken to calling it, 'The Battle of Silverport.' It wasn't a Lerdenian battle, or a Daezun battle, or even a dragon battle, it was a matter of taking back the city of Silverport from the corrupt leaders and putting it back in the hands of reasonable folk who would see that it was run for the good of all the residents, not just the magically empowered.

Once this coronation was over, the jetty would become a new docking place for ships, enabling them to pull alongside, drop ramps and unload. This would be much more efficient than the small boats previously rowed back and forth from ship to shore. He could envision the fleet all tied up and the goods from the mainland rolling off onto the dock. The ships were due back soon. The council had promised the Daezun supplies to take back with them for their efforts in helping repair the city. Sordith could see a great future for all in Silverport.

His gaze wandered up to the council tier. It, and the fifth tier, had been heavily damaged during the battle; dragons were ferocious fighters. The only mansion that was left standing unscathed was Luthian's, and Alador had ordered it torn down after all that was needed had been removed. The only part he spared was the garden. The whole council tier was growing into a park, which all could access, from trench residents to the council itself. There would be no designation of levels based on magical powers any longer. The people were encouraged to mingle as much as their finances would allow.

The third tier remained mostly shopkeepers, but other than that, the whole face of the city was slowly changing.

The council chambers were being rebuilt. Five powerful mages took refuge there during the battle and the dragons fought valiantly to rout them. The whole roof and one side of the chambers had been destroyed in the process. The castle being built for the King would become part of this grand building and what they could save of the original structure. It would take many years to complete. He wondered if Alador would even live in it.

Alador and Nemara had chosen to maintain their residence in his manor on the fifth tier. It was damaged in the battle, but they made repairs, making improvements as they went, much as Sordith himself had done with the Trench Lord's manor. Alador's home now had a terrace overlooking the seaside.

It had not been easy, picking up the pieces of their lives. Some of the dragons, including Keensight, stayed on after the battle to help with the cleanup. The big red dragon said, 'since we did the most damage, we will help with the repairs.' Of course, Sordith and Alador knew it was because Alanis and the rest of Henrick's family was still here. Alador had officially recalled Henrick, but he was not due to 'appear' until today, for the coronation of his son. Prior to that, he had been a somewhat grumpy red dragon giving other dragons orders.

Some of the Daezun stayed on after the battle. They proved to be great builders and truly helpful to those who accepted their assistance, but that was not without issues at times. As Trench Lord, Sordith had broken up more than his share of fights. He missed Owen, who was still recovering from his wounds, and often finished up his day at the big man's bedside catching him up on what was going on outside. Sordith had been forced to use some of the Blackguards Bariton loaned him for a bit of high profile law enforcement.

But, it was not all bad either. With the help of the new council members led by Alador, Levielle, Aldemar, Bariton, and the Trench Lord himself, there was a plan and the city would move forward into the future fully integrated, Lerdenian, Daezun, and the mixes of the two. They also had to bring the rest of the Lerdenian cities to heel.

Sordith shielded his eyes with his hand as he watched the carriage carrying Alador make its winding way down the tiers. It was followed by another carrying Alador's family - Henrick, Alanis, Dorien, Tentret and Sofie. These were followed by a walking procession of the mages sworn earlier to the service of Alador and the city's governing council. Nemara, Keelee and Mesi, who had become good friends, were among these. After the mages, some of the general public were falling in behind to trail down the tiers in order to see the event closer. Most of the folks stayed on the tiers raining handfuls of petals on the passing procession.

Alador had refused the idea of being crowned the "Dragonsworn" in the council chambers. He wanted the whole city to be able to celebrate and he wanted to honor those who had died in the trench during the storm. He said he did not want people to look up at him... he wanted to be one of them.

Sordith could hear the cheering of the crowd as the carriages passed. He was somewhat taken by surprise when the dragons, who had positioned themselves on the rock barrier between the harbor and the sea, roared their approval as Alador stepped from the carriage at the foot of the jetty.

He was the picture of a perfect king, adorned in blue with silver accents. Alador had always preferred his leathers under his mage's robes, so he wore leathers tanned to such a dark blue, they were almost black. His shirt was the blue of a spring sky, and his cape a royal blue velvet with the silver dragon embroidered on the back for all to see. He came fully armed with both sword and dagger.

Alador slowly move along the stone dock. Henrick followed a short distance behind. He held the crown on a blue velvet pillow.

Alador had argued against the crown, but Henrick, in his decades of wisdom as a dragon, said the people deserved to see their king crowned properly. Alador's father was chosen to do it to prove that there was no animosity on his part for Alador killing his brother, and no desire on Henrick's part to claim the leadership of the isle for himself.

When Alador arrived at the end of the jetty, he stood to one side and let Henrick take the lead. Keensight had suggested he might bring the throne from his hoard for Alador to rest in, but the young mage had drawn the line at that suggestion. It was enough just being king. The crown would not rest gently on his brow.

Henrick handed Sordith the pillow with the crown on it. Their father turned back toward the city and motioned Alador to take his place in front of him. Using a magical amplification of his voice, he addressed the residents and guests of Silverport.

"People of the isle, I hereby present to you Alador Guldalian, the Dragonsworn. All you who have come this day to do them homage and service, raise your voices."

A great cheer arose from both mortals and dragons.

"Alador, are you willing to serve the people of this isle no matter their origin, in equality and with due respect?"

"I do," Alador loudly answered, a spell magnifying his voice for the crowds.

"Will you uphold the laws of both the council of mortals and of the dragon council?"

"I will," he replied again.

"Present your sword, my king," Henrick intoned.

Alador drew his sword and presented it on his sleeve, handle first.

"Please kneel," Henrick instructed.

Alador knelt before him, his head bowed.

Henrick raised Alador's sword and enchanted it with dragon fire. He laid the sword first on the new king's right shoulder and then on his left as he spoke.

"King for humans… King for dragons…"

The sword's flames did not burn or even threaten to harm the young mage.

Henrick snuffed out the flames and handed the sword to Sordith. Sordith presented the crown.

Henrick placed the large crown on Alador's head. "Please rise."

Alador rose and turned back toward the city and the huge crowd of onlookers.

Henrick raised his hands and shouted. "May I present your King, Alador Guldalian, the Dragonsworn!"

At this sign, dragons who could create visual effects took flight arching high over the newly crowned King. The visual display was mesmerizing and ended with the green flight sending rose petals down upon the King and his people.

## Chapter Forty-Three

The city was in full festival per the King's decree. Other than the scorch marks of magic, the remains of the coup had been cleared away. Banners of silver with the features of Renamaum danced from every free pole throughout the tiers. Food and mead of equal measure regardless of tier had also been set out. While some may still mutter harsh words about their half-Daezun king, or the fact that there was a king, they kept it close to the chest. Alador had even employed musicians throughout the tiers, creating a light-hearted scene.

Latiera had been brought out, and thankfully the baby was maintaining her mortal form. She was the highlight of the King's personal party. Alador had surrounded himself with friends. Lady Aldemar and her newly reunited daughter, Ruby, graced the ballroom. Many of the mages who had fought at the side of Sordith and Dorien were also present. Of course, he had lifted Henrick's banishment.

The most special guests were his Daezun kin. His mother had accompanied the force of arms that had gathered to assist in the taking of the city. She did not look a bit out of place in her Lerdenian fancies, as she called them. He was proud to have them here where they could meet his daughter. They would leave tomorrow, keeping how they had emerged not far from the Trench's door as their secret.

When Pruatra had held his daughter, she had been a beautiful blue hatchling, the silver edges of the egg retained in her own scales. He recalled the wonder when he had taken the hatchling only to have her change into a mortal baby. Silver hair and deep sapphire eyes were the only hint that it was the same child.

Latiera's hair had been the topic of many conversations tonight. How unusual it was to see a baby with such clearly metallic looking hair. How long it was already. Everyone assumed that some element of the silver came from him, his eyes being akin to liquid silver. Neither he nor Nemara commented when there were observations that while they could see him as the father, the baby did not seem to resemble Nemara at all.

Latiera began to fuss and it caught Alador's attention immediately. Twice now, she had converted half to hatchling while crying. It hadn't happened in a few days, but he was taking no risks. He swooped his child out of Dorien's great arm. "Nemara may need to feed her." He whisked her away, soothing the baby as best he could.

He interrupted and excused Nemara from where she was talking. By this time, Latiera was all smiles as she pulled on Alador's hair.

"Is she okay?" Nemara asked in a whisper.

"She seems to be. However, let us avoid further risk." He bounced the smiling child in his arms gently.

"I will take her up," Nemara said with a nod, reaching for the baby.

"You, my dear, have her all the time. Enjoy the party," he admonished. "I will take her up. If anyone is looking for me, let them know."

"Of course," Nemara actually looked a bit relieved. He knew that Latiera had been keeping her up at night, but Nemara had not allowed him to help during the wee hours, stating that he needed a sharp mind.

As he headed out the door, Mesiande caught up with him. "One minute, you are not getting away with her that easily. I haven't gotten to hold her."

Alador was a bit uncomfortable with Mesiande and the baby, but Mesiande did not seem as if the fact he was holding another woman's child bothered her at all. He reminded himself that health, not parentage, was what mattered in the village way of life. He handed her the baby.

"She is getting tired, so I thought to go put her down." Alador said, hoping the baby would not decide in this moment to reveal who her true mother was.

"I will only keep you a minute," the young Daezun reassured him. She cooed at Latiera and was rewarded with two large eyes. Then suddenly, the baby growled.

Alador groaned inwardly and watched Mesiande for a reaction. "Oh, she must have some air in there. Best you make sure to burp her well before you lay her down." Mesiande offered. As if Alador was unaware of such parenting behavior, she demonstrated how to lay the baby across the shoulder and produce a burp. Alador was too busy being relieved that Mesiande thought that Latiera had burped to take note of her advice.

He gently took the baby back. "I need to get her down and get back," he offered as explanation.

"Before you go, I didn't get to tell you," she began.

"Tell me what?" Alador was not really comfortable with this conversation. He had a baby that was not hers and a woman at his side that claimed to be its mother.

She leaned up and kissed him on the cheek. "Thank you," she softly uttered next to his ear. "I have been thinking of your words after Luthian's death. To stay here as your bondmate was once all I wanted, but I don't want to be a Queen." She put a hand to his cheek as she pulled back. "I can't stay here with you.

He looked into her eyes, their souls melding for a brief moment. "I know," he returned.

"Besides," Mesiande stepped back as she spoke. "I like Nemara. We SHALL cause you all kinds of grief." She turned and went back into the ballroom.

Alador smiled inwardly; he knew Mesiande well enough to know that this was not a threat, it was a promise.

He adjusted Latiera in his arms and started up the stair to put his little girl to bed. He was sure there would be many surprises in store for him in the future. Life was not going to be dull.

Alador was stunned when he opened the nursery room door. The lightstones seemed to have dimmed, and the air was chilled.

The Goddess Dethara stood by his daughter's crib.

He clutched Latiera to his chest and immediately threw up a protective shield.

She turned toward him. Her former guise as Lady Morana had been dropped for her true appearance. She seemed held in the air by the upturned folds of her long ebony gown. Her glossy black hair flowed down to the floor beneath her. Both her hair and dress undulated under the breath of sheer power like waves on the ocean.

She floated toward him, reaching out one immaculately manicured hand toward his child's soft silver locks. He put his hand over Latiera's head protectively and tried to fold his arms tighter over her tiny body.

Dethara's hand dropped. "Such a lovely child, and so very special," she purred hypnotically. She raised her eyes from the child to him. The depth of their black pools mesmerized him for a moment before she spoke again. "My little pseudo-dragon... the dragonsworn... You never cease to amaze me."

Alador glared at her. "You are not welcome here, Goddess."

She placed her hand on her heart, the pale white of her skin standing out starkly against the black of her robe. "Oh, you pain me…" she cooed in mock surprise. "I only wished to see your child… Your dear little one." She smiled and it held both a challenge and a promise. "I can hardly wait until sweet little Latiera comes of age and appears in the Gods' Circle to receive her gifts. I have planned a very unique gift for your very unique child, Alador."

Her voice, speaking his name, lingered in the room long after she had disappeared.

## Glossary

**Blackguard** – an elite army of half-Daezun and half-Lerdenian who have shown the capacity for spell-casting. First school of mages established on the isle.

**Blood-mining -** The practice of feeding a chained dragon to full health then cutting it so that its magical powers and blood meld into the ground. The mixture is harvested and planted into dirt in a nearby mine to congeal into bloodstones. Process takes a minimum of one two turns.

**Bloodstone** – A magically embed stone created from the magic and the blood of a dragon. These combine into a hard substance that can be drained or used for item enhancements.

**Circle-** In an attempt to control birthing and population, Daezun use this ritual for coming of age, reproduction and celebration of high summer.

**Daezun** – A shorter stocky race proficient at mining and other trades involving the use of hands. Daezun cannot cast spells. They revere the dragons and the Gods.

**Geas** – an obligation or prohibition magically imposed on a person. In this case, the geas was established to whoever harvested Renamaum's bloodstone.

**Korpen** – Korpen had originally been slow moving pests that traveled in herds and are now domesticated for farm use. Their massive heads had double, vertically-oriented horns. The upper horn curved forward from behind the head, while the lower emerged from the head itself. As a protection from predators such as dragons, the spikes along their backs were almost impenetrable. That was useful to the miners as well: korpen were strong and a great amount of weight could be attached to each spike

**Lerdenians** – Lithe and lean, many have white hair due to magical drain. Most Lerdenians are capable of some spell casting.

**Lexital** – These unique flying creatures had a strange curved beak with what seemed to be like the sail of a boat rising above both beak and eyes. Their neck was long and serpentine, moving side to side as they steered through the sky. Their eyes were red and rimmed in blue. Their wings were varying shades of blue with a ridge of red that seemed to arch out mid-feathers. There was a natural dip in this neck right before the body that could carry the rider.

**Medure-** Medure was a hard metal that glistened with flecks of blue; it was difficult to find and harder to work. Used as currency in rectangle pieces.

**Panzet** – large birds with long legs, prized for their long purple feathers. Often used in comparison for those who have a focus on appearance but lack intelligence.

**Prang** – A local herbivore, their white and brown coats made it easy for them to blend in with the dead foliage of the cold winter months. An adult prang could weigh up to two hundred and fifty stones – too large for individual families. A prang's up-swept and back-curving horns could be used in medicine for headaches and eyesight.

**Slips-** Another name for medure that has been formed into currency. These are small rectangles of the medal with a small hole in one end so that they can be strung into strings of one hundred.

**Trading Tokens** – Smaller form of currency for day to day items. There are fifty trading token in a single slip.

**Trench-** A below ground level area carved out with a central canal that takes the city sewage out to sea. Many denizens of Lerdenian cities that do not have spell casting abilities are forced to live there in abject poverty.

**Turn** – How the denizens of Vesta measure time. A turn is approximately eight earth months and is measured from winter to summer solstice.

## THERESA SNYDER

I need to tell you about Theresa. We met after working to collaborate on publicity. She has become a big sister and mentor to me. Her books are a joy to read and are lunch time lengths. I recommend Theresa without reservation.

Theresa Snyder has a wealth of life experience to pull from to write her character driven novels, novellas and stories. Born in California, she has lived in every state west of the Mississippi. She grew up in what most people would consider a huge family with two natural born brothers and twenty-three foster and adopted brothers.

Her mother, who was a librarian, gave her a love for the written word. Her father, a high school automotive teacher, instilled in her an interest in how things work.

Writing has always been her passion, but jobs from zoo keeper to legal assistant, make-up artist to marketing coordinator, and retail clerk to print shop manager have paid the bills over the years.

All this experience has led to very richly developed characters, plots and settings.

Her internationally read blog has a following of over 168,000 and has over 4,000 hits a month. She also has more than 50,000 followers on Twitter after less than three years on the site.

Theresa Snyder is a multi-genre writer. She grew up on a diet of B&W Sci-Fi films like Forbidden Planet and The Day the Earth Stood Still. She is a voracious reader and her character driven writing is influenced by the early works of Anne McCaffrey, Ray Bradbury, Robert Heinlein, and L. Ron Hubbard. She loves to travel, but makes her home in Oregon where her elder father and she share a home and the maintenance of the resident cat, wild birds, squirrels, garden, and occasional dragon house guest.

Website:
http://TheresaSnyderAuthor.com

Twitter:
https://twitter.com/TheresaSnyder19

Facebook Author Page:
https://www.facebook.com/booksbytheresasnyder

Goodreads:
https://www.goodreads.com/author/show/7077138.Theresa_Snyder

## ABOUT THE AUTHOR

It is always a pleasure to interact with my fans. You can ask me questions and follow me at these locations.

Facebook:
https://www.facebook.com/dragonsgeas/

Twitter: @balanceguide

Blog: http://dragonsgeas.blogspot.com/

Web page: **Http://dragonologists.com**

I am an independent author. This means I do all my own formatting, uploading and publicity. There is no big company paving the way to the New York Bestseller List. I need your help. If you liked this book, please tell others about my series. Most importantly, even if you just fill in the stars and say good book, please leave a review on Amazon and/or Goodreads. That, more than anything, will help free me to write more frequently and put work out faster. Even if you didn't like all of it, I can take the bad with the good. Thank you so much in advance.

Cheryl Matthynssens

Made in the USA
San Bernardino, CA
08 April 2018